R.D. COLE

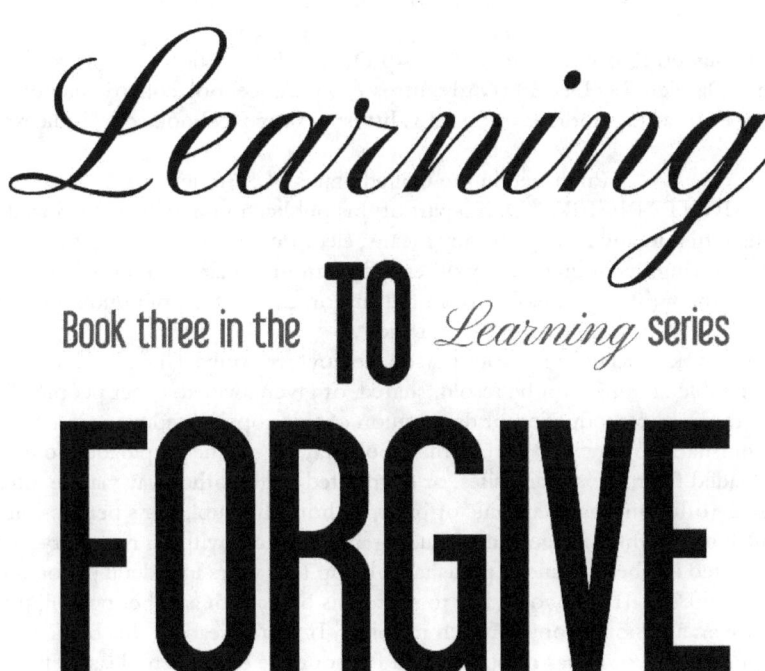

Learning

Book three in the **TO** *Learning* series

FORGIVE

Learning to Forgive by R.D. Cole
ISBN-10: 0-9912894-3-9
ISBN-13: 978-0-9912894-3-1

Book Cover- Berto Designs
Photographer: Chuck Condron with XE Photography
http://www.xephotography.com
Designer: Rebecca Berto with Berto Designs http://bertodesigns.com
Model: Damien Ray Decent (Dirdy) https://www.facebook.com/damiendecent
Editing/Formatting: Indie Express LLC https://www.facebook.com/Indieexpress

Published in the United States of America

DEDICATION

If you're reading this, then it's for you. I dedicate this book to all the readers who take chances on Indies, support us, and love our stories as much as we do. <3

.

TABLE OF CONTENTS

Acknowledgements

Thank you's

And

You Rock

Can I just say that I love and hate this part of writing a book. I have so many people to thank for inspiring me. Believing in me, and pushing me. This year we had a lot of family isssues that cam up, but through it all I never lost my support group.

First, I have to thank the Lord for giving me this imagination and letting me take this journey to meet all these wonderful people. It's a dream come true that I can do this and meet all the readers. Either on FB or in person. You all Rock.

Then my wonderful hubby, Jordan. Thank you for dealing with a dirty house, no dinner, and my emotions throughout this story. I hope you didn't take any of it personally. I love you with all my heart. You've taken on a lot to allow me to write full time. You've supported and encouraged me. Thank you.

Bethani, my miracle. I know you can't see this but I love you. And when I write about the love between child and parent, I think of you and hope I justify how much I love you. Without you coming into my life, I wouldn't be what I am. I wouldn't be period. I love you Princess. Always.

Jammie Cook my Best friend, PA, and half of 2Bookoholics Book Blog. Thank you. Thank you for brainstorming with me, telling me if something is stupid, and pushing me toward great ideas. You are someone I can't do without now. So You Can't Leave. I'm locking you up and keeping you. LOL!!! I truly love you and your witty attitude. Even when we're around people that don't care about us Indie Authors, you make it tolerable… And fun.

If you're reading this THANK YOU. Thank you for taking a chance on my book. I hope you loved Lyric and Blaire's story just as much as me. You are why I write these stories & I hope I made you proud.

I hope they excited you and you'll continue with Ryan's story...

Thank you, Damien, for having such a great physique and personality. You're a wonderful Lyric and I look forward to showing you off at the signings.

Brandee's Bookendings for giving me an Amazing series tour and who's working so hard setting up Lyric's big tour. You're a sweet and real person and I thank you for taking a chance on me.

HEAbook ShelfBlogger. Thank you for the friendship and the Blitz tour you helped set up to introduce Lyric to the world. I know I can count on you to help me or answer any question however weird it is. MWAH!!!

Mari Brown. Thank you for being so strong and introducing me to some amazing people. Thank you for always taking time to read what I send you. You and your family are in my thoughts, girl.

LU Ann & sweet Leah. I loved meeting you both. It's so nice to have someone who understands somewhat of the experience I go through. Thank y'all for embracing me in your circle.♥□

Katie Mac. Thank you. Your kindness in being a friend and editor was a life saver. I hope you enjoyed Lyric, too. I know it was rough in the beginning, but with your keen eye, we made it what it is... ♥□

Francette Phal, thank you for giving me Nicholas Grayson. And for writing a book that blew me away and inspired Lyric. You are truly gifted and deserve to be a BESTSELLER. That book deserves a movie and an award. It was brilliance.

Kimber Dawn, my smut sista... Lol!!!

I love your wicked mind. Thank you for being a True Indie supporter. MOTOR BOAT!!! ☐

Abby & Lisa. Y'all have stuck by me since day one and love all my characters. I've shared and teased you with tidbits of Lyric, so now you can see the final piece put together. Thank you for sticking by me. Oh! And Abby, when we meet, I'm soooooo touching your hair. LOL!!! <3

K. Langston, Thank you girl. For making me feel important and for your dirty mind... Thank you for being funny as Hell. Your posts have been great research and inspirations. Yak!!! Lol☐

Aine Kelly Author aka Shannon. Thank you for making my first signing so great. Loved sitting with you. Also loved losing our signing VCard together... ☐ I got your back.

Heather Gunter, thank you for accepting me from the beginning. Your smile and happiness is something that brightens my day. You're always positive and it helps to push me forward. ❤☐

HJ Bellus. Thank you for writing Cree and your craftiness. Thank you for being down to earth country Girl and a True Indie supporter. My lady crush. ☐☐☐

Lydia and you need to come south. ☐

Trudy Stiles, thank you for your on going support and kindness. Thank you for always answering my questions and being a great down to earth person. Thank you for understanding me more than just on a writer's level. ❤□

Ilsa Madden Mills, thank you for writing such inspirational stories and being a great friend. I loved meeting you and love talking to you. You're so sweet and deserve the best. ❤□

Jennifer La Rocca, thank you for being another supporting indie writer. You're so much fun and I'm coming to visit you one day in P' Cola... Fair warning. □ oh... And thanks for letting me grind on you. I hope you enjoyed it as much as me. □

Bethany Castaneda with HEA Bookshelf blog. Thank you for always being there to support me. For pimping me as a writer and friend. I hope to meet you and Hadley one day... Oh... & Thank you for pointing out what my brain can't. Lol!!! My sweet Grammar Cop.

The blogs who have stuck beside my rookie ass, either from the beginning or not. You all Rock and deserve a hug. I can't name you all because I'll surely forget someone.

I love bloggers and believe in supporting them just as much as my Indies. To me, if one doesn't exist, the other will vanish. So don't make this a competition. Make this a camaraderie. Friendships that reach from country to country. Words that touch millions and then some.

My Street Team of Risqué Readers and BETAS

Thank y'all so much for pumping me up and pimping me out...

I love you girls

Josette

Emma

Bella

Danielle

Colleen

Suzie

Taylor

Bethany

Samantha

Patricia

Caroline

Lindsey

Danielle

Ebony

Misty

Katherine

Helen

Jamie

And more... I know I'm missing a few. <3 Just know I love you all.

Y'all will never understand how much y'all made this happen. When I got low and wanted to give up, y'all's belief in my stories kept me going.

.

PROLOGUE

Nov 4, 2012

Blaire

Today is the day I say my final goodbye, but the words refuse to leave my tight-lipped mouth. It's not supposed to be this way. We have so many plans we've made that we still need to do. Plus, I'm not ready to lose you. I'm not ready to never see you again. You're the one person who always went first to make sure that it is safe for me... The person who shared every secret with me and vice versa before we even took our first breath.

You were my protector and knight, the reason I kept going when I wanted to give up. You hid my darkest secret and never looked at me differently. You promised you would never leave me. But you lied. Just like everyone else.

Now, I stand above the wet ground, watching as the brown box lowers deeper in the earth while you rest in there... cold, alone, not breathing. Except... I'm the one who can't breathe without you.

My mind travels from just a few days ago to the present. The finality sets in, and no matter how hard I try to wake from this nightmare, I can't. My hands grip the sides of my metal chair as my head starts to swim, and black spots enter my vision. The crack in my heart opens more with every word that passes the minister's mouth.

Benji may be resting in peace, but I'm the one who will never know peace. A lie and a needle have ripped my peace away. I can't fix this or go back in time, but I can make a promise to my friend... my brother... my twin. I will never forget him, or the reason he's gone from me. Never forget his laughter or his love. And especially the last thing he told me. Of the life that will never be because of one person.

Two weeks later

"No... no... no! Come on, you piece of crap. Go just a little further, please? I promise, as soon as I can, I'll get you whatever you need. Just please, for the love of all that is holy, keep going."

My prayer lands on deaf ears. Or whatever this old Toyota uses to listen to my rant because it sputters as smoke pours out of the hood.

I know it runs hot, but I put my last two gallons of water in the stupid thing a few miles back. *Fuck my life.* Why is this happening to me? Why didn't I take the time to get the stupid thing fixed? Because Benji always told me not to let people take advantage of me, and the idiot at the automotive place wanted me to pay an arm and a leg to repair whatever is wrong. I only have so much money left and that would have left me broke.

Feeling forsaken, I pull over and punch the steering wheel over and over again. *Please, let this be a damn nightmare.* What am I supposed to do now? I'm not used to being on my own. My whole life, I've had Benji, but not anymore. Now I have nobody. *Who did I piss off in the universe that has it out to make my life a living Hell?* Tears form as it dawns on me that there's nothing around and no traffic coming my way on this deserted road. I'm somewhere in BFE, Nevada with a broken down '83 Toyota

Camry and two hundred dollars to my name.

After stepping out of the car, I kick my tire and scream, desperate that someone will hear me before I rot on this road to nowhere. *Hell!* Call the crazy bus to come get me. I don't care. I just want to… to… *Crap! I have no idea what I want anymore.*

It's my own fault I'm here. The need to get away had me packing up and running from what I knew and what my old dreams were at one time. All I ever wanted was one moment of pure happiness. Something I've always seen in others. But I'm left feeling disgusted with myself and with nowhere to go.

More screams emerge before the tears try to come once more. But I'm tired of crying, tired of feeling sad. Wiping the moisture away, I focus on my anger and look toward the sky before I shout again. *"Ahh!"* When my voice starts to feel scratchy and cracks, I stop and catch my breath.

My eyes look up toward a cloudless sky as I try to think of my next move. Except my mind can't help but notice how its beauty is so opposite to how my life is. Where it's serene, I'm such a damn mess. While growing up, peace was something I never knew.

Breathing deeply, I can't help but wonder if Benji is up there somewhere. If he is, I hope he can see the finger I'm holding up. "What did I ever do to deserve this? Huh? Well, I got news for you, Benjamin, I'm going to go to Vegas and live our dream *without you.* You hear me? I'm going to make it big and have all the money we always talked about when we were growing up. While you just sit up there, or wherever, and do nothing."

But I'm only filled with gusto because I have no desire to sing or touch an ivory key ever again. I don't know what I plan on doing when I get to Vegas, but it won't be music. Maybe I'll become a showgirl. *Yeah right!* The very thought of random people watching me sends shivers down my spine. I'll probably waitress like I'm used to doing. Maybe I'll get a cat so I won't feel so alone.

The wind blows my hair in my face and makes a chill overtake me. It's December, and it's cold. I only have one jacket and a few pairs of jeans in my back seat, so if I need to camp in my car tonight, I'll have to bundle up. It won't be the first time, and I've certainly slept in worse conditions. Maybe I'll die and give the birds something tasty to eat. That way I'll have done something in my life.

So I wait. And wait. Now the sun has vanished, and the chill from earlier has dropped to almost freezing levels. The car battery eventually died so now every exhale is visible, and my fingers are almost frozen. My last cereal bar has been devoured, but luckily, I haven't had an appetite lately. It's been at least an hour since the last car passed, but a lot of help that prick was. He just kept going, not paying any attention to the freezing girl stranded on the road. *Fucker!*

I rub my chilled fingers together, desperate to gain feeling and warmth in them, and when I look up, white lights are coming my way. Should I let myself freeze to death or try again? I don't want to die in my car, so I decide to try once more. The last time I hitchhiked was with Benji when we left our own personal hell the day of our eighteenth birthday. It was the best gift we could have received. Freedom. Or at least we thought we were free.

I stand beside my car and wave my hands in the air while jumping up and down. Deciding to show whoever it is that I'm a helpless girl, I take my hoodie off and bring my fading red hair over my shoulder. When the SUV keeps going past me, I feel frustrated and pissed, but then I watch in amazement as its brakes light up and it turns around. Excitement and fear cause my heart to beat fast. "Shit!" Was this a good idea? I know desperate times call for desperate measures, but what if this person is on the run? There's no turning back now, but I'm pretty fast if I need to make a quick getaway.

When the vehicle pulls up to my side, I hold my breath as the window rolls down. Sitting in the driver seat is a woman who looks to be only a few years older than I am, so I exhale in relief.

"Need a ride?" She speaks around her cigarette.

Her blue eyes show no threat, so I decide she's harmless. Maybe a little wild, judging by her large, showcased breasts and tight clothing. However, wild I can handle, I think.

CHAPTER ONE

"Another lessoned learned. Another wall up."
~Blaire

10 Months later

Blaire

"Hit me, Blaire. Hit me," Mandy yells from above me as I lie on the mat trying to catch my breath. "Don't be weak. Don't cower. Fight, damn it. Fight." She comes to kick me, but I grab her foot causing her to fall beside me with a heavy thud.

My entire body aches from her blows, but I stand up anyways ready for more. My wrapped fist swings out to hit her, but she's too fast and dodges it. My uppercut doesn't graze her. It's always like this with her. No matter how many months we practice she's just too damn fast. We rented out the entire gym tonight while visiting Los Angeles. Tomorrow night we hit the town, but tonight we practice and ready ourselves for the worse situation possible.

We circle one another preparing for anything to happen. She side steps, and before I know what's happening, she has me in a backwards chokehold.

"Fuck, Blaire. When are you going to learn?" Then I feel the cold metal against my temple before I hear the pull back of a gun.

1

"Fight. For. Your. Life," she whispers menacingly in my ear.

It's a do or die situation. She's taught me how to fight and get even. Since she found me on that highway, she's made sure her life mantra is with me every day. *"Fuck them over before they fuck you."*

So I fight the best I can and rear my elbow back with everything I have until impact to her midsection is made and I'm rewarded with her releasing me with a grunt. My fist extends out with force to hit her the way she wants me to, but I'm faced with the pistol she never released. My body freezes with fear. "Bang. You're dead." Her voice is void of emotion as she pulls the trigger. Relief washes over me because it's empty, and only a clicking can be heard. My heart is pounding in my ears, and my knees are shaking. She shows no remorse and never apologizes. She is the epitome of the word bitch.

Mandy is wild, and I can't deny she's a bitch, but she's also a businesswoman who gave me a job. Not a typical one that is five days a week, but one that's only on Saturday nights, pays a hell of a lot of money, and provides expensive clothes, hotels, and new experiences. Now, I don't dwell in my anger as much. I use it on some of the world's richest sleazes. It probably is the only reason I haven't gone crazy. I find jerkoffs with too much money and not enough sense to stay loyal to their wives, or they have some other dark secrets. Mandy has a *men are the enemy* mentality, and believes they're all scum. She says our weekly lessons are for my protection in case one tries to overpower me. You never know what some lowlifes might try even though they're dressed like gentlemen. So I keep my eyes and ears on alert, trust my gut, and have my gun stashed in my clutch.

It's Thursday night, and I'm sitting at a five-star hotel bar in Los Angeles, drinking my glass of Cabernet and scoping out the place discreetly. I'm still sore, and needed extra makeup to cover my lip, but Mandy is a Jack-Of-All-Trades. She can shoot, fight, lie, and even turn a nobody like me into someone unrecognizable. She sits at a nearby table talking to an older gentleman in an Armani suit with graying hair and sporting some heavy bling on his hands. Her usual meal for the night.

Turning my stool around, my attention goes back to the young bartender in his crisp white button down before taking another sip to calm my nerves. Nausea always tries to set in before I meet my unsuspecting client. The thought of some fucker's hand touching mine is enough to make me change my mind and walk out those glass doors, but I keep reminding myself I'm trained and strong. Not weak. Not vulnerable. Nothing like I used to be. I concentrate instead on the itch this stupid ass wig is causing my scalp. Disguise is key in this business, and my bright red hair would cause someone to pick me out of the crowd too easily.

Tonight I chose one that's long and black because it brings more attention to my hazel eyes. Plus it complements the skintight pencil skirt I'm wearing with a three quarter sleeved white blouse that shows off my cleavage. It also hides my tattoos because snobs like this bunch would be real quick to judge a person like me. Add a pair of square, black-framed glasses and voilà. I'm Ms. Crystal Galloway, a graduate of Stanford University, who's looking for a new job. It's neat to play dress up and become someone different for a night. But sometimes, even covered with new clothes and a new name I still feel like the same Blaire from so long ago.

As I give myself another mental pep talk, I get the familiar, creepy feeling that I've caught someone's attention. My stomach rolls, but

I know the game, so I take a deep breath and internally count to ten trying to calm my nerves. I've been doing it for a while now so you'd think I'd be used to the feeling. But it's never gotten easier.

The weekend after Mandy rescued me on the Nevada Highway, I was introduced to this lifestyle. The cash is too plentiful, and I have become a greedy bitch. Having money to buy what I want is new to me. I've never been able to go and buy a brand new Gucci bag or some designer clothes before this. Plus I'm no longer Blaire Morgan from a fucked up family who's alone in this world... I can be anyone I want.

Before I make my move, I look at Mandy, who's also in disguise. She gives me the signal by rubbing her neck seductively. That's my green light. If she had tapped the table, I would have known to wait for the next one, but Mandy knows her men. She knows who has the real money and who's just bullshitting. I swear the woman was in the CIA or some shit because she can always detect a lie. And even though she's taught me her secrets, I'm not as skilled as she is. She always says it's the details. Watch their eyes, their movements, and feel their pulse to see if any changes are made. Feel them out. Start with simple questions and always trust your gut.

After I stand up from my stool, I make a subtle walk past my new target as he and another gentleman sit at a table. Luckily, the restrooms are this direction, so this is easier than acting as if I'm meeting someone else further back or talking on the phone. After about three minutes of checking my make-up, I walk back out and *accidently* drop my clutch in front of their table. Like a helpless woman. "Crap." Boobs faced in their direction I bend over to pick it up, but like always, he's there to help.

"No, let me." He stands back up, and I take in his balding head, dark goatee, and broad shoulders, He's stocky and obviously likes

4

to indulge if his double chin and gut are any inclination. "Here you go, Ms...?"

"Galloway. Crystal Galloway." I give him my hand, and just like the rest of the pricks I've met this past year, he kisses the back of it. *This one is in the bag, baby.* Deciding to stoke his ego I kick up my smile and downcast my eyes. My naivety will make these peacocks believe I'm just a young stupid girl. "Thank you."

I go to turn, but he stops me by calling my name. "Would you like a drink Ms. Galloway?"

Turning around to stare in his direction, I bite my lip. He smiles in victory imagining him have a go at this young, clumsy girl in front of him, but he has no clue he's the one getting fucked tonight.

Walking into our room at a cheap motel a few towns over, I notice Mandy hasn't made it in yet. I take a shower and try to wash the ever-present disgust away, but no matter how hard I scrub my skin, it remains. After all the hot water is gone, I get out and wipe the foggy mirror with my hand to see my reflection. I think of the money I stole from that man tonight and swallow down my guilt. Life is about give and take, though. It's survival, and he had it coming. Right?

Taking a deep breath to clear my thoughts, my eyes land on the half sleeve I started while in Vegas. Since I have no desire to play music without Benji, I chose a black Fender guitar smashed into several pieces. Not just any guitar either, but an exact replica of Benji's scratched, beat-up Fender. Even though I don't have the heart to part with it, I let my tattoo do the talking with its shattered pieces- just like our dream of making it in the music business.

Poetry and music pieces float around its shattered form. I branded myself with my own loneliness in each script that's embedded in my skin. I want people to see it, so they know I'm damaged goods and to back the fuck off. My favorite of all is *"Breathing unwantedly in a world that's not worthy of my existence"*.

Why haven't I given up? I have no goddamn clue because I've thought about ending it all… Finding Benji again, in whatever heaven I've heard about all my life. But I was a coward and still am. Plus when I started making a thousand dollars in one night, I became addicted to money. I've saved a sizeable portion and blown the rest on materialistic things, clothes, and hair being the main things. It makes me feel normal and not poor or lonely.

After packing my bags for our early getaway, I take a long, deep swig of my dear friend Jack and fall into a dreamless sleep for once. When I wake the next morning, everything changes because I have another knife in my back and no money.

"From Mouse to Bitch. Is that really a bad thing?"

~Blaire

As I step off the bus in Alabama, memories of the day Benji and I arrived here try to surface to the forefront of my brain. We spent our last dime on the bus tickets to Mobile with only an old guitar and some talent in our possession. He swore this place would be more promising than the last, and I trusted him. We set up on the streets of downtown and played all day for enough money to sleep in a motel, but on most nights, the streets were our beds. It's pretty messed up how I felt safer living on the streets than in the house I grew up in. But I never felt like I was home until Janet found us.

She walked by while we performed *Open Arms* by Journey and gave us a gig with real jobs at her and her husband's bar, Jay Jay's. I remember feeling some excitement for the first time in my whole life while huddling behind Benji. He was always the one to guard me.

For years, I feared what people would see when they looked at me. One day I decided to have some control of my life and colored my blonde hair red. I felt hidden, improved... even braver. Now that girl that stepped off that bus all those years ago is long gone... dead. Just like my brother. Just like my soul.

I block out my inner rambling and try to concentrate on what I'm going to say to Janet. I ditched my phone long ago as well as anything or anyone to remind me of what I lost, and I ran. With any luck, she still has my stuff that was left when I took off. Maybe my job is still open. Since Mandy left me high and dry, I gotta start from scratch. Again.

Most of all, I hope that that bitch Trudy isn't working there anymore. She deceived my brother and dated some rich guy. Benji was so broken. Maybe she quit, dropped out of school, and married that Jax guy. Or maybe she lost her job and the guy. That would be even better, even though she deserves far worse for what she did to Benji.

As I make my way down the street, I notice the stares I receive from everyone I pass. It's not from the guitar slung over my shoulder or my bright red hair. I'm sure it's from my fuck me boots and ass kissing shorts I'm wearing. That bitch Mandy took off with all my shit and only left me a few of the slut outfits we purchased for some jobs. And let's not forget that I'm braless in a white tank top. She didn't even leave me a bra to hold up my tits, just a mere hundred dollars and a few pieces of clothes to cover my ass. I don't know where that bitch went, but when I see her again,

I'm going to go ballistic. Every time I think of her, I become more livid. Not to forget that today, I've had a shitty bus ride, and I'm starving. So yeah! I'm bitchy.

"Hey, baby. Want to party with me and some friends?" Some drunk guy stumbles by my side as I make my way down the crowded sidewalk. It's Saturday night, and the college kids are on the prowl. But this loser needs to work on his hunting skills because I am not his next target.

"Fuck off." I continue while passing onlookers and familiar buildings. When his arm slings around my shoulder, a familiar fear creeps in, and my heart kicks up its pace. But I remember I'm not there anymore. I'm not *her* anymore. "Don't fucking touch me, you prick." I throw his arm off.

"Oh, come on, baby."

Before I can set this annoying little shit straight and tell him I'm not his or anyone's baby, I reach Jay Jay's parking lot and stop dead in my tracks. My eyes spot a piece of my past that I wasn't expecting. Parked a hundred feet in front of me is Foxy, Benji's pride and joy for the last year before he died. He saved for so long just so he could buy that ugly bike. Well, it used to be ugly. He spent all his tip money and spare time just to make it run and look good. He swore he'd get me on it one day, but I was scared to death of getting in a wreck. I told him over and over again how he'd die one day from being his usual risk-taking self on it. How wrong was I?

Stepping closer, I see the tag still on the back, displaying its stupid name. He loved this fucking piece of junk since the day he laid eyes on it. He made it into something and always believed in the underdog. I guess because that's what we were growing up. Plus, he hated sharing the Camry and stated I was messing with his game. So he brought home Foxy from some junkyard. But what I'm looking at isn't the same bike I left behind.

Instead of being dull black with chrome pipes, it's polished with silver and red flames on the gas tank. I rub my finger along the cold metal and let what I see sink in. Something I left in Janet's possession for safe keeping... Something that was too heavy to take with me, unlike his guitar, but means just as much or even more... Something that's one of the last pieces of my brother I have left. Something drove here tonight by someone who's not Benji. *What the hell!* I don't know why the fuck it's here or who the fuck drove it, but they are going to pay.

When I turn around, I realize more people are watching me—some smiling like idiots, some sneering like bitches. I hike my guitar higher on my shoulder and walk over to the line, shoving past the people waiting to get in the door. I hear a lot of *"Heys"* and *"Fuck yous"* behind me. Don't care. I have tunnel vision and want some fucking answers.

The closer I get to the front, the louder the yelling coming from inside becomes. When I reach the door, another fucking hand on my shoulder stops me. "What?" I yell and turn.

Carlos, one of the bouncers I used to work with, scrutinizes me with his freaky dark eyes. Yeah, it's nice to see a familiar face, but there's someone else I need to see, and someone else who has something of mine that I want back.

"Blaire?" He looks as if he's been hit with a two by four, judging from the surprise that's on his round face. I know I look different from a year ago, and I know I'm dressed like a street walker, but if he licks his lips one more damn time I'm going to bust them with my fist.

"Is Janet inside?" I don't wait for an answer. I shove my guitar in his arms, and then make my way past his large frame and into the crowded bar. My nails dig into my palm to keep from freaking out over all the close bodies pressing against me. I also try to ignore the ever-present memories, but being here-the place that held my brother's happiest memories- they feel stronger and like it was just yesterday, we were on that stage. I let his face and last words enter, but direct it all into anger. Let my sadness fester and build into something that's slowly killing me. Hatred.

I head in the direction of Janet's office that sits down the hall that is beside the stage but the place is like a fucking mad house and I can't get a few feet in the door without people getting in my fucking way. *Breathe... Just breathe, Blaire.* 1...2...3... I continue to count like I always do when I feel overwhelmed and do my best to avoid having another panic attack. Too many people mixed with too many emotions are not good for me without some form of alcohol in my system. I can't relax and feel more and more agitated and closed in with every second that passes. I'm almost ready to run but continue instead.

Finally, I reach the crowded bar and yell for Chris, who is running his ass off. He comes over, but before he can reach me, I look over and see Janet walking my way. She still looks the same, worn out from working many hours at the bar, and worrying about money. She's had it hard for the past few years, and I'm sure me disappearing didn't help. Her hair color is a dull brown now instead of the bleached blonde it was last year. She also has some graying at the temples.

The only word to describe the moment we lay eyes on each other is bittersweet. I've missed her, but I'm so pissed and confused. She smiles and comes over to give me a hug, but my arms remain at my sides. I don't want her affection. Not now. It brings back too many memories of what I used to have.

So I keep my walls up and skip the pleasantries. "What the fuck, Janet? Why the *hell* is Benji's bike outside?" I yell over the loud music, and she's immediately taken by surprise at my new tone. I'm not the same girl that she consoled all those months ago nor am I the quiet Mouse she used to call me. I'm a loud bitch with a voice who wants to be heard.

Her smile vanishes, and I'm glad. I don't want to be reminded of her friendship or kindness. I just want Benji's shit back and to earn some money to get my ass out of here. To disappear.

"Nice to see you, too," she says sarcastically.

"Dammit, Janet. I'm serious. Do you still have my stuff?"

She studies me for a second with tired eyes. I can only imagine what's going through her head. I look like a fucking streetwalker. "I still have some of it. But you vanished. I'm not gonna hold onto someone else's shit so it can rot. So I sold most of it." She starts to cough, and a part of me wants to pat her back, so I place my hands on my hips instead.

"*What?* It wasn't yours to sell. That was Benji's and mine." My voice is full of anger as it raises and starts to grab people's attention. "I left it with you, thinking it'd be safe."

Her eyes narrow. "What the hell was I supposed to do Blaire? You vanished. I called a million times, and you never picked up. Not one damn time. Then your phone was disconnected, and for all I knew you were dead in a goddamn ditch somewhere. So lose the fucking attitude or get the hell out of my bar." Glints of moisture enter her eyes, but she wipes it away. She's always been hard to everyone but me. Until now.

"I'll get out after I get what's mine back." Making my way to the stage, my mind is in a blood fog. Ready to take back all that's been stolen from me. My soul feels as though my brother has been ripped from me all over again, but this is something I can get back. Even though it's just a material thing, it was his, and if I need to take it back with force, I will.

I stomp my ass-kicking stiletto boots up on the stage, ready for war. After I snatch the mike out of someone's hands, I flip everyone in the crowd the bird and address these fuckers hoping for some answers. "Tell me one fucking thing and I'll leave. Who the fuck is riding the black '88 Harley FXRS parked in the staff parking?" I'm lucky to remember the model of the bike because Benji talked about it so much. Especially whenever I called it 'just a bike'. He had to correct me.

As I wait for an answer, heat blankets my naked flesh on my right side, but my eyes stay focused on everyone in the crowd. Then I hear the culprit's answer. "Me." Chills surface everywhere on my body from the rich yet menacing tone. It encases me in its warmth and my mind loses focus.

When I see the voice's owner in all his fucked up glory, my anger morphs into something I've never felt before. Something that sets my belly to quivering. Tall doesn't express his height, and toned doesn't define his frame. He's like a walking, talking, tattooed, sex god with a dark faux hawk that's spiked up just right and some facial hair on his high cheekbones and strong jaw. His full lips twitch up in one corner, and heat starts to rise in my cheeks, so my eyes leave his face.

Seeing the red Les Paul in his arms only adds to his rock star appeal and snags my attention. I want to say he's a poser, but he looks like the real fucking McCoy. I already hate him just for the fact that he has my brother's bike. But add in how my heartbeat skips when his eyes land on me, and I fucking despise the air he breathes.

Without warning, my body walks closer to him, until I can see the beads of sweat on his forehead. To stop my gawking, I allow my inner rage to show through my hazel eyes. I hope that hell's fire shows around my irises and scares the shit out of him. However, from the way his pupils start to dilate, I'm having a different effect on him than what I've planned. So before my female body can get the best of me for the first time in my life and make a stupid move to lick his labret piercing, I act without thinking. I allow my fist to connect with the fucker's chin. With my hand throbbing, I jump off   stage   and   disappear   into   the   crowd.

CHAPTER TWO

*"My fucked up Reality is your
Worst Nightmare."*
~Lyric

Lyric

After our last set, I snatch a beer while continuing to search for the girl with the mean right hook. I don't see her, but I want to know what the fuck her deal is. When she'd disappeared earlier, I'd gone outside and checked on my bike to make sure the crazy bitch didn't touch it. No bombs were attached, and no key marks were visible, so I returned to the stage to finish the show. I would have left and chased her ass, but I promised Ryan's friend Mason that I'd play tonight to celebrate his wedding.

However, I regret my decision as soon as my fingers pass over the strings on my guitar. I have a love/hate relationship with my music. It helps me feel like just a normal guy in a band, but the feelings it stirs in me can bring me to my knees. My self-hatred always surfaces as I sing, but tonight, it seems on overdrive. It must be all the fucking love from the newlyweds.

My inner demon boils over, and my rage builds as each word passes my lips. I'm a prisoner by my own hand and my rage is my guard. It reminds me that happy endings are a fucked up fairytale told by people who are blind to what hides in the dark.

Maliciousness can be dressed in suits as well as orange jumpers. People will do evil shit to survive, and I'm one of them. All I have to do is think of *her,* and of how I fucked up that night, to know the truth.

Looking around, I eye the young drunk crowd that is always nearby these days. College kids are annoying as hell. The drinking doesn't bother me, but acting like a fucking idiot does. I'm not perfect by any means, but I don't stick my dick in everything that walks either. The girls do anything to get attention from either someone they want to hook up with or someone they want to make jealous. Stupid bitches. But the pretty boy cocksuckers are no better, walking around in clothes with premade rips and hundred dollar shirts. They don't know what it's like to go hungry or to be barefooted in wintertime I'm sure. Most probably still suck on their mother's tit.

When I was told this place had an opening for entertainment, I knew I'd be playing around a younger crowd. I also knew I'd hate it, but I didn't think I'd detest it this fucking much. Happy isn't my thing. At The Hole, I was constantly around the rougher, older crowd: fighters, bikers, prostitutes, and thieves. It's where I could be found most nights, hanging out or handling business matters. The owner, Joe, thinks I'm hanging around here to keep attention off his place. In reality, I'm stuck here, babysitting. Playing with the boys is just a perk.

I'm fortunate enough that I only have to be here a few nights a week and most of these kids have finally learned to leave me the fuck alone. If I had my way, I'd sing, fight, and avoid this place like the plague. But duty calls, and right now, I have a serious problem, which has nothing to do with Jay's crowd.

"Jimbo?" I yell to my bassist who's also one of my runners. Lately, rumors of his constant dipping have reached my ears, and from the edginess and constant touching of his skin, I'd say the rumors are accurate. I have one rule in this band. Keep clean. I don't use, and I don't want my members using either. This band means more to me than all the dope money I've made in this business.

He scratches his red beard when he stands in front of me. "Yeah, boss?"

Tonight isn't my night to do pleasantries. I lean down and give him a grimace. "You gypping my clients?"

I watch his glassy eyes widen before he swallows down his guilt. "Nah, man."

Lies are written in all of his movements. "What's the one fucking rule, Jim? The one thing I ask of you and Ryan?" I don't let him answer before my fist cracks against his nose. Ryan watches the encounter and just shakes his head.

"Ryan. Get Carlos, will ya? Tell him to drag this piece of shit out and not to let him back in." I look at Jim on the floor clutching his bloody nose. "You're through with Lyrical Obsessions and me." I watch Carlos drag Jim's ass out and hope I never see him again.

"What the fuck are we gonna do now?" Ryan asks from beside me watching the same thing. He's my drummer and probably the closest thing to a friend I have. He's a pain in my ass, but seems loyal, so I keep him around.

"The fuck if I know." And I don't. Now I need another goddamn bassist.

We head to our usual table and I sit in my vacant seat while glancing around. As they talk of the earlier commotion with Red, I just nurse my beer and observe. David and Ryan are both playboys and always seem to be trying to get in between a different bitch's legs every night we're here. Tonight is no different, and they're sitting with their traditional whiny bimbos. The short blonde chick and her new husband Mason are making gooey eyes at one another across from me. Sailor mouthed Cory is with her country boy date. Then I see the real reason I'm sitting here dealing with this shit. Trudy sitting in her boyfriend Jax's lap.

I've been told that my nemesis wanted her as payback for a kilo of prime powder that he lost when her ex's house was raided a year ago. The ex is now in jail, but when he gets out, I'm sure he'll be dead. That is unless Trudy is taken as retribution. I don't plan for that shit to happen on my watch.

She was supposed to be taken last year but the guy ended up dead in the end. After that, I was told to keep an eye out while waiting to get my hands on Polesky's Russian ass and bring him down.

Nicholas Polesky is the drug lord to the Russian Cartel, who's downright fucked up in the head. If he gets her, either she'll be sold, made into his personal slut, or killed. He has major connections in this country and is the principal supplier for the Southeast. Last I heard, he was sitting low in Atlanta somewhere. So far, no one can pinpoint his exact location. We do know his shipments come in on Georgia and South Carolina's coast. And before I came into the picture, he tried to get his hands on the Gulf coast. And I dare that sonofabitch to try and take it from me.

My eyes focus on Trudy for a moment, and I notice she's drinking for the first time since I met her. She's always been quiet, and I hope she stays that way. The last thing I need is a loud, annoying girl to babysit. Even though all has been quiet, I still watch her. Jax seems to have a handle on things right now, but I'm not sure how he'll do when shit goes down. And it always does in time. Especially in my line of business.

Luckily, Ryan's the only one who knows of my Cartel job out of this group of young kids, and not by choice. He's a persistent pain in my ass who's hung around The Hole enough to figure it out. But instead of putting a cap in his ass for knowing too much, I keep him around. He's been loyal and keeps my mind in a better place when it wants to stay in the dark. I need that at times, so I don't go fucking insane and do something I'll regret.

A hand touching my shoulder pulls me from my musings, and I immediately grasp it. I don't like to be surprised. When I look up, I relax when I see its owner. Mari Rivera.

"I'll be damned, sugar. When Ryan mentioned you two were in a band, I had no fucking clue it was like what I just heard." Mari walks around my chair while her hand slides along my shoulder. She sits in my lap, uninvited, but much welcomed at the moment. Usually I'd throw the chick off who attempts to do something like that, but Mari is someone who is more than welcome. Especially tonight. I need to get rid of this frustration and what better way than to have a quick fuck. She's also someone who can hold her own and I respect. Which is something not easily gained.

She fights at the gym and last year, she started competing. Ryan and I actually spar with her because female fighters are few and far between. And it's improved her skills and strength a considerable amount. If she keeps it up, she'll be able to go pro as she's dreamed of, in no time.

She's not looking to be Sally homemaker like most women. She wants to win a belt in the UFC, so she doesn't want anything other than an occasional fuck. And that is totally cool with me. It's like getting in the ring. We go at it a few times and then go our separate ways. That is until we get ready for another round. Like now.

I grip her ass as she turns and straddles my lap in her tight jeans. "What did you think we did? Played in Ryan's uncle's garage where we stash our Playboys?" Grabbing her cigarette, I inhale a deep drag while trying to calm my body's repressed cravings. After years of being clean, you'd think they'd quit, but when I get real fucking agitated, they like to surface, and I know exactly who has me fucking frustrated. It's not Jim, either.

Mari licks her pink lips, and I see the glint of the tongue ring that knows all sorts of tricks. "Playboy, huh? I have something warmer than a magazine and a lot more vocal. You want to see a real centerfold tonight?" Her hand travels from her shirt-clad breasts down her tight body and reaches my denim-clad cock that's straining to be set free. "Where's that cute redhead from earlier? She can play too if she likes it rough."

"The hell if I know or care. She's just some crazy chick who's lucky she's a she." I pull her hard to my mouth and fuck her lips with my tongue. My fingers pull roughly on her dark hair, so there's not a millimeter of air between us. Most girls pull away when the demon takes over. Not Mari though. She always seems to like it when I get rough. I wonder if Red would like it. Maybe her hair color isn't the only thing on fire. She might like… *What the fuck? Get a grip.* That crazy ass girl will not ruin my fucking night anymore. I pull away and enjoy how Mari's dark eyes are halfway closed and her panting breathing fans my face. "Let's go."

After she stands, I shoot a quick text. **Headed out**.

Lou knows to keep his distance. He's one of my warehouse managers and watches for anyone crazy wanting to cause trouble where trouble shouldn't be. Or if we have unwanted company from the Russians.

"Your place or mine, sugar?" Mari asks as we make our exit. I just look at her because she knows the answer. Very few people come to my house. Too much liability. She nods her head, hearing my response in my silence. "Gotcha. See ya there." She heads out towards her Dodge Ram 1500 that sits on thirty-eights. Guys around here would kill to drive something that big, and when she jumps out, they always want the whole package. Me… I'll stick with my bike. Faster and easier to outrun shit. But I do have my silver Z28 SS at home as a backup.

Pulling into her house off Dauphin Street, I follow her up the steps to her front door. She lives in one of Mobile's historical homes that is being fixed up over time. Real wood siding, old wooden floors, and small rooms, I couldn't stay in something like this. I need space, or I'll feel like I'm back in a cell.

Before I can even get in the door, she discards her jeans while watching me. No sweet words with this woman. Just get down to business and get home. I walk to her after she's stripped down to her black panties and reach around her waist to grip that ass I love. Some guys are into tits. Me? I'm all about the ass on a female. I lift her in my arms before walking forward to place her back against the wall. The feel of her ass in my palms has me kneading each cheek roughly, as I bite her plump bottom lip. I grind myself between her muscular thighs while my tongue explores her mouth before I kiss my way to her ear. "How do you want it, Mari? Here, first?" I reach up and take her mouth roughly, imagining my cock being sucked by those lips. "Or here?" Bracing my legs, I hold her up with one arm as the other reaches between her legs to rub the spot she loves. She moans when I pass her clit with some pressure, and her body twitches in my arms. She's so fucking wet already that I slip a finger in and move it along the walls of her pussy.

"Mouth, Lyric... Fuck my mouth," she pants out. She loves to give head, and I love watching her kneel in front of me, licking the underside of my dick before taking me in her mouth.

I oblige without another word and enjoy as she sucks me till I'm hard as stone and ready to explode. Call me greedy, but I don't give a fuck. She wanted it, and she'll get it after she sucks me up again. "You gonna swallow?" My voice is gruff as I try to hold back for another minute. She looks at me, and with the moonlight through the window illuminating her face, arches her brow. Of course, she'll swallow. This is Marisol Rivera.

21

She adjusts herself on her knees and takes the base of my cock in one hand while the other caresses my balls with just enough pressure to take me over the edge. I grip her head and hold her to me while I thrust repeatedly before I explode in her mouth. As my thrusts slow, she looks up at me and knows what I want next. So she takes my come in her mouth, and spits a small amount back on the head of my shaft before licking it up again.

After I'm cleaned and she's swallowed, I step away and wait for her to stand. Then I walk over and pull her face to me before I kiss her roughly. So hard I'm sure her lips will be bruised in the morning, but right now, I just don't give a shit.

I get home at three a.m., still feeling restless, even after my night with Mari. I should be as drained as she was when I walked out, but my body's set on a different clock. After years of watching my back in the dark, I stay awake when the suns down. A decent night's sleep is something foreign to me. If I've ever had one, I don't remember it. I'll take a nap when the sun rises.

Standing on my front steps, I look up at the moon and flex my fingers over and over while my heart beats against my ribs. Why the hell am I this fucking hyped up? I didn't have a bad run or have to handle some shit ass slinger like a few weeks ago, but I feel like I just fought in the ring and I'm ready for round two.

"It's about damn time. My ass has gone to sleep."

With an ingrained instinct, I swiftly cock my gun and direct it toward the intruder in the shadows. Now I know something is not right with me. Usually I'd know there was someone sitting on my porch. Mistakes like this one can't happen in my line of work. It could cost me my life.

I squint my eyes in the direction of the voice that scratches at my memory. "You have until the count of three to reveal yourself before I pull the fuckin' trigger. One."

"Hold up, Scarface." The figure steps closer until he's in the moonlight five feet away from my gun. "Now will you put that damn thing away? You could put your eye out with it."

Surprise and suspicion war when I finally recognize the person in front of me. Parker Hyde AKA Hyde is the last person I ever expected to see again. The last time I saw him was before I left The Reform, or Hell as the young delinquents called it. He came in when I was nineteen. He was quiet and stayed to himself. If you ask me, he didn't belong there. I stuck up for him a few times since I had been there for two years and most knew to keep their distance. The law says he's a felon like myself, but I don't see it in him. Never had. Even now- with his clean haircut and clothes that make him look like an Abercrombie poster boy. Plaid button downs aren't my thing and neither are khakis. But he's always been able to conform to any environment or situation and eventually held his own. "Hyde?" Shaking my head, I hesitantly put my gun away. "What the fuck are you doing here, and how the hell did you find me?"

He only shrugs and keeps his eyes on mine. "You know who sent me, dumbass. The why is because rumor has it Polesky is in town, and they think you may need me."

Pissed off, agitated, and excited, I pull my hair before I have a chance to punch my door. I'd love to face off one on one, but he always has his thugs do his dirty work. He's nothing but an exaggerated pussy. I've been waiting for him to come on my fucking turf, but I know he's bringing his posse to showoff and protect his ass. I also know there's going to be trouble. Now I have another person to watch out for. *Fuck!* Regardless of my anger, I need to get my shit ready and constantly watch what's mine.

Nicholas Polesky and his entire family are known to take what they want in the past. He was the worst then, and I'm sure he's the same bastard he was nine years ago. Memories of red, warm blood covering my hands from what that fucker's family took from me cause my palms to twitch, ready to take them down again. This was where my reason to hate him and his entire empire surfaced. In that dark alley, I took something from him and got my revenge, but it started our hatred for one another.

Shaking the memory of Carly's lifeless green eyes out of my brain, I unlock the door to my home and try to bring my head to the here and now. I concentrate on the stonework around the fireplace and wooden frame of the mahogany crown molding and high ceilings until my heart slows down. I like this house. It's the nicest I've stayed in, besides one back in New Orleans. The gated suburban community helps me keep a low profile and prevents burnouts and junkies from coming here for their next fix. I keep surveillance everywhere and only have a few trusted men in. Ryan being one of them. Lou, my bodyguard and warehouse dog being the other, and I guess Hyde's ass being the third.

Walking into the kitchen, I don't say another word as Hyde follows behind me. I fix myself a stiff shot of Everclear and let my thoughts try to work out a plan as the warmth flows down my throat. The Reform gives you one man you report to daily with all new information. If something happens and action is needed, *you* make a plan and handle it. If you fail, then you're useless to them after that and disposable.

Hyde leans against the dark granite counter, watching me intently. "So I'm here to help get this mess cleaned up and save your ass. I don't want any lip about it either. You've saved my ass before, and it's time to repay the favor." He sees my dark look that says 'fuck off' but ignores it. "You know we have no fucking choice in the matter, man. So go ahead and think of something to tell the people you associate with, and then figure out where you want me. Either I go into Jay's or the warehouse. I have to keep surveillance on both, but only one needs to know my face. Massey's orders."

He's right. I have no choice in the matter. He's been through the same shit I've been through while in The Reform, so I know he's capable of handling his own. I also know he's talented. His rich parents put him in every extracurricular activity a child could do, music, acting, karate. You name it, this kid did it. He does have skills and his photographic memory will come in handy. Plus he's smart with the tech shit. I'm more of a hands-on guy and computers aren't my thing. And if Massey, our go-to guy, said it, I know it's legit.

As I'm swallowing down my last gulp, I feel like a fucking genius as the perfect solution to one of my problems is formed. "Well, Hyde, if you have to be here, then I hope you brought some different clothes. Cause that pretty boy shit you're wearing ain't gonna cut it. Not for what I have in mind, *Cuz*."

CHAPTER THREE

"I am who I am for a reason. A reason I wish to forget and therefore forget who I am."
~Blaire

Blaire

I'm cold as I lie here hiding under my blanket. He's home, and beer cans were scattered around the living room floor when I came home earlier, so I know what's coming. The sun's lowering, but soft light still reaches my eyes as I bury deeper in my blanket wanting to disappear. However, its smell is my reminder that I'm still here. Even though I've washed it a thousand times, it still smells of stale beer and him. I wish Benji didn't leave me again. I wish I asked to go instead of staying here, but his life is so different from mine. Where I fold into myself for solitude, he reaches out and socializes. Laughing and flirting with all the local girls. Girls who look so happy and carefree. Not me. I'll never be like that.

Hearing the television click off, I hold my breath and pray. Pray he'll pass out... Pray my lock works tonight. When I hear the handle jiggle, my shaking escalates while a cold sweat breaks out all over my body. My fear of monsters still lives at fifteen-years old, but this monster is all too real.

Grabbing my pillow, I bury my face in the cool case and breathe in and out... in and out while counting to ten.

Concentrating on my breathing and the feeling of dizziness, I don't hear the door open or his approach. When the bed dips, I freeze all actions and wait for what's to come. Wait for it to be over.

"Blaire? Wake up, honey. Coffee and bacon are ready."

Startled awake by Janet's voice, I inhale a large gulp of clean air and sit up so fast I feel dizzy afterwards. On the third inhale, I notice the air smells of coffee and vanilla incense instead of sweat and agony, of safety instead of a threat. Looking around, my eyes adjust, and then I notice I'm still sitting in the old, green chair I fell asleep in. However, the visions remain, and the feelings they cause don't leave so easily.

I'm shaking as my nightmare encompasses my entire soul. I think of all the years of disgust and feel my stomach roll like a tidal wave. Covering my mouth, I stand up and run to the kitchen sink to vomit. I'm gagging so hard that tears form in my eyes, but they could be from the dream I just had. No! Not a dream. It was a memory. A fucking memory that leaves me with nightmares. Nightmares that only Benji could make better. Nightmares that trigger my whole spirit to deteriorate.

"Mouse? Are you okay, hon?" Janet stands by my side as I turn on the faucet to clean my mess. She gently touches my shoulder, but I stiffen and she releases me. I know she means well but touching anything or anyone right now is not an option. I stare down as the water eventually cleans away what little contents that I had in me, while wishing everything could be wiped away and cleaned up so easily. My knuckles are white, and my fingers have lost feeling from my grip on the countertop, but something cold on my hand has me loosening my hold. Janet places a wet cloth on top before she turns to finish what she was doing.

I'm thankful she doesn't say anything else. I don't want to talk about what I went through or what I caused Benji to experience because of it. I shut off the water and wipe my face with the damp rag before I go and jump in a scalding hot shower where I scrub and scrub, desperate to feel a sliver of cleanliness. My tattoos can't cover the filthiness that I have become used to over the years. But I'm hopeful. Hope is all I have left in life besides being a coward. I'm too scared just to stop it all.

Time passes, and the water becomes cold. Forcing myself out, I dry off. When I open the door, I see a pile of neatly folded clothes on the floor and recognize them right away. My old Guns N' Roses t-shirt seems to fit the same, but the old jeans have me lying across Janet's bed to zip them up. They used to leave some breathing room, but now my ass looks like it is covered in body paint. I guess it's from wearing heels and the classes I took this past year. Or I put on some weight in the ass area. I don't care though. At this point, I'd wear a trash bag to get out of my earlier prostitute attire I wore back here.

Making my way back in the dining area, I see Janet sitting at the table, reading the paper, and drinking coffee. She looks tired from last night's shift and I see the shadows under her dimmed eyes still.

When I sit down across from her, she slides an extra cup of coffee I didn't notice before in my direction. Instead of bringing up what happened earlier, she gets to the point. "First thing I want to know is how'd you get in here? I didn't see any busted windows, so I know you didn't force your way in."

Looking at her, I arch my brow. "The spare key you leave under that fake rock thing. It's in the same place that it's been in since I met you."

She nods her head before grabbing her pack of cigarettes off the table. "Okay. Then after you pulled that shit last night, why'd you show up here?"

Looking down, I let last night replay in my mind. I shouldn't have acted like that to Janet. Maybe to everyone else, but not her. Looking up, I stare in her direction and tell her the truth. "This was the only place I had to go." Her face softens a fraction, but I don't want her pity. I just want her to know how sorry I am. "I know I shouldn't have yelled at you, but I've had a shitty forty-eight hours. I was robbed and left with only some whore shoes and Benji's old guitar. I had just enough money for a bus ticket and a bag of chips. So I was pissed seeing Benji's bike outside of Jay Jay's last night and starving and really, *really* hurt, Janet. Hurt because I feel like someone else has betrayed me by taking something from me. But after I came here last night, I realized how stupid that was because you were right. I shouldn't expect you to keep my things and then disappear like I did." I wipe an errant tear away. "I'm sorry." My voice cracks as I apologize. Taking a deep breath, I make an effort to calm my crazy emotions the best I can.

She walks up and touches my shoulder again. This time I don't freeze or let it trigger a memory. I absorb the fact someone cares for me. Someone whom I trust out of everyone on this earth. "All right, hon. Enough of this mushy shit. I need some sleep before we open tonight, and you have a job to get ready for."

Just like that, I'm employed, and she's forgiven me. I wish forgiveness was that easy for me.

Walking into Jay Jay's at three in the afternoon on a Sunday is surreal. I am surprised Janet started opening again on Sundays in the first place because we were usually dead. However, she said with business booming every other night, the old regulars requested one night of quiet drinking. So here I am, in my old black T-shirt that says STAFF on the back, walking through the familiar place.

I'm feeling hesitant because I'm unsure how tonight will play out. When Janet mentioned Trudy was in charge of the wait staff, I felt my back stiffen as I went on alert. Even though I want that bitch to pay for making my brother miserable, I promised Janet I'd behave while on her clock. I let her know real quick that Trudy wasn't my boss, and I refused to take orders from a gold-digger. Of course, she quickly jumped to Trudy's defense. I guess the little hussy has everyone fooled.

The lunch shift is closing up and getting ready for the night crowd as I make my way toward the back staff lounge that sits across from Janet's office. It's cleaner than I remember, and it's even sporting a new red couch against the wall and a small TV. I guess business has picked up this past year for her to be able to afford such amenities for the employees.

After placing my bag inside and closing my locker, I turn and see the *princess* herself walk in, wearing the same smile that used to fool me. When our eyes meet, she stops short and loses it.

"Blaire... um... I'm so glad you're okay." She tries to smile, but it won't hold. The last time we saw one another was at my brother's funeral when my palm landed across her face. That was truly the worst day of my life. Out of all the pain I've suffered through in my life, seeing my once happy brother lying in a satin lined casket with cold skin, and no smile hurt worse than anything ever could. It literally felt as though a blade was cutting me in half. I begged for his eyes to open. For this to be some sick joke of his. But he didn't, and I knew this would be the last time I saw him. That image is forever in my mind, and the feelings of loss will always be there, no matter how much time passes.

Shaking off my grief, I roll my eyes as my anger resurfaces. I will not fall for her lies. "Look, bitch. You might have everyone deceived around here, but I know what you are. I know what you did to Benji. I'll work with you because I need the money and I'll keep my hands to myself because I respect Janet, but don't think you can tell me what to do. Don't even talk to me or breathe around me. Got it? I don't want your poison near me."

I see her eyes widen and watch her mouth open, ready to speak, but before a word comes out, another voice intervenes. One that I haven't forgotten, and once again, chills come to the surface while heat pools in my lower half. "Trudy? Everything okay here?"

"Y…yeah Lyric." She stutters.

Lyric? What kinda fucked up name is that? It repeats in my head and my heartbeat picks up with every syllable. I glance at him for one second to see his penetrating eyes burn me alive. Eyes that are malicious and beautiful at the same time. Murky gray-blue encircled by dark lashes and appear to see every part of my anatomy as they continue their evaluation. I feel naked and vulnerable while they calculate every beat my heart makes as well as the movement of my blood in each vein.

Breaking our stare, I bring my eyes back to my enemy who is intently watching our interaction to one another and try to shake off this reaction. "I see you already have someone else wrapped around your greedy finger huh? *Man…* you don't stop, do you?" I walk past them and through the door to escape, but when a large hand wraps around my bicep I'm pulled to a stop. I know who it is without looking behind me, so I keep my eyes ahead, staring down the empty hallway instead of looking into his. I need to be tough with this guy and keep my defenses up.

He bends low and hisses in my ear. "Leave Trudy alone. You keep your poison away from her. Got it?" He throws my words back in my face. But all I can concentrate on is the warmth of his breath on my ear and the calloused tips of his fingers as they rub my arm ever so slightly.

My breath hitches for a semi-second on its own accord, but I know he's noticed when his grip tightens once before he releases me. Still feeling the heat of his murderous stare, I walk quickly to the ladies' room to gain my composure, but I know I'm hiding. Hiding from whoever that monster is because he could make me hate someone more than Trudy. And I'm not sure if I can handle any more bitterness.

As the night goes on, I stay behind the bar while the other bitches run the tables. As far as talking to anyone, I stick with short conversations with customers and eye rolls with everyone else besides Chris, mixologist of Jay's.

I've always respected the guy being a soldier who was honorably discharged. He entered the Army right after high school as a way to stay out of trouble and because he wanted to follow in his father's footsteps. He ended his first term with a missing limb. No one knows his left leg is amputated because he wears jeans all the time while at work. Even though he gets his check once a month from the government, he still wants to make his own way.

He swats my butt with a rolled dishtowel to gain my attention. And I smile before giving him my middle finger.

"So, Mouse, what's with the new bitch look you're sporting?" Chris passes me a Cosmo to take to some hussy at the bar who keeps squealing like a fucking pig. *Who the fuck orders a Cosmo on a Sunday?* I wish I had an apple to stuff between her surgically amplified lips.

Grabbing the drink, I'm tempted to spit in its red contents, but decide against it. We'll wait and see what she tips me. "To keep people like that," I nod my head in the annoying girl's direction, "from talking to me." I've never understood people who see sunshine and rainbows in life, and they get on my nerves. Maybe it was more jealousy at one point in time, but sometime in my past, it's morphed into detesting them and what they stand for.

33

Ignorance.

Can't they see the ugliness that surrounds us as we sit here? The liars, cheaters, rapists? The people who beat down the ones they love? But no, they're too blind and too focused on themselves. They crave compliments on their looks to bring a sense of empowerment over the opposite sex. They don't know that this attitude is an actual weakness and could be the cause of their death. Maybe not a physical death, but a spiritual one because they won't watch their back until after the knife is already embedded. Mandy was the last person I trusted and turned my back on. I'll depend on myself, and if I happen to fail then it's okay. At least I'll walk out without another knife in my back.

"Yeah. They're always here for the band." I give him an eye roll, and he laughs. "Well, I'm glad you're back. I've missed Benji and you. But at least I can have my Mouse back, and I'm sure Benji would want you to be here with the people that care about you."

I don't respond. No one but maybe he or Janet actually gives two shits about what happens to me in life. Honestly, I'd rather no one care. Regardless of their concern, when I have enough money, I plan to leave again. I might keep in touch, but I doubt it. Janet would lecture me about being a wanderer on my own, but she doesn't know what I did this past year to survive. All the money I've stolen and marriages I'm sure I ruined. I'm sure she'd look down on me or chew my ass. Maybe I should tell her. That way she knows how truly fucked up I am, and she'll stop caring so damn much. I know one thing for sure. After Mandy left me without two pennies to rub together, I've decided that I'm tired of liars. So from now on, I plan on being a straightforward person, no matter whom my words hurt.

The night creeps on, and I watch the clock, waiting for my shift to be over. Thank goodness today is Sunday and we close early. If not, I'd have to take drastic measures and run out in front of a train if one more chick asks me when Lyrical Obsessions will be playing. I think I've had at least fifty show up wanting to hear them. Lucky for me, I haven't seen Lyric since our little clash earlier because I seriously don't like that guy. He's just too much. Of what? The hell if I know. I don't like people that think they know me and can put a hand on me. So I, being a bitch, enjoyed telling his groupies the ass-wipe lead singer was out doing a circle jerk with his buddies and how they can find him on YouTube doing bestiality videos. The looks of disappointment and disgust were hilarious. Let that fuckwad threaten me again.

CHAPTER FOUR

"It truly is a small yet, fucked up world."
~Lyric

Lyric

Breathing in and out, I hit the heavy bag over and over again. The sting of the vinyl against my bare knuckles is what I need to concentrate, not the red blood that covers them. It reminds me of someone's hair color that won't leave me night or fucking day. I need to concentrate on Polesky. Even though no one has seen the fucker in town, I'm sure he has eyes taking notes. It's what I would do if I were visiting another area. Especially if someone who equally hates you and wants to rip your heart out with his bare hands runs that territory. But no matter how much I try, I can't get Red out of my damn head. The one on my shoulders or the one in my pants.

I've seen her several times this week, coming and going from Jay Jay's as if she owns the fucking place. When I asked Janet about it, she tells me the girl has had it rough the past year and to let her pick the staff. I guess those two are close because they usually leave together. Trudy keeps her distance, but I see too much damn niceness when she looks in Red's direction. I need to get to the bottom of why Red hates such a nice girl so much. Maybe then, I'll stop expecting her to slit someone's throat.

"Cool it, Rampage. King Mo called off the fight."

Breathless, I grab the black bag to make it stop. My arms burn and my heart feels like I just snorted a few rows of some prime cocaine. Ryan walks up, sporting his trademark bandana and wrapped knuckles. Probably something I should have done, but I wanted the sting. Craved it. "What the fuck are you doing up so early?"

"Hey, you're not the only one who can't sleep some nights, you greedy sonofabitch. You already took my girl. The least you could do is share the damn gym." He places his bag by mine against the brick wall and begins to stretch.

"What do you mean? I didn't steal nobody's girl."

"Well, how many times have you and Mari fucked?" He continues because he knows I don't talk about my business like he does. "Even if it's just once, it's still more than me. That is one fine piece of ass, and I've been trying to bang that for a while."

I can't help but laugh at this kid. He dives in more pussy than a Gyno. Me? It depends on my mood. "Hey, champ, I haven't stopped you from making a pass at her. Go for it. You're the one who's always hooking up with someone else."

He turns to where his back faces me and leans on the wall to do some calf stretches. "Yeah. But the other night was the first time I've seen her at Jay's, and my mind was occupied."

"Don't you mean your hands were occupied?"

"Well yeah! But my mind was full of that Blaire chick Jazz and them were all talking about. That is one fine and fiery POA. I think I might try and talk to her. Ya know? Sweeten her mean ass up so I can lay on the cock while she wears them fuck me boots."

With every word that comes from his mouth, my anger goes up another notch. Just picturing Red with anyone brings out something in me I haven't felt in a long, long time. Jealousy so strong, I sense anger form in its depths, which has me wanting to rip off Ryan's hands for even contemplating touching her. Touching something that, for some unknown reason, has become a fucking obsession since I met the crazy bitch. He turns around and stops dead in his tracks when his eyes meet mine. "Dude! Why the fucking death-glare?"

Shaking my head, I focus on the bag again. "I just have a ton of shit on my mind." I continuously pummel the bag to keep myself in line. *Can't knock the hell out of my drummer.*

Ryan goes to a separate bag and pops in his earplugs to listen to some music. Me? I stay in my thoughts. Plus, I don't need a distraction when I have my back exposed. After another hour in deep thought about Polesky and now Red, I finish and pack up to head home since the sun is up, but receive a text that has me making a pit stop.

Pulling into the warehouse, I see Lou, my right hand man, with a few guys I don't find significant enough to remember their names. I remove my sunglasses and step off my bike before I pat my side feeling my Glock. It's gotten me out of some major shit the past couple of years. Especially in New Orleans or NOLA as us locals like to call it. It's my hometown, but the only family I have is either dead or in jail.

"Lou?" We don't shake hands when I get to his side. We're not gentlemen, so why pretend. Suits aren't right for my crew or me. We keep it casual and maintain a low profile. I'm sure Mobile County police department would love seeing a bunch of suits hanging out at the dock. Anything to get their dicks hard and fatten their wallets. "This better be important."

He nods his head. "It is, boss. We found out this fucker here," he nods his head to a mangled body in the center of the crowd, "has been lacing our shit before he sells it. Had two OD's last night because of it."

I nod my head as I take in the heap of limbs lying on the warehouse floor. His clothes are torn, his face busted, and he looks as if he's had enough. But I'm strict when it comes to my shit. It's clean and pure. I have the best heroine, nose candy, and cannabis shipped from all over, but Brazil is my main contributor. If you sell under my name, it better not be tampered with. I look at Lou. "Any minors?"

"Yes. One was a sixteen-year-old girl."

Now I'm pissed. The fucker in front of me opens his eyes (or eye, since one is swollen shut) and watches me walk to stand in front of him. I recognize him. He pulled this same shit a year ago. He sold it for more when it was laced, and then kept more money than he should have. Killed a close friend of mine, and I would have handled it then, but I'm a believer in second chances. Minors are a no to me. I don't fuck with them. Too much liability because they like to run their mouths and get shit stirred up. Knowing he killed one only brings more heat to me and my boys and depletes my pockets when I have to cover this shit.

"Pete. Pete. Pete," I say through a sigh. "I warned you last year about your habit of fucking with my shit. Didn't I? And didn't I, being the gracious person I am, let you off with a warning?" Pacing in front of him, I keep my stare on my boots. "And since I'm such a nice person, I'm going to give you one more chance." Now I look at him. His fear is apparent, but a small, bloody smile forms. I really hate when I can't beat the fuck out of him from the beginning, but seeing how my boys have already done it, it leaves me with only one thing to do.

"Yes, sir. Thank you..." He pauses when my hand goes up.

"Don't thank me yet. I'm giving you thirty seconds to run as fast as you can before I shoot you. And I won't kill you right off.

I'll take out your legs first. Then your kidneys and just work my way up. I'll use every last bullet to make you suffer like that girl suffered before I finish you off with the last one." His face is pale as he sits there in fear staring at me. "I suggest you get off your ass." I grab my gun out of the holster. "Lou, get your timer started."

Pete stands and starts when Lou says go, but I'm a helluva shot, which he learns right before he dies.

Leaving the men's room at Jay's, I step down the hall and yell in Chris's direction for a beer before we go on stage. I sit down at our regular table and notice Ryan's ass sitting on the table, drumming his legs while watching the bar. I know who has his attention, but there's not a damn thing I can do about it. Finally, his eyes move my way. "What?"

"Hyde here?" I ask, trying to take my mind off Red working behind the bar in those tight jeans that caress her ass. My palm would look great on it. *Cool it, dipshit.* "Where the fuck is my beer?" I need a quick cool down before thoughts of a certain bartender fuck with my head more than she already has.

Instead, I look around and try to keep my mind on the band because tonight's our first performance with Hyde as the bassist. I made him burn his momma's boy clothes and loafers in exchange for some jeans and t-shirt. I was surprised to find some ink under his clean cut clothes, and noticed the scar on his left upper back. Not my business. Not my problem.

"Yeah. He's behind stage, setting up or some shit. Where'd you find the guy anyways?"

"He's my cousin from NOLA." That's all I say because that's

all he needs to know. I like the guy and don't want him to end up dead. He nods knowing the subject is dropped.

"Figures you two are related. You're both grumpy shits. Don't talk. Don't smile." He looks at me. He rubs his palms together while his trademark smile makes an appearance. "Want to see what a smile and some conversation can get ya? Then watch me work my magic."

Before I know what he's talking about, I hear her sweet, husky voice that causes a stirring in my dick. "Here." A cold Corona lands in front of me with a loud thud. When her arm is in front of me, I grasp it to hold her in place. "Let me go, you fucktard." She yanks in an attempt to get free, but she's no match in strength. My hand encompasses her small wrist and forearm, and I take in every millimeter of skin. Her softness is amazing and something I've never noticed before in any female.

I turn my body to face her and tighten my hold just enough to make her eyes flinch. "Not until you learn some manners and bring me my beer nicely." I look in her eyes that stand out against her pale skin and red hair, wondering what the hell I'm doing? I have no fucking clue, but I can't seem to control my temper around this chick. She tries to give me her meanest look, but she doesn't scare me. She might act like a bitch, but I'm sure it's a front. I'm also sure she's an attention hog needing everyone's eyes on her like most of these girls. She'll probably blame her anger on daddy issues.

"Don't take it personally, but I don't do nice."

"Well, that's a shame. You'd be downright pretty if you occasionally smiled." *What the hell was that?*

She's just as surprised by my comment because her eyes widen, and she stops pulling and looks at me questionably. After a minute of the awkward stare down, she finally speaks. "You want me to be nice and happy? Then give me my brother's bike back."

Now it's my turn to be caught off guard, but I'm an expert when it comes to not letting my feelings show. Her words about the bike have one thought surfacing in my mind. This can't be the sister Ben spoke about. She's not timid or shy... or sweet looking. But as I search her face, I see it. The similarity is small, but it's there.

"What the fuck are you looking at?" While lost in thought, my grip must have loosened because she yanks her arm free and rubs her wrist. "Jesus! You're the one who needs to learn some damn manners."

"Oh, don't worry about *The Demon* here. He's as mean as they come." Ryan, who I forgot about, scoots around me and stands by Red. "Now me, baby, I'll be whatever you want. Polite, sweet, kinky... Let me take you out after your shift tonight. I'll show you how nice I can be." He wags his brow and gives his best smirk.

Red tilts her head while narrowing her eyes at him. "I'd rather bath in a gonorrhea-infested hobo's urine. *So fuck off.*" She takes her tray and shoves past Ryan while my lips form a smirk that can't be helped.

He turns my way, looking like a two-year-old, and she just took his favorite toy. And I guess she did, because pussy is his favorite thing to play with besides his drums. My smile slowly builds into a laugh as I watch his face. I haven't laughed in years, it seems, and it actually feels pretty damn good. Different, but good. Along with the laughter, I feel relief that she wasn't affected by his charm.

Ryan now watches me inquisitively. "What?" I wipe my smile away and down half my beer.

"You know, I've known you for almost two years now, and I've never heard you laugh. Not once. And I'm funny as hell. But this chick comes along, and now you're smiling like a fucking Disney character. What the hell is wrong with this town? First Cory starts dating some fuckin' yee-haw, David keeps fucking moping around, and you're fucking laughing?" He runs his fingers through his hair while shaking his head. "And to top it off, a chick turned me down. What. The. Fuck."

As he continues to vent, my mind goes toward Ben. He always wanted to play in Lyrical Obsessions, and man, he had some serious talent. But he couldn't stop using. I offered to pay for his ass to go to rehab, but he always refused, saying he was going to get clean on his own because he couldn't leave his sister. But that's a song that has been worn out over and over again with addicts. *This is the last time. After this bag is gone, I'm done.* I know because I've been there, and it took some major shit for me to stop. And by major, I mean life changing.

It's apparent not even his sister was enough to get him to put down the pipe and needles because he overdosed almost a year ago. Pretty fucked up that it was my shit he tweaked out on all the time. Even though I don't sell it to individuals, my clients and their runners do. Unfortunately, most have to lose something important to wake the hell up and finally pull their shit together.

Ben was good at hiding his habit from people and refused to bring his sister into this lifestyle. I didn't even know he had a sister for months after we met. Even then, he only mentioned her when he was fucked up. He told us how she was a quiet girl who was terrified of everyone who looked at her wrong or said something the wrong way. But he also bragged about how smart she was and how she was the most talented one out of the two of them. She wrote the music, played multiple instruments, and she could sing. He also mentioned scars that are on her. I'm not sure if he was talking metaphorically or physically because he'd usually pass out before he said more.

I'm not going to lie. This mystery girl he talked about always intrigued me, but the girl glaring at everyone as she works behind the bar is not what I was expecting.

Maybe she's not Ben sister. Maybe she's lying. *But why would someone fake that?* No. I know she's his sister. If Ben wasn't right in the head, I'm sure she's just as fucked up. Who's not this day and age though? I'm fucked up in my own right, and I kill in my job, but I'm not a complete monster. Well, not to the innocent. I don't believe in hurting women or children. I believe if you're guilty then you need to pay, and my gut tells me this chick has a story. And as much as I don't need this shit, right now I want to know what it is.

Feeling a sting on my left ear, I turn and swing my fist, barely miss a laughing Ryan. "Did you just flick my ear?"

"Fuck, yeah. You're daydreaming, and we need to get on stage." He spins his drumsticks in his fingers. "Now, let's rock this shit so I can mend my broken heart and get between some warm thighs." He jumps on stage with more energy than a damn monkey on meth.

Putting my guitar strap over my shoulder, I climb the steps. Looking at Hyde tuning his bass and Ryan sitting on his stool, an idea starts to form. Hopefully, it'll prove if Red is, in fact, Ben's sister, and if she is, I finally get to meet this enigma of a girl I've heard   about.

CHAPTER FIVE

"Games are meant to be fun for all parties involved.
I guarantee you won't be laughing when it's over."
~Blaire

Blaire

The night has been going relatively pleasant since I left asshole's table. The crowd of girls has doubled since they started playing, and I hate the fact I still have a few hours to endure this shit. Chris's side of the bar has been slammed with just as many horny college girls as the dance floor was earlier. Luckily, Lyric is off stage, but he's still making his presence known as the band sits at their regular table in the corner. I'm busting my ass trying to avoid his eyes on me.

Thank goodness the annoying vaginas help to keep my anger in check and my stare from clashing with his intense one. When they introduced Hyde earlier, I swear I got a busted eardrum from the squeals. Get your libidos under control girls! These guys are all about fucking you and leaving you with either a baby, STD, or low self-esteem. Okay, so maybe some of these girls need to be brought down a notch, but do I have to witness all the lap grinding? I swear it's just how I imagine Disney world. There's a fucking line of girls that are waiting for a ride.

"You know you'd make more money if you'd smile every

once in a while?" Chris says as he pulls the lever to the draft beer.

"I don't smile. I work. I breathe. I sleep." I slide a shot of Jack to the asshole in a rented suit with slicked back graying hair, and laugh with sarcasm as he tries to look down my shirt. Again. He's been like this for twenty damn minutes, and it's starting to piss me off. "You gotta fuckin' problem with my tits, dude?"

His drunk, red, hooded stare meets mine. "Yeah, baby, I do. They're covered. Why don't you show me what you're hiding under them clothes?" He reaches out, trying to take hold of me while licking his nasty chapped lips.

Immediately, I start to shiver as my hidden terror surfaces. Without a thought, I throw the whiskey in his face.

"You bitch!"

Chris has me behind him before the ass can reach over the bar. "Back off, asshole."

"Look what that cunt did!" He points to his wet face and upper body. "You're gonna pay for this suit. You're gonna pay for this." His finger is directed at me as I peek over Chris's shoulder. The guy is older and well dressed, but I know a fake when I see one.

I step out from behind Chris, remembering I'm not Mouse anymore, or Blaire from years ago. I'm smarter… tougher. "Look, tiny dick. You can't ask girls to flash you their tits and expect them to show the goods to you. Especially if you live at home with mommy and rent a suit just to make yourself look respectable. Your gel-smothered hair needs a cut, and the dandruff you're sporting is reason enough for us to run for the hills. Add your fucked up, perverted ways of approaching a girl and you might as well go back to your blow up doll because the real thing is out of your league."

His face pales and narrowed eyes widen, confirming my thoughts were dead-on. He's a poser. Mandy might have taken my hard-earned money, but she left me with some pretty keen observation skills. Before he can defend himself, Carlos breaks through the gathered crowd to snatch the guy up and leads him out. With everyone's eyes now on me from the commotion, I feel panic set in as my adrenaline lessens.

"I need a minute to myself." Chris gives me the okay but offers me a shot of something clear before I leave. My shaking must be obvious. As the burn flows down my throat and settles in my stomach, I pass onlookers and push my way to the lounge. Sitting on the couch, I put my head between my legs and take deep breaths and count. Hopefully, the liquor will kick in soon and help calm me, but the emotions from moments ago are still there. I'm not used to defending myself. It's still new and can be very overwhelming. The burning clog in my throat starts to build, but I refuse to cry. I'm tired of being weak. *You're okay, Blaire... You're okay.*

"Everything will be okay, Blaire. I'm sorry. I shouldn't have left. I'm so sorry. I won't let him touch you again. I promise. We'll tell someone and get out of here. Grandma will help." Benji rambles and cleans my back as I lay on the floor huddled in myself shaking. I'm in a dark place, but his words still reach me. With each touch of the cloth on my flesh, a sting causes more pain that reminds me of earlier while I suffered. It's my fault I'm in pain. I fought back. He always warned me not to, but I was stupid and did it anyways. Now my brother knows my darkest secret and it's my fault. Now this blackness shadows not only me, but him, as well. And I can't change it.

A thumping noise arouses me from my trance. Looking up through a few errant strands of red hair, I see Lyric watching me. "What now?" I ask and look down to get away from the way his stare makes my insides squirm. Not from fear that he'll hurt me, but fear he'll see me. Judge me and accuse me of what happened to not only me, but also my brother. And that's something I don't want anyone to do. Especially him.

He shrugs his broad shoulders that are covered in his tight orange t-shirt. I see the tattoos on his left arm and respect him a little more. Is that stupid? Yes. It makes no sense, but I think some weird bond is forming from that, and from the fact that he's here. Obviously checking on me. And his art isn't done on a desperate drunken night. It's calculated and detailed. It obviously means a lot to him just as mine does me. "Just wanted to come see if you were okay before I get on stage again."

I exhale before standing, but suddenly I feel dizzy and sway. Before I know it, his large hands are resting on my shoulders holding me steady. I grab his wrist in reaction to his touch and feel the speed of his pulse. "Sorry. I guess I stood up too fast after the shot Chris made me." I look up expecting him to let me go, but he doesn't. He just holds me and rubs his thumbs along my collarbone in a soft touch while staring. My skin tingles and I feel my stomach begin to flip. "You can let go now. I'm fine."

He studies my face for a good minute while holding me in a trance. "No... No you're not fine."

He lets me go before he turns around and walks out the door. I'm frozen in place staring at the door he just walked through feeling pissed off and confused by his words.

After the bar closes and everyone is gone, I head to the kitchen and shut off the lights. Before Chris left, he asked if I needed a ride, but I feel like being alone tonight. I might sleep here instead of taking the bus. Janet had something to handle so she was off today and I don't want to depend on her to pick me up like a kid.

I sit on the freshly wiped down bar with only the blue lights from the stage surrounding me and drink a beer. Why not get fucked up tonight? I feel like I'm coiled tight in a ball and ready to snap open and cause havoc. So instead of setting this place on fire I might as well drink. And with any hope pass out without a nightmare waiting for me.

My eyes take in the drums before they move to the left. I see an old acoustic guitar sitting in its stand, and I feel a pull. It reminds me of the one we used to practice with when mom was alive. When we were happy.

Music was how I always coped with my feelings and past. Now I don't deal with them. I bury them. Just like I did my brother. Before I know what I'm doing, I'm jumping off the bar and slowly making my way past all the wiped down tables and stacked chairs until I'm standing in front of the steps that lead me to the place Benji and I actually bonded and felt at peace. I wonder if peace is still on that worn floor, or is it gone too? Like everything else.

I take a deep breath before I step up the first then the second step. Taking another swig of my beer, I look around the stage and freeze. *What am I doing?* Why do I need this shit? *"Fuck it!"* I throw my beer against the wall across from me. Climbing off stage is a lot easier than it was climbing up. Because even I know, there's no going back and changing what happened. Tonight I plan on finding solace in the bottle instead of the music.

The red couch in Jay's lounge has become my bed most nights during the week, but I still go shower at Chris's house. He's the only one who knows that I'm staying at the bar and has asked me on several occasions to stay with him, but I know he still suffers from PTSD and likes his solitude. Janet hasn't said or asked me any questions about my whereabouts and I'm not surprised. I know I make her uncomfortable. If I didn't then she'd be around more, but lately, she's been MIA while Chris and Trudy run the joint. Besides, I feel more at home at Jay Jay's than I do at her place.

Just the idea of a shower sounds perfect, and since it's early, nobody is here yet, so I can get back before the lunch staff arrives. Heading to my locker, I snatch a fresh pair of jeans and a long sleeve shirt because it's getting cold. And that sucks if you don't own a jacket. After my bag is packed, I shoot Chris a quick text, slip on some knockoff Toms, and wait for his reply. After I get the okay, I head out and run straight into Trudy. *Great.*

"Ouch!" She yelps before bending down to pick up some papers she dropped. "I'm so sorry Blaire."

I ignore her and go to grab my shit off the floor. When my shampoo and the Ziploc bag holding my toothbrush and some other toiletries lands on the floor by her feet, I know I'm busted. My hands reach to snatch them up before she can. "Thanks, but I got it." Jumping up, I make my way to the exit.

Just as I'm almost to the door, she calls out my name. "Do you need a ride?"

Rolling my eyes, I put my back to the door and push it open while I face the girl who fooled my brother with her lies. Even with her perfect hair pulled in a ponytail and green eyes that seem as sincere as all her gestures, she can't fool me anymore.

When the door cracks open a cold wind blows in and causes me to shiver and think about her offer. Should I face the elements outside and freeze or take her up on her offer? When my teeth start to chatter from the icy breeze, I decide to let her take me. *Why?* You know that old saying keep your friends close but your enemies closer? Well this is case and point. I'll tolerate her to find a way to hurt her the way she hurt me.

After we're in her Civic, an awkwardness encompasses the small space. We haven't been this close in a long time.

"Don't worry, I won't tell anyone."

Swallowing my pride is hard but necessary to get inside her head. "Thanks. So what's new around here?"

Her eyes widen a fraction with surprise before she tells me all about Jax's sister, Jasmine and her new family. When she mentions the kidnapping incident that happened a few months ago, it floors me. That stuff is something you only see in movies or read in books. I smile, thinking of Mason. He was always quite like me and observed everything. Left good tips too. "What happened to the girl who took the baby?" I ask with innocent curiosity.

"She's spending time in Metro jail. She still refuses to talk, and we're all pretty sure that there was an accomplice, but we have nothing to go on." Pulling into a foreign apartment complex, I give her a questionable look. She ignores it, smiles, and keeps driving. "I have a better idea."

Attempting to hide my aggravation, I wait to see what she has up her sleeve. After she parks, we make our way up some concrete steps. I'm pretty sure we're at her place because of how meticulous the landscaping is, as well as the structure of the two story red brick building. When she opens the apartment door, all the pictures of her and Jax decorating the foyer walls confirm my suspicions. Dark hardwood floors trail down the hall, and the living room is open to the kitchen on the left. I hear a loud barking and immediately jump. It's so loud and deep I'm sure she has a lion or something in the back.

She sees my face and enlarged eyes then gently pats my shoulder. "He's harmless. I promise." I walk along the hard wood floors and stand behind the dark brown sectional, waiting to see what's next. Trudy goes to the back and returns with a dog large enough eat me. Luckily, he's on a harness. "Say hello to my friend Blaire, Hero." Watching her talk to him as if he's an actual person is weird, but maybe that's because I've never had a pet before. He barks twice, and she pats his head, tells him what a smart boy he is, and then turns her attention to me. "This is Hero, my sweet baby."

"That thing needs to be in a zoo. What is he?" With fear of being bitten, I hesitate before sticking out my hand toward his snout. A small smile forms when I feel the coldness of his nose on my skin.

"He is an African Rhodesian Ridgeback."

He licks my hand, and the sliminess has me pulling away to wipe it on my leg. "I bet your neighbors hate y'all at times."

"He's harmless unless provoked. Jax bought him for me since he's starting med school soon and wants me to have protection while he's doing rounds. As far as the neighbors," she shrugs, "they'll get over it."

She looks at Hero and uses that same high-pitched voice from moments ago. "You need to go outside?" His tail wags as she walks toward the front door before addressing me. "The bathroom is down the hall on the left. Make yourself at home. No one ever uses it. Well, besides David, but he's clean... I think." She smiles before leaving me standing there alone in her apartment. How can she trust me or *anyone* like that? Shaking my head, I walk toward the bathroom to take a much-needed shower.

After I'm dressed in fresh clothes, I make my way to the living room and see Trudy and her giant ass dog watching TV. He stands alert when he sees me, but she easily has him on stand down with one word. "Do you need a hairdryer? Mine is in the master bathroom. I can go get it for you."

I run my fingers through my soggy hair. "Sure." After she leaves to get it, I walk around and take in her home she shares with Jax. I see the love in their eyes as they pose either with family at the beach or friends at the bar. Then a particular picture catches my eye; it's of my brother and me on stage. My finger traces his handsome face that could make me smile on a whim or piss me off just as fast. He was my only family, the only person who believed me, and that was because he endured just as much as I did. If he hadn't come home early and if I hadn't fought that night, then he wouldn't have suffered.

"Here you go."

I hear her voice but keep my focus on the picture and the girl I used to be. Sad anger tries to take hold, but I push it away until I can get away from her. "I'm ready to go." My voice is a rough whisper due to my sudden grief. I don't want this girl's charity or sympathy. I don't want to use anything that's hers. But I know if I want to hurt her, I need to get close. I close my eyes for a second while I calm myself enough to face the girl who took it all away. When I open them up, I see her weakness and know exactly how I'll hurt her and take all she loves away.

Later that night I announce that I want to work the floor. Everyone looks at me as though I'm crazy because people and me don't mix, but eventually concede when I force out the word please.

When Saturday finally arrives, I go to Chris's to get ready instead of using the lounge. Tonight is the night I plan on using the skills Mandy taught me all those months ago. Since I don't own anything like I used to wear, I have to improvise. I trade out my usual jeans for the ass-kissing shorts I was wearing when I came into town, and then pull on my Jay's tank top and some black heels that I picked up at a local second-hand store. My makeup is heavy and dark, my lips are as red as my hair, and I have to say I look pretty damn good. After a little teasing and hairspray, I put a high bump on my crown before I tie it to the side. Last, but not least, I pull down my shirt to show just enough cleavage and *BAM!* I'm ready for round one.

As soon as I walk in the door, I feel eyes on me, and no matter how hard my heart is pounding, I'm determined to pull this plan off. People left, right, front, and even Chris behind me are staring. In fact, Chris has been ogling my ass since I stepped out of his bathroom half an hour ago. And on the drive here. He's lucky I like him so damn much or I'd throat punch him. Just because I'm dressed for attention, doesn't mean I like receiving it. This is strictly business. I head to the lounge to put my stuff away while scoping the place and walking like I own the place. Tonight I'm not only working for tips. I'm working for revenge.

As the night goes by, tips are flowing with every smile and wink I give. Girls compliment me on my hair as guys just stare at my goods. If I have to smile to get revenge, then so be it. If I have to act as if I actually give a shit about what they have to say, then it's a small price to pay. In the end, it'll be worth it.

It's going on ten when I hear a whistle come from my left. Looking, I see that annoying drummer as he passes by, wearing his usual sleeveless t-shirt and bandana. Tattoos cover both his arms and flow up past his collar. When he gets to my side, he takes a drink from my tray that doesn't belong to him.

"Excuse me, you little shit," I yell before snatching it back.

"Come on, Blaire. Since you won't take me out, the least you can do is give me a beer." He pouts in a cute, but annoying way. I quirk an eyebrow before I get ready to leave, but the idiot does the unthinkable. He drops to his knees and grabs my waist. "Please, baby. Don't leave me." He yells loud enough for everyone in the bar to hear. "I promise she was nothing. I promise you, baby, I'll marry you now that your preg– *Ouch... Shit.* " He yells when my fingers brutally twist his ear as I yank him to his feet.

"Has anyone ever told you that you're a pain in the ass?"

"All the time. But my grandmother's favorite name for me was dumbass. She really loved me. Get to know me and you will, too." He winks before grabbing the beer off my tray again. This guy is pure arrogance, and I can see why girls flock to him after every performance. He reminds me of Benji, and I can't help the smile I give.

"See, my effects are already workin' on ya."

"Oh no! Don't think so highly of your charm on me. I was just thinking that you remind me of someone."

"Oh yeah, who? Wait... let me guess. Your fantasy guy... Magic Mike... that Edward guy who sparkles but young and hung?" He wags his eyebrows playfully, and a laugh escapes me.

"No, you dope. My brother."

His smile falls. "Wait... You have a brother? Should I be scared?"

My smile slips as Benji's playful banter with every female crosses my mind. "No. He's dead." I stop him before he can do the "I'm sorry" bullshit. Why apologize when you didn't do anything? I've heard it enough this past year, and I'm tired of it. "Um, excuse me, but my tables are waiting." I push past him and get back to my job.

My mind focuses on Benji and why I'm here. Why I'm doing what I'm doing and could cost me my job, plus Janet. His sobbing words enter my brain and why he was so miserable and I know I'm not backing down.

Turning around, I head to the bar and see *her* smiling and talking to the guy that I've been waiting for all night. A nervous excitement builds in my gut. I've never felt this type of rush. Maybe because this is for my brother. When Jax turns and walks toward the table in the corner, I take a deep breath and push up my boobs. Then I make my move.

CHAPTER SIX

"Trouble's here and she's in heels."
~Lyric

Lyric

"This everything?" I ask Lou while he counts the crates that were just unloaded off the barge. Each one should hold a few kilos of superior Brazilian cocaine and heroin. This shit's not cheap and costs me close to fifteen grand a kilo because it comes from one of the finest coca plants with an extremely high level of alkaloid.

Lou opens one with a large crowbar and sees the large TVs. After he busts the back out, the bags of white powder are made visible. There should be five kilos in each TV, so with fifty crates, you're looking at a great amount of money. But I run this business right, and I'm not greedy. People think dealers or the cartel are like Scarface and Antonio Montana. But I'm just an everyday guy who's twenty-six, hates wearing anything but jeans and boots, and loves getting new ink. I have about fifty workers helping, and I pay them a sizeable amount after every shipment we get.

At first, they didn't want to take a twenty one year old seriously. But when I was released and stationed in NOLA, I took up fighting. Before long I was approached by Theo Dell who ran the local drug trade. He wanted me to be his guard, and after a while, I became his right hand man. For a year, I had his back and gained his trust. Then I had to take him out, and since then, I've run the business. Eventually, I was ordered to move here and run both New Orleans and Mobile's drug industry. Not by choice. Nothing is ever my choice.

When Lou takes a hit and tastes the supply, he rolls the taste on his tongue. I turn away and watch the workers instead. The temptation to lose myself in the bitter flavor when it fills my nostrils and drips from my sinuses can come on strong on nights like this. I can't wait to finish up so I can get the hell out and go play at Jay's. I need a dose of normal. "Yeah, boss. This is some wicked shit."

I just nod my head to signal Javier to release the men who were in charge of the shipment. They'll get back on the boat in one piece. If I were screwed in any way, one would live and carry the other's head in a box as a message to Senior Juan Andres. I've been dealing with that fucker for four years now, and he's only tried to fuck me over once back in NOLA. Just once.

We keep everything business in this life. No friendships because friends don't exist. But Juan and I do share a hatred for Polesky. So he stays on my good side and I on his.

Rumors of how Juan wouldn't budge on the cost of his supply for the Russian meant Polesky wasn't happy. Before he left Columbia, he wanted to make Juan pay for hurting his pride, so he raped and tortured Juan's fifteen-year-old niece, and carved Polesky in her back. The girl lived, but she's fucked up for life because of that monster. My hatred for Polesky comes from a darker place, and I delivered some revenge on him and his family because of what they took from me. Now I'm waiting on a chance to kill him myself. The world would be best without him in it. He's a sick sonofabitch and will do anything to get what he wants. And when the Reform got word he was after Trudy, they gave me a call since I was already running Mobile.

I pick up the guitar case filled with money for Juan's delivery. After I confirm the cash is real, his two leeches return to the ship.

"Lou? I'm out. Get this shit unpacked and sorted. We'll give the runners their usual, and you know what to do with the rest." I walk toward my bike after he nods his head and I head toward Jay's.

After I park and head inside, I let my eyes wander to look for anything out of the ordinary. When I see Tru working the bar with Chris, I don't think much of it. However, when I make my way to our usual table, I see *her*. That little fucking vixen with red hair. I stand back a little and watch her long pale legs in black heels as she walks, but my eyes have a connection to my dick, I guess, because they travel to her ass. It's barely covered by some white cloth. An urge so strong to take her over my knee and spank the shit out of her, surfaces. I'm an ass man, and her ass definitely grabs my attention. Especially as her hips sway from left to right when she carries her drink tray like she owns this place.

When she stops, I finally shake my way out of my wet dream and adjust my dick in my jeans. I part the crowd, watching her the entire time. Her demeanor is different tonight. She talks to the people at the table and smiles seductively as she bends down in front of Jax. I'm sure he's got a clear shot of her tits like everyone on this side can see her ass while she posts it up.

At first, this girl showing her goodies like one of the Candy store strippers confuses me, but I remember her anger with Trudy. Turning my head toward the bar, I see Trudy as she waits on another customer. It's obvious she hasn't seen anything yet. The girl's too sweet for this chick to come in and try to ruin her.

It's time to take control of this situation, so I make my way toward the stage and have the DJ cut the music. I planned to do this the other night, but shit happened before I could. The crowd isn't too happy at first, of course, but when they see me walk up and grab the mike, they go fucking nuts. I give a crooked smile, and then look at Blaire who is still trying to whore herself out to Jax.

"How's everyone doin' tonight?" Screams pierce my ears, but I keep my eyes on Red who's now standing and looking straight at me. Right into my eyes. I wonder if she sees my sins or the souls of all the people I've killed.

"Now, I know I'm not supposed to come up here yet, but we have someone very, very special in the crowd tonight. Someone who, I've heard through rumors, is pretty damned talented. So I'm gonna need everyone's help to get 'em up here. But first I need a fucking beer." The crowd holds their drinks in the air and hollers. After they calm I once again address my target. "Red?" She arches her brow. "Bring me a beer, would ya? And make sure it's cold."

I'm sure she is calling me every name in the book as she makes her way over to the bar to grab my beer. Honestly, I'm surprised she does it at all, but it seems she wants to leave a favorable impression on good ol' Jax.

She makes her way to the front of the stage and holds the bottle in my direction. "Here." she says with pure irritation.

I stare her down and shake my head no. "Come up here. You're holding us up." As her eyes narrow, my smile widens. Pissing this girl off is my new hobby.

She makes her way on stage, and fuckers in the crowd make lewd comments. An urge to tell them to fuck off takes hold, but I bite my tongue. I don't do emotions when it comes to women. I'm not a guy who wants what others have in this world. I accept my life how it is–the good, bad, and fucked up–because I've been through worse. But I feel something very close to jealousy with this messed up girl. Why else am I trying to piss her off and help her cope with her fucked up life? To accept this bad hand life's dealt her? I might feel it, but I don't fucking like these feelings of anger and fear that she might want one of those asshole's attention. Fear that she might actually like one of them. Just like with Ryan the other day... I was ready to take her away when he asked her out. Keeping my smile intact, I hide my inner thoughts and realizations. I can't afford this shit. Not now and not ever. But that doesn't change the fact that I want her.

When she is beside me, she once again holds out my drink, but I ignore her and address the crowd instead. If pissing her off is my new hobby, then I'm having a field day. "Isn't she nice everyone?" The crowd whistles and I look over and see her eyes harden at the same time pink crawls up her neck. *Dammit, that is hot.* "But not only is she a great waitress, she's also one hell of a singer. So as a treat, I think she'd love to sing for us. Isn't that right, Red?"

When I try to pass the mike, she shakes her head no before attempting to leave. My hand encases her small wrist, halting her. She refuses to look at me so I can't see her reaction, but it doesn't deter my tries in pissing her off. "Don't let us down, Red. Let's see what you're made of."

In slow motion, she turns my way. The crowd starts to chant 'Red' over and over. I see a hint of sadness before it morphs into anger again, then she snatches the mike and shoves my beer in my empty palm. "Fuck you."

The crowd laughs as my heartbeat picks up. I love a good fighting partner. I enjoy having these moments of just being a guy in a band, instead of someone who kills people and smuggles drugs. Getting her riled up is icing on the cake. In fact, I might have just found my new habit.

Grabbing the other mike with my free hand, I decide to entice her to do my bidding. I don't know why I give a fuck, or if any of this will help her in any way, but my gut tells me it will. I'm pretty fucked up, but I hate seeing someone innocent like her become another walking disaster. I've seen a lot of shit, growing up on the streets. "Red? How about we make a bet? You and me sing one song apiece. The audience votes for the winner."

She stops pulling away, and her delicate features are cast in the colored lights of the stage. When her green eyes land on me and remind me of Carly, I release her. The likeness is so uncanny that I feel as though I'm standing beside a ghost.

"And why would I go along with this stupid idea of yours? I don't perform anymore."

"Because I have something you want."

"I don't want anything from you."

"Not even a certain bike?"

Her chest heaves and her brows knit while her brain works. "You'd wager the bike?" I nod my head and hope she takes the bet. Within a heartbeat, her eyes become determined. "Okay. Let's do it."

I feel relief and fucking excitement coursing through my veins. Almost like I've went a few rounds with some asshole and kicked his ass. And it's just because of some chick agreeing to perform a song. Hell… I bet Ben's bike. The one thing I've always wanted to buy from him and took advantage of the opportunity after he died.

Janet had it stored at Benny's shop, and after six months of it just sitting there, I approached her and bought the thing. Now I may lose it because I have a need to see this girl do better for herself. People go through shit in life that can make them or break them. She deserves to make it.

"Let's get this shit started then." Yelling to the roaring crowd, I look at Red. "Ladies first."

Her eyes are hard as she picks up the acoustic guitar I had placed on stage all those weeks ago. Ryan comes up to add some drums to whatever she chooses to sing, but she just shakes her head no and sits on the stool before adjusting her microphone. The entire room becomes silent and waits. She takes a deep breath before time slows down and I watch her lips pucker as she exhales. My entire body feels the sensation of her breath on me even on the sidelines. I involuntary shiver. With shaking hands, she tunes the guitar, and guilt tries to set in my gut. I don't let it though because I know she needs this. I don't know how or why I know... I just do.

Finally, she's ready and speaks to the crowd that patiently waits. "All right, everyone. I haven't done this in a long... long time. Please bear with me. This song means a lot to me. It's called *1000 Sundowns*." She clears her throat as silence descends the mass of people.

Then the first chords of the guitar start and shudder from the gentleness of her fingers as they make contact with them. When her angelic voice starts the song, I feel like I've died. Like I shouldn't be allowed to listen to something so clean while I remain covered in filth. The innocence her vocals portray is something I've never heard before. A feeling I've never felt before sets under my skin and warmth and heat build. There's only one word I can call this feeling, and it's a word I never thought to feel or experience. Peace.

She's singing for her brother. Her emotions are in every word and chord. I watch, transfixed on her face under the stage lights not wanting her to stop. Everything else before this moment means nothing. It's all vanished and washed away. A feeling of salvation settles deep inside me and I'm free.

As the last chord echoes around me and the last word is sung, I feel bereft because I don't want it to end. She seemed so different while singing, but before I can figure out why the crowd goes crazy with applause. Red doesn't smile however. She just stands with hatred in her eyes as she passes me to disappear off stage. Without thought, I just nod my head in Ryan's direction and tell him to take over. He's happy to do it because he loves being the center of the crowd's attention.

As I make my way off stage, people come up to slap me on the back or just to get close. Especially the girls. I usually only have a few approach me, but tonight they've seen a rare side of me. Someone talkative and somewhat sociable. I just do what I always do. Ignore them until I finally make my way to the lounge door and walk in.

"Oh my God! Can't you just leave me alone?" She stands by the window, looking outside and never once taking her eyes away from the night scenery.

"How'd you know it was me?"

"Because you're always doing this." She waves her hands between us, and finally looks at me. Tears stream down her face, and I automatically take a step towards her. "Following me every time I just want to be alone. You're always around."

She's right. It seems whenever she's ready to be alone I can't let her. I don't have an answer to her question so I'll ask my own. "Why are you so upset? The crowd loved you."

She doesn't answer at first. She only turns her face away and stares out, so I get closer… and closer. Until I'm standing directly behind her. I need to pull away… to turn around and walk out. She doesn't need to be involved in my lifestyle. But I can't stay away from how she makes me feel alive, excited, and normal. I can't stay away from *her*. I keep eyes on this place as she sleeps at night knowing that's not part of my job, but I can't help it. *Fuck! What am I doing?*

"Why do you care?" she whispers in a hoarse tone from the tears she's hiding. I can't stop myself from wanting to make her stop crying. Hold her like I used to do Carly. When my front is just a few inches from her back, I hear her breath hitch. I like the way I affect her. "If I tell you, will you please back off?"

No. But I tell her what she wants to hear. "Yes."

She turns and looks up at me with so much emotion portrayed along the angles of her face. Eyes that show a lifetime of sadness, a full mouth that never smiles, but if it did, mountains would move. "Because that's the first time I've performed in a year. Do you know that last Halloween was the last time I felt like I did while on that stage tonight? Like everything was suddenly better? But that feeling is a lie because my brother died that same night. He was the one who was always there for me, and then within a few hours, he was just gone. Me playing only makes me realize how much I miss him and how it used to be. But when the song's over, I'm slapped in the face with reality." She stops and just looks at me. "Is that not enough? Do I need to tell you my whole life story now?"

Her lip trembles and I lose rational thought. My hand reaches up and cups the back of her head before I lower my mouth down to hers. I try to be tender and slow, but I'm not a gentle person, and I want this so damn much.

Before long, I realize I'm the only one participating, so I open my eyes.

She's standing in front of me like a statue with her hands still by her side, and her eyes wide. No movement. No blinking.

Fuck... I don't even think she's breathing. "Red?" I whisper and cup her cheeks but get no response. She looks stunned and scared to death. Now, what the hell do I do? "Red, talk to me."

But she doesn't. She just stands there watching me with no other reaction so I back away. Then she shakes herself out of her trance and runs out the door.

"Fuck... Fuck... Fuck!" Feeling angry and fucking agitated, I punch the lockers hard enough to leave a dent.

CHAPTER SEVEN

"Oh Shit!"
~Blaire

Blaire

I hear a bang right before I hear Lyric yell. Leaning against the wall, I catch my breath while my mind runs in a thousand different directions. He kissed me. My first real kiss was from that... that asshole. Guys have tried to kiss me before, but I've never felt like I did a minute ago. Warm, excited, and tingly. I'm too fucked up for this shit. I just need to stay away from him from now on.

Working the lunch shift sucks. Well, the money does. Sober people don't tip as well, or it could be my 'lovely personality,' as Janet likes to call it. But at least I don't have to deal with assholes trying to grab me while the sun's up. When I decided to stay away from Lyric that night, I meant it, and I've succeeded so far. The only bad thing is I had to leave my lounge couch and take Chris up on his offer. I haven't even approached the subject regarding the bike or who won two weeks ago. I'd rather keep my distance and take the bus.

Besides my fear of walking in on him masturbating, living with a guy isn't that bad. Chris is neat as neat can be. In fact, I think he has OCD. He sleeps most of the day, and I come home after he clocks in at Jay's, so we never see one another. Unless it's early Saturday before he heads out to therapy, and I'm up for work. I've been looking in the paper for a second job so I can save some more money. I'm either leaving or getting a place of my own. But nothing has come up that I'm qualified for. Even though I received my GED a few years ago, I still don't have the experience every place is requesting.

So as I bring another round of Gumbo and sandwiches out to a table, I concentrate on my next move, instead of reliving the feel of Lyric's lips touching mine. Usually, if a guy touches me, I run to go vomit. It's an automatic trigger for bad thoughts to swamp me. It even happens when people hug me, but I've learned to bear platonic touching. Except Lyric's kiss was not platonic. It wasn't threatening either. If I'm being honest with myself, I might even admit to liking the feel of it. Which is more reason why I can't be around him. I don't need to have someone else in my life hurt me. I wouldn't survive.

"Excuse me."

I turn toward the female voice and see a girl with long black hair, blue eyes, and a baby face. She's not sitting at my table, but she waves me over with her bangled arm.

"Yes?" I notice a car seat carrier beside her in a spare chair but no baby.

"You're Blaire, right?" Before I can answer, she continues. "I'm Cory. I used to fuck Ryan. "

Oooookay? I lift a brow at her to show my confusion. But she looks so serious, and I kind of want to laugh.

Finally, she clarifies. "You know? The tatted drummer boy

from the band that plays here."

"Oh, right. I'm sure you and half the population have probably fucked him."

"I haven't."

I turn and see Jax's little sister Jazz taking a seat in the vacant chair across from Cory. She has a dark haired little girl about six months old with the fattest cheeks and the bluest eyes I've ever seen, sitting on her hip. I can't help but smile at her when she stares at me.

"What's her name?" I find myself asking. I'm not used to kids because I've never spent any time around them. However, this little girl has an effect on me that I'm not used to.

"This is Princess Finlee."

"Oh, Sweet Yoda Jazz! Would you stop introducing her as Princess Finlee? Someone is going to think you're crazy."

"She is a princess. I'm the queen and Mason's the King. So you might as well face it Cory." Jazz sticks her tongue out in Cory's direction.

"Fine. Then I'm the Fairy god-bitch."

"And what is Bo?"

Cory shrugs. "The hell if I know. He can be the royal guard or somethin. Better yet. He can be royal crop farmer. Because heaven forbid he tries anything else in life."

"But he's goal oriented. And super sexy."

"Can I help you two with something?" I ask before this ridiculous conversation continues. "If not I really need to get back to my tables."

"When do you get off?" Cory asks.

"Um… and why would I tell you?"

"Because you want to. Besides, as Tara Sivec would say, 'Vagina's For Life.' So unless you tuck, we need to stick together."

"Who's Tara Sivec?" I shake my head, trying to gain some sense after the most ridiculous five minutes in my entire life. "Never mind. I get off in two hours."

Cory nods her head as they stand to leave. "Good. I'll pick you up then." She passes me a twenty. "Here's your tip."

"This isn't my table." I say but they continue out the door.

Sure enough, when I walk out Jay's door, Cory is outside waiting for me. "Hey hoochie! Where to?"

"I'm going home. What you do is up to you."

"Sorry, hon, you're stuck with me for tonight. I think you need a friend and one with tits." She cups her boobs. "And I got you covered in both areas. I'll have your back, and you can feel me up if you want. But remember, no matter how hot you are, I'm stickin' with the dick. So get in." She gets in a newer Volkswagen Beetle that's as black as her hair and has a Mickey Mouse head on the antenna. I scrutinize her for a minute and debate on what the hell am I going to do, but then she honks the horn, causing me to jump. "Get your ass moving."

Rolling my eyes, I get in the passenger side and feel something heavy hit my lap. "That's to answer your question from earlier."

I look at the large white book decorated with cupcakes. "A cookbook?"

"Ha! No. That is so much better than a fuckin' cookbook. That is Tara Sivec's bible to bad days and vaginas that need a pick me up and maybe some masturbating visuals." She wags her eyebrows. "She's better than Oprah."

The Chocolate Lovers Series by Tara Sivec sits in my lap, and I don't know what to do with it. Reading is not my thing. "I don't have time to read."

"Make the time. You'll be a happier person. Especially if masturbation is involved."

As she drives, I skim through the pages instead of watching the scenery pass outside my window. On the title page, I see written in pretty script 'Vaginas for life' and Tara Sivec signature below. I guess Cory sees what I'm looking at because she tells me she met her recently at an Author signing. She also tells me her three favorite things in life are Sci-Fi conventions, Disney, and smut. My only thought is this girl is crazy.

When we come to a stop, I'm already on chapter three and laughing as quietly as possible. I didn't think I'd enjoy reading about some chick wanting to lose her V-card. But honestly, anything is better than real life.

"See...I told you. Pure brilliance to make even the meanest bitches smile."

Looking up, I see we're not at Chris's house. Instead, we're on University of South Alabama's campus in front of an old building, which I assume is a dorm. Before I can ask questions she's already out and walking toward the ugly green door. I follow behind and up two flights of stairs because the elevator is out of order before we finally reach her room.

"Look Cory. I appreciate the ride, but I really need to get back to my place."

"Nope. We are going out tonight. Just the two of us and my dear friend Jose Cuervo." She throws her purse on her bed as she continues. "Before you argue about it, answer this question. When is the last time you laughed or had a friend?"

"I don't do friends."

"Because you've been duped one too many times or burned? Well Blaire Bear, you're not the only one who's been shit on in life. I learned to take a shovel and toss the shit back at 'em or hit the fuckers over the head with it. Either way is fine with me. I saw how you've handled yourself at Jay's and I think we could be friends. Yeah. I'm loud and weird. I speak my mind and could care less if I offend a preacher. I own my individuality no matter who doesn't approve or who tries to change me. Not even my boyfriend can change me. I'm a liberal, raised in a conservative family, while living in Jersey. And hell! I'm proud of it."

"So you want to fix me? Is that it? I'm not a charity case for you or anyone." My anger boils from this girl's nerve to call me out like that. Why do people want to fix me when I'm too damaged?

She comes to stand in front of me and loses her smart-ass attitude. Her blue eyes are stern, and her back is ramrod straight. I stiffen when her hands land on my shoulder. "No. I don't want to fix you. You're not broken. You're you." She takes a deep breath and continues in a whisper. "But you do live like a victim. And what you need to learn is how to be a survivor."

She sees right through me. My head swims with confusion from her words. I feel exposed and accepted all at once, and it's such a bittersweet moment that tears form in my eyes. "How... how do you know that?" My voice is strained and low, but she hears me.

"Because I was you."

Her arms wrap around me, and instead of running, I welcome it. No one knows what I went through, my dark secrets. Benji only knew by accident. He never made me talk about it, and deep down, I knew he didn't understand. But this girl does. She does, and I don't have to talk about it and worry about reliving it any more than I have to.

All of the sudden, she lets go and smiles, transforming her into the girl I met earlier. "So? You up for a few hours of living and not reliving?"

We decide not to go to Jay Jay's. Well, she decided not to after she hung the phone up with her boyfriend Bo. She said he'd look for her there. She told him she wasn't feeling well, but he's still called several times, so she finally turned her phone off. I want to ask why be with someone she needs to lie to or escape from, but that's not my business. Besides, I know she doesn't want to talk about it. If she did, she'd bring it up. So after two shots of Jose, she dresses me in black jeggings with a white and silver off-the-shoulder shirt. I slip on my flats, and we head out toward downtown. We walk around, eat at a local pizza place, and head to Grand Central.

"You want another shot?"

"Yeah!" I yell in her direction. The music is blasting my eardrums and the liquor is flowing in my blood. I'm feeling loose and relaxed. That's the only word to describe it. She grabs my hand, and we make our way to the bar and take a seat where no one stares. Being incognito and unrecognizable feels wonderful and reminds me of my time on the road with Mandy, and I can transform into anybody I want. But who? I don't know yet.

My eyes go to the band on the small stage. Two guys and two girls play some cover songs from the early nineties. The lead singer is wearing tighter pants than me, and he appears to be a glory hog while the girl on guitar is dressed to show off her gorgeous hourglass figure. Her long, dark hair is garnered by a red headband and her bangs roll up like a sixties pin-up model. She shows off her ass in ripped jeans, and a red bustier displays her ginormous boobs. The guy on bass and her give one another annoyed looks. The other girl with white dreads bangs on the drums in the back clueless as to the singer making his own rules as he goes. I would hate to work in a band that can't communicate with one another.

"Hey, beautiful." Someone whispers in my ear. I turn to see a well-dressed guy that looks to be my age. "Can I buy you a drink?"

"Sure. But you have to buy my friend one, too." I nod my head toward Cory who's chatting it up with the bartender.

"Okay. But first tell me what your name is."

This is it. The moment when I can be Blaire or someone else. I hold my hand out and say the first name that comes to mind. "Call me Red."

Three shots later, I feel no pain and have no memories haunting me. In fact, I'm not me. I'm some sexy girl, rubbing myself all over some guy in the middle of a crowded dance floor. I feel his hands on my hips as they rotate and I start feeling hot. Not just temperature wise, either. Soon, the urge to go to the bathroom overrules my libido, and I yell my intentions to Cory who's just returned with more shots.

"Hurry back." My mystery guy tells me, and I can't help but laugh for no reason. His face blurs before it morphs into the one I've seen too often tonight, the one person I've imagined watching me, over and over again. I've tried making him jealous at times, but knew how stupid that was. It's just the alcohol because the drunker I become, the more my visions morph into the guy with the badass tattoos and sultry voice, Lyric fucking Devereux.

Luckily, I'm not in heels because I don't think I would be able to walk if I were. I've never drunk this much before. But hey! I like it. I like not feeling like shit. I like being normal for the first damn time in my twenty-five years of life. Maybe alcoholics knew what they were doing after all. I push open the bathroom door and hurry to relieve myself. *Man! Peeing is the bomb.*

After the euphoric feeling is gone, I wash my hands and make my way out the door, but before I can look up, I'm against a wall in the back, looking into those beautiful eyes that I've imagined on me all damn night. "Hi, you," I slur with a big smile on my face. He doesn't look happy though. "Hey. Anyone home?" I flick his nose, and he scrunches it up. Still pissed though. What a party farter. *Ha! I said fart.*

"What the fuck are you doin?" Now the fucking vision wants to get an attitude with me.

"Hell to the no!" I quickly cover my mouth. "Oops! Thought I was thinking that thought. Any who. I'm par-tay-ing. Wasssss it looks like, Mr. Sexy?"

His lip lifts up in one corner, and my mind thinks of our kiss. I wonder, if he were to kiss me again, would I freeze like before, or would I kiss him back? Could I initiate the kiss? No! You can't kiss a vision. Can you? I did flick his nose though. "Hmmmmm…"

"So you think I'm sexy?"

"Do I have a vagina? Duh! Did you know Tara Sivec has a girl code? Va-Jay jay's for life." I even attempt to show him the hand signal Cory showed me earlier but fail epically. "Shit! I gotta find Cory."

"She's with Ryan. Now let's go."

"No!" I say as he pulls on my arm. If I leave this dark corner, I know this vision will vanish, and I won't be able to kiss him like I want. Because when the liquor leaves me, I won't feel like this.

"What the fuck do you mean *no*?"

"No. I'll not leave until you do something."

"Do what?" he asks with pure exasperation in his voice. How can he make my body hum when he's annoyed?

"Kiss me." His eyes widen before that smirk comes back. I try to put some sexiness in my voice. "Kiss me and I'll leave."

Then he says something I wasn't expecting. "What if I don't want to kiss you?"

"Huh? You did the other night." Now my feelings are hurt. Even my vision just turned me down. And I'm supposed to be in control of this hallucination, too. Swallowing back my rejection, I shove his very real feeling shoulder. "But... but why?"

He stares at me before he leans down and inhales deep. He's smelling me, and it's so damn hot. I feel like squirming and rubbing my legs together, or better yet, wrapping them around his imaginary waist. And I'm certainly glad he's not real because I'm sure I've smelled a lot better before I sweated out Jose on the dance floor.

"Because Red. When I do kiss you again, and it will happen, I want you to remember *every fucking detail.* Every caress of my tongue as it slides in. Every scrape of my teeth on that sexy, plump bottom lip of yours. And everything you feel inside as I do it." He sucks my earlobe between his teeth and a moan escapes on my next breath. "Because after that, I want to be all you fucking think about. Understand?"

No words form. All I can do is grab his shoulders and hold on before my legs give out. Between the alcohol and the heat I'm feeling from my *very* overactive imagination, I'm not feeling so good. When I lay my head against the cool wall, I close my eyes before slipping into darkness.

CHAPTER EIGHT

Point of No Return
~Lyric

"What the fuck are you doing?"

I barge in my front door with a wasted Red in my arms and look at Hyde. "It's my fucking house so don't worry about it. I'm handling it." I walk down the hall and kick my bedroom door open.

"Fine. Handle it, but put her in my room. I'll sleep on the couch."

The thought of her wrapped up in his sheets makes me furious, possessed even. I will not have her in his damn room where he jacks off at night. "She's sleeping in my bed."

"Are you su–?"

He stops his argument when a fucking growl erupts from my chest. I don't know why the fuck I brought her here when I sent Cory home with Ryan, but I just couldn't let her go yet. And still can't. Even after she threw up on my best fucking boots, I didn't let her go. And even as she blew chunks in Hyde's car, I didn't let her go. But I know I need to. And I'm not just talking about now.

Placing her on my king size bed I look at her limp form before I start to undress her. I'm aware what an asshole move this is and shouldn't, but I need to make her comfortable here. In my home. I slip off her black flats before I gently slide her pants slowly down her long legs. The whole time I watch her face, no matter how much I want to look down. But my hands love the feel of her cool skin as they skim down every inch.

I wish she was awake and asking me to kiss her again. Her flirtatious attitude was enough to cause my dick to harden earlier, but now with her pale and clammy skin I just want to take care of her. She doesn't look good and hasn't moved a muscle for the past half hour. She must be dehydrated from all the fucking liquor she drank and all the vomiting.

Without hesitation, I make the decision to continue breaking the rules. I walk in the kitchen and go to my locked pantry. Inside is my storage unit of guns, ammo, bulletproof vest, grenades, and some medical shit in case I ever need stiches or intravenous therapy. I grab a bag of fluid and the IV kit before heading back to the room. I like to keep myself prepared in case I'm ever shot again. I also have several pints of A negative blood on hand.

"You're seriously gonna stir shit up if you give her a fucking IV man. She's going to know something's not normal. I mean, who in the hell has this type of medical shit in their house or has the training to do this shit? Not a mechanic who plays guitar."

Hyde's right. I could earn myself a bullet, but she looks too damn pale for me to care. I continue to ignore him as I head back to my room to be the rule breaker I've always been.

After she's hooked up, I sit in the chair across from her and wait in the dark. She hasn't stirred or made a noise, but her breathing is steady, so I'm sure she'll be fine. I hear a knock on the door and stand to go answer it. Hyde stands there with a cup of black coffee and a red folder. He doesn't say anything just passes it to me and walks back down the hall.

I open it and see a picture of the guy Red was dancing with, along with an arrest record. His name is Alex Bishop, and he's twenty-eight years old from Atlanta, Georgia. He's been charged with D.W.I's and domestic violence. He's also been caught running drugs. He recently had all charges of abuse dropped when his ex-wife stated she was using and was confused. I seriously find that hard to believe. Then I see some surveillance pictures of the fucker talking to someone in a suit and sporting a fucked up ponytail. The image is blurry, but I know exactly who it is. Polesky.

I sit and wonder if it's just a coincidence that Red and this guy talked most of the night, or if they actually know one another. I knew he had eyes in Mobile, and I've been waiting patiently for a chance to run into one of them. But I don't want to interfere with that Russian bastard coming to Mobile. I want my chance to take him down. I don't think Red has any ties to Polesky, but the coziness these two showed on the dance floor could be from more than the alcohol. Another question surfaces. How did Hyde know to pull these files? Fuck if I know. I haven't slept in over twenty-four hours, and my mind needs some damn rest.

Standing, I stretch my body to release the kinks while trying to be quiet. My eyes open to a sleeping redheaded vixen, and my body automatically makes its way to stand by her. She looks at peace like this. No worry lines around her eyes or mouth. Not like someone who works for someone willing to do harm to the innocent. I pinch the skin around her wrist to check her hydration level. Relief fills me when it shows improvement. My fingers linger longer than necessary as I take this private moment for granted. Even though I seem to break the rules every time it comes to this girl, I know there's one I can't break. I made a promise years ago, and I plan on keeping it, come hell or a redheaded distraction. One thought is in my brain when I exit the room, and it causes my stomach to knot up. If she is involved with that bastard in any way, I know I'll have to kill her.

Hyde's on the couch with his computer, and when I walk in, he shuts it. "How is she?"

"Fine." I sit across from him and analyze the guy before me. He's smart and knows more about me than most because he witnessed it. The beatings. The humiliation. The kills. And as far as I know, we're on the same side. "How did you know that guy Alex worked for Polesky?"

"I recognized him. That's why I left early. I needed to get his file together to show you when you got home. I was in Atlanta for a bit after my release and knew he spent his time kissing Polesky's ass. Likes to flaunt the dirty money he makes with his clothes and his black Corvette." He stops and scrutinizes me. Then his eyes travel to my bedroom door, and I know exactly what he's thinking before he says it. "You know. She seemed pretty friendly with him. Do you think…?"

"No!" I yell, agitated from the whole fucking situation. She's innocent in this shit. I pull at my hair, take a deep breath, and slowly let myself calm down. Getting worked up over assumptions is dangerous. I'll get proof, and then we'll see who's on whose side. After a minute, I open my eyes and look at him in all seriousness. "No. She's not part of this. She was just drunk. And drunk girls get friendly, you know that." At least that's what I want to believe.

He just nods his head and stands up. "You know if she is and you can't do it, I will." Then he heads into his room and shuts the door.

"Ah!"

A high pitched scream coming from down the hall wakes me, and has me jumping up, grabbing my gun, and heading in that direction. When I bust through the door, I see Red sitting up and clutching my gray sheets to her chest.

"What the fuck is going on?" she yells and looks from me to the gun. Her face pales, and she looks like she might vomit again. Thankfully the I removed her IV earlier.

I let my eyes roam the room and see no danger, so I put my Glock back in my holster. "Mornin'. Or should I say evening."

She looks around and then at me again. "Where am I and why do you have a gun?"

"My place. And I carry a gun with a permit to keep the crazy fuckers away. People will rob you for a piece of gum if they're hungry enough."

She lays her head back on the pillow. "Ugh! Why do I feel like total shit?"

I walk over and take the glass of water and aspirin off the dresser. "Take this. You'll feel better." She looks at me with one mascara-smeared eye. "Here, take it. I don't have all day." Grudgingly, she sits up and slowly takes it from my hand. I ignore the shock waves that travel up my arm, but when I look in her widen eyes, I'm sure she feels it, too. "Now to answer your question. You decided to try and drown yourself in tequila last night. It's called a hangover."

"Why am I here?"

"Well, I could have left you passed out in the hallway of a

strange place, but I'm not a complete dick."

She says something under her breath and hands me the water back. "I need to call Chris to come get me. *Shit!* And Janet. I'm sure she's so pissed I didn't show up for work." She tries to stand, but she's weak and unsteady, so she grabs the corner of the side table. Then I watch her eyes widen when she notices her pants are gone, and she's wearing a pair of basketball shorts that are four sizes too big. She sits and covers herself back up. When her cheeks become pink, I can't help but smile. For someone whose every move screams sex, her actions couldn't be more innocent.

"I called Janet already. She was fine with it. She wanted me to tell you that you're off for the week. She knows how tomorrow night is Halloween." I'm waiting for a reaction, but I don't get one. Tomorrow will be a year since her brother's death. She doesn't realize I know this, though. "I'm taking you home after you rest."

"I don't need to be off. I'm fine," she whispers quietly. "I also don't know if I should thank you for helping me, or kick your ass for interfering and taking my pants off. But I'm too damn tired to do the last, so I'll just say thank you." She gives me a small smile. "Thank you."

That little gesture is a lot for her, I'm sure. Her hair is a mess, and her eye makeup is smeared, but to me, she's still a vision. Shaking my head clear, I try to gain some insight before I join her in that bed. "I'll make you something to eat." I walk out the door, fighting my basic instinct to take what I want.

The drive to Chris's house is tense and quiet. My mind was absorbed with thoughts of her and Polesky while she was resting. However, now my thoughts swarm with images of her and Chris.

This jealousy shit is new to me, and I loathe it. But then again, anger is something I've lived with all my life and has kept me alive when I should be dead like everyone I've ever loved. I can't help but picture ripping Chris's hands off if he touches her, smells her clothes after she showers, or him just having her in his house while she's sleeping. Without meaning to, I squeeze the leather steering wheel so hard, I'm sure finger indentions will be left. When she starts anxiously tapping her feet, I can't take it anymore. "Are you nervous about something?" I ask harshly.

She ceases her foot tapping. "No." She doesn't say anything else for a few minutes while her whole presence engulfs my car. Then she turns on the radio. "Do you mind?"

"Nope."

She sits back after she turns it to a hard rock station. Korn's *Twisted Transistor* is blasting through my speakers, and it only fuels my anger. I reach to turn it down, and she gives me an inquisitive look. "I have a headache."

"O-kay."

I decide to take advantage of the time I have her to myself. Since she's moved to day shifts at Jay's, I don't know when I'll see her again. "Did you have fun with that guy last night?"

Her guard goes up, and her back straightens. "Why is it your business?"

"It's not."

"Exactly. So don't ask."

Taking a breath, I try a different tactic. She's stubborn, but I have patience. "He just looked like he was up to no good. That's all." Her face is illuminated by the streetlights, and I see her arch her brow. "What?"

"He looks like he's up to no good? Ha! He was dressed like a gentleman and smiled. Unlike you, who looks like a complete asshole."

If she's trying to offend me, it's not working. "I am an asshole. It's no secret. And you're a bitch. But he looked like a creep dressed like a gentleman. You know. A wolf in sheep's clothing, or however that saying goes."

"Geez. You know how to sweet talk a girl." She rolls her eyes and turns to look out the window to dismiss me, but I continue to push.

"Have you ever seen him before?"

"Oh God! What is up with the twenty questions? You know, for someone who doesn't talk much, you sure don't shut up when you start."

"You still didn't answer my question." I park the car in Chris's driveway. The porch light is on, but his car is gone, so I know he's gone to work.

She reaches for the door handle. "And I'm not going to." She gets out and slams the door, but I turn off the ignition and follow her up the steps. I'm not ready for this thing to end. I need answers. After she opens the front door and walks in, she tries to slam it in my face, but I catch it with my hand. "Do you need something?"

"Yes." I walk in, but leave the door open. My eyes stay on her as I approach. I see fear at first, but she pushes it away and replaces it with that stubborn trait I'm learning she has. She crosses her arms and looks up when I'm close, refusing to move. "Last night, you asked me for something. Remember?"

"To go to hell?"

I smirk because this game we play is a fucking thrill for me. "Oh, honey. I've already been to hell." I stand in front of her an inch away expecting her to cower, but she doesn't. Should I make this soft and gentle like before or should I make it punishing for possibly being a part of Polesky's team? I roll my neck and let it pop in several places before I swiftly grab her by the waist and pull her tight body to me. Her breath hitches and she freezes, but not in fear. In anticipation. It's written all over her face.

My other hand grabs her by the nape of her neck, and I feel the softness of her bright, red hair between my fingers. "You asked for this." Then I lower my lips to hers. I want it to be punishing, to show her how much of an asshole I am, but I can't. I have a deep feeling she needs the exact opposite.

Nipping her bottom lip, I taste her cherry lip-gloss while I massage the tension in her neck. She exhales softly and tentatively opens her mouth. My tongue dives into the moist warmth between her lips, and I savor every fucking millisecond I'm there. I don't know when or if I'll be able to kiss her again. Timidly her tongue starts to move against mine before her hands reach up to grab my shoulders. I feel her nails bite into my skin through the fabric of my t-shirt, but it feels fucking amazing. After this, I stop moving and let her take control. Let her feel me like I said she would last night. Let her savor every touch, every feeling I arouse in her. But in all honesty, I'm feeling her. I know without a doubt that this kiss is one I'll never forget.

The hand on her waist slowly traces up her ribs, over her exposed collarbone, and across her erratic pulse. When both hands are cupping her cheeks, I once again take over the kiss that is on its way to becoming feverish. She moans, and a growl forms in my chest. She swallows it just as her hands grab at the nape of my neck to hold me close.

Feeling my dick become stone hard against her stomach, I pull away. We stand there, breathing hard enough to fan one another's face, while my hands remain cupping her flushed cheeks. Then I let go of her, turn around, and walk out the front door knowing, without a doubt, I'm in deep shit.

CHAPTER NINE

"All girls dream at one point in life. And we all hurt when they're crushed."
~Blaire

Blaire

When he's gone, I just stand there, watching his headlights disappear from the driveway. My heart is beating so fast and I'm literally shaking from that kiss. He's nothing like I initially thought he would be. Yeah! He's an asshole but not a fucking asshole. He took care of me all day today. Brought me eggs and toast when I woke up, and washed my clothes for me. And even though he keeps giving me the most evil looks when I meet his eyes, he is always watching me. *And that kiss?* I touch my lips and feel a smile form. I feel butterflies swirling in my stomach, and all I can think of is one word. *Happy.* I'm happy, and it feels so damn good. And I want to see him again. To feel this way again.

I grab my phone and call Cory to see what she's up to. "Hey. How are you feeling?"

"Oh my fucking Yoda-god! Where have you been? I forgot to save your number, and then nobody knew what happened to you. Well, Ryan did, but that shit wouldn't say. Let me just tell you, I have been looking for a picture to put on a milk carton and pricing billboards."

I laugh because I'm just so happy. And this girl was worried about me. I think I might have my first friend. "I'm good. Just got back home. Listen. Tomorrow is Halloween, and I know Jay's has its annual costume party. Do you want to go shopping?"

"Um… sure. Aren't you working tomorrow?"

"No. Janet gave me a week off." However, I plan on going back to nights so I can see Lyric. I know everyone thinks I might crack because tomorrow is a year since Benji's death, but after tonight, I think I'll be okay.

"Okay. Can Jazz and Trudy come? We already had plans."

I think about it for a second. I handle being around Trudy for work, so a shopping trip should be okay. I think. "Um… sure. You'll be there, so I think I can manage."

The next day, the girls pick me up, and we head to every Halloween shop in Mobile. I keep quiet most of the time because I'm still not sure about Trudy interacting with me in such a friendly manner. Thankfully, Cory has a way to involve me when I feel left out, which unfortunately, is a lot.

"So, why did you buy something so sexy to wear tonight?" Cory asks me.

I clutch my bag and wonder if I made the right choice in attire. This is not the job I used to dress up for. Tonight, I don't want to ruin a life or con a cheater. I want to catch someone's attention. This is my first crush, and I have no clue what I'm doing. So instead of dressing like the usual slutty cops and playboy bunnies on Halloween, I chose to dress sophisticated with some sexiness, like my favorite cartoon character growing up, Jessica Rabbit. I already have the hair, so I didn't need to buy a wig. Besides, it kind of fits with the others' costumes.

Cory, of course, is going as princess Leia. Jazz is going as the Queen of Hearts, so Baby Fin will be Alice, and Trudy is going as Audrey Hepburn. All are some sort of iconic female movie star.

She must see my blush as I think of last night's kiss and why I'm taking such a risk. Her eyes widen, and she smiles. "You little skank. You like someone, don't you?"

"Shhh!" I look at Jazz and Trudy as they walk ahead of us to Jazz's SUV. "No… maybe." I shrug my shoulders and smile. "I don't know."

"What-ev. You so do. It's all over your face. This girl in front of me is smiling without her bitch card out. So… *who* is it?" She nudges me with her shoulder.

"I'm not telling. I don't even know if he likes me." Well, I think he likes me. He did kiss me and took care of me. My heartbeat picks up from just the thought, and another blush envelops my cheeks.

"Well, whoever he is would be crazy not to."

I don't argue with her. She might see someone who's likable, but I don't. I haven't in a long time.

We load up and head back to our houses to get ready. Cory says her boyfriend and she will pick me up after she's ready. Jazz and Mason are taking Fin trick-or-treating, and Trudy is working. I head inside Chris's house to get ready for my first attempt at flirting. I re-dye my hair because my blonde roots are starting to peek through. After I'm done, I rinse and watch the red water disappear down the drain. Watching the color disappear has me thinking of Lyric's name for me. *Red.* I'm not Blaire to him, and I'm not so fucked up that I'm keeping him at a distance. I'm just Red. Maybe even sexy to him. If not now, however, I plan on being sexy tonight. I want another kiss and that feeling it caused in me. The warmth, tingles, and butterflies. I want it all.

So tonight, I take care in getting ready. I actually lotion my legs, and do my old ritual of beauty that Mandy taught me. That woman might be a thieving bitch, but she was a beautiful thieving bitch who knew all the tricks in the book when it comes to makeup and hair. I'm shaved smooth in every place I want to be touched. Maybe not literally. But I did kiss someone without my usual terror resurfacing. So maybe more could possibly happen.

After my purple above-the-elbow gloves are on, I hear a knock on the door. I quickly take one last look in the mirror, grab my red sequined wristlet that holds some money and my ID, and rush to the door. Opening it, I see the oddest pair. Cory in her princess Leia attire with smoky-eyed makeup, and a large cowboy whose smile showcases his dimples.

"Howdy, ma'am." He tips his hat in true cowboy fashion. "You sure look awfully purdy."

"Um... thank you?"

He winks and offers his elbow. I look at Cory who's on the other, and she just rolls her eyes.

"Don't worry. This is how he always is." She pinches his butt. "Save that shit for the bedroom."

"Yes, ma'am."

I lock up the house and take his elbow. Then we head to Jay Jay's while my heart is pounding a million beats a minute. I block everything out but the one question I continue to ask myself. *What the fuck am I doing?*

After we arrive and make our way to a table, I decide a drink might settle my nerves. I know the band will be showing up to sit with everyone soon, and I want to be cool. Not jumpy or nervous. I'm trying to act as if this is a job, thinking it will help, but I know when I see him, those thoughts will disappear. So I head over to the bar.

Trudy approaches, looking lean and beautiful in her black dress just like the original Audrey Hepburn. "Wow, Blaire. You look stunning," she says, and I know her words are sincere. I don't know when my hatred for this girl started depleting, but it has. Or it could be because I'm focusing on one feeling and one person right now?

"Thanks. Can I get a Jack on the rocks?" Since Jose and I are no longer friends, I'm sticking with my usual.

After she slides it my way, I sip it, but with my nerves still on overdrive, I decide to swallow it down fast. The taste and burn cause goose bumps to surface, and my face twists to show my discomfort. But who truly loves the taste of alcohol? It's the effect I crave… need. Especially tonight. Then I order a second while I wait for the tranquility I felt the other night to hit.

I sit for several minutes, watching the crowd, while I feel my body finally start to loosen up. Then I see Ryan come in first followed by the bassist, and then Lyric walks in. But I can't move from my seat, and it's not from my vanishing nerves either. It's from the brunette walking in with him. She's tanned, toned, and fucking gorgeous.

I grab my drink and shake the ice, wishing it wasn't blocking the golden liquid. It clinks on the side, and that's all I hear. The blood rushing in my brain has everything else fading, the crowd, the music from the DJ, everything. I concentrate on the clinking, and breathing in and out, and begin my counting ritual. I learned a method while I laid in bed scared or in pain. *Breathe in… breathe out.*

Closing my eyes, I continue until the commotion surrounding me comes back, and I can hear more than my own blood pumping. Then I open my eyes and see the two kissing while she straddles his lap in her referee outfit. Watching the two and thinking of our kiss has me feeling stupid and naïve. Filled with shame. My endless anger returns just as my happiness from earlier falls on the floor for the world to stomp on.

I feel the walls crowding in, as the voices get louder and louder. No amount of alcohol is going to erase the image of the one person I was starting to trust kissing another. Instead of walking out, I decide not to show him how much I'm affected. I order another whiskey straight so no ice blocks me from the feeling I crave. Now the burn isn't so bad. My throat is numb, and I can feel my disposition slowly become the same. Emotionless… dead. I try to concentrate on the karaoke singers as they screech in the mike. However, my mind still sees *him*.

"Hey, you. I didn't think I'd see you again. You disappeared the other night."

I look up from my empty glass and see my dance partner from a few nights ago. He's decent, with his crooked nose and dark hair cut short to the scalp. He has a faint scar above his right eye. He smiles slyly, showcasing his freakishly white teeth. But it's a nice smile, and he seemed enjoyable enough the other night. A little cocky, but if I was making money like him, then I'd be cocky too, I guess.

He works for a pharmaceutical company and travels to introduce his products to doctors everywhere. It's funny how I don't remember much about that night, like his name, but I do remember his work status. But I was pretty drunk.

I return his smile, happy the desired effects from the alcohol are finally kicking in. I'm feeling warm, loose, and ready for anything. "I'm sorry, but what was your name again?" I lick my lips seductively and receive his full attention as his eyes follow the movement.

"Alex. But my friends call me Bishop." He taps the empty glass with his finger. I automatically notice no ring, but a very elegant diamond Gucci watch adorns his wrist. "Need another?"

"Sure."

We keep light conversation for the next thirty minutes until I hear someone announce it's time for Lyrical Obsessions to take the stage. I spin the bar stool around as Alex throws his arm around me, and we snuggle up like a cute couple or some shit. As much as I want to push him away, I don't. I'll just drink when the familiar feelings take hold. My free hand automatically starts to fist and leave nail imprints in my palm until my drink arrives. I quickly swallow it down then watch the band strut on stage like they own the fucking place. Or at least the lead singer does. *Fucker!* I say under my breath.

"How are you motherfuckers doin' tonight?" Lyric speaks into the microphone, and his voice bounces off the walls. I feel Alex jump from beside me, and when I look his way, his eyes are now on Lyric. I guess he fucked him over, too because he looks pissed. Before I can ask, the crowd goes insane as girls and guys scream and whistle, so I ignore it and turn my attention back to the stage. I hear a few girls scream, "Fuck me, Lyric," but he just laughs and picks the chords of his guitar. With the deepness of his voice bouncing from the speakers, I feel my heart rate pick up while my numbness starts to disappear, and my anger begins to smolder.

"I need to make a phone call," Alex says before disappearing into the crowd.

I could care less if he stays gone, but since he is giving me free drinks, I won't argue if he comes back. I decide to look down and block the sound of Lyric's voice out as much as possible, but it does nothing for my hurt. I don't know why I feel so fucking betrayed by that sonofabitch, but I do. And I feel stupid for it. For once, I was hopeful to feel normal... to be a girl. But now I know I'll never be like all these other females in here. At least not sober, anyway.

The band starts Evans Blue *Cold,* and I start to feel restless as Lyric's voice reaches my ears and causes my body to awaken. Warmth spreads and longing mixes in, and when his words about his hand sliding on my neck like he did last night, a detailed picture of us in his bed invades my mind. I feel restless and have to cross my legs and squeeze my thighs together before I do something stupid like go to the front of that stage and act like a groupie.

My dress automatically opens at the thigh from the side slit. A large hand slides across my pale skin, and I look up to see Alex. He must see the lust in my eyes, because he leans in and kisses me while his fingers inch closer to my panties. His kiss isn't like the one I want. Instead, it's rough and demanding. It's violent and full of dominance. His lips are chapped, and his breath is stale, but with Lyric's raw singing in my ears, I endure it.

When Lyric's voice stops, I pull away from Alex, unable to stomach anymore. No matter how much I want to look at the stage, I keep my eyes trained on the guy who just stuck his tongue down my throat. But I know, without a doubt, Lyric sees me. Every inch of my skin burns from those deceiving eyes of his. I smile, feeling victory, and hope he feels the way I did when I saw him kissing that girl. I hope he knows that I think he's a fucking asshole, and he can go back to whatever hell he came from. However, he once again starts to sing and finishes the song.

Grabbing my clutch, I lean in and tell Alex I need to go to the restroom. Cory is in a heated argument with her cowboy as I pass her table. She gives me an apologetic smile that I don't return. She didn't do anything to me, but I don't feel like adding someone to my life, anymore. Friendships and relationships of any kind make me feel too many things, and I don't like it. Especially when I get fucked over.

As I wash up, I hear the band start a different song and sigh. Maybe deep down, I wanted Lyric to follow me and rescue me again, but I'm stupid for thinking he would. So instead, I decide not to let one kiss change me to a senseless girl who depends on one guy's attention to feel happy. Plenty of guys show me attention, and one with money is out there right now waiting for me. So I'm going to take my life back and live by my own terms.

I walk back out to the bar and see Alex. He stands straight and smiles until I reach his side. "So handsome, you wanna get out of here?" I let my hand slide up his broad chest and feel his heart beat pounding hard and fast.

We pay our tab and make our way to the exit, but before we reach it, the music stops again. With my eyes on the exit, I ignore the interruption and the all-consuming stare on my back as we make our way to a new black Corvette that is my chariot for the night to my newest fuck up.

After Alex rolls over, I run to the bathroom to cry. Luckily, I turn on the shower before retching in the toilet to mask the sound. The tears come harder every time my stomach heaves whiskey. I was fine earlier. I was okay with fucking some random guy when the liquor was flowing through my blood. Now I'm feeling again, and it's not a good feeling.

After I finish, I sit naked on the cold tile floor and sob for what I just did. Maybe Benji didn't see me. *Oh God! Benji. The anniversary of his death, and I do this? Fuck some guy because he bought me drinks?* My stomach rolls again with the thought, and I once again throw myself over the commode to empty my stomach. Nothing but green bile comes up because I have nothing else to give. I continue to question my stupid thought process for sleeping with someone. Why did I think I'd feel some semblance of *normal* from the action? Instead, I still feel like the lowest person. Is it customary to feel guilt over a one-night stand? Or is it just my twisted and fucked-up mind?

After I turn off the water and rinse my mouth out, I open the door to see a sleeping Alex. What happened to the suave guy who made my toes curl from earlier? *Oh yeah! He was never here.* He was rough and uncaring. But thankfully, quick. Now it's time for me to leave, so I don't have to face him again. I grab my phone and call a cab before heading down to the lobby to wait. I can't stand to look at my mistake any longer.

The first thing I do when I finally get to Chris's is shower. It's only one a.m. so I know Chris is still out, and I have time for myself. The water is the hottest I can get it and leaves my skin the color of cherries, but I need to get clean. Sterilized even. Then my brain shows flashes of Alex over me, kissing my skin, before I envision the person who was supposed to protect me in life doing the same thing.

That's a good girl, Blaire. Show Daddy how much you love him. Daddy loves you.

Screaming, I scrub harder. My nails scratch my skin until

blood surfaces. But nothing helps. Nothing takes it away.

This is our secret. You'll keep our secret, won't you? No one will believe you if you tell. They can't understand a love like this.

"Stop it. Stop. Please. *Benji!* Help me." I hit the shower wall, wishing the nightmares would leave. I cry out for my brother, but I get no reply. He was the one who saved me and took me away. But now he's gone, and I have no one but myself. I'm so weak. Just like Mandy always said. So fucking weak and stupid.

Standing, I turn off the water that now runs cold. My legs slowly carry me to the sink, and I see the naked reflection of the girl I hate. Quickly, I open the medicine cabinet to escape her stare and see several medicine bottles full of prescriptions for Chris's pain and PTSD. I open the one for sleep labeled Ambien and take three, desperate for nothingness to consume me so that I can forget. After I crawl into bed naked, my eyes become heavy, and my mind goes blank. Finally, I've found a void.

CHAPTER TEN

"Integrity is doing the right thing even when no one is watching."
~C.S. Lewis

Lyric

I put down my guitar and storm off the stage. My ever-present rage has reached new heights tonight, and no matter how many times I tell myself to leave Red alone and let her go, I *fucking can't*. After I kissed her last night, I knew instantly I was in too deep and needed to cut ties with her. I have too much shit going on in my life to add fucking emotions and some insane girl to the mix. Definitely not what I need.

Running into Mari at the gym today seemed like the perfect distraction. A way to remember I just need to get laid every once in a while and nothing more. We fucked in the gym showers, not caring who heard or saw us. But when her back was to me as I slammed into her, all I saw was red hair and pale ivory skin. All I saw was Red, and I never wanted it to end. And all I felt was guilt when it was over.

Seeing her tonight with Polesky's guy, and watching as she left with that motherfucker, gutted me. I felt like I was punched in the stomach so hard I wanted to hit my knees. But I just hollered louder in the mike and played my Gibson until it felt like fire was going to erupt. The entire time on the stage, my mind was seeing the two of them wrapped in one another or working together. I can't figure out what thought is worse. The one of her being a pawn in the Russian cartel or her having feelings for that cocky ass sonofabitch Bishop.

Now, I'm free to leave. I bypass every fucking person and go straight to my bike. They're lucky my ass stayed and finished the fucking set. Instead of beating the shit out of Bishop, my music took my abuse tonight. Now though... now, I'm ready to find those two and get some fucking answers. Where has she been since she left town after Ben died? Did she get caught up with Polesky somehow? And most importantly, what is her fucking problem?

I travel the streets of downtown Mobile while thinking of Blaire and ignore my phone that continuously beeps and vibrates in my pocket. Finally, after I pull to a stop along the curb, I watch the building in front of me. I un-straddle my bike and put up the kickstand, preparing to wait and watch to see if either Polesky shows up or if Red makes an appearance.

Just as I'm lighting a cigarette, I see her bright ass hair coming out of the building before she jumps in a cab. She seems to be in a hurry, and from this distance, her face looks like she's been crying. My blood starts to pump hard as I think of that fucker hurting her. Even though she went willingly to bed with him, she shouldn't be crying about it. I feel for my Glock 45 under my leather jacket as tendrils of smoke rise around my face. Before I can take a step in the hotel's direction, a car stops in front of me.

"Don't do it, man. Think about it before you go in there and kill the motherfucker. Be smart. You're asking to make this situation worse than it has to be." Hyde knows I'm a short fuse waiting to explode, but he's right. Tonight is not the night to put a bullet in that guy's head.

Smoke blows from my nose as I give Hyde a go to hell look. Then I flick my cigarette away and get back on my bike. Without saying a word, I head home. I have some research to do on Blaire Morgan.

Walking inside, I slam the door before grabbing a beer and going into the computer room. My mind wants to find Red and shake her for answers, but I know that won't get me anywhere. Especially after the way she looked tonight.

When I register into our confidential archive of personal information, I have high hopes of finding some sort of answers. Reading through the small amount of records, I see nothing on her known whereabouts this past year. Even Hyde has nothing on her being with Polesky in Atlanta. So I search further in the past. After about ten minutes of sorting through several girls with similar names, I find my Red. At first, I don't think it's her. The photo is of a little girl with pale blonde hair smiling with her sixth grade class. But I'd recognize those hazel-green eyes anywhere. I follow up with the next year, and then the next, and soon, I don't see any more smiles on her face. Just a lifeless stare. Then I look for Ben and notice the same thing. However, his smile doesn't fall until his junior year.

"Look at hospital records," Hyde says as he takes a seat beside me, eating an apple.

Taking his advice, I look for the local hospital records and find Ben and Blaire's birth certificates. I run their parents' names next. Mother Dianne Morgan passed away when they were around ten years of age. Father Joseph Morgan was a single father who worked at a steel mill but was let go several years later. He also volunteered at the local fire department and was an active member of the church. He's now remarried but no current record of employment. And that's it. Nothing more. I know all of their blood types and social security numbers but have no answers to my questions.

I take my work phone, not the one for the drug cartel, but my real work phone, and dial the number to the guy who's been like a big brother to me for years. The guy who taught me how to keep a bullet out of my skull. One of the first people to show me respect in life. My one connection to The Reform. "Sergeant Massey? It's Lyric. I have a request, sir."

"Fuck, Lyric. This shit better be good. I just went to sleep."

"Yes, sir. I need to take a few days and go out of town. I'll leave Hyde here until I get back."

"Leave? Why the fuck?" He breathes heavily over the phone. He's about fifteen years older than I am and is one bad sonofabitch from his tours overseas. He's a well-decorated Marine who worked with us kids when it was time for our training. He also knows that when I call for anything other than relaying information, it's for a legit reason. Just like the kidnapping a few months ago.

After a minute, he answers. "Dammit. How long do I have to cover your ass again?"

"Two days. Three tops."

"Alright. But I want your ass back ASAP. Got it?"

"I got it." I go to hang up, but he calls my name. "Yeah, Massey?"

"Does this trip involve personal matters or is this business?"

"Both."

He sighs with exasperation before the phone goes dead.

Hyde is watching me as I stand from the desk chair. I know he's wondering what the fuck I'm doing. But I don't even know, so I ignore him and print the address for Blaire's father before I go pack. Instead of taking the bike or my car, I borrow Ryan's 67' GTO and head to South Carolina to do some recon. It's the least he can do for my putting up with his ass.

When I reach the one red light town of Dunbar, South Carolina, I check into a local motel and get a few hours of sleep. Later that day, I scope out Blaire's childhood town before I set eyes on the home she grew up in. It looks empty, but I still decide to park behind a few trees for cover.

The small, ranch-style house is in the middle of an old farm that doesn't appear to be operating any longer. A rusted barn that's falling to pieces sits fifty yards in the back, and an old corroded tractor has overgrowth and weeds covering it. The wood siding is old with chipped paint and a few boards missing on the front and left side.

When I get to the back of the property, I run into an old basset hound tied to a post. She's starving, if her ribs showing are any indication. So I walk back to the car and grab some beef jerky before making my way back to her. She growls as I approach, so I toss a small piece. "That's a good dog." She gobbles it up, and I get closer to toss her another. When her tail starts wagging, I'm close enough to squat on my haunches, set a piece directly in front of me, and wait. Her large brown eyes watch me, unsure of what to do, but soon she comes closer and takes it. After the third time of doing this, I finally reach up and pat her behind her ear. That small touch has her in my lap, and she's eating the rest of the jerky out of my hands "Poor bastard. You were hungry, weren't you?" I know what it's like to starve.

After a few more head rubs, I know it's time to go back to my car and wait in the shadows for someone to get home. When I'm back at the car, I notice the windows from my vantage point are boarded up. The place isn't abandoned because I hear a TV inside. Plus fresh beer cans are left scattered on the porch and throughout the yard. Whoever lives here is a drunk and a slob.

Lighting up a cigarette, I wait. An hour later, I see an old, red Dodge Dakota coming up the drive. When it parks in front of the house, the door swings open and an older man with a balding head and large gut gets out, a paper bag in one hand. He stumbles up the steps, and the fall breeze carries the smell of liquor in my direction. The poor dog barks and howls non-stop, probably begging for food, but the man doesn't do anything other than yell for it to shut the hell up.

After he goes inside, I hear someone else. Turning my head, I see a woman get out of the passenger seat, and I'm sure she's his new wife. She reaches in the back, and at first, I think she's getting out another bag, but then I see the little girl she lifts and carries on her hip, while a cigarette hangs out of her mouth and comes close to burning the child.

The girl can't be any older than four years, and she looks like she's been crying if her red, blotchy face is any indication. Her strawberry blonde hair looks to be a knotted mess, and her bare feet are black on the bottom. Just then, she turns in my direction and looks where I'm hiding by the large oak tree. My heart almost hits the ground because I know, without a doubt, this is Red's little sister. She has the same hazel eyes that continue to stare at me. Almost as if she knows I'm here. Thankfully, she never makes a sound. Only rubs her eyes and nose.

"Frankie? Where the fuck is the remote?" I hear a yell come from inside.

"I have no idea. Savannah was watching cartoons dis mornin'," the woman says around her cigarette as she walks up the steps. "Joe. I gotta get ready for work since no one else in this damn house wants to make any money. So you gotta watch Vannah." She walks inside and slams the door closed.

Leaning against the car, I wait and before too long the wife goes to work. She's dressed in a McDonald's uniform so I'm figuring she works a distance from home since I didn't notice one in town. A few minutes later, the man comes out and sits on the front porch. He opens a white ice chest that sits beside his plastic chair and pulls out a beer. For two hours, I watch him as he finishes a whole twelve pack. On several occasions, the little girl has told him she's hungry, but he either ignored her or yelled something while staying in his chair. When the sun's gone down, I decide enough is enough. I walk out of the shadows and make my way toward the house.

He belches loudly and looks up when I emerge from the shadows. "Huh?" He squints and shakes his head before he stands up on wobbly legs. Wise man. He needs to be on alert with me. His flannel, buttoned down opens up and underneath is a dirty white shirt. "Who the hell are you?"

I don't smile. I never do, so why waste it on this piece of shit? "You Ben and Blaire Morgan's father?"

"Blaire? You know Blaire?" He relaxes, and I see the excitement when he says her name. "She here?" He looks over my shoulder.

"Nope." I walk up the steps and tower over him. The excitement from moments ago leaves his red eyes. "Aren't you going to ask about Ben? Your son?"

"Oh yeah? How's that lowlife doin?" He smiles and shakes his head. "Probably got a shit load of kids, huh? That boy couldn't keep his dick in his pants. Real ladies' man." He grabs his crotch. "I guess he got that from me." He laughs as he sits back down. "Like father like son."

"I don't believe so. He wasn't a piece of shit."

He stops laughing and stares at me. "Excuse me, boy?"

I lean my shoulder against the porch column and cross my ankles. "I said he wasn't a piece of shit. And he wasn't a child abuser."

He stands up so fast, the plastic chair tips over. "Whatever those shit kids told you is all lies. Everyone knew they were crazy back then. Especially Blaire. The girl made shit up in her head all the time. Didn't have any friends after her momma died. So I tried to help her fit in. Lot of good that did me. She and that so called son of mine started rumors."

"Rumors, huh?" I stand straight and cross my arms. "What kind of rumors? The ones of you being a bad father? Because if that's the case, I don't think that's a rumor."

He face turns red with anger, and he steps toward me, but doesn't get too close. "Now, hold up one–"

Before he can finish, I grab him by the collar of his dirty shirt and get in his face. "No, you hold up. You're the one who's been drinking while a little girl is inside, alone, and starving like that dog out back. You're the selfish piece of shit that would rather have your cheap beer than get a damn job and do something besides getting drunk." I shake him hard. "I can ruin you, you sonofabitch. And I might just do it. But I want some fuckin answers, and you're going to give them to me."

"You can't come here and threaten me," he says, but I hear the tremble in his voice.

I tighten my hold. "I'm here, and I just did." His throat convulses as he swallows hard. "Now, I want to know if you have ever hurt Blaire? And I want the truth." I let him go and watch as he falls on the floor of the small porch. As he stands back up, my eyes keep up with his every move. If he tries to run or if he lies, I'm ready.

"No." He answers in hesitation. His eyes widen for a fraction, and I see a tick in his jaw. The Reform might have been hell on Earth, but if you survived, you learned some pretty heavy shit.

"Wrong answer." Before he knows what happens, I grab the back of his head and ram his skull on the porch railing. He yells and blood spurts from his now crooked nose. "Wanna try again?"

He holds his nose while leaning over in pain. "Ugh… dammit! You're fuckin' crazy. I'm gonna call the cops."

"No, you won't. You have a neglected child inside while you're two sheets to the wind. You could have fallen down the porch steps in a drunken stupor." He stands up while holding his nose. "Now answer me. Did you *ever* hurt Blaire?"

He stares at me, and I see his internal debate. I know before he answers me what his answer will be. I want him to say it though. I want him to acknowledge what a sick fuck he is. Instead, he smiles with pure maliciousness. I might kill, and I know I'm not a saint, but this piece of shit is sick in the head and I'm tempted to put a bullet in it.

"Yes. She liked it when she got older. She was always a slut. She wanted it. Always brushing her hair and wearing them clothes that left nothing to the imagination. I'm only human. After her mom died, it was her responsibility to be a good daughter and to take care of me. But then her brother had to brainwash her. I warned them nobody would believe 'em, but he still told." He starts to laugh with pure insanity. "Don't worry. That bastard got his. Especially when the cops brought them home after they ran away that first time."

My head nods slowly as my fists clench and unclench. I imagine crushing this guy's windpipe as he continues to talk. I imagine him suffering and causing him excruciating pain. So much pain, until he can't take it and screams for mercy. My heart and adrenaline start to race in unison. As much as I want to kill this motherfucker, I know I need to be careful. This isn't my job and there are rules. Nevertheless, it will be handled, and that little girl will be taken away from it.

Before I leave to make the call, I give in to my desire to cause this asshole pain. I ball my fist and land a clean right hook to the left side of the fucker's face. He lands with a loud thud, knocked out cold. When I look up, I see a miniature Blaire watching me with wide eyes through the screen door. All of the sudden, I'm encompassed with a need to see her and hold her because of what she went through. It takes a few hours, but I make sure the girl is in safe hands before I get in the car and head back to the motel to grab my shit. Then I load up and head back to Red. Luckily, the ride isn't boring or as lonely as on the way up. Ryan's going to be pissed his car smells like dog though.

It's early morning when I reach my house, so I let the dog inside and give her a bath. After she's taken care of, I go and wake up Hyde to get the run down since I left. Nothing major happened at the Jay's. He does mention that since I left unexpectedly right before our busiest night at Jay's, they had a girl named Cookie play in my place.

"Was she any good?"

He shrugs his shoulders. "Yeah. She's alright. Anyways, how was the trip? Get any answers?"

"Yes and no. What band is this girl with?"

"Um… Serenade? Suave?" He scratches his head as he thinks.

"Sinister?" I ask, and he nods yes. He's lying about not remembering. His memory is too damn good. But I don't push.

"I've heard them play at the Hole. They're decent." I decide to ask the one question that has been on my mind the whole time I was gone. "Has Red been back to work or been seen anymore with Bishop?"

Even though I wanted to go check on her myself, I decided not to. I promised myself on the way home I'd keep away. No matter how much I want her, I don't fucking need her or the trouble she'll cause. I know my life would fuck her up more than she is. She doesn't need the baggage I carry or the threat that follows me. She needs better.

"Nope. Chris said she's been staying in her room. Never comes out while he's home." He stands and stretches. "I'm gonna go for a run."

As he leaves, I debate on doing the same, but I know my feet will take me to the one place I don't need to be. I don't need to take the chance of breaking my promise to myself. Instead, I head into my room with my old acoustic guitar. My fingers start strumming on the chords as my thoughts return to Red, her sister, and Polesky. Everything is falling apart, and I don't know what the fuck I'm going to do about it. Lie to the world or to myself?

Crowned with Obscurity

There's no light I see

Shadows are the sunlight to someone like me

Waves of coolness travel my skin

Wishing it was your flesh instead once again

But I'm nothing

Nothing that is good for you.

Nothing, but the Devil's closest kin.

The you I want is not what I need

My need for you is not real

It's nothing to me

Forgotten to this realm of hate

Forgiveness is what they fake and portray

But you're a liar too

They all are

Just like me

Darkness is the only light I understand

Shadows are the sunlight to this soulless man

Rays of coolness that travel on my skin

Skin that's burned and black as sin

Because I'm nothing

Nothing but the Devil's closest kin

Keeping the faith in something unseen

Knowing you're lost and nowhere free

Hatred for me is what you should feel

Yearning for fairness is someone else's will

Not mine

Never mine

CHAPTER ELEVEN

"New Beginnings are often disguised as painful endings."
~Lao Tzu

Blaire

I'm so warm and comfortable. Wrapped in a void of nothingness. No worries or fears. No nightmares. Everything is like an abyss and dark. However, I'm not scared of this darkness. I feel like I'm floating even though I'm heavy. Then I float deeper into nothing.

My oblivion disappears, and I wake feeling the aftermath of another night of drinking. This one seems worse than the others. Then again, it could be from the annoying dog yapping outside. With every deep bark, my head pounds harder. My eyes open and everything is blurry, but after a minute, they adjust and my heart drops. *Where am I?* Judging by the wall covered in tacky wallpaper, I'm not in my room at Chris's house. And judging from the snores coming from my left, I'm not alone either. What the hell did I do?

I think of my late night of drinking. I remember having an excruciating headache, so I took two more of Chris's pain pills.

Then I became restless. So I decided to go out for a drink. I walked into a dance club wanting to people watch without being recognized. After that, my mind goes blank, and my head hurts too much to continue recalling last night's events. I know I need to get out of here… wherever here is. Angry and confused, I kick my bed partner and climb out the bed to look for my clothes.

He grunts but doesn't wake. I see blond hair sticking out from the top of the blanket but refuse to look. Maybe it'll disappear that way. People say ignorance is bliss.

After I slip on my jeans, I notice a brown leather wallet on the floor open with a few twenties sticking out. Feeling my old ways creep up, I decide to take what I feel I deserve. Why not? This guy obviously had a good time. He's not the one who feels like used trash afterwards. As I take this guy's cash, his ID reaches my line of sight, and I feel sick because I recognize him. He's one of the biggest playboys to enter Jay's, and it looks like I was his latest game. David Lawrence.

Before I vomit from being one of his bimbos and girls I've always hated, I let my adrenaline get me the hell out of there. As I'm leaving, I pass a bunch of guys in the kitchen and know I'm in a frat house. When they see me, I hear a bunch of whistles and rude comments. However, I don't feel like confronting them. Panic is setting in, and I need to get away.

Once the cab drops me off, I run inside and lock the door. Quickly, I clean up and feel the need to forget another fuck up. I open the medicine cabinet and see the orange prescription bottles. They sit there, taunting me, as I debate taking more of Chris's medication. I know it's wrong, and he's a friend. But the devil on my shoulder wins the battle. After I swallow them down, I go in my room and lay down, waiting for the dark cloud of nothingness that is my best friend, to swallow me up once more.

Bang. Bang. Bang. Hammering on my door invades my sweet unconsciousness and wakes me. When I open my eyes, there's no light coming through the window so I know it's night. Only the light from the moon shines through. Luckily, I'm in my own room this time.

"Blaire? Can I talk to you?" Chris bangs once again. His words are curt, and I have a feeling deep in my gut he knows I've been taking his medicine.

Shame and fear set in, knowing I deceived my friend. Dreading the confrontation to come, I grudgingly make my way to the door. When I crack it open, I see his angry features take in my disheveled form. "Yeah?"

He holds up the bottle of pills. "Do you need to tell me something?" I answer with silence. "Okay, let me try this again. Have you been taking my pills?"

I still don't answer. What am I supposed to say? *Um... Sorry, Chris, I swiped your meds cause I'm too fucked up to sleep without nightmares?* No. And I'm not going to lie. So I turn around and go sit on my bed. I can't face him. He took me in and helped me when I was in need, and I stole from him, knowing how fucked up he is with his leg and nightmares.

"How could you do this to me? Are you that fucking selfish? Did you not think I might actually need these for a reason? Do you not think I have insomnia and pain? I called the VA today for a refill, and I can't get any more for another two weeks. What the hell am I supposed to do until then?"

"I'm sorry. I'm fucked up," I whisper and feel like the worst person breathing. I didn't let his needs affect my decision in taking his meds.

"And I'm not?" he yells and hits the door. "I only have one damn leg. I have fucking night terrors of my friends dying every fucking night." I sit there, refusing to look at him as a tear falls. His breathing is heavy, and I feel him watching me. "You need to get your shit and leave. I can't trust you anymore." With those words, he slams my bedroom door, and I jump. Five minutes later, I'm still sitting there when I hear his car pull out of his driveway before I do what he says.

After my bag is packed, I sit on the steps while I try to come up with a plan. All I have is my clothes and my pride. I have no car, no home, and no friends. And it's all my fault. I did this to myself, so there's no one else to blame. I'm sure Chris is telling everyone we know I'm a dope head who stole his medication. And I'm sure David will tell everyone I'm a thief. Maybe it's time I head out and do what I've always done. I've saved some money, and with the two hundred I took from David, I can get a room and maybe a new disguise. I just have to do one more thing before I go. Visit my brother.

I adjust my bag on my shoulder and carry Benji's guitar to sit in front of the stone block. I haven't been back here since the day he was put in the ground, when I lost him. When I lost everything. Now I feel as though I lost it all once again, and I'm in the exact same place. Funny, huh?

I place my bags down and sit on the cold ground. My icy fingers trace the words inscribed on the marble stone that I'm seeing for the first time.

Benjamin Quinton Morgan

Wonderful Brother, Ladies' Man, and Rock Star

February 23, 1988 – November 1, 2012

Janet did good picking out what to say on the headstone. The words are so true. I inhale the night air, letting the November chill rush in my lungs as I think what to say. So I start with the one thing I know is true. "I miss you, bubba. And I'm sorry I haven't come by. I just couldn't do it."

While I sit there in silence, I feel a tingle crawl up my spine. Looking around, I see no one else. Maybe it's Benji, letting me know he's listening. "I'm not good at this stuff, ya know. You were always the talker. Just the sound of my own voice bothers me." After a few minutes of only the smell of wet, dead grass in my nose and the whistle of the wind, I decide to do the one thing Benji always loved me to do. Sing. My heart knows exactly what song he'd want to hear too. *Home* by Gabrielle Alpin.

It was our life wrapped in lyrics, and we sang it together on several occasions. It was our reminder that we had one another, and he was my home, and I was his. Now I'm homeless.

My heart breaks at that very thought, and my voice cracks, but I push on until the last word passes my lips. My fingers dig into the cold, dead grass that covers his body, and I hope he hears my words and knows how much I love him.

As the tears slowly fall, my mind wanders to why I'm homeless, why my brother is no more. His life isn't with me any longer because he loved someone who didn't appreciate what he did have and what he could have given her. She just threw it away and broke his heart.

Closing my eyes, I picture his face. And even though I try to see the happy Benji, I can only envision the last time I saw him. He wasn't smiling. Instead, he was sobbing. He refused any comfort and went to his box. His magic box that held his comfort and took him from me. No matter what I said, he always leaned on that box.

"Benji, don't do it. Please! It's not worth it. She's not worth it." I bang on the door, but he refuses to open it up until he's done.

Walking out the door, his glassy eyes meet mine. I'm so angry that he continues to let his drugs, and now Trudy, take him further away from me. "Why are you doing this to yourself?" I sob. "Why won't you let me help you?"

He stumbles past me and leans against the wall where he sinks down to sit on the floor. "I can't save anyone." He looks up at me, and tears fill his eyes once again. "Not you. Not her. Baby died," he mumbles. The drugs are making him incoherent, and I can barely make it out. "She wants a new life. Now that baby is no... no more. Now she's happy."

Remembering that night, the anger is fresh. That bitch aborted their child so she could be with rich boy Jax and have a new life. I know her and Ben were intimate. I saw the flirting and the kiss. He even told me how in love with her he was. He smiled more when she showed up in our lives and not just the smile he showed the girls who always were around. He smiled when he woke up in the mornings. He even used less. Then Jax showed up and ruined it.

After his confession, I left. I couldn't stand seeing him like that, so out of it until his eyes rolled in the back of his head. I went to the diner down the road to cool off and to get him his favorite steak omelet to eat when he woke up. But I was too late, because when I got back, he was dead. I shook him for what seemed like forever trying to wake him up. But he wouldn't come back to me.

When I'm done, I stand and wipe away my tears. My heartbreak feels as fresh as my anger. I'm once again ripped into pieces and alone, and with every beat of my broken heart, more and more of my soul gushes out.

Grabbing my stuff, my eyes linger one last time on the words that represent the most important person that ever lived for me. Then I make my way down the road and pass people who are full of laugher and blind to my grief. As the chill gets worse and the wind causes me to shiver, I decide a drink would help warm me up and possibly calm me down enough to think of a plan. So I go to the first bar I see.

I sit on a stool at the bar and order a whiskey straight. The guy with the long gray beard reminds me of ZZ Top and Sons of Anarchy's lovechild with his tattoos and a black leather vest. He doesn't say anything, just places my drink on a napkin and moves on to the next customer. I turn in my seat to observe. It's what I always do. The crowd is different here. It's full of people who don't have much, and if they do, they don't rub it in with their attire. Most women are wearing jeans and judging by the assortment of motorcycles out front it's probably because they rode with someone. Pool tables are in the back, and cigarette smoke floats throughout the building. A small stage sits in the back as well as a small dance floor covered by people line dancing. Nobody notices me. If they do, they don't stare. I'm sure my face is red and blotchy from crying and the wind. I'm thankful not to be grabbing anyone's attention. Tonight, I'm just a girl in a bar.

"Joe. Get me something strong and big, will ya?"

"Ah, Cookie. I got something for ya strong and big."

The bartender playfully comments to the girl who just walked up. When I turn, I recognize her as the guitar player from a week and a half ago. Instead of her pinup attire, she's wearing jeans and a black leather jacket with a yellow shirt underneath. And instead of rolling her eyes, she's smiling.

"Not tonight, doll. Jackass is with me. But remember, you're the real man of my heart." She winks and grabs her drink before sashaying away. The bartender smiles to display his white teeth underneath all that gray hair. He catches my stare. "You play?" He nods his head toward the guitar case by my stool.

"Some."

He nods his head while I nurse my drink and hope he doesn't

ask any more questions. I'm not in the mood for him to lend an ear while I chat about my sorrows or whatever bartenders are supposed to do.

He eyes my empty glass. "You need another?"

"Sure." He pours the amber liquid while I listen to the commotion behind me: Bad Company plays from the jukebox, people laughing, and the clacking of balls breaking on the pool tables. Then I get the same feeling that I had in the graveyard. Like someone's watching me. But I shake it off, blaming it on my nerves and how today has been really messed up.

I look at my phone and am shocked to see it's one a.m. This day from hell has flown by. Even though I want it to end, I still have nowhere to go when I leave here. I feel weary, and I know it's more emotional than physical. I could head to a local hotel, but I hate wasting my money.

By the time I finish my second drink, I've decided to head to the bus station and let fate take over. The first bus out of here is the one I'll take, and wherever it goes, I'll try to make my home. Try being the key word.

After I pass a twenty to the bartender, I grab my things and once again face Mother Nature and her bitchy chill. It's late, so hardly anyone but a few partygoers or drunks are out. Yellow streetlights and shadows dance off the brick buildings and sidewalks. I know this isn't the safest part of town, but Benji and I used to live on these streets. Regardless, I keep my steps steady and my grip on my bags tight. Then that feeling returns. I look behind me and don't see anyone, but my feet involuntarily speed up as well as my heartbeat.

In a flash, it happens. I'm grabbed from behind, and my mouth is covered before I can get out a scream. I'm thrown into the shadows and hear my bags hit the ground. Instinct takes over, and I slam my elbow backwards and am rewarded with a male grunt. When I'm free, I run, but before I can make it out of the shadows, someone steps out in front of me.

"Please… please, help me," I beg.

"Shhh, pretty girl." He wraps his arms around me and starts to walk me backwards into the alley and dread sinks in. I try to remove myself from him, but his grip only gets tighter.

"Bout damn time. This one is a firecracker."

The guy who holds me turns me around and grips my arms so tightly that I know I'll have bruises. "I told you I wouldn't miss this one." He smells my hair. "Firecracker is right. She smells like heat. You hot, baby?" He kisses my neck, and I jerk away.

The one I elbowed comes to stand in front of me as he starts to undo his pants. He's bouncing on his toes as if he's excited about what he's about to do. I still can't see him clearly from my tears, but I can make out a slender frame. Watching him in slow motion, I start to feel helpless and wonder if I should just give up. My eyes start to lose focus with the realization that there's nothing I can do. I'm destined to be damaged. Life has truly fucked me over. "What you lookin at, bitch?" he questions me.

Frozen and unable to talk, I just stare. My voice has disappeared with any hope that I'd be okay. Then he punches me across the face. Excruciating pain radiates through my entire body and spots dance before my eyes. I fall to my knees as my mouth fills with the coppery flavor of blood. When I spit, I see the dark liquid fall to the ground. My palms dig into the broken asphalt and dirt as I try to hold myself up. I know I'll be doomed if I pass out, so I continue to fight. After a few deep breaths, I look up and see a third guy has joined the other two. He hasn't approached me, and I don't feel any fear from seeing his large frame. Squinting, I see he's fighting off my attackers.

He punches one, and I watch as the guy falls down beside me. My shadowed rescuer has the other one against the brick wall, and I think he's yelling, but I can't be sure. It's all in slow motion, and my hearing isn't right. All I hear is a high-pitched ringing. Plus my vision is starting to fade in and out. But I do get a glimpse of the other guy starting to stand before he reaches into his pocket for something. My gut tells me it's a weapon, and my stomach drops with pure fear. Straining through the pain, I gain my voice and scream. Before I can finish, two shots are fired. I close my eyes as the sound ricochets off the brick walls that surround the alley. I don't know who went down or if I'll be next, so I just count.

1... 2... 3... 4... 5...

"Red?"

Hearing that name, I know who is here with me. My eyes crack open to see his shadowed face. "Lyric?" I squeak out, but more blood fills my mouth, so it's inaudible.

I hear his deep sigh as he lifts me in his arms. My body aches all over, but knowing I'll be okay, and I'm protected, it's endurable. Then I let the black spots take over and welcome my friend nothingness once again.

CHAPTER TWELVE

"The world will not be destroyed by those who do evil, but by those who watch them and do nothing."
~Albert Einstein

Lyric

Red's face flashes through my mind-swollen, bruised, and unrecognizable- as I sit beside Janet in the hospital waiting room. I've been here for the past two hours, waiting for the doctor to come out with an update. I'm not the only one either. The cops are waiting to ask her questions as well, but I've already had Joe clean up the alley. As far as they know, I scared them off before she was actually raped. I just hope she doesn't remember me killing the two sonsofbitches.

Anxiousness sets in so I turn to Janet to keep my mind off of Red. "How are you doin', Janet?" Not many people know how sick she actually is, but since we discuss business, she told me.

She looks my way, and her skin is thinner and pastier than usual. "I'm making it. Doctor says chemo would only prolong my life by a few months. Told them to shove those few months up their ass if they expect me to be sick the whole damn time. I'd rather just get it over with." She looks toward the door to where Red is. "I just can't leave until I know Mouse will be okay. She and the bar are my only babies left on this earth. And I know you'll take care of Jay's. Now I just gotta make sure she's okay. Then I can die in peace."

I don't know what to say. I know I bought Jay's out of debt, but I can't guarantee to take care of Red, too. She doesn't need my shit. Unsure how to answer, I just sit there and nod my head. Before long, the doctor walks out.

We stand and Janet claims to be Red's mom when the doctor asks. He tells us she's awake, and the officers are talking to her now, but she's on pain meds and incoherent. She's suffered a ruptured eardrum and her lip needed a few stitches, but she'll make a full recovery. Even though I know it all ready, hearing no rape had taken place has me exhaling in relief.

"Can we see her?" I ask. I should leave since she's not in any more danger, but I can't. Not until I see her not beaten and bloody.

"After the officers are done. I want to keep her overnight, but she should be released by tomorrow."

Not long after he exits the waiting room, a nurse comes in to get Janet and me. I let Janet go in first and prop my leg on the wall. As I wait, I think of tonight's events and how it could've been a lot worse.

On my way to speak to Joe, I passed her at the cemetery. Not wanting to interfere, I forced myself to keep moving, but when she walked to The Hole, my guard went up. I stayed at a back table and observed her. She wasn't flirting or even talking to anyone. She looked lost, and with her bags packed, I knew she was leaving. When she left, I sat there thinking it was for the best. Let her leave town and let my life get back to normal and let me get my priorities straight. She's better off.

But after a few minutes, I stopped lying to myself and went after her. I needed her in my life.

She has become an obsession to me. She makes me feel something other than hate. She makes me want more than this lie of a life I'm living. *Dammit! I sound like a fucking Hallmark card.*

"Lyric?" I open my eyes as Janet approaches me. "You can go in now, but she's out of it."

I nod my head and walk through the heavy door. The lights are low in her room, but I can see her. And my decision to stop lying to myself feels right. Her face is dark with bruises, and her lip is swollen and stitched on the bottom, but she's still here. Alive. Whole. And she's still beautiful.

Not wanting to disturb her, I stand a foot away from the bed. Tonight was very traumatic, and even though she's been through a similar hell, her mental state is fragile. Watching the steady rise and fall of her chest, I think of a plan. She's too reckless and obviously needs someone. Should I move her in with me so she can recover, or let her return to Chris's and crave her company from a distance? I don't know just yet, but I need to figure it out before she's released tomorrow.

Before I leave, I reach out and touch her open palm. Her fingers close around my finger for a second then she whispers my name. I look up and see her good eye barely open.

"Thank you." Her voice is muffled and hard to make out. But I know what she said. And I know I'd kill anyone to protect her.

She closes her eyes again, and her breathing once again becomes steady. I leave to let her rest, and Janet meets me in the hallway. "Are you gonna call Chris to come get her tomorrow?" I ask and push the elevator button.

"No. I'll take her. Chris kicked her out tonight. I'm guessing that's why she was down there with her bags."

"What?" My fist clenches, ready to knock the shit outta someone. I'm pissed that he would kick her out in the middle of

the fucking night with nowhere to go.

She watches my reaction, not saying anything at first, but I see her wheels turning. The whole walk down, there's a tension, because I know she has something to tell me. I just don't know what it could be. I do know it's about Red.

When we reach the parking lot, she stops me by placing her hand on my arm but never makes eye contact. "I see the anger in you, Lyric. It's not pretty. However, I also see the way you care about my Mouse. She's had a very rough life and tends to run when things get rough. It's how she's survived. Now it's time for her to face her demons, and she can't do it alone. I'm dying and can't be there with her, and Chris isn't ready to help." Her eyes meet mine, and she straightens her spine. She's a fierce woman, and I see why most back away when she looks at them this way. I'm not most. "Are you ready to?" She gently squeezes my tattooed forearm before walking away toward her truck. I can only stand where I am as the sound of her footsteps fades and ask myself that exact question. *Am I?*

But another more important question surfaces. How can I help protect her from her demons when I'm a demon myself?

On the way home, I decide to make a pit stop. When I walk up the steps, I smell cigarette smoke before I see Chris sitting in a plastic chair. He eyeballs me while blowing out the vapor through his nose before looking ahead once again.

"You know why I'm here?"

He nods his head. "Yup." He pops the 'P' and continues to sit there not looking at me.

Lighting my own cigarette, I give him more time to talk, but he doesn't. He only sits there and smokes.

"You gonna talk then? Or do you like me hanging out on your porch at four in the morning?"

"I don't have to explain shit to you." He flicks out his bud and slowly stands. "What I do in life doesn't need your damn approval."

My hard eyes fall on him, and my spine straightens, ready for a fight. "When it comes to you throwing Red out on the goddamn streets, and her almost getting raped, then it does. She could have been killed tonight."

"Did you just come over here to make me feel like hammered dog shit? Because you're too fucking late," he says with angry remorse, and then takes a deep breath. "Look. If I knew that she wasn't going to go somewhere safe, I wouldn't have kicked her out. I was just so damn angry that she betrayed me the way she did."

"What did she do?" My curiosity gets the best of me. Even though it's not my business, I tend to make it my business if it involves Red.

He limps to the front door, walks inside, and then calls in my direction. "You coming in?" Following behind, I take a seat on the couch across from him in the living room. Stretching out my legs, I get comfortable and wait. "She was stealing my pain and sleeping medication. I was pissed because I can't get any more for a few weeks and just blew up on her. After she was gone, I knew I shouldn't have, but it was too late. I figured she got to Janet's or even that girl Cory's."

"Why the hell are you exposing her to that shit?" I ask in a low angry tone. I know my attitude is unwarranted, but I can't help it. Especially after witnessing her getting beat tonight. It should have never happened.

"Look, Lyric. I understand you're pissed at the whole fucking world, but you're not the only one who cares for Blaire. I've known her a lot longer than you have. I never thought she'd pop pills for a high. Especially after what happened to her brother. But people change. Shit happens. And everyone copes differently." He lifts up his pant leg. "And to answer your question, not that you deserve one, I have my own fucking reasons for taking medication." He taps on the aluminum leg that hides under his jeans. "I also have PTSD and need prescription medication for sleep and to go about my daily life. And this shit here," he unstraps the component that holds his prosthetic on and slides off a rubber stocking, "hurts like a bitch most days."

I examine his amputated leg and the scar that rests below his knee for a second before I pull my eyes away and see the military pictures on the wall. It's not my place to ask what happened, so I'll leave it alone. I also can't bring myself to apologize for being pissed about how the situation was handled, but I understand why he has the medication. This guy isn't a low life looking for a high like my mind wanted to interpret when he mentioned pills. I guess it's because I deal with people like that on a regular basis that I thought the worst. He's a vet who got fucked at a young age and deserves my admiration. What he does and what I do are on two different playing fields. "She just doesn't need any more shit, ya know?" I won't say anything more than that because what I know about Red is something so messed up, I'm sure she doesn't brag about it to her friends.

"I hear ya. And I didn't mean to flip my shit. I really hope she's okay." He sighs and lays his head on the couch. I stand to leave, but he stops me as I open the door. "Do you think they'll catch who did this to her?"

My eyes stay fixated on the cuts that mar my hand as it's

wrapped around the doorknob. "I guarantee those bastards got exactly what they deserved."

The whole day, I can't sleep as images of Red drift in and out of my mind. What she's doing and feeling now verses what she was feeling last night. I want to make sure she's safe for once in her life. So I get up with the decision that I'm bringing her to stay here. It's irrational and dangerous, but I can't think of any other way to keep her safe. Now I need to make some changes throughout the house.

Moving my artillery out of the kitchen area and into the third bedroom/office was a bitch, but I went ahead and cleaned my M-16, MP-5 submachines gun, and a few of my pistols. I also changed the lock just to be on the safe side. Wanting Red to not need anything, I went to the store and picked up all kinds of girlie shit. I just threw any damn thing I saw in the cart. Even went to the mall and bought her some dresses and those stretchy pants I see chicks wearing at the gym. Unsure of Red's size, I asked a random woman who had a similar build her size. She was happy to tell me and even offered to try some on for me. I tried not to be a complete dick and threw a hundred dollars at her before walking away.

Now I'm back home, placing everything in its place before I go pick her up. Before I can concentrate too much on her in nothing but the tiny piece of black cloth, I shut the drawer and double check everything. All this reminds me of my old life with Carly. We only had one another and lived on cereal or grilled cheese most days. My life then is nothing like my life now.

Hyde isn't happy with me bringing her here, but when I told him he could get over it or find another place to live, he shut up. I knew he wouldn't leave. He keeps me up-to-date on any new information regarding our job or Polesky. Plus, I know he's worried more than anything, because it's not part of the deal. And if she is working with Polesky, I'll basically be cutting both of our throats. But my gut tells me she's innocent in all of this, and it's never let me down before.

With nothing else to do around the house, I call Janet. When I tell her about my plan, she isn't surprised. In fact, she tells me she had no plans to get Red from the hospital today because she knew I was going to do it. The thought of her knowing my decision before I did is unnerving, but I shake it off and get in my car to head to get Red. I don't know how she'll react, but I don't care either.

CHAPTER THIRTEEN

"Knowing you care is enough. I hope."
~Blaire

Blaire

"I have to work so I won't be there. I don't want you to worry though because someone's picking you up for me. Okay, Mouse?" Janet asks on the other end of the phone.

I can't help my mind from wondering if she really has to work, or if she's just ashamed of me. I don't dwell on it though. My body hurts too damn much.

"Yeah." My lip throbs with every movement as the fresh stitches pull. But that pain is nothing compared to how my soul suffers. Every time I close my eyes, my new nightmare morphs with the old. And I can't shake either one. So, to make it tolerable, I concentrate on the only good thing I can. Lyric.

I see him coming to help me and saving me from harm. I know it sounds stupid, but in my head, he doesn't just stop last night's frightening incident from taking place. He prevents both.

We hang up the phone, and I let the silence of my room invade my mind as I lay on my side. I can't help but do the same thing I've done since I woke up. Look out the window of my hospital room and try to see something- *anything*- good in this world.

133

Something that will make the suffering and pain I've felt for as long as I can remember worth it in the end. But it's not there and hasn't been since before mom died. It seems things have only dwindled and turned out worse. Every inch of me and every layer of mass that creates this body I find myself in feels tired and lonely. How are there so many people in this world, if all life gives you is something else to fear and cry about? I don't have an answer and fear I never will. I can't see anything beautiful or worth living for any longer.

As the nurse pushes me out in a wheelchair, I grip the card from the lady who came and talked to me earlier in my hand a little tighter. She was respectful of my silence and never pushed me to talk. Even though I didn't like her, I didn't push her out or ask her to leave. My lip hurt too damn bad.

Her soft voice never reprimanded me for my whereabouts last night. I figured someone in such nice clothes would tell me I shouldn't have been out drinking alone in such a bad part of town, but she didn't. She just told me about herself and business. She works with people who've been in similar situations and wants me to contact her if I want to talk about anything. Even though I don't, I still can't bring myself to throw away the card in my hand. It's a lifeline, and I'm terrified of letting it go. All my other ties have been cut, so why not have a false friendship in my head that lets me believe I'm not completely alone in this world?

Sitting in the hospital front lobby, I wait for Janet's friend to pick me up and take me to her place. When I see that familiar silver sports car pull up, my heart starts beating wildly. How am I supposed to face him after last night?

Lyric steps out with his sunglasses on and black leather jacket blocking the fall chill. He looks menacing, and I guess he can be. But he was just protecting a friend, and it was two against one, so in my head, he had no choice. When he struts into the lobby, everyone's eyes turn his way. My throat convulses when he's directly in front of the wheelchair, towering over me, and he takes in my face. His sunglasses block his eyes from my sight, but I feel his stare. Feeling self-conscious all of a sudden, I look down and see his fist clenching so tight that his knuckles are white. My palms become sweatier with every second that passes. Does he blame me for what happened, and for his having to take not just one life, but two?

Trying to distract my thoughts, I study the words on the card. Then a shadow overcasts me and I look up. He bends down and easily lifts me in his arms. I automatically latch my arms behind his head, but keep my head down, so not to make eye contact. I hear the nurse tell him sternly how that's not how they're supposed to discharge patients into their waiting vehicles. Lyric just ignores her and deposits me in the passenger seat. He even buckles me up like a five-year-old who can't take care of their self. Either he thinks I'm stupid and incapable of the small act, or he cares. Somehow, I think it's the former and not the latter.

I don't feel like talking, so the drive is silent and awkward. Should I tell him thank you again? Or does he not want to be reminded of last night's incident? Turning to look out the window, I get a glimpse of myself for the first time. My right eye is swollen and three different colors, and my bottom lip is stitched and puffy. My fingers go to touch it, but another hand gently grabs my fingers before they make contact.

"Don't touch it," he says. He keeps his hand on mine for a few more seconds before releasing me.

Not wanting to argue or talk, I do as he says with my heart

135

slamming against my chest. I avoid the mirror at all cost and close my eyes, or eye, instead. When the car engine cuts off, I look up wondering why I'm at his house. I can't help but speak up, no matter how much pain it causes. "Why are we here?"

"Because this is your new home."

I'm puzzled and give him my full attention. "I thought I was staying with Janet?" When he doesn't say anything, my mind thinks the worst. Janet doesn't want me around her. Why else would she turn me away?

"That's for Janet to discuss with you, not me." He goes to open the door and my hand lands on his heavily tattooed arm.

"Is it because of what happened at Chris's?" I ask in a whisper while shame surrounds me. He doesn't say anything and I start to panic. I need him to know that's not the real me. "I'm not a drug user."

His words are clipped and gruff. Void of caring. "I'm not your judge, so you don't need to explain anything to me." Then he exits the car and slams the door.

I've broken everyone's trust in me? Just because I wanted sleep? After a few deep breaths to calm myself and keep the tears away, I finally drag myself up the steps. I'm grateful to have a place to go and not be alone, but I didn't expect to be so close to Lyric. And I don't want him thinking the worst of me.

When I walk inside and pass through the foyer, I come to the living room. I see Hyde on the couch looking at his laptop. He looks up but gives no reaction to me standing there in a large t-shirt and jeans. He doesn't even say anything. Just gets back to looking at whatever is on his computer screen. It's as if I'm not there.

"Blaire?" I look forward and see Lyric down the hall. "You're staying in my room."

Following his lead, I tail behind him to his room. He's grabbing some clothes and putting them in a bag. I start to panic because I don't want to be alone. Even if he doesn't trust me. "Are you leaving me?" I grip the card tightly in my hand.

He stops and looks at my face before his gunmetal eyes land on my hands in front of me. He shakes his head and continues to pack. "I'm sleeping on the couch."

Relief washes through me. The thought of being alone is frightening. I've been alone for off and on this past year, but now, I don't think I can do it.

"I have one rule in my house. And I expect it to be followed." He carries his bag over his shoulder and approaches me as I stand by the door. "No one comes here. No one knows where I live, and I expect it to stay that way."

I nod my head even though that request seems strange. I won't question it though. Most people have things they don't want others to know about them. Plus he's allowing me to stay here until I'm better.

After he leaves, I sit on the large, wooden bed. I feel drained physically and emotionally, but I'm too scared to sleep. I don't have any medication to make me numb and so out of it that I can't dream. I've never felt more alone than I do right now. Even after Benji died, I knew I could call Janet. In the back of my mind, I always had somewhere to go, and someone to count on. Now I don't know what I'll do when I'm recovered enough to leave. As I continue to think, I feel my eyelids get heavy, so I lay my head on the cool pillow. The smell of Lyric surrounds me, and I inhale deeply. I'm so sore, and my head throbs, but with that smell, I feel okay. I feel like I'm not totally alone and that he's here with me.

When I open my eyes again, the sun's down. I slowly sit up and stretch, amazed that I fell asleep. I look on the bedside table for a clock or my phone, but instead, I see a bowl of soup and a glass of water. My stomach growls when the chicken soup's aroma reaches me, and my mouth starts to water.

There's a light knock on the door, and Hyde walks in carrying my duffle bag. For a moment, I was excited about not being alone again, but seeing his face pulled into a frown lets me know he doesn't want me here. "Here." He places it on the floor by my feet and makes his way out again.

Without thought, I ask, "Where's Lyric?"

"Out." Then he shuts the door.

The next two weeks are pretty much a continuous cycle. I get up, eat by myself, watch TV by myself, and eat lunch and dinner by myself. I have no friends in real life, and I don't do the whole social media crap. Well, I'll take that back. I find Sissy. A timid basset hound that lives inside this lonely house. Since no one was around for me to ask about her, I named her Sissy because she's scared of her own shadow. Her eyes look so sad that I can't help but try to make her feel better. She wouldn't come to me at first, but I started leaving table scraps on the floor while I ate. In time, I was able to rub her gently behind the ear, and now I have her sleeping in my bed with me at night. So other than Sissy entering my life, the only thing that has changed in the past two weeks is me. Physically, anyway. My lip's healed and my eyes are no longer different colors.

I still wake at night in a cold sweat though. The nightmares are worse, and I blame it on the silence of the house and the unfamiliarity, which causes me to feel like I'm a child all over again. Seeing shadows and figures that aren't there. But they feel real. And the fear I experience is so very real.

This morning is no different. Sitting up, I wipe the mixture of tears and perspiration from my face and forehead. After a few deep breaths, I realize where I am and stand to make my way to the bathroom. I take a hot shower and try to enjoy all the body washes that were here for me on my first day, but I can't with the nightmare still playing in my head.

Lyric isn't helping me anymore in my dreams. I think it's because I haven't seen him around much. I haven't even seen Hyde. They're usually off doing things that guys do when I'm awake. But I do hear them sometimes in the early mornings arguing about me being here. Actually, Hyde is doing most of the arguing. I never hear Lyric's retort. They don't know that I'm awake because of my ever-present nightmares. But I hear them.

I've explored Lyric's home since I came here from the hospital and found the weirdest things that just don't add up. Yes, it's beautiful and big. And yes, it's in a fancy gated community. But there are no pictures on the wall or personal touches other than a few guitars. Paper plates, plastic and Styrofoam cups, and plastic utensils are all there is to eat on, and I've only found two cooking pots. Most of the food is microwavable, so I guess it doesn't matter. Why would someone want to live in a fancy home unless there was something of value? And what is in the third bedroom, or what I think is the third bedroom? The door has a lock that requires a key. Maybe the value is in there? Or is Lyric staying in there when he comes home?

The one thing I found that surprised me most of all is my old companion that sits polished in the formal dining area. The black grand piano was my pride and joy when I played at Jay's with Benji, and if we had more people and instruments in the band, I would have sat behind it all the time instead of using the keyboard. Even though I discovered it two weeks ago, I haven't touched it. I don't know if I'm ready to just yet. This one instrument holds so many memories of good times with my brother that I know, once I open that door, something in me will break. And I'm not strong enough to break anymore.

As I step out of the bedroom, I don't hear anyone. It's eight in the morning, and that usually means I'm by myself for the rest of the day. After I let Sissy out the back door, I walk into the kitchen and start up the Keurig for a cup of coffee. I hum to drown out the quiet, but my voice bounces off the walls due to the vacancy of life. Taking my coffee into the living area, I'm shocked to see Lyric lying on the couch watching me. I jump, dropping my cup, which causes the hot liquid to spill all over my hands.

"Shit." He jumps up, grabs his shirt off the couch, and wipes down my reddened skin.

The heat on my scalded hands is forgotten as a blush rushes from my toes all the way to my face. I feel only the warmness from his inked skin that covers his bare chest as he stands a few inches from me. I lick my dry lips, avert my gaze to his face, and see he's watching me with his dark gray eyes full of secrecy.

"You okay?" he asks me.

"Um, y... yes. Sorry." I take a breath and try to regain my wits. "I'm not used to seeing you here."

His lip lifts on one side, and his hands are still enclosing mine. "It is my house."

I quickly pull my hands away from his because it's too much. My stomach does flip-flops and my heart pounds with nervousness from his close proximity. "I know. It's just... I'm always alone.

And…"

Before I can finish what I'm saying, his hand comes up and touches the fresh scar on my lower lip. "It healed nicely." The feel of his calloused finger gently touching my skin has all thoughts leaving my brain. My eyes close and I absorb his touch while my emotions take a different turn. *What's this feeling I'm experiencing?* I can only feel. "Do I make you nervous, Red?"

I debate on lying or telling the truth. Both have consequences, and I swore that I wouldn't lie anymore because of all the trouble it causes. I choose to stick with the truth. "Yes," I whisper.

He's silent for a minute, but I still feel him there. "Do I scare you?" His breath is now fanning my face, and I know he's close. So close. I remember the last kiss we shared, and I want to feel like that again. I want that exhilaration to come back.

"Yes." My lips gently touch his as I speak that one syllable, and I want him to ask me something else just so it can happen once more. My body is reeling with so much responsiveness. What I feel right now with him, and how I crave that happiness, is scary, but when I lick my lips and my tongue touches his Labret piercing, all thoughts leave me.

"Good."

"Woof… woof!" Sissy barks at the back door and my eyes open. Lyric's watching me, and his eyes hold a question. Or maybe a dare. I can't be sure. All I do know is we are nose to nose, and our lips are less than a millimeter apart. But when I hear a second round of barking, I pull away. "I… I really need to let her in. She doesn't like to be alone either." I tuck an errant hair behind my ear and turn to go let Sissy inside. A nervous eagerness to get back to Lyric has me hurrying my steps, but when I do return to the living area, I notice he is nowhere around. Then I hear his car start up out front, so I walk to the window and watch as he pulls away.

CHAPTER FOURTEEN

"She drives me to my breaking point."
~Lyric

Lyric

I ran. For the first time in my damn life, I ran like a fucking bitch. Why? That's easy. *Red.* Even her nickname gets me stirred up. But I did the right thing. Didn't I? Ever since I met her crazy ass all those weeks ago, she has been on my mind. She goes deeper than the ink on my skin. Everything that she is just wraps around my soul like a damn vise. And I don't need that shit right now. I want it though.

In my mind, I see her reaction to my closeness. Her skin erupting in chills, her breath fanning my face. *Fuck!* I rear back and slam my fist on the steering wheel, trying to decide what the hell I'm going to do. All I hear though in my brain is her heavy breathing. The feel of her tongue touching my piercing is still there. The girl has put a spell on me. I'm someone who's trained to hide his feelings, but with her, I absolutely can't, no matter how fucking hard I try.

As I speed down the highway, I come to a rash decision that could be the death of me. Literally. But I know if I don't do this, I'll have never done a damn thing for myself since I was seventeen

143

years old. I yank the emergency brake and do a reckless, illegal U-turn.

After I park, I get out and slam the door shut before running up the steps. Opening the door, I don't see her, but I hear her. The keys to the piano in the other room play an eerie tune that reverberates in the vacant house. My steps take me to the dining room entrance and I stand there, frozen in place. The pulse of the melody is fast then slow as she allows her slender fingers to press the ivories in a tune that I've never heard before. Chills erupt my body, and I swear it's as if her fingers are touching me instead of the keys. Her eyes are closed, and her head jerks as the keys are hit with forceful passion. The way she absorbs herself in the music and expresses her feelings in her actions is mesmerizing. It's as if she's performing in an orchestra, wearing a gown instead of black sweats and a tank top. The longer I stand there, the more jealous I become of a damn instrument.

She is so engrossed in the music, she doesn't notice when I approach or when I'm standing behind her. My eyes focus on her pale shoulder and the pattern of freckles. A few strands of her red hair have fallen from her ponytail, touching her skin like I want to. So I allow my hand to reach out and make contact with the softest skin I've ever felt.

She jumps and looks up at me with wide eyes. Bending down, I whisper against the shell of her ear. "Don't stop." Silence encases the room with only the sound of her heavy breathing. Inside, I'm begging for her not run from me and hide. When she plays, she's free and passionate. It feels like forever when she turns her attention back to the piano.

As her fingers press the ivories, I sweetly kiss her earlobe. Then my tongue tastes her warm, sweet skin as I work my way down to her erratic pulse. Her fingers misstep on the keys, but she recovers and continues the stimulating melody. My palms caress her shoulders and feel their way down to her wrist. I'm enjoying the tremors my touch provokes before working my way back up again and starting over. But I need more. "Do you want me to touch you, Red?"

She can only nod her head due to her breathless awareness of my presence. "Do you know how long I've wanted to touch you? Every. Fuckin. Day. Since you walked into my life that night," I say gruffly into her ear, and I'm rewarded with a moan. "I've imagined you while I fucked other girls. I dreamed it was your legs wrapped around my waist. I've felt your hands claw my back. Your sweet juices flowing as you squeezed my dick from within you." I bite down on the sensitive skin between her neck and shoulder. "Now I'm tired of imagining, and I'm ready for the real thing. Are you?"

My hands go down the sides of her rib cage until they reach skin at the hemline of her shirt. Reaching around her waist, I caress her abdomen. My hands inch their way under the thin material right before her breathing hitches.

Feeling the weight of her breasts in my palms, my thumbs glide over her bra, stimulating her nipples to pucker. My dick jumps to attention and strains against my denim jeans.

I lick her from pulse to collarbone and lean over to watch my hands play with her tits under her shirt. Her taste makes my mouth water and makes me feel fucking greedy. As I squeeze their weight in my palms, she moans, and my whole body heats up. So I go further as beads of sweat start to build on my forehead and back.

My left hand works its way down her skin until I'm at her bellybutton. I stop and wait for permission to continue. I don't want to do anything she's not ready for. But God, I'm craving her. The breathy noise she's making, added to the powerful music she's creating, is causing a beast to rise in me. But this is about something more than just fucking her. This moment is about her trust. Being lost in one another's bodies. Losing yourself fully to each other. I know I'll never find someone that makes me feel how she does.

I bite down gently on her shoulder. "Tell me to stop. Tell me to leave and walk out that door."

She leans her head back on my shoulder and shakes her head. "No," she whispers huskily.

My hand continues exploring her skin and travels underneath the fabric of her black sweats. That's when I notice she's not wearing anything under them but soft skin. The lower I go, the more I feel as though I might explode in my jeans. When my fingers slide between her folds and become wet from her juices, I have to stop and count before it actually happens.

Her playing has now become messy before she stops, but I whisper for her to continue and kiss her ear. When she resumes the tune, I let one finger sink in her tight opening. Her inner muscles clamp around it as I twirl and pump in and out slowly. Her back arches as her fingers sloppily hit the keys, but the blood rushing through my head and down to my straining cock blocks the music. Adding another finger, I spread her sweet, wet pussy a little wider. But it's still so fucking tight.

Breathy moans erupt from her chest and out her sweet mouth as my thumb starts to brush gently against her clit. My teeth dig in her shoulder as I retain my self-control. Even though all I want to do is fuck her right here on top of the black grand piano, I know how important my control is with her. I speed up my movements as her walls start to contract. "Come for me, Red. I want you let go."

"I can't... I can't." She shakes her head and pants. But I can see her trembling and feel her body becoming tense. Getting ready for release. She's holding back, though.

With my opposite hand, I uncover one of her breasts and caress her soft flesh. Electricity shoots up my arm from the contact. I shouldn't be surprised. What this chick does to me is better than a hit of the best Columbian nose candy. My heart is beating faster than a speeding train, and my dick is so fucking hard that I'm sure I could bust the strongest steel known to man. And it's because of Red.

When we're together, sparks fly, and it's enough to consume me. Every fucking piece of me, leaving me nothing. Not even ashes. I roll her nipple between my thumb and forefinger, which triggers her to rotate her hips. She starts to ride my hand as the music builds. Back and forth, her hips rotate. Pushing down harder and going faster, ready for climax. With one more touch to her clit, she lets go, and I have her singing my name like she's on stage, blowing the minds of every goddamn person who's watching.

As her body quivers and she descends from her high, I remove my hand. I turn her around to straddle the bench. Her eyes remain closed, but her breathing is still irregular. If I still had dreams, she'd be it, exactly like this. Mussed hair, flushed cheeks. The only thing missing is swollen lips. So I stroke her blushing cheek and kiss her, allowing my tongue to explore her warm mouth and dance with a friction that's as old as time.

When I pull away, her green eyes open. I'm unsure of how she's going to respond to what just happened. Will she run, or will she take a chance on me? As the weariness starts to set in, I hit my knees while keeping my concentration on her reaction. "Red, if you want to go further, you need to show me. If you don't, then I'll leave. It's up to you."

Her eyes widen a fraction with my last words, and I'm sure she's going to pull away. I'll not rush or push her to do something she doesn't want. She's had a traumatic experience as well as a horrid past. It's her choice in the next step. She stands and walks behind me toward the door. I'm sure she's leaving because I've pushed her too far today, and her emotions are frayed. The door clicks closed before I hear her feet come forward. Then I feel her cool touch on my shoulder. My eyes close and I absorb the intimacy of the gesture, of the decision she is making.

I don't move, but stay where I am. I'm fearful of this being a dream. Maybe I'm still high from the aftershocks of watching her come from my touch. Of her thrashing against me as she hollered my name. It was sweet torture. So I stay on my knees because if she's willing to give herself to me, then she can have me any way that she wants me.

Her touch journeys around my shoulder to my clavicle as she walks to stand in front of me. In a submissive gesture, I keep my eyes ahead so my face is parallel to her slender stomach. For this woman, I do submit and want to feel her touch as long as I can. I swear she's generating a heat that has my cock throbbing. It's unlike anything I've ever experienced in my life. The more I have of her, the more I hunger for her.

When both her hands travel up my neck to my cheeks, she pulls my face up until our eyes lock. I'm drowning in the trust I see and feel unworthy. But I'm a greedy fucker, so I'm going to take it.

Slowly she bends down until our lips touch. I leave my mouth closed as she explores my lips with hers. Then she gently bites down on my bottom one until I give her access. I watch her eyes fill with bliss before they close and a moan leaves her. Her fingers thread in my hair at the base of my neck as her demeanor changes from timid to aggressive.

After a moment of leaving my clenched fist on the side and not touching her, I give in and clutch the back of her head. Soon, we're nothing but lips, tongues, and heavy breathing as we explore each other. She slowly climbs in my lap and reaches for the hem of my shirt. Raising my arms, I allow her to remove it before I attack her neck.

"I want you, Red. I want to fuck you so hard. I want you to know I was in you. No one else." I reach for her shirt, and when she raises her arms, I remove the piece of cloth that's separating us. Her breasts are covered in one of the bras I purchased for her, and a sense of pride sets in. She's wearing something I was able to provide for her. "Pure beauty." I kiss between her breasts and she shivers. Looking up, I watch her reaction. Her sultry hazel-green eyes are heavy with longing. Her pupils dilate as I bend down, take a lacy covered nipple in my mouth, and suck. Her hips jerk against me, so I suck hard until she moans and threads her hands once again in my hair. Then I do the same with the other breast.

After I finish assaulting her beautiful curves, I wrap her legs tightly around my waist. "Hold on."

"Where are you going?"

I look at her and kiss her lips. "I'm going to the bedroom."

She's quiet for a moment as I make my way down the hall. "Oh. We could have stayed in there."

I walk in the room and kick the door closed before making my way to the bed. The smell of her is everywhere, and I can't wait to get inside of her. "If you think I'm letting our first time be on a floor, then you're wrong." Bracing my knee on the bed, I let her body gently slide off of mine. She lays back on my charcoal gray comforter and her red hair fans around her luminous skin. I can't help but kiss her again. "You're worth more than that."

She doesn't say anything else, and I'm glad. I don't want her thinking too much about this. I don't know how this will affect my job or her safety. All I do know is I can't go without tasting every fuckin' part of her. When I lay my body on top of hers, I can't help but let my hips grind between her legs. Nuzzling her neck, I ask, "What do you want, Red? What do you want me to do to you first?"

She swallows and licks her lips as I suck on her neck. "Th-th-that thing you did earlier. Touch my breasts." Her voice quivers with nerves.

"Are you scared?" I allow my mouth to go lower.

"Yes." I look up on alert. The last thing I want is for her to be scared. Before I can say anything, she covers her face. "Not of you, ass."

"Okay. Then what?" I ask even though I'm sure of the answer. She doesn't need to know that I'm aware of her past.

Her cheeks bloom with heat and turn crimson in color. "Of... God, I can't believe I'm saying this." She takes a deep breath and closes her eyes. "Of disappointing you."

That is not what I was expecting. I push myself up above her and arch a brow. "Red, I've wanted you since you walked on that stage and knocked the shit out of me. You're beautiful." I trace her scarred lip with my finger.

She looks away. "N-no. You're wrong. I'm painted. Not beautiful."

"Painted?"

"Yes. Painted. Like an old house that's been covered with new paint to hide the damage. Damage so deep that nobody wants to live there unless it's hidden. Damage that can't be fixed."

Her eyes start to glisten, so I sit up and take her hand. Today isn't about sadness. Today, I'm going to show her how amazing she is. "Come with me."

I lead her to the walk-in closet with the full-standing mirror along the wall. I stand her in front of me to look at our reflections. She only comes to my sternum and has skin like ivory. Her bright red hair allows her eyes to stand out more, and I watch them consider my bare skin. I'm decorated in colorful tattoos, and her upper arm's adorned with black and gray ink. But she, as a whole, is more colorful, and a greater piece of art than all my tattoos combined or even Michelangelo's Sistine Chapel.

"You're wrong. You're not painted. You're everything beautiful." My arms wrap around her waist to hold her tight. She starts to shake her head no, but I refuse to let her think less of herself. "Look at me, Red." Her eyes land on my reflection, and I get weak from the pain I see in their depths. "Yes. You. Are. Do you get how I know this?" She shakes her head as a lone tear escapes. Turning her to face me, I take her face in my hands. My thumbs wipe the tears away as she gazes up at me. "It's because something or someone that's so damaged and just painted," I take a breath to get the words out, hoping she understands, "couldn't have restored me."

CHAPTER FIFTEEN

"Every crack, every smear, and every mistake isn't a mistake at all.
It's something that's just simply meant to be and made me who I am."
~Blaire

Blaire

His words have me wanting to look away. But the truth in his eyes tells me he truly believes this. He believes I've helped him. When he's the one who's been helping me. He's allowed me to feel the way I've always heard about from movies or other girls. Giddy, anxious, hot, and excited. I should continue to argue, but I'm left caught in a labyrinth of emotions that I don't know how to evade. And honestly, I don't think I want to. It's more than I've dreamed of feeling for another person. Especially someone I've known for only a short time, but it's there. He's standing in front of me, helping me in more ways than he knows. I brace my hands on his arms before pushing myself up on my tiptoes. Then I kiss him, ready to lose myself.

As we continue exploring one another's hot mouths, he walks me backwards toward the bed. When he sits, his hands grab my hips to push down my pants and leave me in nothing but my bra. The look on his face as he takes in my form produces another new emotion. *Powerful*.

I reach behind me and unclasp my bra, releasing my breasts from their fabric prison. When his throat convulses, I step forward and climb on top to straddle his large, colorful body. The morning sunlight shines through the window, and the feel of its warmth on my naked skin only adds to the heat Lyric is causing me to feel on the inside.

He lays back and places his arms above his head. "I'm all yours."

And so I take this opportunity to explore his body from his head to where his jeans meet his skin at his waist. I trace every portion of him that's colored with ink, and outline his art with my fingers. Then I become brave enough to add my lips and tongue to my inspection. My eyes drift closed as I savor his taste and smell. Clean, masculine, and mouthwatering.

His breathing is labored, and quickly morphs into a deep growl that vibrates through his chest, especially when I scrape my teeth against his nipple. As I go lower, my hand reaches for the button of his faded jeans, and with skills I never knew I possessed, I unclasp it with one hand.

He lifts his hips, so I pull his jeans down to expose more skin. This bit is unadorned with colorful ink, but no less enticing and sexy. I kiss the V indents that direct me to go lower until I'm face to face with his cock. And it's fucking pierced. Holy shit, that's hot.

"You like what you see?" I hear the smile in his deep voice.

I pull my gaze away from his length and look up to see his metallic eyes watching me while he's sporting a smirk. Instead of returning his smile, I want to wipe it off his face by doing something I never thought I'd do. Grabbing him in my hand, I kiss the head. The feeling is soft until the cool metal makes contact. But when his hips jerk, I lose my train of thought.

His reaction from my touch changes me into someone I don't recognize. Someone who wants to drive this naked, sexy, secretive man to the brink of insanity. I take him in my mouth as far as I can but keep eye contact. I have to know it's him. I'm scared of my past interrupting and taking this one moment from me.

His hands land in my hair, but instead of pushing me down again, he pulls me up. "Not yet. I can't come until I've been inside you." He pants.

I slowly crawl up his body, letting my naked breasts trail up his chest. When we're face to face and my wet heat is sliding against his length, I kiss him long and hard. I suck his tongue in my mouth before biting his lip.

He rolls us over, and before I can wrap my legs tightly around him, he breaks the kiss to stand and reach for his jeans. "What's wrong?" I ask, breathless.

He digs out his wallet while eyeing my naked body from head to toe. "Not a fucking thing." He pulls out a condom and rips it open with his teeth. I watch, mesmerized, when his hands wrap around his length, and his thumb rubs around the piercing on the head. Moisture builds between my legs, and I rub them together, eager for him to come back to me.

When he crawls over my body, it's unhurried and affectionate. It's his turn to explore me, and explore he does. When he kisses the creases between my legs, I come unglued. A moan from deep down erupts as his tongue slides between my folds. But it's just once. "I'll come back for a larger sample later."

He licks and nips up toward my belly button to my breasts and all the little pieces of my skin between. Then once again, we are face-to-face, fanning one another with our labored breathing. This time I lock my legs around his waist. "You ready for this?" he asks.

I don't answer. Instead, my hands clasp behind his head, and I pull him down for a kiss that answers his question. With one deep thrust, he's inside me, and the understanding that there's no going back hits me. But I don't want to anymore.

As he moves in me, we never break eye contact. I want to see him. I want to know he's the one causing me to feel these intense sensations. Nobody else. With every thrust of his hips, his impact is like a collision. Shock waves shoot throughout my entire body, and my heels dig into his ass. Heavy breathing and guttural sounds fill the room. Maybe it's the piercing adorning his cock, or maybe it's him. I don't know. What I do know is it's different this time. Sensual. Erotic. I feel high from the look on his face. Even though the sun is shining golden beams of light on us, his stare is dark, dominant, and raw. Almost on the verge of primal.

He sits up, and holding one leg in place around his waist, he puts my other legs on his broad muscled shoulder. This position allows him to slide in deeper, and I moan loudly.

"You like that, don't you?" He thrusts harder and harder.

My body is starting to tense up, and I know I'm close. He grips my thigh before reaching up to pinch my nipple. My hands are restless, and my head is thrashing. I don't know what to do. But his voice is there. Commanding me. "Let go, baby. Let it all go."

And I do.

We lie naked in bed for the rest of the day. Even though we've explored one another many times, we can't seem to stop. He's shown me things and caused me to feel emotions I never imagined.

Never dreamed of.

His phone rings again, and like before, he leaves the room to talk. I don't dwell on it though. He's here now, and I'm sure it's Ryan or Hyde. But this time, he comes back in the room and pulls his pants up. My heart stops because I'm sure he's leaving and our time is up.

"Where you going?"

"Work." He grabs a shirt out of his drawer and pulls it on. "You goin to stay, or you gonna get ready?"

"Um… I haven't seen anyone in two weeks." Should I go to Jay's and face them? Face Chris? "I don't know."

"It'll be fine." He walks over and kisses me as I lie on the bed. "Come on, Red. It'll be okay. If you feel uncomfortable, I'll beat the fuckers up."

His words cause me to smile and ease my nerves. "I'll have to get ready. It could take a while."

"I'll wait. Take all the time you need. Besides, they won't start without me." He winks and walks out the door, and I'm questioning who is this guy? He's so different than before, and all we did was have sex. But in the end, I dress in new jeans that I found in the drawer along with a black and white chevron blouse. When I walk out to Lyric, he whistles before bending down to kiss me where the shirt shows off a good amount of cleavage.

"I might have to kill the fuckers anyway. Huh?" He hands me my jacket before studying me from head to toe. When his eyes land on my black heels, he grabs my waist and pulls me close. "Leave those on tonight while I'm fucking you."

Instead of his erotic words pissing me off, I get a visual of us back in his room. Fucking. Our sweat drenched bodies sliding in sync. But, before I can attack him, he pulls away and walks outside. I mumble 'asshole' as I follow behind.

The rest of the weekend flies by. Unless Lyric has to play at the club, he's in bed with me. The only interruption we have is his phone and Sissy. He's been attentive and has brought me food in bed every morning. He's run me baths and has even washed me. It's the first time in my life I haven't been scared or fearful of a man other than my brother.

Nobody questions our closeness at Jay's, or at least not that I know of. David only gave me a knowing look when I saw him, and Chris continuously apologizes for his reaction. Of course, I'm the one who's sorry, and he's forgiven me. He even offered to let me stay with him again, but before I could answer, Lyric started to sing on stage. So I gave him the only answer that came to mind. No. And as soon as the band exited the stage, Lyric grabbed me, and we left. Together.

Now it's Monday, and he's gone. But this time, it's different than before. I'm not lonely. Plus, he left me the keys to his car so I could leave. Janet called to check in and wants me to come back to work, and after some inner debating, I decide to start again tonight.

When I walk in the door at Jay's, I hear a loud scream before Cory jumps in my arms and straddles my waist. "You're alive!"

"Of course I'm alive," I say and place her on her feet.

She pushes my shoulder. "Bitch. I've been a fucking wreck. You just disappeared, and then I heard about what those bastards did." Her blue eyes become angry. "Makes me want to castrate them with my nail clippers." She opens one of the lockers, pulls her sweater off, and shows her goodies to whomever is in the lounge.

"Are you working here now?" I ask when she pulls on a Jay's shirt.

"Yeah, I needed the cash. Parents are being dicks. I really hate asking them for a dime anyway." She shrugs and throws her hair in a ponytail.

"Sorry."

"Don't be. I'm not. We've never really gotten along." She walks out the door, and I follow. "Thank Yoda, Lyric showed up when he did. I mean, kinda romantic on a fucked up level, if you ask me. Like fate or some shit. And luckily, for you, he's hot. Could you imagine some Peewee Herman being there instead? Or better yet Richard Simmons? He'd have pulled his booty shorts up another inch and run away instead. That or jazzercise on their asses."

I really feel uncomfortable with where this conversation is going, but before I can divert it, I feel warm breath on the back of my neck. I look over my shoulder at Lyric as his arms slide around my waist, pulling me close.

"Mmmmm... You're one lucky bitch, Blaire." Cory winks in our direction before walking behind the bar.

"Why are you here? The band doesn't play until Thursday." I ask, enjoying his closeness a little too much. I'm too addicted to stop, or walk away from it. This guy has me hooked.

"I got done early at the gym," he says in my ear. His warm breath makes my body heat up. "Went home expecting to see you waiting for me. Naked," *kiss,* "wet," *kiss,* "those long, beautiful legs spread wide open," *kiss,* "on my bed." *Kiss.* "But my car wasn't there. So I figured you'd be here."

"So you were worried?" I ask hopeful.

"No. Just *really* horny." I hear the smile in his voice and go to elbow him in the gut, but he moves out of the way, grabs my arm, and spins me around. His face loses its smile at his eyes meet mine. "You sure you're up to working again?"

"I need to do something before I go bat shit crazy. Plus, I'm not a freeloader. I want to make my own way."

"I could pay you..."

I'm instantly angry and don't let him finish. "For what? I'm not a fucking prostitute."

"No shit, Red. I'm talking about you cleaning the house. Plus you're taking care of that dog."

"*That dog* is your dog." I cross my arms over my chest. "And I like taking care of her. I don't need to be paid."

He takes a deep breath and scratches the back of his head. My eyes involuntarily travel down to where his t-shirt raises and I get a glimpse of skin. When I hear his deep laugh, I look up and blush. I quickly cover my embarrassment with mock anger. "I really need to get to work, jackass. So if you'll excuse me..." I turn and leave with his laughter in my ears and a smile on my face.

Cory works the bar while I'm stuck working the floor with Trudy. I still refuse to talk to her. Every time I see her, I envision Benji's grief stricken face and hear his words. Whenever we run into one another, she apologizes, but I ignore her and continue making my rounds.

As I head to Janet's office after closing time, I can hear her coughing from the other side of her door. When it ends, I knock for permission to enter. She's sitting at her desk, looking at her computer screen. "Hey, Mouse."

"Are you busy?" I take a seat across from her, building courage. This conversation is long overdue, and I need to know why she's been so distant.

"Always. But you can bother me." She starts coughing again and takes a sip of water. Her weathered skin is pale and heavy with deep wrinkles as she looks at me.

"Are you okay?" My gut tells me something isn't right. Either she's disappointed with me or something else. She's never around and hasn't been for a while. "I'm sorry for what I did. You have to know the meds I stole from Chris weren't to get high. I would never do that after what happened to Ben. I..." I look at my hands as shame sets in. "I just wanted to forget and sleep."

She's quiet, so I peek up through my lashes to find her studying me. "Mouse. You don't need to explain anything to me. I know about your nightmares. You did live with me for a year. Besides that, we all fuck up in life." She has another coughing fit, and I hear it gurgle deep in her chest. When I try to stand and help, she shakes her head no and holds up a finger. After the fit ends, she sighs and says with remorse, "Me not being around has nothing to do with you, Mouse. I wanted to tell everyone after Thanksgiving. But I'll go ahead and tell you." She gives me a serious look. "I'm selling Jay's."

"What?" I ask in disbelief. Jay's is her baby. She's struggled for years to keep it afloat. It's also the last thing she has of her deceased husband. It can't be financial reasons, because we're always packed. "Why?"

She stands up and walks around to sit in the chair beside me and my stomach plunges. "I'm dying, Mouse. I have lung cancer."

"What?" I say in disbelief. The idea of another person I love leaving me has my whole world shifting. I blink as I try to bring everything back in focus. *This has to be wrong.* "Have you seen a doctor?" She nods and I start to calm down. People do treatments and go in remission all the time. Janet is the toughest woman I know, and this should be a piece of cake. "Then when do you start radiation or chemo?"

She grasps my hands with hers. They're cold and worn instead of their usual warmth. "I'm too far gone for treatment. It won't do any good."

My throat starts to burn, as her words sink in. "No!" I yell in anger and stand. "You're gonna be fine. I'm sure there's something we can do. And maybe the tests are wrong. People mess up all the time."

She shakes her head no and pats my chair for me to sit. "Now, Mouse. You know I love you. You and Benji were always there for me after James died. You two were like my own kids. And I don't want you to be sad. I want you to be prepared. Just like I want to prepare."

The tears refuse to stop, but I fight them. As I count and breathe, I try not to picture my life without her in it. "How long have you known?"

"A while. Before you came back." She embraces me in a hug. Her trademark fragrance of cigarettes is ironically comforting, considering what she just shared. "You'll be fine, Mouse. Don't worry." I pull away and she wipes my tears. "You're stronger than you ever gave yourself credit for. I see it. Ben always saw it. Hell, child! Everyone but you sees it. Now it's time for you to recognize it. Okay?" I nod my head to placate her because she's stubborn and won't let up if I don't. I'm not sure I believe it though. The only thing I'm sure of right now is that life isn't fair.

When I'm back at Lyric's, I get a shower and crawl in bed to cry and mourn for a loss that hasn't happened yet. I toss and turn as my emotions take over. Lyric hasn't made it home yet, and loneliness sets in, so I let Sissy crawl in bed with me. But even with her warmth and sweet kisses, the tears won't stop. I'm scared for the friend who's more like mother to me. And selfishly, I'm terrified for myself. Deep down, I always knew she was somewhere willing to help me. She always took care of me. Even when I fuck up, she's there. Who's going to be there for her?

CHAPTER SIXTEEN

*"Face reality as it is, not as it was
or as you wish it to be."*
-Jack Welch

Lyric

I got the call earlier today and went straight to the meeting place. Someone supposedly has an in to Polesky. So here I am, sitting in an old diner in the middle of nowhere, waiting for the informant. Whoever it is. Hyde wanted to come, but I told him to stay and keep his eye on Blaire. Something has been bothering her, and I noticed it after her first night back at Jay's. I don't want to pressure her though, and possibly push her away in the process. But I hate seeing her upset. So I decide that if she's still upset, I'm going to ask her what's going on.

After ten minutes, I hear the jingle of the door. Looking up, I see a woman walk in wearing a hoodie and sunglasses with her dark hair pulled back neatly. I can't see her eyes behind the tint of her shades, but I know they are on me. My left hand hovers over my Glock waiting for her next move. Then she raises her hands before she slides in a seat across from me.

"Mr. Young. I'm Anya." She uses my alias in case someone's listening. Then she removes her sunglasses and stares at me with pale cerulean eyes.

"Anya. Can I get you anything?" I ask as the waitress passes.

"Yes. But what I want isn't here." I see the coldness as she stares me down. "You and I have something in common, *Lyric*, I mean, Mr. Young," she says in fake apology.

My hand hovers over my gun because this chick obviously knows more than what she's letting on.

Her eyes lower, and I know she's aware of my actions. "I'm not here to hurt you. I need your help. I also know you won't pull out a loaded gun with all these innocent people around. Not your style. So go ahead and move your hands on top of the table. Because I will not flinch when it comes to killing any of these people." Her eyes taper to a slit as she waits for my response. My gut tells me this chick isn't bluffing so I do what she says and move both my hands to the handle of my hot coffee where she can see them. If she pulls any shit, she won't leave without a mark.

"Now that I have your attention, let's get down to business. We both want retribution for our losses. Someone who took away someone we loved." She reaches in her bag, pulls out a folder, and hands it to me.

I open it up and see images that I've tried to erase for nine fucking years. Carly dead in the alley. Blood covering her body from where her throat was slashed. Her swollen belly unmoving. Her dead eyes staring at nothing. Rage fills me as I stare at this bitch across from me. "How the fuck did you get these?" I ask through clenched teeth.

She arches a black brow. "I found them. And believe me, I have plenty others." She tilts her head and smirks. "My uncle loves to keep souvenirs of his work."

"Uncle?"

"Oh yes. Didn't I tell you my full name? How very rude of me." She smiles and even though her features are strikingly

166

beautiful, I see pure evil. "I'm Anya Polesky and I believe you want to kill my father, Nicholas."

This has got to be a fucking joke. "Anya Polesky? You're supposed to be dead." I heard about her body being found a few years back in the Nevada desert. She's heir to Polesky's fortune as his oldest child. She was on her honeymoon in Vegas when her husband was found dead in their hotel room and she was found miles away from the crime scene.

"I'm alive and well." She calls the waitress over as I let her words sink in as she orders. I'm sure The Reform is goin to have a fuckin' field day with this new info... if it's true. When she's done, her attention is once again on me.

"How is it possible when they found your body? And your uncle never left that alley." I wave the file, wondering how these pictures came to be.

"It's called technology, Lyric. He had them emailed to his personal address. I actually have some of the actual act if you'd like to see them." She smirks in my direction. "Now, as for the other question, it wasn't my body. It was a random showgirl." She leans in and her voice goes to a whisper. "Do you really want me to relive that night? Because I can make you relive yours if you want to play that game." She taps the folder that holds confirmation of my worst nightmare.

"You know I need proof, *Anya*. And doll, I relive that fucking night every damn time I close my eyes."

After a minute of studying me, she concedes. "Touché, Mr. Devereux. Touché. I'll tell you." The waitress interrupts us at that time and brings her food. "After I eat, of course."

I'm headed back to Mobile with information that will change every fucking thing. Anya Polesky is alive and out to put a cap in her father's ass. I only hope I get to make him suffer first. It's pretty fucked up to want to kill your own father, but the chick has warrant. She wants to avenge her deceased husband who she married for love. Polesky didn't think he was good enough for his business and knew whoever she married would get his fortune. He said he was weak, but she defied her father's wishes and married him anyway in Vegas behind her father's back. Polesky, being the selfish asshole he is, didn't like not getting his way and made other plans. His thugs interrupted their newly wedded bliss with a torturous hit. She wasn't supposed to be killed, but when they tried to leave with her, she ended up stealing one of their guns and killing the sonofabitch before escaping. She's been on the run ever since. When I asked her about the body they found, she said she did what needed to be done so they couldn't find her. And with that last sentence, she became quiet and said no more about it.

According to her, the bastard is still in Atlanta. Figures the chicken shit is too scared to come on my turf. But he does have eyes watching, and she believes that if they see her, it will get him in Mobile sooner. She promises, if I help her, she'll give me a file with names to all his trafficking partners from all over the world.

But I don't need to worry about that right now. More important things need to be handled this week back in New Orleans. I have another shipment coming in the port in a few nights and it's a big one. Not only am I expecting the finest heroine from the South Pacific, but also enough weapons to utilize a few hundred men. I'm talking military issued M9 Berettas and AK47. My buyers are well known in this business because they don't fuck around when it comes to their money. The Knight family is a close-knit mafia crew from up north. I dealt with them last year with a similar shipment and it went smooth with no fuckups.

They bring in their trucks, load them up, and leave. Of course, this is after compensation. Even though they've never given me shit before, you never know what will go down. I've met Cole Knight for the first time last year. He's a cocky motherfucker but runs his crew and takes no shit. Even though he's younger than most, and even me, I respect him and he returns that respect. Trusting is a different issue. Trust is something earned and not given. I can only hope this shipment goes as smooth as the last one. But my gut is telling me something different and I've learned to trust it over the years.

As far as this Anya shit goes, Massey will give me orders before long. Now I want to enjoy my time with the redhead at my house. I know Red can't be a part of it or whatever is going to happen in the future with Polesky. What I don't know is if I should push her away or protect her the best way possible? But that's a stupid question because after what happened to Carly I know her distance from me is best. Shit just became fucking real and my hands are tied. Luckily, I have some time to get everything figured out. And I plan on taking full advantage of every fucking second I have with her. I shoot a quick text to Hyde to see where he is.

Me: **You headed home?**

Hyde: **No. Friends.**

Me: **Don't come home for the night. Tell everyone Blaire and I went out of town. And I know I'm fucked either way so don't give me your lip.**

Hyde: **Fine, but Ryan's gonna be pissed for canceling another gig.**

Me: **Fuck the gig.**

I can picture him shaking his head and telling me again how being with Red is a bad idea. We're convinced now that she was just an innocent bystander and not part of Polesky's team. But

Hyde doesn't like her so close to us. And I don't blame him. I just can't turn her away even if dragging an innocent person into this shit isn't right. I plan on walking away. Eventually. But I haven't had enough of her yet.

When I enter the living area, she's sitting on the couch with the dog watching TV. "Hey you," she says and smiles. She's really opened up the past few weeks. She's healed more than just her physical bruises. We spent Thanksgiving at Janet's and I think she's had time to accept the fact that Janet is sick. Hopefully her next upset in life won't cause too much emotional damage and she remains strong because there's a little girl she still needs to meet.

When I don't return a smile, hers disappears. But I have no reason to smile after today because in my mind it's one day closer to letting her go. Instead, I walk over to her, bend down, and kiss her, ready to fall into her depths as far as she'll allow. I don't just kiss her. I own her with it, exploring and memorizing the taste of buttery popcorn and something that's all her.

My blood heats up as I envision her under me, over me, and beside me. My cock sliding in and out of her heat. "I want you." Her fingers take hold of the base of my skull to pull me closer, and soon, I've pinned her to the couch.

She helps me lift my shirt over my head before my mouth attacks her slender neck.

"What if Hyde comes in?"

"He won't." I reach for her tank top and push it up to expose just a tiny amount of skin. Bit by bit I unveil her, taking my time to savor her reactions. I unwrap her like a gift. Something precious, because that's exactly how I see her. My gift. The first thing I've wanted for myself in a long time. But I know I can't keep her and she's only a temporary happiness. I just thought I could enjoy it for a while longer.

I kiss her stomach and hipbones, loving the laugh that erupts from her. Before I can go lower and finish unwrapping her, she scoots her body out from under me and sits up to remove her top, revealing her beautiful breasts to me. My mouth is drawn to them and I can't help but suckle them one at a time. I blow warm air against her pink skin to watch in amazement how they tighten and pucker in reaction. Her breathing is lusty and erratic, and when I look up at her beautiful face, she's watching me with hooded eyes. I lick my way up to her collarbone, throat, chin, until finally I'm letting my tongue once again invade her mouth's warmth.

She climbs on my lap in only her soft, cotton pants. I grip her ass and push her down to feel her heat. But it's not enough and I'm desperate for more. My thumbs hook in her pants to push them down as far as I can. She stands and discards them the rest of the way. After I unzip my jeans and expose myself to her, she hits her knees and grips me in her hands before her mouth descends on my dick. But I need to taste her first. "Not yet."

She stands up with a confused look upon her flushed face. "What's wrong?"

"I need to taste you." I stand and let my jeans drop to the floor before picking her up to make my way down the hallway and to my room. After placing her feet on the floor, I lay back. "Come here." She smiles seductively and climbs above me, once again straddling my naked body. I kiss her. "Now turn around." She smiles slyly before she turns and places her sweet, wet heat in my face to devour. I lick her folds and suckle her clit over and over. Then I feel her mouth once again wrap around my dick and about lose my shit. But I hold out. I will not come until she does. Blaire always has a way of getting me off faster than I'm used to.

Adding a finger, I start to pulsate it in a rhythmic motion. Her administrations ease up on me as her inner muscles clench and squeeze me before I add another finger. Just as I capture her clit and suck, she explodes and moans loudly while riding my face. My tongue savors the tangy flavor of her juices. I've eaten plenty of pussy in my day, but this here is prime and perfect.

When her convulsions have ceased, I swiftly roll us over and push her on all fours before entering her from behind. No barriers separating us. Nothing but our bodies, together.

We stay lost in one another's sweating bodies, actions, and sounds for the rest of the day. Afterward, I watch her doze off in a peaceful sleep while my mind wars with my heart.

The next morning, I wake to the best smell- besides Red- invading my nose. Bacon. I stand and stretch before I go take a piss. Then I walk into the kitchen and see her. She stands out against the white cabinets and dark granite like a single red rose in the snow. Her red hair is up on top of her head and she's wearing my tee shirt from yesterday. Guilt stabs me in the chest because I know there's no future for us. Not yet. Maybe one day. First, I have shit that needs to be taken care of.

I shake myself from my conscience and go steal a *very* crispy piece of bacon from a plate on the counter.

"Hey. I was wanting to surprise you."

"Oh, don't worry. You did. I actually didn't know bacon could be burned to the point of being inedible." I shove another piece in my mouth and evade her hand as she tries to slap me playfully.

"Hardy har har." She teases. "If it's so burnt, then why are you eating all of it?"

"Because it's bacon." I shove another piece in my mouth. She rewards me by sticking her tongue out at me before reaching for plates in the top cabinet. Her shirt rides up and her pink and black-stripped panties flash me. I can feel my body awaken so I turn to fix a cup of coffee for us both. We need fuel after last night's activities and for what I have planned for today. "So what kind of surprise did you have in mind?"

"Well, I was wanting to bring you breakfast in bed. But I guess I'll do it another day." She looks over her shoulder and winks.

"Really. You know I can always go lay back in bed."

"It won't be a surprise though."

"Maybe not for me. But it will for you."

"Huh?" she asks in confusion and places some food on our plates. I palm my dick and her eyes follow my movements before she gives me a quirked eyebrow. "I think you've already shown me all your tricks, Mr. Devereux."

"Is that right, Red?" I walk up to her slowly and press her back against the counter. "You positive about that?"

She looks up to make eye contact when we're pressed against each other. Then she shows that rare brave and confident side of hers and grabs my dick through my shorts. "Yes." Slowly, she strokes me and I growl as my eyes close from the sensation. "Looks like I'm the one full of surprises." She releases me and ducks under my arm to make her getaway.

However, I have a few tricks up my sleeve, which she quickly learns when I grab her and place her on the counter to have my favorite meal of the day.

I take in the busy streets of New Orleans and observe the people walking up and down the sidewalks, cars passing, and trollies running the rails. Bums walk up and down asking for money, dancing, or just panhandling discreetly. Watching it all and smelling the beignets, I feel like that same punk kid who used to sling dope and steal. Too many bad memories live on these streets so I only come here when I have to. Usually I stay outside the city but I want to give Blaire a different kind of experience…something unforgettable. So we head to the Voodoo Villa, which is in the center of the Fauborg Treme, also known to be the birthplace of Jazz. It's a two hundred year old house with two suites that give anyone the N'awlins experience. No hurricane has torn it down, only marked it to add character. Worn brick and stucco with intricate iron walk around the porch.

I see the excitement in Red's eyes as we park along the busy street and she takes in our surroundings. Grabbing her hand, I lead her inside the old house and check in before leading her to our room. Our suite has old N'awlins class with a fireplace close to the wrought iron bed, a very updated bathroom with a Jacuzzi and large shower, and its own little courtyard blocked from the busy street for more privacy. Wicked thoughts of how many ways I can make her come enters my brain. However, I need to wait because I plan on taking her shopping and spoiling her while she's mine.

I made reservations to Morton's of Chicago steakhouse and it's pretty fuckin' fancy. I've never been there myself because shit like that was never in my budget and now that it is I've never wanted to take anyone out. Hell, this is my first date. Might as well pull out all the stops because I don't know if I'll ever do it again.

Once we're settled, we walk around the city and I show her some voodoo shops before we go shopping. When we walk into Saks Fifth Avenue, I watch her eyes take in the surroundings. I have to force her to walk into an actual store.

"Look at that." She points to a black Louie Vuitton bag, picks it up, and inspects it. "I don't see a price though."

I take it from her hands. "Don't worry about it."

She quirks an eyebrow at me. "How do you have enough money not to worry about it?"

I shrug my shoulders and tell her the same answer I've rehearsed over the years. "Parents left me life insurance." I see her eyes widen with regret that's really unnecessary. My parents are only God knows where. I left their drunken asses when I ran away at twelve. "Don't." I bend down and kiss her lightly on the lips.

She returns my kiss and nods with understanding. "I still don't want you to blow money on me though."

"Get over it, Red. I'll blow money on you and you can just blow me. If you want, of course." I wink in her direction.

Instead of blushing and being embarrassed, she walks up to me in the middle of the store. When she's directly in front of me, she stands on her tiptoes to lean into my body. She licks my earlobe and bites down gently. Swarms of chills inhabit my body. Then she cups my junk in her hand and blows gently in my ear. "Done." she whispers with a smile in her voice before walking away, her ass swaying.

I shake my head while smiling and see the young girl behind the counter watching with wide eyes. "Only in NOLA." I adjust my now-aroused dick in my jeans and promise to make her squirm later.

CHAPTER SEVENTEEN

*"Opening yourself to someone is harder than closing off the entire
world.
The question I ask myself is, are they worth the struggle?"*
-Blaire

Blaire

I feel like everyone is staring at me. I'm so out of my element sitting here at a cloth-covered tabletop decorated with a beautiful centerpiece, different crystal glasses, and cloth napkins. The room is decorated with black walls and silver accents in different shapes. It's very contemporary and elegant. And very much not what I'm used to. At least not as myself.

The only time I've ever been in a place like this is when Mandy and I scoped out our new prospects for the night and I was in disguise. Not Blaire Morgan, but someone who was used to places such as this. That feels like a lifetime ago instead of only a few months.

Every time I try to ignore the unwelcome feeling and concentrate on the beauty of the atmosphere, I catch someone's stare. When we first walked from the elevator into the restaurant, I felt all eyes land on us. Even though the mid-thigh black, strapless dress and beautiful black, sequined heels cost more than my last car, it's obviously not good enough for these people. Our ink covered arms gain disapproving stares from the staff and the elders sitting at different tables when we remove our winter jackets.

"I don't think we should be here." We've been sitting for fifteen minutes without anyone coming over for our drink orders.

"No. You're hungry so I'm gonna feed you." His eyes wander the facility once again but nobody makes eye contact with him. I feel his frustration. "Give me a second." He stands to make his way in the next room. I admire his butt in his black slacks and his broad shoulders in his slate gray button down before he disappears around the corner.

After a minute, I hear raised voices before he storms over to me. "Come on, Red. Let's get out of here. It seems we make these fuckers uncomfortable." I grab his hand before we make our way out the same way we came in, grabbing our jackets in the process.

"What happened?" I ask to break the silence in the mirrored elevator.

His breathing is heavy and his jaw is tight as his teeth grind together. He continues to hold my hand and squeezes gently. "One of the customers complained that we made them uncomfortable or some shit. So it was either them- a regular- or us."

"I'm sorry." I say and lay my head on his shoulder. He looked really excited about taking me out tonight. Just thinking of the clothes he bought for such a fancy dinner makes me hurt for him.

"What do you have to be sorry for? It's not your fault."

We step out of the building and start walking the streets. The sun's down and the night crowd have emerged, ready to make New Orleans their bitch. Guys and girls alike laugh and carry on as they head in different directions. Wind blows my hair around my face and I huddle in my black pea coat looking for warmth. "I know how much you wanted to go out tonight. And the money you spent on this outfit. I'm sorry I won't be able to enjoy it like you wanted me to."

"Don't worry about me enjoying you in that sexy dress. Believe me, I plan on enjoying it tonight when we return to the hotel." He winks at me and I'm immediately warmed from the inside out. "If you think we're done for the night *mon cher*, then you're insane. This is N'awlins and I plan on showin' your fine ass the nightlife." He throws his arm around my shoulder and we head towards Bourbon Street.

Instead of steak, we eat boudin and jambalaya. Instead of fancy tablecloths and stares, we eat on a worn wooden table and talk about random shit. The bike being one. He says I won it fair and square, so when we return to Mobile it's mine. When I ask him if he's interested in buying it, he looks at me like I'm crazy.

"What?" I take a bite of the spicy concoction of rice, peppers, and crawfish tails.

"You want to sell it to me? But you made such a big fuckin deal about the damn thing." He laughs.

"Well I don't know the first thing about motorcycles or how to drive them. And the reason I made a big deal was because I was having a shitty day. Plus it was my brother's and I didn't expect someone else to be driving it when I returned to Mobile." My smile falls as Benji and my past enters our conversation. I shake my head and look up to see Lyric watching me with inquisitive eyes. I decide to change the subject before he can ask me anything I'm not ready to answer. "So Mr. Devereux, I've heard of your big bad fighting skills in the ring. Why haven't I seen it?"

"Big and bad huh? Who said that?"

"Just people at Jay's. I'm sure none of them were right though. I haven't seen you fight once, well, except that night." I stop and look at him with wide eyes while heat travels up my neck. We haven't discussed that night in the alley and what took place. I haven't really thought too much about it. He was defending me, so it's not like he did anything wrong. But I can't help but picture how he didn't hesitate to pull the trigger on both men.

He doesn't seem affected by my question or my hesitation. "Well, I try to not fight in the ring anymore. But sometimes Ryan likes to brag and book a bout or two without my approval. He loves the ring and thinks it's good for me. He likes to think he knows everything." He shrugs. "Now, since you got to ask a question, it's my turn."

I take a deep breath to gain my courage. It doesn't matter if I want to continue this conversation. I know it's inevitable. "Okay. Shoot."

"Where did you go after you left Mobile?"

No lies, Blaire. No more lies. I remind myself to be honest and straightforward. To keep my promise to myself, no matter how tempting it is to lie. Lies have caused nothing but trouble in my life. "Um, I traveled a lot. I met a girl a few years older than me outside of Vegas and we traveled together, actually. She was really smart and outgoing." *And a thieving bitch.* But I keep that to myself.

"Then what made you come back?"

I shake my head no. "No way. You don't get another question. It's my turn." He gives me that lopsided grin that always causes my stomach to flip and my head to spin. But I try to think of a question instead. "Do you have any family?"

He runs his hand through his dark hair and sits back casually. "Other than myself, there's no one left. When I left, I never looked back. I have friends that are my family."

Understanding of our connection and my pull toward him sets in. From that one statement, it makes sense why I feel the way I do. Safe and protected. How a home is supposed to feel. "No wonder we get along," I say before I can stop myself. He quirks an eyebrow, waiting for clarification to my statement. "It seems we're alike in that area. Ever since Benji, my brother, died, I don't have anyone either. I guess like knows like after all."

"I guess so." He drums his fingers on the table just as the blonde waitress brings the check. She flutters her lashes and sticks out her ass just a little more as she talks to him. Then she bends down to whisper in his ear, and I can't help but give a loud false laugh. Her moves are so obvious and annoying. Besides that, her actions cause that green snake to wrap around me. Jealousy really sucks. After she walks away, I catch Lyric watching me. "What's so funny, Red?"

"Ha! I bet it's hard looking so good to every woman. Having them pick you up wherever you go. That," I nod my head in the direction of the waitress, "doesn't happen to many people, you know. How do you hold girls off your man package all the time?" The beer has me feeling vocal. Or maybe it's the jealousy. Either way, I can't seem to shut up. "I'm sure women would cheat on their husbands for one night with you."

"No, thanks. Married women are trouble. And don't worry. The only girl I want to deliver my man package to is you. Besides that, she was asking for your number, not mine."

My laughter ceases and my eyes widen with surprise. *"What?"* I ask in shock. I'm kind of flattered that some cute blonde wanted my number. "Really?"

"Nah. I'm joking. She really wanted my *man package*." He laughs and dodges the balled napkin before he finishes off his beer.

"I'm sorry, dad. I won't do it again. I promise." I cry out, but he doesn't listen and refuses to stop the beating. The car antenna slashes against my back, causing excruciating pain to radiate throughout my entire body. Tensing up only makes it worse, but I can't stop. This time is worse than before. This time I'm scared for my life. I hear Benji yelling on the other side of the door. And I hate he's listening. He went out to smoke a cigarette while I showered so we could leave before dad came home, but he got home earlier than usual.

We've been avoiding him since Benji found me that day. He makes sure wherever he goes that I'm with him or he stays home with me. But dad stepped through the front door before we could escape. And I'm paying for it.

"You think you're so fucking smart, Blaire? You're just a slut like your mother. A fucking slut who needs to learn her lesson."

My cries for help are muffled as my face is shoved in my pillow and I hear a loud banging on the door. The impact is so hard it shakes walls. I'm praying Benji will hurry. I hear the unbuckling of his pants and my heart speeds up with fear. Then a loud crash shakes the bed and my dad's weight is lifted off my bloody back. I take a much need breath when I lift my head and see Benji fighting my tormentor. They throw punch after punch as I huddle in the corner where my mattress meets the wall. Benji is on top of him, hitting him over and over, calling him hateful names. But before I can blink, dad grabs my lamp and slams it against Benji's head, knocking him completely out. I cry out my brother's name but he doesn't stir. I'm too scared to move to check on him because once again, my nightmare stands and stalks in my direction.

I wake up saturated in sweat and tears from my nightmare. It's fresh and I feel it to my core. Running to the bathroom, I hit my knees and vomit in the toilet. The burn of bile as my stomach tenses is nothing new to me. It's been a while though. This is the first time I've had a nightmare since Lyric started sleeping with me. I was hopeful that it would be over. That he was my cure to be whole, but that's just stupid. Having a gorgeous guy in bed with you doesn't make it all go away. Nothing makes it all go away. So I vomit and retch, desperate to purge my body of my dark secret.

The feel of a cool cloth hits my neck and I know Lyric is witness to my humiliation. But he doesn't say a word. He holds my hair back until I'm done. Then he helps me stand, but I can't be touched right now so I slap his hands away.

"Don't push me away, Red. Let me help." He pleads but I shake my head. Touching anyone is off limits.

Guilt fills me so I refuse to look at him. I know he's just trying to help, but I'm embarrassed and feel too disgusting. My body feels heavy so I lean on the tiled bathroom counter and look at my reflection. I try to remind myself that I'm not the same scared girl. But I see her. I see the blonde hair and dead eyes. Tears cause her to blur as my anger rises.

"Why did you have to yell for help?" I ask her. If she didn't cry out, it wouldn't have killed Benji. He wouldn't have been tortured and turned to drugs for an escape. Fury surfaces as my heart breaks for my brother... for causing him his own nightmares he needed to escape from. My hands squeeze the counter edge, desperate to rid myself of these emotions, but I still feel as though I'm drowning in them. So I reach over and grab the first thing my hand wraps around before slamming it into the face of the girl who ruined her brother. My brother who won't let me live in peace. "I hate you." Glass shatters, but I can't stop my actions. I need to make her pay for what she did.

"Stop." My hand is halted after the deep command is yelled. I drop the object and watch in slow motion as it falls in the sink followed by red drops. Blood. I'm turned around and come face to face with Lyric. He grabs my face and brings himself to my level. His mouth is moving but it takes a minute to hear his words. "Baby? Can you hear me?" I nod my head as I blink away tears. "Good. I'm going to look at your hand, okay?" As he inspects it, I keep my eyes on his head and think of nothing, feel nothing. I'm numb and broken from that night.

He wraps a cloth around my palm before walking away. The bath water starts, and when Lyric comes back, he starts to undress me. Even though he's seen me naked many times before, I feel exposed for some odd reason I feel as though he sees more than just my naked skin. This time, he sees my scars. The ones visible and the others that only I can see.

I start to shiver from the cold before he lifts me gently in his arms, carries me over to the large tub, and gently places my feet in the warm water. "Sit." He commands when I just stand, staring in shock as he walks away. The frothy bubbles cocoon my aching body, and when I place my hand under the water, I yelp from the sting. Then I remember the wound on my hand. I look at my open palm and see the cut. It's an inch long but not deep.

"Keep pressure on it." Lyric kneels beside the large tub with a cup in one hand as well as a clean washcloth. "Lean back." I do as he says the best I can without getting my hand wet. He fills the cup with water and pours it over my scalp until my hair is wet. The scent of jasmine fills the air when he squeezes shampoo in his palms and massages my scalp. His fingers gently dig into my hair and I start to relax. Afterwards, he once again uses the cup to rinse the pink tinged shampoo from my hair. I feel my nightmare flow away with every drop of dirty water that leaves my scalp.

Once he finishes my hair, he washes my back, shoulders,

breasts, and all the way down to my feet. His touch and ministrations aren't sexual this time but more like those of a caregiver. A deep sense of trust forms inside of me. Trust for this man in front of me on his knees. I feel no judgment from him for what just happened. I also feel he will never judge me for my mistakes. So my mouth starts to move, and for the first time, I tell my deepest, darkest sin.

"My mother died when my brother and I were ten. She was in a bad accident on her way home from choir practice. She played piano for our church." I smile with the memory of her angelic voice teaching Benji and me to play multiple instruments and sing while growing up. Music has always made me feel closer to her.

"After that, our father started drinking. He would come home every day and drink. Eventually, he wasn't the same. The alcohol morphed him into something more evil. Like a monster. He started yelling at us over the smallest things. If a cabinet door was left open. A light left on. Anything. My brother started to rebel and hangout with the bad kids at school just to escape. I didn't want to make it worse, so I stayed home. I tried to take care of the house and keep us fed. Besides, I didn't have a lot of friends while growing up. Benji was the social one between us.

"One night, Benji was gone and dad came home angry. I always tried to stay in my room when he was in one of his moods. I was sitting in front of my mom's old vanity mirror brushing my hair and singing." I look up at him. "I used to love my hair because it looked just like Mom's. Long, thick, and pale blonde. I took extra good care of it because it was the last thing I had besides music to keep her memory alive." I envision that day in my head while I continue to speak. I try to detach myself from that thirteen-year old girl, but I see what she saw that night and feel everything she felt. "When I looked up, I saw his reflection in my mirror. He was watching me while leaning against the door. I thought I'd done something wrong. It was the only time he'd ever approached my brother or me."

The fear is fresh and my body starts to tremble. "I didn't know if I was going to get yelled at or hit again, so I stood up and started apologizing for whatever it was. He didn't say anything. Just came in and shut the door. Then he opened his arms for a hug. I was confused and stood frozen because he never showed affection to us. Not one time since mom died. I didn't move until he yelled at me to do what I was told. I thought it was odd, but I did it anyway because I was scared. But... but deep down, I was excited. I wanted him to care for us like before." Shame envelopes me for wanting his affection that night. "But when I was wrapped in his arms, he called me by my mom's name, and no matter what I said, he didn't care. Then... then..."

I lose it and break down. I can't continue talking, but I can't stop my mind from reliving that first time. The pain and confusion. When I fought, it was more brutal. He slapped me and called me a slut. When it was over, he told me what a good daughter I was. How my own mother would be proud that I was doing what I was supposed to do.

"Benji found me one night, the one night I fought back. He tried to keep me safe after that night. He couldn't though. He couldn't stop him, and when he did try, he suffered." I wipe my tears with the back of my hand. "At times, he was forced to watch. I remember his eyes apologizing and pleading with me. I remember his tears. I ruined him because I fought back. He would have been fine if I'd never cried for help. He would still be here."

I look up and see Lyric watching me. He shows no surprise over my confession. No verdict of guilt. No disgust. The only sign that he heard me is when he picks up a wet piece of my red hair. "Is that why you color it?" he asks.

I look down at the pink water and see the red dye I hide

behind. It never fails to disappear a little more with every wash. "Yes." I only wish that the Blaire I hide from the world would stay buried as easily as the fake one vanishes.

CHAPTER EIGHTEEN

"Holding her while she breaks is hard
when she slips through my fingers."
-Lyric

Lyric

Red has finally fallen asleep beside me when my phone vibrates. I look and see Lou's name so I step outside to take the call. "We good for tonight?"

"All set. Dock at twenty-two." He confirms the time and hangs up.

I light a cigarette and lean against the building, wondering what I'm going to do with Red while I handle this deal tonight. The only option I can come up with is to lie. Lie about some shit I need to do on my own. But I really don't want to leave her alone. Tonight was the first time I've witnessed her relive her nightmare and I felt fucking powerless. None of the shit I deal with in my job nor all my life experiences could have prepared me for what I witnessed tonight. There wasn't a damn thing I could do to ease her pain as she broke.

When she smashed the mirror, and I saw blood oozing from her hand, I was scared to death. I felt a fear so strong as I watched her breakdown that I admitted something for the first time to myself. I love her. I love her so fucking much that I'd kill for her again while people watched if that's what she wanted. She's revived feelings I've long forgotten. Raised me from the dead and awakened me into more than what I was before. I want her to be around me every day so I can smell her skin, hear her soft voice, and make her smile. Not just for this short time we have together, but for the rest of my life. I want to protect her from the nightmares that haunt her. Even if that means giving my job a big 'fuck you', I'll do it. After this mission is over, then so am I. I flick my cigarette and head inside. After I crawl in bed, my arms automatically go around Red's waist to pull her toward me. I can't help but smile like a damn pussy when she willingly snuggles deeper into my chest.

It seems no lies are needed after all to keep Red distracted while I handled tonight's trade. We're headed back to Mobile this morning because of a phone call from Trudy. Janet's in the hospital and isn't doing well. We don't know much, only that she's been out for two days, and when Trudy went to check on her, she was passed out on the floor.

I look at Red as she sits in the passenger seat looking out the window. No words have really been spoken since last night. She's silent, and I don't know if it's from the phone call or from embarrassment over what transpired between us last night. Either way I don't like this distance so I reach over and grab her hand. "She'll be fine." I lie. My gut tells me Janet won't be fine. She's dying and refusing any treatment. She's been preparing for her death for a while. That's why she sold me Jay's. It's all finalized but I refuse to let everyone know it's sold until after we know Janet's truly finished. She didn't want to wait, but I don't want her to lose any part of her normal, everyday life. So I told her I wanted to hold off on telling people so they won't treat me different. She was satisfied with that. Now, I have a feeling it's time.

Finally, her eyes turn in my direction. "Do you really believe that?" she asks angrily, narrowing her eyes.

I feel as though this simple question is a test. Lie to give her possible false hope or tell the truth and break her spirit early? I squeeze her hand. "No." I tell her honestly.

She only nods her head instead of breaking down the way I initially thought she would. "Me neither."

When we reach the Infirmary, we head straight to the fourth floor. Janet is staying in the Medical Intensive Care Unit to make her as comfortable as possible. Since visiting hours are specified, we meet Jax and Trudy in the waiting area. Trudy's eyes are red and swollen from tears when she looks up and sees us.

I'm not sure what today will bring for these two girls' relationship and Jax must be thinking the same thing because he keeps her firmly by his side when they approach us. Red is the surprisingly the first to speak. "How is she?"

"Sleeping. The doctors said she's had several seizures overnight and they did a scan which confirmed that the cancer has moved to her brain." Trudy's voice breaks so Jax squeezes her in a comforting embrace.

"She's refusing treatment of any kind. More fluid is building on her lungs, but she's supposedly signed something to stop any of us from intervening." Jax says.

"Damn Janet and her head strong ass." Red whispers, grief lacing every word she speaks.

Silence falls between us after that as we all let our morning brains absorb everything that's going on. Jax leads Trudy back to their seats, and Red finds one against an opposite wall. I stare out the large glass partition separating the waiting area from the hallway leading to the large automatic doors to ICU. Nurses in bright, colorful scrubs pass by but pay us no mind. My mind wanders to what's going down tonight, but Red is never too far from my thoughts. Now that I've admitted to myself how I feel about her, I want to do better and be worthy of her trust. And the shit I'm into isn't the best ways to make that happen. So I'm stuck trying to think of a plan for our future.

After a few minutes of musing, I sense someone standing next to me and know it's Red. We don't touch or talk, but I recognize her closeness. The hairs along my skin stand on end because my body automatically wants to touch her. "Thank you for bringing me here. I'm sorry you had to leave."

"It's cool." I look down at her profile as she watches a smiling brunette on the other side talking with another nurse.

"Do you think it's hard for them?"

"What's hard for them?" I ask.

"To watch people die all the time. To know that the patients they care for today will be taking their last breath tomorrow or the next day." She tears her eyes away from the young nurse to meet mine. "To know that, when they leave here to go home and laugh with their family, the family of their dead patient is grieving. Or is it easy to wash it all away with the soap they shower with?" A lone tear falls down her face.

Reaching up, my thumb wipes it away. "I don't know, Red. I hope they appreciate their lives a little more when they leave here. But I honestly don't know. Everyone's mentality is different and everyone handles death differently. And I'm sure they see a lot of it."

"Like you?" Her eyes bore into me.

She's referring to the night I killed those two guys in the alley. We've never discussed it even though I know it's crossed her mind. I see how she eyes the gun I always have on me or by the bed at night. Instead of being brave and standing there to take in her persistent stare, I grab her in my arms and pull her close to avoid it. "Yes, Red. Like me," I whisper in her hair and kiss her temple. She wraps her arms around my waist, and we stand there holding on to each other as if it might be our last time.

Just then, a nurse comes in and tells us two people can go to the back. Trudy tells us to go ahead, so I grab Red's hand and lead her down the hall through the automatic door. There are about twenty single beds in their own curtained cubicles and a nurses' station in the middle of them all. Janet's area is toward the back, and when we pull the curtain back, all I can see are her sunken cheeks and pale skin. She's still asleep but it doesn't seem restful or peaceful. Instead, you can hear every gurgling breath she takes. Her chest retracts and sinks in as she struggles to breathe.

Red walks over and touches her hand. "She's so cold," she whispers to no one in particular.

"That's very common during the last stage of the disease. So is the shortness of breath and noise. Her lungs have built up fluid but she refuses any draining." The nurse walks over and tampers with the IV that rests in her neck.

"What's that you're giving her?" Red asks.

"Morphine. We want her to be as comfortable as possible. And since her veins are so thin, we had to put in a central line." She writes in her log and gets ready to leave.

"How long do you think she has?" Red asks.

The young lady looks uncomfortable with the question, but answers anyways. "You never know with this disease. Everyone is different. But with my experience, I'd say a few days. A week at the most." She smiles gently and exits.

We wait for hours but Janet still sleeps. Jax takes Tru home to rest and I take Red back to the house to grab some fresh clothes. She's determined to stay at the hospital and as much as I want to stay with her, duty calls.

Heading back to New Orleans, I try to concentrate on business. I need to call Massey and find out what the plan is with Anya, but I just can't at the moment. I know I won't like it. And as much as I'd love to just quit and leave, I know it would involve Red uprooting her whole life and living on the run. Maybe I should just tell her and see what happens and how she reacts. But so much shit is on her plate now with Janet being on her deathbed that I really don't want to add any more weight. So I'll just wait and call Massey on the way back to Mobile.

I pull into my house in New Orleans and push the button on my key for the garage door to open. I've come here just to trade out vehicles because I don't need to take the risk of having my Chevy recognized. I'll drive my black Escalade to the dock tonight instead. After I park, I decide to head inside to take a piss. Stepping into the dark laundry room off the double garage, I smell something off and unwelcome. I remove my gun from my holster and give my eyes time to adjust to the darkness before creeping in the kitchen. My eyes land on the island where a candle burns beside a wine glass with a red lipstick stain. Then I see the flick of a match that illuminates a feminine silhouette and know exactly who's here. "What the fuck are you doing in my house?"

"What does it look like?" Anya holds up her cigarette. "Smoking." She smiles seductively and makes her way toward the candle. The yellow glow shines on her feminine features and she looks at my gun. "You can put that thing away, you know. I'm unarmed." She spins slowly in a circle. My eyes take in her tight black pants and white sequined top. She catches my stare and her smile grows. "Like what you see Lyric?"

Let her think what she wants. I still don't trust this chick even though she supposedly wants the same thing I do. "Seen one set of tits, you've seen them all." I place my gun back in my holster and head to the half bath off the kitchen. When I finish, Anya is exactly where I left her so I go to the fridge and grab a water.

"What took you so long anyway? I thought you'd be showing up before tonight and I've been here since yesterday. Oh and by the way, you really need to stock up on some food." She walks over to reach for her own water and places her hand on my back.

I turn around swiftly and she takes a step back. "For one, that's none of your damn business. Two, this is my house and you broke in. Three, how the fuck did you find me?"

"I've known about your whereabouts for the past several years. I knew if I wanted to piss off my bastard father before I send him to hell, I'd have to team up with someone he hates and is threatened by. So I've done my research on you, Lyric Devereux. And I have an idea."

"I'm not interested in any of your ideas. Besides, that doesn't give you the right to break into my house. I should just put a bullet in your head."

Her eyes narrow. "You probably should, but you won't. You want to kill him just like you did Uncle Vladimir after what he and his thugs did to you. Don't you remember how they killed... what was her name again? Carly?" She arches a brow. "Yes. Carly. And

195

wasn't she pregnant with your son?"

"Shut the fuck up." I growl.

She ignores me and continues to taunt me with my past. "Don't you remember all the blood, Lyric? How he raped her and slit her throat? How several of the men had a turn with her, while she struggled to breathe? She was there all alone that night. Remember?"

I remember that night with fresh emotions.

"Damn it, baby. You have to stop this shit. You said you'd get an actual job before I deliver. I can't work at McDonalds for a while after."

Carly's voice is behind me yelling, but I concentrate on cutting my white lines. I know her speech by fucking heart now. She's given it at least every other day since we became pregnant. She doesn't realize this shit keeps the roof on our head. I just snort every once in a while. I give her the same answer. "I'm goin to, baby, I promise." I roll up the twenty and snort my way into heaven.

I feel a hard sting on the back of my head. "What the fuck?"

Carly stands there in all her dark skinned beauty, her light green eyes shining angrily at me. "You always say that same shit, you know. And I'm fuckin' sick of it. You're either running around with those idiots or getting into trouble. I'm fuckin' sick and tired of living in this piece of shit one room piss bucket of an apartment. My son... your son deserves more. But it seems I'm the only one who actually gives a shit." She leaves and slams the door behind her, which causes the framed sonogram picture to fall off the wall and shatter as it hits the floor.

"Great, Carly. Fuckin' great." I yell. I don't chase her. I just let her leave. She'll cool down like she always does and come home. I eyeball the white powder and decide to sit down and finish

the last two lines, but my eyes land on the broken picture. A bad feeling sets in my stomach and fear takes hold. I can't ignore it, even after I finish snorting, so I grab my keys and my gun before heading out to look for Carly.

I head toward her girlfriend April's place. It's late and dark even with the lights from the stores. When I cut the corner, I hear a few guys laughing and speaking some weird language. The wind blows and I smell it. Blood. The copper scent fills my nose. Then I smell Carly's favorite apple scent. I break out in a cold sweat, and before I transform into something evil and unforgiving, I run.

With only that night in my head, I put my gun between Anya's eyes before she can blink. "Shut. The. Fuck. Up."

In the dim light, I see her face pale from fear. Her hands go up in surrender. "I'll stop. Okay? I'll stop." I uncock my Glock and lower it from her head. "Now that you're remembering why you hate that bastard, I want to tell you my idea. I know I can help you."

"What did you have in mind?" I ground out. My mind still sees the blood, and I still feel hatred when I think of what that bastard and his brother took from me.

She crowds me with every step she takes in my direction. I know this game. I see dumbass girls playing it all the time at Jay's. They seduce or try to, so they can get what they want. Her hand tries to land on my chest, but I grab it to keep her from touching me. She only smiles. "A union of immense proportion."

"No."

"Just think about it Lyric. If father thinks we're together, on an intimate level, he'd run fast to get me away from you. He'd pull out all stops to get me back." She winks and yanks her hand from my grasp before turning around to jump on the counter. She runs her fingers through her long black hair and eyes me. "And when he's close, I'll kill him when he least expects it."

"Like I said before. No!" I grab my keys before heading over to blow out the candle. "Lock the door before you leave." Walking out to my Escalade, I feel anxious and ready to get this shit finished.

The Port is lit up as tankers and ship workers come to work to make an honest living. Lou sees me pull up and meets me at the warehouse doors. "They here?" I ask.

"Yup. So are the packages. Most have already been broken down and separated."

I look around the worn down warehouse with its sixty-gallon drums lining the walls and more being rolled carefully off the ship.

"Well. If it isn't Lyric Devereux."

I look to the back corner and see Cole Knight walking up with an extended hand. He's my height and has a similar build, but I don't wear Polo shirts and neat jeans. He likes to dress in the finest clothes because it's what he grew up knowing. Me? I wore what I could find. But if my father ran the Knight family and construction business, I'd probably be the same way.

When we shake hands, we both squeeze hard before letting go. It's a guy thing. "Cole," I say and light a cigarette. "You bring enough trucks?"

"Fuck, yeah! Just look." He nods his head toward a large opening and I see three black Mack trucks with chrome pipes, grills, and side steps. Bright lights decorate the three beasts and the purr of the diesel engines lets me know they're ready to roll. The trucks' long dry boxes showcase *Knight* in bold black letters on each side, and the ramps are down as some of his men start loading the shit up. "So who's getting the H?" he asks as we walk to the back to handle payment. He has his man Pete by his side while Lou stays with me.

"Some locals. Most of it Lou is taking back to Mobile. Shit sells like golden pussy out that way."

After counting the green twice, we head back out just as the last truck is being loaded. I see two blacked out Land Rovers parked close to my Escalade and the hair on the back of my neck stands up. When I look around the trucks once more, I see the red light coming a few hundred feet away and aiming straight at us. Without thought, I immediately jump on Cole and we land on the hard cement just as the bullet flies past us. Everyone pulls out a weapon and takes cover, but no more shots are heard. I crawl behind a large post and Cole does the same, both with our guns drawn.

"Pete." Cole hollers and Pete automatically gathers up several men to go see who the fuck just pulled that trigger.

"That was either meant for you or me. But I guarantee they're long gone. That was a fucking sniper and they have their exits already planned before a shot it fired." I stand and dust off after I put my gun back in my back holster. "If I had to guess he's under that dark ass water and his gun is too."

"Well fuck." Cole lights a cigarette and waits for his men to return. Sure enough, they come up empty handed. Everyone remains on guard until everything is loaded. Cole once again extends his hand. "Thanks bro. Your ass just earned a Knight's trust. You need anything you know who to call."

CHAPTER NINETEEN

"Sometimes your lowest point is exactly what you need." - Blaire

Blaire

The past twelve hours, I've been here at the hospital either holding Janet's frail hand or sitting in the waiting room. You'd think losing people you love as often as I have would make the heartbreak easier. You'd think that I would be used to saying goodbye. First, my mom leaves, then Benji, and now the one person who I could count on for years. Telling myself she won't suffer any longer doesn't help my selfish need to keep her here with me. But my needs seem to be the last on God's list.

My neck aches from sleeping on the plastic green couch and I want a shower. However, I refuse to leave Janet's side. I'll stay here until she wakes up or takes her last breath. It's the least I can do for everything she's given me. Even though I feel like crying, I refuse to. I'll mourn for my friend after she takes her last breath and not until then.

While channel surfing beside Janet's hospital bed, I hear the curtain pull back. Trudy walks in carrying a tote bag. Ignoring her, I turn back to the TV. She hasn't been back since her and Jax left yesterday. I was hoping she'd stay gone, but I should've known better. She's the ultimate gold-digger and suck up. She loves to make sure everyone loves her, and she continues to put on some stupid sweet girl act. I'm the one who saw how she broke Benji. An urge to go postal on her ass sets in so that I have to grind my teeth together to keep me from making a scene. My mood is already fickle and all I need is one more thing before I lose my shit.

"I brought you some food." My eyes stay on the TV even though I don't know what the hell I'm watching. "I also brought some snacks. I know how hospital food can be and how expensive the machines are."

Geez... does she ever stop being fake. Screw being calm. My eyes narrow on her. "Do you think I need your charity? Do you want an award or standing ovation for your good deeds? News Flash. You're not getting either from me. You can't bribe me to be your friend. If you really want to make me happy, then leave me alone. You can't change the past or the fact you took Benji from me." My heart is pounding and my head feels light by the time I'm done.

She loses her smile and sits the bag on the floor. "I'm not trying to do anything, Blaire. I'm trying to help someone who I care about. I didn't take Benji from you. I didn't want anything bad to happen to him. He was my friend. *You* were my friend. And I think it's time you told me why you hate me so damn much." Her voice is stern and anger masks her face.

"You know what you did, so don't play stupid."

"No I don't know, Blaire. If I did, I wouldn't ask. I try to own up to my screw-ups because I know I've made them. I try to learn from them. So unless you can tell me why you hate me, I'm not leaving. I'll stay right here and annoy you until you *do* tell me. And if you think you want to kick my ass, then let's go at it. Because I'm so fucking tired of your attitude."

"Fine. If you won't say it, then I will." Standing, I look her into the eyes. "Because of what you stole from this world. Not just a great person but also the child you aborted. Benji wasn't enough for you, was he? If rich boy Jax found out you were pregnant by my brother, then you wouldn't be able to use him for his money." Angry tears start to leak from my eyes as my brother's words replay in my head. "He would have been a great father, but we'll never know because of you." My grief gets the best of me and I fall back in my chair while sobbing.

Only the sounds of the TV can be heard over my weeping. My face stays covered and I try to compose myself, but I can't stop sobbing. It's too much. Everything is too fucking much.

"Benji and I never had sex, Blaire."

"You can stop with the lies. I know, so just leave me alone."

She refuses to leave though. Instead, she gets closer. "No, you don't know. You might think you do, but you have no clue. Your brother and I were never anything more than friends." She exhales loudly. "Look at me, Blaire. Tell me if I'm lying."

Taking a breath to calm the roar in my head, I look up and see the tears in her eyes.

"I'd never... ever... abort my child. Do you understand me? *Never*." She wipes her cheek and comes closer. "If something had happened between Benji and me, and we did get pregnant, I'd have loved that baby for the rest of my life, Blaire. But it never... *ever* happened."

"I saw the kiss, Trudy." My tone is vehement.

"What kiss?" she asks in confusion.

"That night. When the guys grabbed you and Benji cleaned you up in Janet's office. I walked in while you two were kissing."

Her eyes widen as the memory surfaces but she never loses

eye contact. "Blaire. Are you sure you saw us kissing, because I pushed him off. He only kissed me for a second. I didn't see him that way. And I told him that I was, and still am, in love with Jax." Her stare is unwavering as she watches me. No ticks or flinches take place. No pupil expansion. A sinking feeling enters my gut with the knowledge that she's telling the truth.

Confusion and disbelief have my head spinning. "What? The baby though. He said the baby's no more. He couldn't save it. That you moved on. That he was too late. He was so upset after that kiss. He left for a few days, and when he came back, he wasn't the same." I remember that night. The words. The slurring after he shot up. "I don't understand."

Her face starts to crumble with grief. "Blaire. Before I came to Mobile, I had a baby. He passed away. That night in Janet's office, I told your brother about it."

My chest tightens and panic sets in. I can't breathe. "I need some air," I whisper before leaving the room. Dazed, I bypass everyone and everything. *What do I do? What do I believe?* Confusion over what I believed morphs with what I just learned. What was once black and white is now so foggy.

If she's telling the truth, then lies of my own making have ruined me. I believed them and let them fester into such hatred that I'm not sure it can be fixed. For a whole year, I've thought the worst and wanted revenge. I was going to break her like she broke me. I was willing to ruin lives as some form of justice. *And for what?* Because I listened to the half sentences of my brother while he was so high and out of his mind?

Eyes cast down, I continue on my way. Soon my vision blurs, but I refuse to stop. I don't want people to see me. If I listen to my gut, then all this hatred I've had for her was for no reason. Why was I so stupid? Not once did I think of his state of mind. Not once. My mind is so fucking muddled and my emotions are on a thin wire. Breaking is all I want to do. Break into a million pieces until this sadness, hatred, and guilt is buried in the ground.

When I reach the lobby, my feelings aren't resolved, so I continue to walk until I can't walk any more. Then I break, not caring who passes me. I don't know how long it's been or how long I've been gone, but when I return to Janet's side, I'm alone. Trudy left the bag she brought earlier, so I dig for something to eat. I pick out a bag of Doritos and a bottled water. When I reach inside for a sandwich, my hand touches the metal of a spiral binder. Curious, I take it out and inspect the cover, worn with scratches and ink marks.

Just as I sink back in my chair, a nurse tells me visiting hours are over so I pack everything up and leave. As I walk down the hall, my eyes land on Lyric sitting in the waiting room. His presence is like a salve to my wrecked and broken soul. Whenever I believe no one will be there, at my darkest point, he always shows up. I watch him from the other side of the glass and feel so grateful. My raw emotions have tears building along my lids, but these aren't like the ones from earlier. These are happy ones, relieved that I don't have to be alone anymore. He's my happy ending when I believed fairytales weren't for the damaged. But he's mine.

He looks up and his eyes collide with mine before he says something in his phone and hangs up. Without thought, my feet start moving in his direction, and when he stands to come toward me, I could burst with love.

He grabs my face and wipes my tears. "Red, baby? What's wrong?"

I'm choked up from it all. I never thought this would be my reality, but it is. Never knew I'd fall for someone. Or that they'd always be there when I needed them. Only three words float around in my head. And I can't help but say them even though I could risk scaring him away. "I love you." They come out broken but still strong.

He only searches my tear-filled eyes. No words come from his beautiful mouth and that's okay as long as he holds me close and doesn't push me away. He saw me at my lowest the other night and still stayed. I'm sure my nightmares will be a future fight, but I no longer have to battle them alone. Because even though the words don't leave his mouth, I know he loves me.

He brings my body closer to hug me tight. My face rests against his chest and my arms wrap securely around his waist. His warmth and scent envelope me. Even with today's events, I start to calm and know that, without a doubt to blind me, I'll be okay today. Confidently, more than okay tomorrow.

Three days later Janet is gone. Five days later, we lay her beside her long lost love James. I hope she has peace now. I hope she's no longer holding worry on her shoulders for Jay's or even me. The bar has been closed since she took her last breath, but everyone is coming tonight for a celebration of Janet's life. Trudy and I haven't talked to one another since that day we had words. I think she knows I need time to accept the truth. I also have to accept the fact that I was wrong. She deserves a big apology that I plan on delivering tonight.

We're also meeting the new owner of Jay's for the first time. I don't know what to expect, but whomever the person happens to be, they still won't be Janet. Working for anyone other than her will be strange. You always knew where you stood with her because she spoke her mind regardless if your feelings were hurt. I've been tense all day, so before he leaves, Lyric runs me a hot bath. He and Hyde are meeting the caterers and setting up at Jay's for tonight's services.

Sissy's barking and scratching at the backdoor interrupt my musings. I grab a towel and go to the kitchen to let her in and see the bag of items Trudy left at the hospital. I have completely forgotten about it with all the crap that's been going on. After Sissy runs inside, I take out the spiral notebook. After closing the bedroom door, I pull on some panties and a bra. Then I sit down, open it, and begin to read.

I immediately know whose this is from the handwriting. Benji always had a neat script compared to mine. I always told him God mixed that one thing up between us, because I write more like a boy than he did.

Drawings, songs, and some of his memories fill page after page. Some date back ten years ago when he lost his virginity, to later when he snorted his first line. The words show me a boy I never knew. A boy who played pranks and had friends. A happy boy.

From one page to the next, I absorb his words and try to see what he saw. My heart breaks when I read about the verbal abuse our father used to put us through. He always hated us, I think. Always blamed us for mom not being here or because he didn't have money. I'll never understand the why of it just as I'll never forget it.

When my eyes see that date that will forever be in my heart, dread sinks to the bottom of my belly. I have to take several deep breaths before I allow myself to read it.

May 4, 2008

I found Blaire tonight. She was beaten and bloody. Deep lashes marred her back. I looked for that fucker but he's gone. Probably off blowing his paycheck on booze again So I headed to Blaine and promised to be there from now on I told her I was going to kill him when he walked through the door I had a shotgun but she told me no Begged me not to say anything Only to stay with her Who does that? I'm so confused by her tears Why is she scared to tell people what he did? Why can't I help her? When I asked her how long this has been going on, she only cried harder Why did I fail her? All these questions with no answer Why can't life have a magic eight ball when you need it? All I can do is to make sure it never happens again

—Ben

*

Aug 1, 2008

I plan on taking Blaine away from this But I'm scared Not of him but of failing her What if we starve to death or something else happens? She deserves a good life I should have seen the signs sooner I should have been around more But I was wrapped up in my own life, not caring about anyone else I guess I've already failed her

—Ben

*

Sept 10, 2008

She's still asleep beside me I gave her a sleeping pill I sought off a friend of mine I hope it helps with her nightmares She screams and hits me in her sleep and I don't know what to do She stays in my room but it's not enough I need to get her out of here But I can't do it alone

—Ben

Nov, 18, 2008

I told Aunt Fay what was going on. She called me a sick liar and an ungrateful heathen. That her brother would never hurt a child. Even after I showed her the scars he's left from the beatings. Not with his fist. That would be too nice. He likes to use a car antenna. This type of switch cuts deeper and leaves a mark. But even with this evidence, she still stays in denial. I don't care if I have to stay here and absorb it all but not Blaire. She's too good of a person. She doesn't deserve this life. But I know family will do no good in helping her get away. All I can do is interfere like I have been and try to take his anger out on me. Let him wear his drunken self out. But I still feel like it's not enough. Once again, I failed Blaire, and now that I told, I know it will get worse.

                                                        Ben

Tears drip on the notebook paper as I continue reading. Because it did get worse. So much worse. But not for me. No… Ben was always there, and he was beaten so bad that I thought he'd die. He was forced to watch me suffer and in the end, he suffered. He dropped out of school because he was missing so many days. Whenever I tried to stay home and help him like he did me, he would tell me to go away. Little did I know, he was using his new addiction to needles to mask the pain. I should have never fought back or cried for help that night. I should have just stayed on the floor in silence. He wouldn't have found me and found out. He would have lived a normal life and stayed clean. But I did and I can't make it right or change it.

My heart breaks with each word I read from a brother I never knew. Or at least not as well as I thought. The person who wrote these dark secrets isn't the strong one I knew. This one wasn't the one who walked on water as I imagined at times. He might have taken me away from my tormentor and became my hero, but who was his? Who held him up when he needed it? Real happiness evaded him until he met Trudy. His feelings for her are written, from the first day he met her, to the confession she made that night in Janet's office. I feel so stupid and lost for not seeing it. For assuming something I shouldn't. And yet I still haven't apologized to Trudy. How can I? I've believed her to be something she's not for so long that I've had to work it out in my head before I can face her again. But tonight I plan on taking that step. She deserves my apology, and if she doesn't accept it, then I'll completely understand. I need to thank her for showing my brother some piece of happiness even though it ended in his heart breaking.

Before I know it, time has flown by and I'm running behind on getting ready. I close the notebook and place it on the bed, but it falls when I stand. Wiping my tears, I bend down to pick it up but my hand halts midway. The page before me isn't songs or poems. I see a picture of a little girl no older than two years. Blonde hair but not like mine. I have pale hair like my mom. This little girl has strawberry blonde hair, but she does have my eyes. Not just the shape or color, but also the fear and deadness I always saw looking in a mirror.

My finger outlines her cherub face and my knees give out as I read the words below.

Save Savannah...

CHAPTER TWENTY

"You'll never hate me as much as I hate myself. I promise."
-Lyric

Lyric

"What the hell do you mean you're done?" Massey yells on the other line. "You can't just quit, Lyric. You're too fucking close to Polesky. Do you understand that? And now that his daughter has magically reappeared, he's bound to come on your territory."

I knew he'd be upset with my decision to cut out before they're ready, but I'm over this shit. Over the dope and drugpins. Over the violence and death. I'm ready to wash my hands clean and take what I want in life. I want Red. They can try to bribe me with more money all they want, but I don't care about that shit anymore. As much as I respect Massey, his ignorance of what really goes on at The Reform has only added to my resolve to quit. "I've been with The Reform for almost ten fucking years. And I'm telling you, I'm done. Let Hyde take over or send someone else in. I honestly don't care if you find a vagrant off the street. Just not me."

"Don't forget, Lyric, that without us, you'd still be rotting in a prison cell. Besides, Hyde is more intelligence than action. Nobody has the status or connections you have to pull this shit off either. Do you honestly expect us to sit on our thumbs while you blow this mission and go play house? We'd be starting from point A all over again and we don't have that time, Devereux. If Polesky isn't apprehended or killed, he's going to threaten this country. He's bringing in more scum and we can't locate his ass."

I'm so tired of The Reform running every aspect of my life. Since they transported me inside its walls, I've had to sleep, shit, and shower under their eyes. "You know, the only fucking reason they chose me was because I killed Polesky's brother. I'm basically fucking bait. I didn't choose this life. It was either this or face the death penalty. I was a scared kid who'd just lost the one fucking person I cared for."

"You might not have chosen, but you stuck with it. You excelled in all areas of training. You showed respect and grew. Now you're one of our best." He sighs heavily. "Look, kid. If you get Polesky, I'll see what I can do about cutting you loose early, but we need you to take him down."

Trapped. Again I feel like a caged animal, and I'm ready to attack whoever stands on the other side of the barred door. "And if I don't?" I ask with dread. I know they have a wild card to hold against me. They always do. In training, they loved to threaten to kill your bunkmate by holding a gun to his head if you couldn't complete a mission. Not Massey. He's one of the good ones. The ones who were higher in rank were more power hungry.

The Reform's mission was to make me a man, and if you couldn't change, then you weren't useful and were disposed of. They loved to take young delinquents and runaways. They made it clear from day one where we stood on the hierarchy of living. We were the lowest, just future criminals who had a chance to change and help the government. People wouldn't miss us and if they did, they'd never find us. We were unable to have any contact with our past until granted our freedom. Something rarely given, if the rumors are true. Nobody knows.

You might think we're some sort of military or homeland security. But we have no label. We get no medals. Our reward is to live, and if we're lucky, we get freedom and a new life in the end. Some of the best in the country train and school us. Not at first, though. They didn't want to give a bunch of punk kids with invincible mentalities the resources to kill. We had to earn it the first eighteen months. We had to show respect to receive it or mercy.

"You know what will happen, Lyric. We'll find you and whoever you're with, be it that girl or someone else, and then we'll kill you. Not by my hand, but by someone else's. Understand?"

My fist clinches with the thought of me endangering Red in any way. I knew deep down that she wasn't a good idea. Being with her isn't a good idea, but I couldn't then, and still can't break loose from the hold she has on me. Now I have no choice but to continue with this fucked up plan and risk losing her in my life forever. At least she'll be alive somewhere and I'll make sure she and the kid are taken care of. No more worrying about shit. *Fuck!* This is going to suck. But I need to get over it and do what needs to be done. I just hope she can forgive me when it's over. "Yeah, Sergeant, I understand."

I walk back into Jay's as everything is being set up. Caterers run around with food trays and set up the tables while Ryan helps set up the instruments. The doors don't open for another hour for close friends and family to have time to reminisce and celebrate for a couple of hours. The doors open to the public afterwards for the regular party when the caterers have everything cleaned up. I don't feel like facing anyone right now, but Hyde nods his head when we make eye contact. I follow him to Janet's, or rather my office.

He shuts the door behind us. "How did he take it?"

I sit heavily on the desk. "How the fuck do you think he took it?" I ask.

"Hey! Don't take your beef out on me. I tried to warn you when I saw you getting attached." He comes over and stands directly in front of me. His stance is one they taught us, feet shoulder width apart, back erect, and brace for anything. "That vanilla shit isn't in our cards, bro. They run every fucking aspect of our lives until they're ready to cut us loose. And there's not a damn thing we can do about it."

"It wouldn't be so fucking bad if I knew she'd forgive me when this is over. I could handle it better. But not knowing if she'll want me after all is said and done is driving me insane. What Massey and those assholes at the Reform want me to do will put a nail in the coffin in what Red and I have." I feel scared for the first time in years. Panic wants to take hold when I imagine the aftermath to my next move.

"But would you rather her end up in a real coffin, bro? Because if you don't do this, and you try to run, that's exactly what'll happen."

Nothing else is said. We both know he's right. Massey said the same damn thing. So I know the choice is out of my hands. Hyde smacks me on the shoulder. "Hang in there, bro. We've been through shit way worse than this." He walks out the door leaving me alone inside the small office. And even though I can't see it, I feel my whole world starting to shake. It's on the verge of destruction.

I tip my third beer back and down it in a few short gulps. The chill flows down my throat and I ignore the bitter taste. I could definitely go for something stronger, but the more I lose myself in alcohol, the more I'll want to lose myself in Red. And that can't happen. I feel like my life is going to complete shit. The one thing I want for myself isn't for me. Not now anyways. Maybe in the future, if I'm lucky, she'll let me back in. It's all I can think about.

I've pulled a favor from Massey since he's fucking me over and owes me. So hopefully, he'll pull through and make it happen. I don't know what Red will do if it doesn't. She just lost Janet and adding to her grief is going to kill me. And I know for a fact that this will hurt her. She's vulnerable and has been handed a shit life, but she's a fighter and has proven herself every day. Her words of love echo in my ears at night when I'm alone. She's only said it that one time, but I know she loves me, and that's something I've wanted for a few weeks now. I wanted her to want only me, and now that it's happened, I have to crush her.

Everyone who loved Janet, and then some, are here, with the exception of one. Red has yet to show up, and as much as I want to go check on her or shoot her a quick text, I need to start distancing myself. So I keep company with the crowd and just sit and wait for the storm to blow over. I smile and nod my head when people approach to tell me how well we played at one point or another or how sad Janet's death is. They are also curious about the new owner of Jay's. I look at my watch and figure why the hell not. I stand and slam my empty bottle on the table before making my way up on stage.

The crowd goes wild and after a minute, they finally quiet down. "How y'all doin'?" Another round of applause. "We're here tonight to remember one of the founders of Jay's who unfortunately lost her battle to cancer almost a week ago. So, I thank you all for coming tonight." The stage lights are dimmed for a more natural look. I search the crowd, hoping to see that long bright red hair mixed in somewhere. People's bodies are packed together as they wait, but still no Red. "Now, I know everyone is curious about what's going to happen to Jay's, but I'm happy to tell everyone it's here to stay." As the crowd erupts with cheers, I see her on the far side of the bar. Her eyes show anger and her finger is in the face of some girl whose back is towards me. Reminding myself to keep my distance, I continue with my speech. "Because I'm the new owner."

Finally, I have her attention when my words reach her ears. Seeing her tears has me digging my feet into the wooden stage. She looks beaten and worn. Janet's passing is only the first piece to the avalanche of emotions she's about to experience.

I turn away. *"Now, let's fuckin celebrate."* I holler into the mike and feel the walls vibrate from the crowd's loud cheers. When I jump off stage, I keep my eyes away from her. Too much fucking guilt eats at me. I don't feel the pats on my back as I make my way to my usual table. I pay no mind to the girls rubbing against me. And I don't hear the music from the DJ. I just sit and order another beer.

When she comes up behind me, I know. There's no need to turn around. I feel her, smell her. My body stands at attention. But I just keep my eyes ahead and drink.

"Lyric. I need to talk to you."

Her voice is strained and I find myself standing. Without a word, I grab her arm and lead her to the office, but keep the door cracked. She tries to hold me, but I sidestep her advances. "Shoot," I say indifferently and look at paperwork on the desk.

"I found something tonight." Her voice breaks. "Something that I'm still trying to understand." She takes a shuddering breath. "Can't you look at me? Please?"

After I do as she asks, she tries to wrap her arms around me again, but I grab them to stop her. "Don't."

Her confused eyes meet mine. "What? Why?"

Here it is. Time to end it. Time to save her while killing myself. My need to make this easy on her has me giving her some bullshit reason. "I'm the new owner of Jay's."

"So? What does that matter?"

"It changes everything, Blaire. You know that."

Her eyes widen as a tear falls. "What did you call me?"

"*Blaire.*" In true asshole style, I drag it out slowly.

"Don't call me that. You always call me Red." Her arms fall to her sides.

"Okay. Miss Morgan. Is that better?"

"Why are you doing this?"

"Doing what?"

"Being this way. Acting like you don't want to be around me. Acting like you don't love me."

Bile rises and I want to vomit from her calling me out. She sees right through me, no matter how deep I hide. I bend over to grab my knees and hold myself up before I fall. Then I laugh without mirth to play it off. "Love you? I'm sorry, *Miss Morgan*, but you're delusional if you think that shit. I think you need to stay out of people's medicine cabinets." She pales and I feel like the lowest piece of shit, but this has to be done. "Is this because I let you sleep with me these past few months?" I take a step towards her and reach down to undo my jeans. "That isn't love, Miss Morgan. That's what us adults call fucking. And it's time to stop. But hey… If you want to go another round." I unzip my pants as her eyes narrow, allowing more tears to fall.

She shakes her head vehemently. "No… no… no! I don't know what's going on. Or who possessed your body, but I know you love me, Lyric." She looks at me and wipes her eyes. "I know you do. And if I have to show you and remind you, I will." She grabs my face and slams her lips to mine.

She shows me with a kiss. A kiss that I'm too weak to pull away from. My hands reach down and instinctively grab her hips to bring her body to mine. I taste her tears on her lips. I taste her sorrow and confusion. But most of all, I taste my Red. The girl I love more than any fucking thing in this goddamn world. The girl I have to release, and so I try to concentrate on what I need to do. But I'm selfish so I absorb her. Every breath, every sound, and every time she tells me she loves me between kisses. I don't think I can give her up just yet. I can't pull away from her to stop. But the image of her lifeless body is my resolve. I grab her shoulders and push her away. But before I can explain, the devil walks in and drives that final nail in between Red and me.

"What the fuck are you doing kissing my boyfriend?" Anya stands in the doorway, smiling like the true bitch she is.

CHAPTER TWENTY-ONE

"The secret to change is to focus all of your energy, not on fighting the old, but on building the new."
-Socrates

Blaire

"Mandy?"

Lyric stiffens beside me before turning his eyes on me. My focus stays on the bitch thief dressed to kill in her red halter top and low-rise jeans. Her dark hair is pulled to the side and curls fall against her large, showcased breasts. All I want to do is make her pay. My fist clenches with the effort to keep myself from pulling the hair off her skull.

"I'm sorry. You must have me mistaken with someone else, dear." She plays stupid and twirls the red stir stick in her cocktail.

My heart rate is speeding and my head feels dizzy from the kiss and then seeing Mandy. Inside, I'm screaming like I did earlier with her when I walked and saw her conniving ass at the bar. When I confronted her with what she did to me, the bitch stated she was just looking out for me. I call bullshit. She wouldn't have taken my money if that were the case. She would have made sure I would be able to make it.

Now she shows up out of the blue, spilling some crap story

219

about being Lyric's girlfriend. Why is she lying? Why isn't he saying anything? What the fuck is going on? "Oh, don't play dumb with me. I know who you are. We lived together for almost a fucking year."

"You're obviously drunk." Arching her brow, she stares me down, but addresses Lyric. "Babe. We need to go. Our friends just showed up."

Looking at Lyric, my eyes beg him to tell me he loves me... to tell me the truth. He doesn't though. He walks up to Mandy and wraps her in his arms instead. My eyes can't break away from the nightmare I'm watching. My heartbeat resounds in my ears and begins to shatter as he bends down and kisses her neck before saying something in her ear.

She smirks in my direction. "I love you, too, babe." Then they walk out together, and I'm left with more fucking questions than answers while losing another person I foolishly trusted.

Time passes but how much, I don't know. Locking myself away from the world, I stay in a void. A black hole of sadness and rejection, feeling guilty for grieving for someone who doesn't deserve it instead of the surrogate parent I had for the past several years. I'm hollow and too unimportant to care.

After Lyric left with Mandy —or whoever that bitch was— I walked out of the bar, confused and unsure. Just like that day in the hospital, I kept walking, hopeful that the pain would stay behind. My feet automatically led me to the one place I've always considered home. Janet's.

Her presence is everywhere. From the air that smells of cigarettes and perfume to the furniture, she lingers. She always kept her home so clean and had incense burning to scent the air The fragrance is comforting but doesn't heal me or make it all better. I'm still hollow... lost.

Wrapped in her blankets, I realize there's nothing left in me. Nobody that I can count on anymore. And I'm so fucking tired. Tired of heartbreak. Tired of giving people all of my trust so they can just leave after they pulverize it. Tired of them leaving me helpless and naked with nothing but another brick to put up. I'm close to being completely enclosed.

Blaire

Upon hearing my name, my heavy eyes struggle to open. Lyric sits there, staring down at me. His features are apologetic and full of sorrow. His touch on my forehead is soft. Maybe it was all a bad dream. Maybe I'm back in his bed and he's with me again.

"Blaire, wake up."

His voice breaks and his form starts to shift. I shake my head, trying to awaken so I can see him more clearly, but also wanting to sleep to avoid him. Even though I want to hate him, I can't. I love him and that makes this so much harder.

When the voice takes on a feminine high pitch, I sit up and see two figures. One sits beside me on the couch and the other is standing in the kitchen. After rubbing my eyes, I see Cory beside me while Trudy works in the kitchen. "What... what are y'all doin' here?" My throat feels dry and scratches with each word.

Cory only sits up and smiles. "Bout damn time. We've been trying to wake you for ten freakin' minutes." She scrunches her nose. "I hope you're done with moping around. Cause you look like shit. And ya stink."

"Cory. Geez. She's heartbroken. Can you be a little more

sensitive?" Trudy defends while unloading groceries from plastic bags. Heartbroken can't describe how I feel. Betrayed. Misled. Like every tear that falls brings me closer to just giving up.

"Hey. I'm only telling the truth. It's been three days since she left Jay's in tears. And she's wearing the same clothes." Cory turns to face me. "Nobody knew where you were and figured you'd up and caught the next bus out of here. However, the lead singer of the assholes told us to look here. Funny how he knew, huh?"

Stretching, I feel all the kinks in my stiff body, but soon my anger numbs my physical pain. "Asshole is right. But it's more like lying asshole. I'm so stupid." Memories of how often he was gone. Even before we started having sex, I never saw him. The late night calls and how he always left the room to answer them. We never went out unless we were out of town. The locked bedroom door.

Did he keep his pictures from his relationship in there? No! Maybe they just met. Maybe they started dating before our trip to New Orleans. He was acting weird but I never suspected another woman. Maybe they met in New Orleans after he left me at the hospital. I know he had something to do, but I didn't question him. Could he have brought her back? Why wouldn't she claim her name? *UGH!*

With each question, more confusion sets in. "I don't know what is up with him and that bitch, but I know for a fact they can both rot in hell." After I wipe another tear, I lock eyes with Cory. "I don't want to talk about him or anything associated with him. Not Jay's, not the band, nothing."

Cory smiles and her eyes take on a devious look. "Good because I don't want to either. I don't want to talk about anything or anyone with a penis tonight. It's time to get down to business, so get your smelly ass up and in the shower. Jazz will be here soon so we can get this much needed party started."

"Party?"

"Hell yeah! I've declared that today be 'Fuck it Day'. Fuck men. Fuck dogs that chew on new shoes. Fuck families and hoochie sisters. Fuck the weird neighbor who looks for gold with one of those treasure-hunting things while in his underwear." She shivers with animated disgust.

"Metal detectors," Trudy yells. I look over and see bottle after bottle of amber liquor, shot glasses, and Red Bull.

"Did you take that from Jay's?"

"Fuck yeah she did. That idiot Lyric might still have my ovaries ready to have his baby, but I think he deserves a big *fuck you*. So we stole some of the only men we can count on. Jim, Jack, and Jäger for some bombs. We're gonna blow shit up and celebrate Janet with the two girls she loved the most."

I'm still in a daze as this all sinks in before I'm forced to the shower. When I'm done, I realized I have nothing here. No clothes or even damn deodorant. Luckily, Jazz came prepared. With fresh pajamas and armpits, I walk into the living room and see three large pizzas. The smell of cheesy greasy goodness mixed in with feeling clean has my mood lifting. Trudy sits on the couch facing Cory and Jazz who are both on the floor, so I guess that leaves me sitting with Trudy on the couch.

My appetite returns as soon as I take my first bite and.it definitely isn't ladylike. But as I watch the others, I realize they are just as crude in manners.

We talk about anything random. Cory brings up whatever comes to mind and it usually has to do with sex. When the word Manicorn comes up, I can't help but ask what the hell she's talking about. Then I see the picture Jazz pulls up on her phone and laugh for the first time in days, while wishing I never asked. My eyeballs can't be bleached to erase the image of guys dressed up as ponies.

So not my thing. But whatever. Free country and all.

Cory places a Jäger Bomb in front of each of us after the pizza is demolished and then raises her glass. "I want to say fuck you to possessive meatheads, parents who judge instead of accept, and horny pricks." Cory downs her bomb and looks at Jazz.

"I want to say fuck you to crazy bitches and bad parents who need to grow the hell up. Oh… And America's look on the perfect body. My boobs were working boobs and are awesome." Jazz downs hers and smiles widely.

Trudy surprises me by standing with her back straight, ready to down her Bomb. "Fuck you, assholes and dealers. Fuck you for ruining and taking lives. And a big fuck you to anyone who hurts my girls here in this room or my family." Her voice is strong and her demeanor is ready to fight. That's not something I'm used to seeing on her shy self.

Feeling determined to make this speech count, I hold my glass up as the anger I feel for everything I've gone through in my past and recently with Lyric surfaces. "I want to say fuck you to liars, thieves, and men in general. After tonight, I will no longer talk to, think of, or see you again, and I hope you rot in your new girl's poisonous, dog meat vagina. If you catch herpes, I hope it hurts and causes you to scratch from asshole to ballsack until you bleed." I down my Bomb, loving the licorice taste and sweetness from the Red Bull. The burn that flows down my throat coats the acid from the words that I just spoke. I'm so fucking ready for another.

We are rude and crude and not giving a damn. We dance like idiots to Ke$ha and when it mentions making it rain, Jazz jumps on the couch and dumps her purse all over the place. Not just cash but actual coins are being thrown. Luckily, it doesn't hurt because we're drunk as hell. We tell our phobias, and I can't help but bust out in hysterics when Cory announces her fear of pomegranates.

She says something about the inside looks disgusting and causes her skin to crawl. It's still funny.

"I think I'm going to breakup with Bo." Cory announces.

"Why? He seems sweet. And his ass in wranglers is so yum." Jazz stuffs an Oreo cookie in her mouth and smiles, showcasing her chocolate covered teeth.

"It's just time. His horse has been rode hard and ready to retire. God knows I've tried this exclusive thing, but honestly, we fight all the time."

"Oh... yeah!" I slur. "I remember y'all fighting once. At Jay's." Gripping the counter for balance, I try to snatch Jazz's Oreos from her. *Damn, I drank a lot.*

"Yeah. I wanted to get yooooouuu," she points at me, "from that weird guy that night. But *Bocephus* said to leave you." Cory sits on the stool and leans on Trudy.

"Bocephus? Wait... is that his real name?" Jazz slurrs.

"Yup. I like to call him that when I fake an orgasm. Ha... which unfortunately is more than I care to admit."

"Does he know?"

Cory shrugs while shoving a cookie in her mouth. "Hell if I care. I don't plan on seeing him or his," she holds up her pinky and wiggles it, "hamster dick ever again."

"Oh, come on. The guy is so cute and built. I'm sure you're exaggerating."

"You're right. He doesn't have a hamster dick. He has a mangina." I spit out my drink, trying not to laugh and choke to death before she continues. "I'm positive he shoots up. He's starting to look like a gorilla who walks on his fist. And if that's the case, he should've put some roids in his weenie instead of his ego. We got into it yesterday. And that's when I decided it's over." Her eyes narrow as she fixes herself another drink. "Do you know what he did? He *RIPPED* my Hans Solo poster from beside my bed. That's when I told him the poster was the only fuckin' way I can get off when I masturbate, because he's not meeting my demands."

Her eyes start to get glossy with tears, and we immediately surround her. Jazz grabs her face and makes her look at her in the eyes. "Don't cry, Cory. Remember we're having a Fuck It party. Not a therapy session. So get that back straight and those tits perky then dry your eyes."

"Okay. I will. But dammit, I'm fuckin' sad now. Do you know how much I miss that poster?"

The following week passes and my mood starts to lift even though unwanted thoughts of Lyric surface from time to time. I've been staying at Janet's place since I have nowhere to go, praying I won't be kicked out anytime soon. I refuse to be anywhere near the reason for my heartbreak. If the thought of him and another woman makes me want to hide in a dark closet to cry, I can only imagine what I'll do if I actually see it. So for the safety of humanity, I keep my distance. Trudy helps me find a new job at Martinis, a swanky piano bar a few blocks away from Jay's. It's only three nights a week, because I'm not the only pianist in town, but hopefully, the tips will help me out.

I'm expecting Jazz and Fin to pull up any minute. She's bringing over some of her dresses for me to try on before my first performance tomorrow night. The whole fancy dress code is going to be an adjustment, but I'm hopeful this is the right choice in my life. It's one I made all on my own. I still need to get the balls to go and grab my stuff from Lyric's, but I just can't seem to make myself face him, or what we had. Procrastination should be my new middle name. So I've been mooching off the three girls who shoved pizza and lots of liquor down my throat the other night, and even though I feel like I'm turning into a freeloader, I'm not going to complain. The day is coming that I'll need to suck it up and just do it.

I'll discuss this with the Trudy, Cory, and Jazz later, along with the fact I have a sister I never knew about. But I'm in no position right now to go to South Carolina and take her away from that hell. I don't even have a real roof over my head, just the one I'm borrowing until Janet's estate, and belongings are distributed or auctioned off.

Hearing the knock, I run to open the front door and see Jazz and chubby cheeks Fin. "Here." She shoves Fin in my arms before running back to her car. She then carries in dress after dress before rolling in a suitcase. When I ask her what's inside, she tells me shoes, and I stand there with my mouth open after she unzips it. Different colors. Different heights. Some with jewels. Some with bows. There has to be fifteen different pairs of heels. Our feet are close in size, but Jazz is a lot shorter than I am. In her clothes, I'm going to be showing my ass off, or look like I'm ready for a flood.

She takes Fin and has me try on every dress. I quickly learn that pink is definitely not my color and clashes with the red of my hair. However, the blues and teals are nice, but like I said before, my ass is on display. If I sit on the piano bench, people will get more than a musical show. Before I give up hope on finding a dress, she passes me another one. The black, backless, halter-top, floor-length gown has a high slit on the left side. The ruched fabric wraps beautifully to the left and stops at a large brooch of silver gems. Struck speechless, I stand in front of the mirror and marvel how beautiful it looks. No wig hides me from the world. No fake names will be used. I, Blaire Morgan, am going to do the one thing I love the most. Play piano.

Images of Lyric and me at the piano the first time he touched me invade my thoughts and I start to feel flushed.

"Dayum girl. That's the one, no doubt."

Jazz's voice interrupts my memory and I take a deep breath to clear my head. *Don't ruin this, Blaire. Don't let him ruin this.* After my pep talk, I look at her petite reflection in the mirror and smile. "Yes. I believe it is." But really, I'm not only talking about the gorgeous dress. I'm talking about me, a girl who's taking her first step of independence and who's determined to be good enough to have someone who will love me. That someone is a little girl who needs to be rescued before it's too late. "It's definitely the one."

CHAPTER TWENTY-TWO

"Knowing your own darkness is the best method for dealing with the darknesses of other people."
-Earl Jung

Lyric

Anya leads Bishop outside of The Hole with a false promise of some sexual favor. His smirk and body language is relaxed. No suspicion is seen on his face and I'm positive he has no idea what's about to take place. He quickly walks her around to the passenger side of his car and traps her body between his arms.

She smiles and looks at him with lust in her eyes. "I love this car. It's so hot. I've never ridden in one before. Will you take me in it tonight?" She talks his ego up.

"Sure, baby. But it's gonna cost ya." He bends down and kisses her neck. "You think you can pay the price?" His hands move to her large breasts, and when her neck tilts, her eyes meet mine and I see nothing but pure evil. No soul or life. I wonder if that's what Blaire saw when she looked at me. I quickly train my mind back on what's happening instead of what's not.

"Time to pay the piper, baby." Bishop opens the passenger door and slides their bodies toward the inside of the car.

Anya smiles seductively as she disappears from view and

drops to her knees. Onlookers and witnesses pay no mind to the two individuals about to openly have sex. Prostitutes are common in this part of town, and unfortunately, rape is too. Cop cars keep their distance, but just to be on the safe side, I have some small town thugs taking watch.

As I step out of the shadows, my feet make no sound. When I see his face morph from pure ecstasy to fear, I know she's pulled her 38 special out, and if I'm right, the cold metal is pointed at his dick.

"Make a fucking sound and you'll lose your tollbooth asshole."

His hands go in the air as he starts to beg. *Pussy.* She's easy to take down if he had sense, but obviously, that's not the case.

Instead of grabbing him from behind, I let him see my face. His eyes widen as his breathing becomes labored from fear and anger. I'm not going to lie. I like scaring the shit out of fuckers like him.

"You." He hisses and spittle sprays me in the face. I just dig in his pocket and grab his keys before disarming him of all his weapons. When I'm done, I smile coldly. "Now pull your pants up and put your shit away." Anya keeps her gun on him as she stands. But then I hear the whistle and know we're running out of time. I hand the keys to Anya. "Don't speed."

She pouts like this is a fucking game. "Aww, babe. You're no fun." Then she slowly pulls her dress up, showing her legs and places her gun back in her garter holster before leaning up and kissing me on the cheek. She's playing this couple act like it's an art and I hate every second of it. "But you'll learn how fun I can be later. That's a promise." She winks at Bishop before walking around the front of the black Corvette and getting in the driver's seat.

"Don't even think about pulling any shit, Bishop. I'll break your neck before you get two inches from me. And your trusty sidekick is already occupied. So don't think of calling him either." Then I see Lou's Cadillac pulling toward us and smile for the first time in three weeks. "I've been wanting to do this for a while now." My fist plants hard on the fucker's face and he falls cold on the asphalt. Lou helps me load him up and we head to the dock.

"Damn, Lyric. I think you killed the muthafucka."

"Nah. Unfortunately, he's still breathing. Plus he'd be useless to me dead."

"I hear ya. You trust this bitch? Cause I ain't gonna lie. I don't."

"We just need to keep our eyes on her. I don't trust her either, but if she brings Polesky to me, I'll take my chances."

Bishop finally comes to after Javier throws cold water on him. He spits and sputters when he wakes to only realize he's tied to a metal chair surrounded by at least fifty men, some Columbian, some American. All of them are with me and all hate Polesky.

Javier laughs while tossing the bucket to the other side of the room. "Mornin' sunshine. You enjoy that nap? Cause you gonna need all the energy you can get." He lights a cigarette and blows smoke in Bishop's face.

"Let me go, you dick. Or you're all gonna pay for this shit." Bishop yells but nobody can hear him outside these metal walls. The boats and machine plants that surround us drown out all noise. Even gun shots. "Do ya know who you're fuckin with? Do ya?"

"You talkin' about that Russian *puta*? Because that's all he is to us anymore. A straight bitch." Javier loses his laugh. "He's pissed off the wrong *capos,* you *pinche pendeja*." He takes his cigarette and lets the red tip land on Bishop's hand, burning his flesh. Bishop screams and tries to yank his body free from the plastic zip ties. But they only cut deeper into his skin.

After a minute, I stop Javier's fun. It was his cousin who was raped and tortured by Polesky, so I allow him some leeway. "Javier. That's enough." I say with command. He laughs before walking over to the side of the building. I approach Bishop and grab an extra chair to straddle backwards and face him. "You know who I am?" He doesn't say anything, which is not surprising. I grab my KA-BAR out of the sheath inside my boot and causally clean my nails. "I'm goin' to ask you again. You know who I am?" Once again, he stays silent, and when I look at him, his eyes are watching my knife. I whistle to get his attention. "Hey, dick. Look up here." His eyes meet mine, and no matter how tough he's acting, I can still see the fear in them. "I'm goin' to ask you one last time. Do you know who I am?" I count down the seconds, waiting for an answer, and when I get to five, I shove my blade straight through his hand directly where Javier burned him. He screams as blood flows from the wound and drips on the cement. "You feel like speaking now?"

"Ugh! Lyric... Lyric Devereux. Murderer of Vladimir Polesky." Sweat breaks out on his brow and his face turns pasty white.

"Damn right, I murdered that rapist piece of shit. And I dream of doin' the same damn thing to Nicholas."

Heels clatter on the cement floor as Anya approaches. Looking over my shoulder, I see the video camera in her hands. After Polesky watches this, he'll know she's alive and I have her. He'll show his face either to get her back in the family business or to end her for disloyalty and deceit. Plus, I'm positive she knows some major shit about what he's done or is still doing, and because of that, she's a liability. Getting close to her was a no brainer for the government. It's not about the drugs to them. It's something bigger. I'm just not privy to that info.

"What is that bitch doin?"

"Aww." She clucks her tongue. "Is that any way to talk to the sexiest woman alive? That is what you called me at the bar earlier, right?" She stands between his legs while recording his face. "I bet you're regretting buying me that drink now, huh?" Then she places one high heeled foot up between his legs on his dick. "Do you know who *I* am?"

"A heartless slut."

Her red lips form a smile that shows no humor and she starts to add pressure with her foot. "Yes. I am heartless. I was raised to be, and when I finally found my heart, he was murdered by your boss." More weight is added, and his breathing becomes erratic. When he's almost in tears and close to passing out, she releases the pressure and lowers her heeled foot on the ground. Then she turns and sits in his lap before turning the camera on them both. "Hi daddy. Look what I've got." She smacks Bishop's cheek. "Wake up. You don't want to miss this. And don't forget to say hey to my dad, Nicholas Polesky."

"You're lying. His daughter is dead," he says weakly.

Her smile widens as she stands and tries to hand me the video recorder, but I shake my head no. This was her idea so she can run this show. She only arches her brow to show her irritation. "Javier. Come hold this." She yells without looking away from my face. After she hands Javier the camera, she slowly walks around Bishop's chair while letting her hips sway. The men in the room are watching her blue skirt caress her ass with every step, but I know she's trying to gain my attention more than theirs. When she passes the second time, she grabs the handle to my KA-BAR and looks at me. "May I?"

"Be my guest," I answer with false indifference. Honestly, I'm wondering what's in store for this guy.

She turns toward Bishop, pops her ass in the air, and leans in. "Brace yourself." She stands before jerking the blade out of his hand, and pays no mind to his screams. "You see, I don't care if you think I'm lying. When my father sees this video, he's the only one that needs to believe I am who I say I am." She gets down on her knees between his legs not caring about the blood on the ground or dripping from his palm. Grabbing his opposite hand, she places the tip of blade under his thumbnail. "Where is he? Is he in Atlanta still, or is he headed here?"

"Fuck you." Bishops spits in her face.

It doesn't faze or disgust her. She just wipes it off. "Growing up with him as a father, I started watching people being tortured when I was ten. You're the first one I get to try it on, though." Using the tip of the knife, she rips his nails off one by one. The machines outside loading trucks and barges drown out the agony in his screams.

After the seventh bloody finger, he screams for her to stop and gives in. "He's n-n-not in either place."

"Then where is he? Is he close?"

At first, he says nothing, but she takes the knife and places it against his cheek with just enough pressure to break skin. "Y-y-yes. Very close," he stutters, "but you won't find him."

She smiles brightly and sits in his lap as blood spray on her hands and clothes. Her knees are filthy, but none of it disturbs her. "I won't have to." She kisses him on the cheek before turning back toward the video camera. "Daddy, I hope you missed me. And I hope to make you proud." She puts the gun to Bishop's head and pulls the trigger.

Blood splatters her face but her smile never fades. "Come here," she says to me and stands up from Bishop's limp body. When I'm beside her, she wraps her free hand around me as her other continues to hold the camera. "And look who I'm with, daddy. Do you approve of him?" She loses her smile and the face of sadistic beauty transforms into pure evil. "If not, then come do something about it. That is, if you have the balls."

This bitch is a true sociopath, and I'm wondering who is the real threat. Her or her father?

My clothes litter the floor of the gym's bathroom. After I shower, I plan to throw gasoline on them, light a match, and watch them burn. My goal is to rid tonight's events from my mind. I'm washing not only blood off my body, but also the smell of Anya's perfume, and the kiss she ended the little video with. The thought of her sickens me, not only her poisonous tongue on mine but the enjoyment she took in killing someone. Pure fucking joy, like a kid at Christmas. She not only tortured him and fired the gun, but she also dismembered his corpse before tossing the pieces in the bay.

I've killed for a while now, but it's definitely not something I enjoy. Pulling the trigger and taking someone's life always brings me guilt until I remind myself what possible evil I've taken out of this world. But I'm sure Anya felt no remorse. Not one damn speck of it. Her actions are proof. The kiss she gave me was as sexual as they come, and I'm sure she was close to orgasm. And the way she wanted to continue, even after the camera was off, was proof that she got off on pulling that trigger As if high, she needed to find another form of release. I guess being raised by a Russian drug lord would fuck someone's head up, but I believe Anya would kill a child if provoked.

She made sure Polesky's other guy, who was at the bar with Bishop, not only personally sent it to her father, but watched the whole ordeal. So now, we wait. Either Polesky comes here for his precious daughter or a war has started. Either way, I'm following fucking orders and can't do a damn thing about it. I just keep my eyes open and wait.

After finishing, I wrap a towel around my waist and grab a black trash bag to throw my soiled clothes in. The door opening causes me to look over my shoulder. Ryan walks in so I relax some even though I'm not in the mood for his shit right now. "S'up?"

"You tell me. I've been blowing your damn phone up for two days. Figured I'd eventually find you here. I got word of Torres wanting to go a round with ya and need an answer." He leans against the wall and crosses his arms. "You interested? Cause it certainly will pay a shit load."

The mere thought of fighting brings that familiar adrenaline rush. Being in that atmosphere is intense and winning makes all the blood worth it. Plus, if I'm planning on getting out of this mess after Polesky is out of the picture, I know I'll need all the money I can get. "Yeah. When and where?"

"One month and in Biloxi. His turf. You haven't fought in a while and he's been talkin' some shit. So when word got back to me, I came looking for ya. Of course we had words, and even though he's in a different weight class than me, I still think I could take his ass down." He rubs his palms together. "I know you're gonna KO him first round. Already getting my Benjamins ready."

I just shake my head. Ryan loves to make quick money, probably as much as he loves fucking those skanks. Me getting on his ass about gambling won't help.

"Where's that psycho bitch that's always hanging on you, anyways? I'm surprised she's not a permanent attachment to your dick."

I shrug my shoulders as I pull on my Ominous shirt and jeans. "Don't know. Don't really care."

"Mmmhmm! Isn't she your girl?" he asks but I don't answer. I haven't said anything about her being anything to me. Anya does all that shit. And no matter how much I want to deny it, I hold my tongue and play her game.

He gets the hint and drops the issue. "Well, Cory and that yeehaw split. Bout damn time. She's not the goat milking type. And I'm sure she'd be living the farm life if she stuck with his ass. Never did like him or how he talked to her. He's too much beef and not enough brain to do anything else, if you ask me."

"You and her still talk?" Cory is pretty much the only chick Ryan ever slept with twice.

"Some. She's been hangin' around that bitch Blaire for..." *Oof!*

He's against the brick wall before he can finish his sentence. My forearm is digging into his throat, cutting off his air and blood flow. I don't give a shit if he's a friend or not. "Don't you ever... *EVER* talk about her like that again, got it?" Instead of answering, he kicks my legs out from under me, but I catch myself before I completely fall on the floor. I like the kid, but I'll fuck him up if need be. "You really wanna do this?" My body gets ready for a fight, feet apart, and arms ready.

He coughs to get air before standing up straight, watching me. "Fuck, no. What I do want is some damn answers. You didn't mind when I called your *girlfriend* a bitch, but I call Blaire one and you get all fuckin crazy. What the fuck dude?"

Taking a deep breath, I relax. "Don't worry about it. Shit's just really fuckin' complicated now."

"I do worry, bro. I know you're into some shit. I'm not sure exactly what, but I know it's deep. But I've never seen you act like the band doesn't matter. All of a sudden that Anya chick shows up, and you're never around for practice, the shop, or the gym. Hell bro, you own the bar now and you're hardly there. And I know you're not off fuckin' her because you wouldn't be such a goddamn ass all the time. Besides that, you cringe from her. Literally fuckin cringe, dude, and that shit's not normal."

"Stay out of it."

"Look, I'll stay out of it, but if you need any-fucking-thing, I'll be ready. Yeah?"

Ryan has been loyal to me for a while now and I know he means what he says. He would be a big help if I ever needed him. He's fuckin crazy and has the fighting skills to back it up, but I don't want him getting killed. "Yeah." I agree. He comes over and slaps me on the shoulder before turning around to leave, but I stop him before he can. "There is one thing you can do. Will you keep a close eye on Red for me?"

"Already handled dude. Cory's been staying with her a lot."

"And?" My heartbeat picks up with just the thought of Red. Once this shit is done, I'm getting her back, no matter what. If I have to beg and grovel, I will. If I have to kill, I will. No matter the cost. My need to feel alive again has me wanting to see her. Touch her. Taste her. Just the thought brings not only my dick to life but my heart, too. I feel no life inside me since that last kiss we shared, and when Anya's around, I sink deeper in my own hell. One I've only recently started to escape from. Anya has pure evil in her and a need for vengeance that swarms and touches everyone she comes in contact with. She's devious and will use all of her assets to get what she wants, no matter who gets hurts in the process. Even Red.

Anya told me how she picked her up hitchhiking and taught her how to hustle for money. Money she later stole. She even told me how she contemplated killing Red because she was too weak to be useful, but couldn't bring herself to do it. I guess her black heart does beat on some fucked up level.

"She's good. Working at a ritzy ass piano bar downtown or some shit. Cory told me Janet left all her assets to her so now she has a place to live and a way to get around."

I nod my head while picturing her face smiling instead of the angry tears from three weeks ago. She finally has a place of her own and has started a life. The only thing missing is me. With any luck, it's not for too much longer.

CHAPTER TWENTY-THREE

"Breaking from the truth that was built with lies."-Blaire

Blaire

When I press my fingertips against the ivory keys, I fall into a trance where all I see is music unfolding and all I feel is contentment. For me, playing the piano is an art. I visualize my masterpiece and know what piece to perform. Then it's all about feeling my way through it until I reach the end, either making it my own in every way or leaving it precisely as written. I'm happy just playing, and it's taken me time and some crazy girls to feel happy again. Every day, my heart heals a little more and I keep pushing forward to get my sister back. Even though I'm still in love with Lyric, I can't do anything about it right now besides keep my distance and get over him.

After the first week of being away from him, realization hit me. I don't need him to fix me like I thought. I need to fix myself. So I've reached out and found some help with the psychologist from the hospital. I've slowly opened up about my past. She doesn't push like I thought she would. She listens and shows no judgment or disgust. With these discussions, I might be reliving those nights of molestation, but I'm also fighting back. I'm refusing to let him take me down and beat me mentally for the rest of my life. Or my sister's.

Lyric was gracious enough to have Hyde bring me all my things. He silently walked up the steps and laid bags and boxes on the porch while I stood at the door and watched, refusing to let him inside. When he carried up Benji's guitar case, I met him half way and snatched it out of his hands. My resentment showed through my eyes and I wanted him to know how I was feeling. He never liked me anyways and had no problem letting me know he didn't want me around. But, when I saw just a glimpse of sadness, my guard slipped and stayed that way until Cory walked through the door later that night.

She found me crying as I rummaged through the boxes that smelt of Lyric when I opened them. We decided a nice bonfire was needed as well as a few drinks. So we took all the nice pretties he'd bought me and torched them. The only thing not there was the dress he bought me in New Orleans. It's fine, though. I don't think I could have destroyed it. As the fire burned, Cory kept my mind occupied. I don't know what I'd do without her around. She always knows how to make me smile when I need it most.

Over the past week, I've talked to a lawyer about getting custody of my sister, but they've been absolutely no help. I have to prove her abuse and, since I only have a photograph of a sad toddler who I've never met, they think I'm crazy. But I refuse to stop trying. Even if I have to go and personally get her out of that nightmare and away from that monster, I will. I'm not sure how just yet. I've had several ideas run through my head. Maybe I need to find out who the bastard married and call her. Who's to say she's not just as evil though and tips him off? If I do go get her, we'll be living on the run the rest of our lives. To do that, I'd need money, and lots of it, hoarded away. The fear of being too late pushes me further every day.

When I open my eyes, I take in the dim atmosphere and can't

help put compare it to Jay's. Beautiful clothed tables with candlelight and exquisite polished dark wooden floors. No crowded bar full of liquor or beer taps taking up space. No drunks lingering. Only my stage on one end and beautiful artwork along the walls. Is it strange that I miss all that, though? I miss the sleazy dressed crowd and their crude behavior. Nothing but black tie attire is welcome here, so tips have been substantial. Even compliments from some of Mobile's wealthiest families and invites to play at other functions have come up. I've had to ask Cory to help me schedule, so I don't double book anything. New Year's Eve is in a few days, and I have an event to play at the Bragg-Mitchell Mansion. It's an old plantation home built in the eighteen hundreds and is now a museum that can be leased out for any event if you have the right amount of money.

Having been asked when I accepted this job that I keep my tattoos covered, I bite my tongue and do it because the money is too good. Shaking my thoughts away, I stand from the piano bench to take a break as people applaud before continuing their meals and conversations.

Passing the tables, I head toward the ladies' room, my black heels tapping out a heavy rhythm on the floor. Before I can make it, a gentleman in a tailored suit stops me. He's average in height, but has striking blue eyes, and his strong jaw is covered with neatly trimmed stubble. He smiles, and it's nice. Not cocky or lustful. Just nice.

"Excuse me, Miss. Sorry to hold you up, but can I say that your playing is exquisite," he says with an accent.

"Thank you. I really enjoy it." Not wanting to lead him on, I break eye contact and look toward the restrooms, hoping he takes a hint. I'm not used to compliments and always feel the need to pick something wrong with me and point it out. Plus, I'm not a social butterfly like Cory or Jazz. Trudy is even more sociable than I am.

If I'm pissed off, then I'm not one to hold my tongue. "Excuse me." Relief fills me when he doesn't argue before I make my way to the ladies' room to take a breather.

After walking in, I take in the Victorian style couch and a set of chairs resting against the wall and the extravagant crystal chandelier. It doesn't even smell like a public restroom, but more like a garden. I walk around the corner that separates the sitting area from the stalls, and stand in front of the large, gold-framed mirror with cherubs watching from the two top corners. Light pink and yellow flowers color the wallpaper with vines that intertwine. Three white, porcelain bowls trimmed to match the golden faucets sit on top of beautiful marble countertops. This opulent bathroom cost more than my home and truck combined. Breathing a sigh, I shake off my melancholy and remind myself that I've come a long way from just a few weeks ago. Just look at my dress. I've purchased the red strapless pencil dress and added a long sleeved, black lace jacket and black heels to the ensemble. To blend the colors even more and change the outfit, I added a black sash to wrap around the waist.

In order to let Red go, I've lightened my hair to more of a strawberry blonde that reminds me of the picture I have of Savannah. Small black flowers adorn my braided French twist. No glitz or glamour of jewelry catches the mirrors light because I don't want to waste money on things like that.

After I apply another coat of lip-gloss, I turn the corner to leave the restroom and my stomach drops. Lyric stands there, leaning against the bathroom wall beside the only exit. My eyes take their fill as I assess his worn boots with whitewashed jeans, then up to his black leather jacket that hugs his muscled physique. The dark color brings out his penetrating eyes so well that my knees feel weak. My breathing speeds up to match the pace of my pounding heart and all that I've worked on the past few weeks feels lost.

Tearing my eyes from his all-encompassing frame, I look at the gold-trimmed marble floor. But I can still feel him there, staring and waiting. Does he want me to scream? Does he want to shatter the few pieces I've worked so hard to rebuild? My mind scrambles for any type of escape from this room and him. I can't deal with this shit right now. Not here. I still have to perform and being reminded that I was just a fuck when I thought I was more will definitely cause me to lose every sane thought and climb back into a black void.

Taking a deep breath, I count to calm myself, and straighten my spine. My plan is to walk past him without showing any acknowledgment to his presence. Just as I reach the door handle and pull it toward me, his large hand slams it shut. His warm breath on my hair causes a shiver to run through me. His actions speak only of want. But why? Should I believe he loves me? He's proven he doesn't by abandoning me that night. Trudy and Cory told me that he and Anya/Mandy are together and she's always with him. I don't understand that whole situation, but I'm finished trying to put it together. *I'm done period.*

His hand touches the hair along the back of my skull. "You need to come with me. Now."

More chills creep along the skin of my arms and down my spine, but I'm thankful the jacket hides his effect on me. "Fuck you. I'm not going *anywhere* with you," I ground out while internally cussing myself for letting him know he affects me in any way, pissed or sad. Once again, I pull on the door only to meet more resistance from his strength.

"Dammit, Red. Don't do this. Just come with me and I'll explain it all."

"Will you please stop this? Go back to your life and leave me to live mine. Besides, shouldn't you be with what's-her-face?" Pure bitterness drips from my voice because the thought of him with her makes me want to lose my shit and fuck her up.

My eyes stay on his large hand holding the door in place in front of my face. Memories of how that hand touched me form. He caressed not only my skin, but also my heart, and my demons. Even though the cuffs to his black leather jacket cover his wrist, I *know* the decoration of his tattoos covering his arms. I memorized them as he slept beside me. Touching him at his most vulnerable moments was my way to figure out this man who keeps secrets. Tracing them with my fingers, kissing them with my lips, I cherished every breath he took. Now, however, he's no longer mine to enjoy or love. *"Now move."* My shoulder pushes against the door.

"No. The only way you're walking out that door is with me. You *have* to trust me, Red." His fingers wrap around my arm to pull me way from the door.

Trust him? Is he fuckin' for real? The rage I've kept inside comes to surface and I lose it. He has no right to touch me. No right to be here. My hand slaps his hand away before I turn to face him. *"No,"* I hiss.

Pain explodes when I reflect how another person took advantage of me and how I was stupid enough to fall for his shit. When I remember how he built me up, only to throw me down. Now he wants to come back and walk all over me, again? I don't think so. "No more talking." My palms slam into his chest as I push him away from me .The familiar tears start to build. My throat burns as my enraged misery takes hold. "You had your chance to talk a month ago. I begged like a fuckin' idiot and you did *nothing*." I shove him again. "Nothing. You turned your back on me when I needed you." With all my strength, I shove him one last time and watch as he lands on the couch. It feels so good to release some of this resentment. And even though I see that familiar tick in his jaw, I continue, not giving a shit to his reaction. *"I hate you.* Hate what you represent. A liar. A cheater."

"I've told you things, Lyric. Things I've never *ever* told another person. Not even Benji. I showed you the part of me that I hide from everyone and you turned away from me. *You lied to me.* You chose her and left. My begging wasn't good enough for you. My love for you wasn't good enough. I'm not good enough." Tears leak down my cheeks, but me ruining my makeup is the least of my worries. "I haven't heard a fucking thing from you in a goddamn month. You never even called about me working at Jay's anymore. I didn't exist to you. Now, out of the fucking blue, you show up wanting to *talk? Hell no!* I have nothing to say to you besides this. *Leave me the fuck alone.* I've moved on without your help, so let me live my life without you in it. Because I'm over you." My eyes close to hide the lie from his all-knowing stare.

"Red." He stands and reaches out to me, but I back away. Without another word, I walk out of the bathroom with him on my heels. "Fuck, Red. Listen to me, you stubborn ass woman." He grabs my arm just as we pass the cigar room and everyone's eyes land on us. "We need to leave. *Now.*"

I'm too angry to be embarrassed because I could lose this job over his stupid ass attitude and I need this job.

"No." Pulling at my arm, I try to break free from his grip, but he refuses to let me go.

Sue Ellen, my boss, comes up and looks from Lyric and me. "Blaire, is there an issue?"

"Blaire is leaving so there's not a goddamn problem." He pulls us toward the exit.

Sue Ellen's eyes are wide from Lyric's attitude. Yanking my arm away, I make a decision that will hopefully close this chapter of my life so I can start a new one. "Sue. Call the cops. This guy is harassing me and needs to be arrested." My eyes stay on my boss, but I can still feel Lyric's stare and know he's pissed. A small part cares, but is quickly overrun by the pain he's caused. *Who gives a shit if he's upset? He didn't care when I was.* I just want him to leave me alone and let me live my life while he goes and fucks whatever whore he sees fit.

Marco, the security guard, walks toward Lyric, but I still refuse to watch him be dragged out. The pull I have for him is so strong, I'm liable to follow and do whatever he wants. I don't want to be the girl who needs him, or any other man's desire, to feel valued. I'm better than that. Better than what he knew. I'm not Red anymore. I'm not his. I'm my own person who's learning to make a life without a crutch.

As soon as he's gone from the building, I feel it. I don't know how, but his presence was there, and now, it's not. So I dig deep inside and try to pick myself up. I clean myself up, take a deep breath, and even though Sue Ellen insists I go home, I return to my piano bench. I'm anxious to lose myself in the song once again… to be where I was only a few moments before. Breaking and showing people my weakness isn't what I want. However, I can't seem to escape what just happened and the relapse I'm feeling. I can't escape Lyric. So I leave. I walk out those doors, wanting to hide from everyone.

When I reach the driver's side door, I hear a screeching noise before the sound of squealing brakes. Looking up, I see that same SS I used to drive and Lyric blocking me in before he gets out of the car.

"Get in the car, Red," he commands and I can definitely see how pissed he is even with the dim streetlights.

"Go home, Lyric," I say while opening my door before I jump in the driver seat.

"Dammit, Red. I said get in the fuckin car," he yells.

When I give him the bird, he hits the hood of Janet's truck. *Ass!* I go to put the keys in the ignition but drop the damn things on the floorboard. *"Shit...shit...shit!"* After I lock the door, I reach down and, ignoring the noises outside, blindly search for the tiny mace dispenser Cory bought me to keep on my keys. Most women would probably feel fear when a sexy, tattooed guy blocks her in and demands she go with him, but I'm not most women. I'm just ready to get away from him.

Finally, I feel them and exhale with relief, until I hear a loud crash and glass falls all over me. My ears are ringing but I still hear my own scream. Before I know it, the door opens and I'm being dragged out of the driver's seat. "Let me go." My hands and feet hit and kick, trying to escape his hold. When I'm about to scream for help, his hand covers my mouth before I get the proper amount of air in my lungs.

"Calm the fuck down." He walks around his Camaro, throws me in the backseat, and then gets in and speeds out of the parking lot.

"What the hell are you doing you fuckwad?" I slap his head but he doesn't flinch.

He speeds down Water Street then hits I-10 only to go faster. "I told you. I need to talk to you and your ass is going to listen to what I have to say." He weaves his way in and out of traffic and shifts gears. My heart continues to race from adrenaline and his driving skills aren't helping it either. A heart attack looks to be in my future.

"So you kidnap me? Not to mention, bust out my damn window. Are you freakin' insane?"

His eyes meet mine in the rearview mirror and narrow. "You could thank me. I just saved your life."

My mind has focused on the cost of getting Janet's truck window fixed when his words penetrate my musings. Saved my life? Is this some kind of joke? Then I look at him and know, without a doubt, he's serious. "W-w-what do you mean, save my life?" That's when I hear gunshots hitting the car.

"Get down." Lyric yells and I immediately do what he says. I burrow down in the floorboard and feel every bump the car passes over as well as every swerve he takes.

I'm thrown from one side to the other and my stomach starts to roll from motion sickness. People honk and yell as we speed past them and more blasts come from the passenger side. When glass shatters on me, I scream. I'm in the middle of a fucking *Die Hard* movie, and I've never liked those action films to begin with.

As the pursuit continues, I feel a heavy impact on the driver's side and know whoever is chasing us is trying to run us off the road. Then we spin around so fast, the force slams me into the seats. Lyric continues to drive like a demon, and I'm sure he's forgotten I'm in the car. He never once checks on me, and I'm a little hurt, but way too freaked out to say anything. Finally, I can tell we've lost them because his driving evens out. When he tells me I can sit up, I ignore him and stay where I am.

"Red. Sit up. We're fine now."

After sitting up, I look at him in the mirror. "What the fuck just happened?"

His eyes leave mine and he doesn't say another word. He seems to be concentrating more on speeding down the highway than me. I sit back in my seat, careful to miss the glass and exhale, trying not to lose my shit. Two thoughts run through my head. What the hell am I into and am I going to die?

After a few moments of silence, he finally speaks. "Red. Look at me." My eyes leave the passing night sky to meet his in the mirror. "You're gonna be fine. I promise."

I don't respond. I only sit there in shock, not only from what the hell just happened but also by his presence. I don't need any of this shit right now. I have obligations. There has to be a mistake. Anger sets in and overshadows my initial shock. My eyes narrow as the urge to cry from fury becomes an overwhelming force. "Dammit, Lyric, either answer me or take my ass home. Now. I don't need this shit."

"No. It's too late for that. Don't you see? I need to take you somewhere safe. They were waiting for you." His voice sounds so fucking calm.

I hate it. Hate this whole thing, whatever *this* is. How can he be so damn composed after what just happened? I could have died tonight. How could he or anyone be so damn calm? Or at least any normal person. All of the sudden, actual fear sets in and more questions form. I'm not sure if I want to know the answers but I need to ask .

"They? Who are they? *Who* are you for that matter?" He continues driving away from Mobile, still not answering my questions. "Where are you taking me?"

He breathes heavily, hesitant to respond. His eyes show his internal debate, and I'm terrified he'll shut down and become his usual guarded self. Then he answers my last question, which causes the others to disappear from my thoughts. "To meet your sister."

CHAPTER TWENTY-FOUR

"At the center of your being you have the answer;
You know who you are and
You know what you want."
–Lao Tzu

Lyric

Pulling into an open service station somewhere outside of Birmingham, I stop to fill the car with gas. Red's asleep in the back seat and I don't want to wake her, especially after all the shit that's happened tonight, but this is our last stop before we reach Massey's.

She's groggy, her hair's messy, but she's still beautiful. When she sits up and stretches, I'd love to stare and undress her, but business comes first. I'm not sure if we're being tailed, so we need to keep moving. "Come on. We need food and drinks. If you gotta go to the restroom, do it now. We still have a few hours 'til we're there."

"And where is there exactly?" she asks with pure attitude while stepping out of the back. She ignores my offered hand and continues on her own. Not going to lie, that hurt. She's lost trust in me, but who could blame her.

"Not here. Now hurry."

She gives me the bird and makes her way into the store. I stay completely aware of every person that surrounds us, keeping watch for anything unusual.

When I received word yesterday about a hit on Red, I knew she'd be dead within hours. Sure enough, when I walked into the door of Martini's last night, she was talking to Polesky's nephew, and I knew it wouldn't be long. I don't know how he found out about her, but he did. Pure fuckin fear of reliving my nightmare hit me, and I dropped everything just to get to her before they did.

Confronting her in the bathroom didn't go as I wanted, but I'd expected it after the way I treated her. Like shit. Like a piece of ass I could just walk away from. She doesn't realize I had to force myself to leave that room. Every step out took all my will power and drove a knife between us. If only she had heard me whisper to Anya how much I fucking hated her, maybe she wouldn't be so angry. But she couldn't. I wanted to keep her out of this war until it was over, but I failed. I became attached and fell in love. Now she's in danger because of it.

With Anya's disappearance a few days ago, the dam's broken loose and I've had to consider entirely new outcomes and take new precautions. I don't think she's joined her father and betrayed me. She has too much hate for the bastard. I believe she's become trigger-happy and has gone to find him. Javier followed Polesky's man until he vanished in Gulf Port, Mississippi. After word of his nearness became evident, Anya's eyes lit up with that same malicious look. A few days later, she left, and her phone has since been shut off. She seems to be pretty damn good at her disappearing act.

Hyde has left the house and is doing recon on it now. Cameras surround it inside and out and he watches from a separate location. Jay's isn't open because I don't need Polesky's men coming in and killing innocent people. Tru and Jax are with Hyde, and even though I don't believe Polesky cares about getting to her any more, I can't risk it.

Now I'm taking Red to Massey's in Tennessee. He and his wife took Savannah in when I found her starving to death. We had to pull some strings to keep her out of foster care, but with his connections, Massey was able to do it. When she's safe with her sister, I'm heading back to Mobile to finish what I started.

Red comes out of the restroom and grabs a basket that she fills with every possible candy and soda the store holds. It's so full, shit's falling out of it, and she uses both arms to hold it up from the weight. I can tell she's doing this shit on purpose. After she dumps it on the counter and the cashier bags it all up, she looks at me with narrowed eyes. "Woops! I forgot my wallet."

Smiling in her direction, I pull out my wallet and throw two hundred dollars on the counter before grabbing the bags. "Keep the change." I say to the cashier. When I open the door for Red, her pissed off expression has me wanting to laugh. I forgot how much I loved doing this with her.

The rest of the way, Red sits up front with her bare feet on the dash, ignoring me. She doesn't say a damn word until she falls asleep again. Even though she appears to hate me, I know it's a front. I might've ripped her apart once, but I know she still loves me. She just needs to learn the truth about who I am and what I've gotten her into. I'll wait until after she meets her sister so she might see some good in the demon I am.

As I pull into Massey's long driveway, sunlight dissolves the night and colorful orange and violet shades appear across the sky. The colors spread all over Red's huddled form beside me. Her strawberry blonde deepens to the familiar bright red that matches her dress. Her half sleeve of intricate tattoos cascades in the light and each word and music note is more evident. This woman looks like a decorated she-devil and holds my heart in her hands. She owns me. Every fucking piece of me.

When I shut off the car, the quiet wakes her. Not wanting to get caught staring like some lovesick idiot, I look out the window. The driveway ends at a large piece of vacant property that used to be farmland. A variety of toys litters different spots in front of the two-story, brick and vinyl sided home. A large red door and a wraparound porch accent the front, and a detached three-car garage sits toward the back.

The only other time I've been here was when The Reform first released me. Massey had wanted me to come home with him for a real Christmas before I started pursuing Polesky. He always did look after the boys he came across. And I know he's still fighting to end the program or destroy the current hierarchy of management.

Before walking up to the door, I shoot a quick text to tell Massey I'm here. Red decides to stay in the car and I don't know if it's from fear or nerves. As long as she doesn't run, I don't argue.

The sound of clawed feet hitting the hardwood floors gets closer, followed by heavy footsteps. Massey answers the door, not looking happy to see me. "You know this is a bad idea, right?" He stands in front of me with his back in a straight military stance. I've respected this man and his opinions for almost a decade, but this is not one of those times.

"You know I don't give a shit, right?"

He rubs his shaved head and answers through a yawn. "Yeah… yeah, I know." He looks over my shoulder, spots Red in the car, and gives me an inquisitive brow. "Come on in. Coffee's in the kitchen."

Turning around, I wave for Red to come on, but the stubborn girl shakes her head no. "The only way you're gonna get her in here is by bringing Savannah into view. I've fucked up in the trusting me area of our relationship."

"I'm not surprised." He shakes his head before heading back up the stairs. When he returns, he has Savannah hanging on his hip with her tiny arms clasp tightly around his neck. Her long, strawberry red hair is in disarray, and when her sleepy eyes meet mine, she tucks her head in the crook of Massey's neck. "I've just now got her warmed up to me and Sylvia. She still doesn't talk much, but she's just untrusting." He grabs a warm jacket off the coatrack to cover her small body before stepping outside in the cold winter air. "Vannah, do you remember us telling you about your sister? Well, she's here to see you. Do you want to see her?" Her head nods hesitantly. "Look?" He points to the car and she peeks through the jacket's opening.

Red's reaction as she sees her little sister for the first time is one of pure wonder. I had no clue she knew about her.

Red opens the car door and slowly steps up to the porch steps. I'm sure she's freezing in just her dress and thin wrap, so I take off my leather jacket and place it over her shoulders. She doesn't shy away. The little girl in front of her has her captivated. Blaire's eyes well up with tears and her chest rises in a steadying breath. I'm sure she wants to appear strong, so she doesn't break in front of Savannah.

With my arm still around her, I gently guide her up the steps. Massey steps back inside the house where it's warm, and she follows without hesitation or argument. Savannah's presence is like a beacon of light and Red is the lost ship. As soon as the door closes behind us, Savannah wiggles out of Massey's arms and stands by him in her footed pink pajamas. She looks from Massey to Red as if to ask if it's safe to go to her sister.

Red bends down to the little girl's level, making them equals. "Hi, Savannah." Her voice breaks, but she clears her throat to recompose herself. "My name is Blaire. I'm your big sister. Do you know that?" Savannah nods with wide green eyes. Blaire sticks out her hand. "It's nice to finally meet you."

The little girl walks over and grabs her hand. The terror is evident in both of their eyes as they look at one another. Red's tears refuse to be held back any longer and leak down her cheeks. Before she can wipe them away, Savannah comes up and does it for her. "No cwy, Bwaire. Be happy."

Red holds her little sister's hand against her dampened cheek and gives a smile that is pure stunning. "I'm very... very happy Vannah."

After that moment, the ice is broken and introductions are made. Savannah watches Red's every move and even tries to follow her into the spare bedroom while she changes into some borrowed clothes. Sylvia comes down and makes an amazing breakfast of pancakes, eggs, and bacon, and after we eat, it's time to explain some things to her. With any luck, her trust will return. But it's going to be hard for her, especially after I almost got her killed.

We sit at the country style, wooden table drinking coffee. Sylvia knows the drill so she takes Savannah to bathe while we talk. I can tell our serious expressions terrify Red. We're rigid and on guard because we're breaking all the rules by telling her about The Reform and why I'm in Mobile. I'm just as terrified. I don't know if she'll run further away from me or decide to forgive me.

"I want you to listen to what I'm about to tell you, Red. No questions until after I get done. I won't repeat what I'm about to say, and I would appreciate if you wouldn't bring it up after today." After she nods her head, I tell her about my groupie mother and her abusive boyfriends and about my running away to live on the streets. I tell her about my early stages of fighting and the gangs I was associated with. Then I tell her about Carly. "She was my first love. Creamy Mocha skin. Beautiful light eyes. She captivated me. We met when I was sixteen and she was fifteen. She found me selling shit to her friends, and when I offered to sell her some weed, she refused with sass and turned her back on me. I was intrigued, so I came around her turf just to see her as much as possible, and soon, we formed a relationship. Her father didn't like me and the feeling was mutual. He was a drunk, so you can imagine what she went through. They had a fight one night and he hit her. Needless to say, I made sure he needed dental work. After that, she left with me and we made it together on our own as best we could.

"I started running drugs for the local gangs and eventually got addicted to not only them, but also the money. I was able to rent a one-bedroom apartment that was really a piece of shit, but hey, it was better than freeloading from friends or sleeping in shelters. A few months later, Carly got pregnant. As her pregnancy progressed, so did my addictions, and with that, she started to lose faith in me." I still see that last fight in my mind and it cuts me deep, knowing I was more interested in snorting that last round than comforting her. "We had a huge fight one night, she left, and I proceeded to get high. I remember the feeling of fear and the worry I felt and it surpassed my high. So instead of giving her until morning to cool off like I usually did, I went after her."

Before I can continue, I have to compose myself. My entire body wants to stop thinking, remembering, and talking. "I found her... or her body, anyways. She'd been raped and was bloody from where they slit her throat. I don't remember much after that but seeing her attacker laughing with two other guys and cleaning his knife. They spoke a different language. It was like killing an innocent woman was a fuckin joke. I remember my sorrow vanishing and pure anger taking over. After that, I blacked out with rage and just attacked. My fighting skills paid off I guess because I killed the fuckin bastard with my bare hands after I shot his goons." She doesn't need to know the details of how I bashed his head in by constantly slamming it into the dirty asphalt, but only after I stole his own knife and stabbed him several times.

"That's when I was dragged off his dead body by the cops and they hauled me away for first degree murder. I didn't find out the name of the fucker until a few days later. It was Vladimir Polesky, brother to Nicholas Polesky, a Russian drug lord here in the states. He was in *N'awlins* doin' business for a trade, and the sick fuck liked torturing innocent women." No more words will come out because it's smothering me, but my eyes don't leave Red. We stare at one another and a calmness settles inside me with every second that passes.

"Lyric was taken to trial and found guilty of murder. Not only of Vladimir's, but Carly as well." Massey says and Blaire's eyes widen. "Polesky has always been on the government's radar, and as soon as he found out about his baby brother's death, Lyric only had a number of days until he would end up dead as well. That's when the Reform stepped in. Instead of being hauled to sit in a prison cell, Lyric, as well as other runaway delinquents, were sent to be trained. Not just in weaponry, but in respect and obedience."

"Like military school?"

Massey's brow furrows and he looks down into his coffee cup. "Nothing like military school. The Reform is about building men out of boys, changing future criminals to something useful, and then each are sent on missions when we feel they're ready. Unfortunately, if they show any signs of disrespect, the boys are severely punished, and sometimes killed. No loss for the government. Either way, they rid the world of a possible fuck up. Well, that's how command sees it, anyways."

"Oh, God!" Red covers her mouth and her eyes meet mine. Understanding dawns as she reads them. "You're here for Polesky? Like bait?"

"Exactly like bait. He wants me dead just as much as I want him dead." Looking at Massey, I silently ask him if I should continue or stop. He nods slightly, so I turn back to Red. "When I was released, I was put back in *N'awlins* to draw him in. I fought in the ring to get my name out there. Soon, another local drug leader took me under his wing as his bodyguard, and when the time was right, I had to take his place. Word of Polesky sending a man to Mobile for payback got back to me, so I stayed close and ran my drug shipments from both ports."

Her eyes narrow, and she looks down at her now cold coffee.

"Red, look at me." With hesitation, she does, and I can tell her reaction won't be good after these words leave my mouth. But it's time. "I supply the majority of drugs in Mobile. It was my drugs your brother OD'd on. My runners sold it to him."

Her face loses all color and her breathing becomes erratic. "I don't understand. Y-y-you're some kind of a drug lord?"

"No. I'm acting as a drug lord to draw in Polesky. He's lost his Columbian contacts and I have them. It was only a matter of time before he came, and somehow, he's figured out you're my weakness. He put a hit on you. I tried to keep you out of this when I walked away. But it did no fuckin, good." I reach across the table to grab her hand. "And I'm so... so... so fuckin, sorry, Red. I didn't want this to happen."

She quickly stands and puts her hand up. "Stop... just stop. I can't hear anymore." She takes a shuddering breath. "I can't comprehend any of this or *you* right now." She turns and walks out of the room.

My eyes stay focused on the door she left through, begging her to walk back in. To tell me she believes me and forgives me. But after a full minute, nothing happens and I know I've lost her.

"Give her time, man. She's just had a fucked up night and day," Massey says as he stands up, walks to a kitchen drawer, and pulls out some keys. "Here. Take the bike. You'll get there faster. Besides that, your car looks like shit with all those bullet holes."

"Thanks, man." Forcing out a laugh, I feel every fucking piece of my heart breaking. Without another word, I grab the keys and walk out the door with Massey promising me he'll watch out for both of them until I return. The question is, will she want me even then?

CHAPTER TWENTY-FIVE

"The weak can never forgive. Forgiveness is an attribute of the strong."
-Mahatma Gandhi

Blaire

Watching Lyric leave from the upstairs window, a part of me wants to follow. But the other is happy he's going, even if I don't know exactly why I'm staying with strangers. Everything he told me makes sense in a way, because it explains his private behaviors, and why he didn't hesitate to pull the trigger that night in the alley. However, it all seems too unbelievable. Am I really in love with some undercover drug cartel leader? Is there really a place that trains young boys to be killers? And most importantly, did he sell my brother the bad drugs that took his life? My stomach hurts with that thought and I feel sick.

Stepping away from the large window, I look around the teal and purple bedroom. It obviously belongs to a girl who loves bright colors. Beauty pageant trophies and crowns decorate the white bookshelf along the wall beside the door. Pictures of a happy brunette with braces growing up from elementary to graduation are taped to the mirror along with photos of the entire family of father, mother, and two teenage daughters. Both have dark hair and brown eyes, and are smiling and look completely happy.

Happy? What is that exactly? The last time I can remember

being sincerely happy was when I lived with Lyric. Then my mind sees Savannah and our moment this morning. A smile forms across my face because she does make me happy. The fact that she's here and safe is still a mystery to me, but I'm too exhausted to seek answers right now. And too scared that I'm not good enough to take care of her like she needs. With the weight of the world on my shoulders, I walk to the full size bed with its lime green comforter decorated with purple polka dots and lie down. My mind can't wrap around what happened from last night to this very second. A headache is starting to creep up my neck so I close my eyes hoping to relax. Maybe after some sleep, I'll wake up ready to face the knowledge I learned a few moments ago, and I'll be ready to accept it.

When I wake, it's around lunchtime, so I make my way down the stairs to face the people who took Savannah in and to find out how she got here. Lyric's friend Massey sits on the couch with his computer. He knows exactly when I walk in the room, even if I am hiding against a wall behind him. "Come on in, Blaire."

With hesitant feet, I step around the corner and he closes the laptop. "Where's my sister?" The term still feels weird on my tongue and sounds strange to my ears. *Sister*. Even though I've known for a month now, but I've never spoken it out loud unless I was talking with the lawyer. I never told my new friends or my therapist. We're still not that far into our sessions. The only person I wanted to know was Lyric. But that was the night I found out and he pushed me away. With that thought, another question forms. "Who's Anya? Or Mandy? Or whatever her name is?"

Massey shows no surprise at me asking this. He takes off his wire-framed glasses and rubs the spot between his eyes as if he has a headache. Maybe he's buying time before he answers. I don't know or care. I need to figure this shit out so I can make a plan.

When he does look at me again, I know I'm not going to get much out of him. He has the same closed off look Lyric wears. "That's classified. But I will say this. Stay away from her. She's someone you shouldn't mess with."

Before I can dig for more answers, I feel someone latch onto my left leg. Looking down, I see a smiling Savannah.

"Bwaire," she squeals happily.

Warmth and happiness set in and I smile. "Vannah." When her arms go up, I don't hesitate to pick her up and cradle her to my body. I love the smell of her innocence and youth. The strawberry scent of her hair matches the color. I could hold her forever I think.

"We've told her about you for months. Since we got her really. But we never thought she'd warm up this easily." Massey's wife Sylvia speaks as she brings in four cups of hot cocoa and places them on a wooden coffee table that sits between the brown leather sofa and matching love seat. She pats the seat beside her. "Come sit and relax."

I carry Savannah over and place her down before sitting beside her. "It took her a while to warm up to me and even more so for Scott. I think because he's always gone on business. She was in rough shape and my heart broke for her. After a few meals and hugs, she started to speak some. Nothing big, but two worded sentences. Huge improvement because she never spoke a word, and the only time we heard her voice was when she woke with night terrors."

Too many memories of living in that house with that monster surface. She's just a baby and I pray he didn't molest her like me. If I jump to unnecessary conclusions, I'm liable to break myself from guilt because I wasn't there for her.

Savannah goes to a toy chest against the wall and pulls out several stuffed animals like a happy little girl would. I feel such gratefulness for this couple that took her in. "Can I ask how y'all got her?" Sylvia and Massey stare at one another in silent question, and I know it's classified information. "Okay. Do you know anything about her... her," inhaling deep, I try to gain strength to ask this question while knowing the answer might not be the one I want to hear, "level of abuse?"

Sylvia grabs my hand and squeezes it tight. "Nothing sexual, if that's what you mean. Just emaciated and some long scars across her back. We don't know exactly what they're from, but they were pretty deep and left marks. I'm hoping that, as time passes, they'll fade."

Without having to see the marks, I know what caused them. It's something we share. "Car antenna," My voice is void of emotion. "It was the switch he preferred." Nausea from thoughts of a little girl enduring such abuse takes hold. But I remind myself continuously that she's alive, she's safe, and she wasn't sexually abused.

My attention turns to Massey and a tear rolls down my cheek. It's the only way I'll grieve for my sister while she's present. I want to be strong for her and protect her from the world's evil. "Is the bastard dead?"

He once again shows no surprise from my question and looks me dead in the eye. His hatred is apparent from his stare and the tick in his jaw. "No. He's in a place with people that will show him the same courtesy he showed his children."

My head nods with understanding. Death would be too easy for him. I want him to suffer instead of having a swift death. "And her birth mom?"

"Money hungry bitch and I'm not saying another word." His

tone is final. It's fine, though. I have all the answers that are really important at the moment. His phone goes off so he excuses himself before disappearing into his study.

While we watch Savannah playing, Sylvia tells me about her two girls, Hanna and Michelle, who both attend college in Tennessee. One goes to Vanderbilt and the other University of Tennessee. She's sad because this is her first Christmas without either of them home, but having Savannah has helped. She also tells me how they both had the biggest crush on Lyric when they met him three years ago.

Hearing his name still causes my heart to pick up its pace, but I'm still bitter after all that I've learned. The life he's been holding back on after I opened up about everything I went through growing up. It wasn't easy to tell him those things, to let myself trust someone with not only my body, but also my heart.

And he knew my brother? He sold the heroine to him? Or made money somehow off his addiction. *Ugh! I want to hit him in his goddamn face.* My trust was once again misplaced, and I talked about my brother, how his death affected me. He never showed any sign of knowing him or guilt for what he had done. *Bastard.*

Sylvia studies me for a second. "I see that look, Blaire. I don't know much about the boys from The Reform, but I know they have no control over their own lives. Absolutely none." Then she looks at Savannah and sighs. "But one, we both know, broke the rules for you."

And with those words, she walks out of the room and leaves me having an inner battle of emotions. One is gratitude for what he did for me and the other is betrayal for what he kept from me. Right now, I just don't know which is going to win.

The next few days are quiet and a routine begins. I wake to a snoring Savannah cuddled beside me every morning so I sneak out from under the covers to get in the shower. When I'm done, she's wide-awake so we head downstairs and eat cereal together while watching cartoons. Lucky Charms is her favorite and I can't help but smile. It was Benji's favorite, too. Every day she talks more and more and I learn that she's smart for a four-year-old.

On the third day, snow flurries start, so we head outside to play together. I've had to borrow Sylvia's daughters' clothes because I don't have anything with me, plus they live too far from any clothing stores for me to go shopping. And let's not forget, I have no money with me. The last thought brings Lyric and everything I've learned to my mind. I can't help but worry that he might be in trouble but there's nothing I can do. Hearing Massey on the phone late at night has me believing Lyric is on the other line. I have no proof of this other than my own intuition. Either way, the phone conversations give me peace of mind so I can sleep.

After we head in for lunch and warm up while drinking hot cocoa, Vannah brings up Benji. "Where is he?"

"Um… he died and is in heaven." The words still hurt to say but she needs to know the truth.

Her large eyes meet mine. "Will he come back? Wike you did?"

"Like I did?" I ask. "I never died, Vannah. When someone dies, they don't come back."

"Daddy towd me you were dead. But you came back." Before I question her further, she continues. "How did he die?" She looks at me expectantly and smiles, showcasing her missing front tooth.

What do I say? How do I tell a four-year-old girl the truth about her brother who did drugs and OD'd? My mind searches for anything that she will understand, but nothing comes to mind. I don't want to lie, but I don't want her to know about that ugly side of life. She's going to find out on her own as she grows up. The world is a horrible place and bad things happen that shouldn't. People die who shouldn't and people live who shouldn't. I hate the fact today's world is probably nothing compared to tomorrow's and I can't protect her from it all. I can only shield her today, and the only way to do it is by lying. That's the one thing I've tried not to do since I became tired of being the one lied to all the time. Even that might not be enough, but it's the only way to protect her innocence at the moment.

As I tell her about Benji's love for adventure and how he had a horrible accident that made him hit his head really hard, I think of Lyric. How he lied to me. How he protected me because of those lies. He tried to hide me from the ugliness of his world just like I'm trying to protect Vannah. How can I be mad at him for that, or for sacrificing himself to bring down a truly evil person?

That night, when I lay my head on the pillow, I do something I never thought I'd do again after our mother died. After all those years of asking for help and never getting it, I pray. Pray that Lyric will be okay and for him to know I forgive him. "I love you, Lyric."

A loud crash wakes me from a dead sleep. It's so loud I sit up and Savannah starts to scream, but I cover her mouth quickly. Putting my finger to my lips, I tell her silently to stay quiet. She nods with wide eyes that reflect the moonlight. The floor is cold on my feet and my breaths are foggy. It feels colder now than it did when we fell asleep. So cold my teeth want to chatter, but I know I can't make a noise. Grabbing a robe off the floor, I slip it on for extra warmth while listening for anything coming from another room.

When I feel something slide against me, my heart rate picks up and cold terror sets in until I see Vannah. She grabs my hand and wiggles her finger for me to come to her. When I bend down enough, she cups my ear and whispers, "Fowo me."

Confused about where she's taking me, I follow. She leads me inside the shared bathroom between the two daughter's rooms. The nightlight that normally stays lit isn't on and I'm sure the power is out. Luckily, a window lets in moonlight to help guide our steps. Movement downstairs has my heartbeat speeding up but I continue to let Vannah lead me. She opens the bathroom sink cabinet door and climbs inside. I don't think we both can fit. but I want to make sure she's okay so I bend down and look. She's not there. "Vannah?" I whisper in the darkness.

"Shhhh!!!"

An involuntary smile forms, because she's four and has taken charge in a terrifying situation. Before I know it, I hear the bedroom door slam open against the wall. Without hesitating, I close the cabinet door and step into the walk-in closet. Whoever it is, I refuse to lead them to Vannah.

No voices are heard, only heavy breathing and things being tossed around. My body goes further into the shadows behind the clothes while I pray they won't find Vannah. The bathroom door smacks the wall, and to keep myself from having a panic attack, I count. *1...2...3...*The door to the closet opens. *4...5...6...* The perpetrator steps closer and starts to rummage through the clothes. I scoot back into the far corner. That's when I touch something at my feet. Slowly, I squat down and feel the cool metal of a softball bat. Wrapping my hands around the grip, I lift it up. Even though I'm terrified, I make a decision that if I'm going to die, dammit, I'm going down with a fight.

Just then, the shadowy figure slings the clothes back, revealing me. I haven't had time to raise the bat yet so I swing low, and with all my strength, hit him right in the balls. He yells in pain and lands on his knees. As I pass him, he grabs my foot and brings me down, causing me to lose my grip on the bat.

He starts to climb his way up my body and I kick him but he doesn't stop. My hands automatically claw until he lets go and my nails rip skin. The darkness shadows over his figure and blocks him from my sight, but it's easy to make out his massive size. I'm sure if he grabs me again, I won't be getting away. As I stand, I grab the bat. Before he can get to his feet, I swing like Reggie Jackson and bash him in the head, knocking him to the floor. I don't know if he's dead or unconscious and I don't care either way. Even though my curiosity wants to know who the hell it is, I'm not stupid enough to stick around. I'm just ready to get the hell out of there.

After I open the cabinet, I grab Vannah who's been watching the whole time. We walk out into the hallway and I stop to listen for any noise that seems unusual. Silence greets us and reminds me of a horror movie. I don't know where the Masseys are but I have a bad feeling.

Taking a steadying breath, I latch onto Vannah's hand and we make our way down the steps. My stomach drops when one squeaks from my weight, but nobody comes after us so we continue. When we reach the kitchen, I find the keys to Lyric's car before grabbing jackets from the mudroom.

The snow flurries and wind have picked up so I carry Vannah the rest of the way. When I see the car isn't inside the building, I exhale with relief because I won't have to break in. It's hidden behind it with a tarp covering it.

"Stay here." After I set her down, I begin removing the snow-covered tarp. When I'm done, my arms are burning and tired, but the adrenaline coursing through my body has me hurrying. I manually unlock it with the key, hoping no one hears or sees anything odd, and put Vannah in. Reaching across her tiny body, I grab the seat belt and make sure she's secure.

Before I can finish adjusting the strap, she grabs my hand with her cold fingers. "I scared, Bwaire."

The light is too dim to see her, but I hear the tears and sniffles in her voice and my stomach clenches. All I can do is lie to her once more to help her feel protected. I don't like her sad or feeling unsafe. No child should ever be scared of death like this. "We're gonna be okay. So, don't you worry. Okay?" I can only hope to keep that promise and get her to safety before whoever is still after us comes back. With a deep breath, I crank the car and try to find my way to safety. Try to find my way to Lyric.

CHAPTER TWENTY-SIX

"You changed me. But do you still want me?"
-Lyric

Lyric

At every stop I make on the way back to Mobile, I call to check on everyone and to see what changes have been made. Hyde's position is still secure and there's been no sign of disturbance at the house. You'd think I'd feel better about that shit, but it's actually the opposite feeling that hits. I'm ready for this to be finished. It's not just about revenge anymore. It's about getting out and making a life for myself.

I call Lou and he assures me all is quiet at the warehouse. I still have a bad feeling though. In my gut, something isn't right, but I can't pin it down. So I do the only thing I can do to try to make myself feel better. I call Massey and check on Red and her sister. Every time, it's the same answer. *"Everything is good and quiet."* So I get back on the bike and high tail it down the road.

After parking, I walk up to the apartment door where Hyde is keeping watch, and knock.

"What's the password?" Hyde asks from the other side.

"Fuck you, Hyde. You know it's me." After I give the hidden camera the finger, the door unlocks. Trudy is on the other side with her big ass dog Hero and Sissy guarding her. I bypass all three and grab a shot of whiskey to help me get warm. Riding with no gloves or jacket on is a bitch.

"Is all this really necessary?" Jax asks as he comes down the tiny apartment's hallway.

Leaning against the kitchen counter, I take in the place. It's a pay by the week, furnished with two futons in the living room, a full size mattress in each room, and thick blinds. It also has a washer and dryer because our time here is unknown. It's not the Ritz, by any means. It's not even as good as a Super 8 Motel, but it's safe and discreet. I'm sure he's used to better arrangements.

"Yes." I leave it at that, grab clean clothes, and head to the shower. Afterwards, Hyde shows me last night's surveillance tape. An unknown SUV drove past my house four times but never stopped. The windows are limo tint, so when we zoom in to try and identify the driver or passenger, we have no luck.

"Any word from Ryan?" He was supposed to get Cory out of Janet's earlier last night since I couldn't ask Lou or Javier to do it. They have no clue I'm associated with the government and that's the only way I found out about the hit on Red. Hyde has been listening to certain satellite transmissions since he got here. They're all in Russian, but luckily, he's fluent in the language.

"Last night he called and had Cory at her dorm. Safe."

"Good. Anya?"

He just shakes his head no.

Now time for the hardest part. Waiting.

Two days later, Hyde tells me he has something. It seems my car is on the move and headed south. When he moved in, Hyde thought a tracking system on all of our vehicles would be good as a backup plan, in case we're left behind somewhere by Uncle Sam. You never know when The Reform will be ready to fuck you over, so we try to watch each other's back as best as we can.

Grabbing my phone, I call Massey to figure out what the fuck is goin on. When he doesn't pick up, I try again and again. After the fifth time with no answer, alarm tries to take hold and cloud my senses, but I reason with myself. Now isn't the time for panic. Plus, I don't need to let him know about the tracking device.

"He could be sleeping," Hyde says as he watches the map on one of the many laptops set up on the table.

"Or dead."

"Don't start now, you fuckin pessimist. Let's just watch the car for an hour or so, and then we'll call him back. Massey has the panic room, right?"

I nod my head in answer. He knows too much inside government Intel and could be at risk. He wanted to protect his family from different enemies, so he built it underneath the house where a basement would be. A special venting system can lead you down from any of the rooms if you can't get there by the trap door in time.

"Maybe it's a trap to lead you out. Massey knows what he's doing. I'm sure they're fine."

My mouth stays shut as I pace the worn, carpeted floor the next hour and a half. Dawn bleeds in around the edges of the thick curtains but the car is still heading south. With tension in my body, I dial Massey's number.

Nothing.

Somehow, Massey has been overrun or he's turned his back

on me. I know for a fact my car isn't there. It's on I-65 south. Nobody can find the tracking device and remove it. It's in the fucking gas tank. My one thought is getting to Red. I'm confident it's her driving this way and I'm not sure how much fuel is left or if she has any money.

After hanging up the phone, I look at Hyde. "Keys." He gives them to me without hesitation. My fury I can deal with. It's one emotion I'm used to. But the fear I've experienced very few times in life is the emotion I'm focused on. "If she stops anywhere, let me know. Got it?"

I don't wait for an answer. I grab an extra Berretta 92FS and some extra mags for it and my Glock. I slam out the door, not giving a shit about Polesky or any other threat who might be watching me. Red's safety is the only thing on my mind. After I get her in my arms, I'll worry about revenge. Not a moment before.

Another hour passes with the car traveling before it comes to a stop somewhere on the side of the main highway. When it stays exactly where it's at for an hour, I'm sure she's out of fuel. It takes me another three hours to reach the coordinates Hyde sends me. I find the shot-up Camaro parked at a rest area, and when I look inside, it's empty. I wait outside the ladies' room, positive Red is in there. And with any luck, Savannah is with her.

As an older woman exits the restroom, I stop her. "Excuse me. Are my wife and daughter inside? Both have strawberry blonde hair. The little girl is about four-years old."

She looks skeptical at first, but finally answers. "Oh, yes. Y'all must have had a long trip to still be in your pajamas." Then she leaves and my heart starts to slow. It *was* Blaire driving and she's here. Safe.

Not caring about the rules, I walk into the tan, ceramic tiled bathroom and stop to listen. Not a sound. As I search out my surroundings, the large mirror to my left reflects the bathroom stalls to my right, and I look for feet but none are visible. "Red." Her ass better be here because I don't know where else to look.

Scuffling noises from the large handicap stall reaches my ears so I head towards it. "Red. It's me."

Then, like an angel in a large coat and rubber boots, she emerges from the stall. "Lyric? H... how'd you know we were here?" She walks up to me, her hair in a messy ponytail and her eyes tired and wide with fear.

When she's within arm's reach, I pull her to me in an embrace that I don't want to end. Thoughts of her in harm's way plagued my brain while I drove to find her, and now that she's here in my arms, I'm scared to release her. But we're needed back in Mobile. "Is Savannah with you?"

She turns her head to look back toward the stall. "Vannah. It's okay, baby." When her sister runs to her side, she immediately unwraps herself from my arms to pick her up. Two sets of hazel green eyes full of trepidation land on me for answers. "What's going on?"

"I'll explain it on the way." I lead them out to Hyde's car and load them up.

After a quick stop for some fuel and food, we're once again on the road. Savannah sleeps most of the way, but every once in a while, she wakes to make sure Red is still with her. While she's out, Red tells me what happened and how she's scared Massey and Sylvia are dead.

"They could be in the panic room." I try to ease her fears.

"Panic room?" Her eyes land on me.

"It's a room he had built for safety. They could have hidden in there."

I ask her question after question about what she heard or saw, but unfortunately, it's not much. She only remembers a loud clattering woke them from sleep, the power being out, and seeing one man dressed in black that she hit with a bat. Supposedly no gunshots or screams were heard, but she admits her mind was on getting Savannah to safety. She doesn't remember an unusual car in the driveway or anyone following her.

After walking into the apartment, Trudy helps Red get Savannah settled. Hyde pulls me to the side and tells me that there was some movement last night at the house. No cars were seen on the road, but video shows people coming in through the backyard and looking through the windows.

"That's it? That's all you special operatives, or whatever the fuck you are, have after three damn days of keeping us holed up in some unknown apartment with no fucking connections to the outside world?" Jax ridicules from behind me. "That could be some perverted teens or neighborhood punks."

When my narrowed eyes meet his, I stalk toward him. My mind is brought back to my first encounter with this clean-cut pretty boy. I was ordered to get close to Trudy so I tried dancing with her, but I didn't expect a pretty boy to come pick a fight with me when I did it. We were nose to nose until Ryan intercepted me from breaking him.

Ryan's not here now. "If you want to leave, then get the hell out," I growl, fed up with babysitting. A fucking tidal wave of resentment has struck me. "The one person I take orders from isn't around right now. So I don't give a shit about protecting you or anyone else besides Red and that little girl."

"This whole thing is a shitty-ass joke. Either that or you two are out of your damn minds."

"Then *leave*." My breathing is labored as my fist clenches on my sides. I'm ready to hit somebody, and if Jax wants to be it, then I'm okay with that.

"Trudy." Jax hollers while his eyes stay trained on mine. "Let's go."

"No, Jax. I'm staying."

I can't help but smile like the sonofabitch I am when I see his stupefied expression.

"What?" he asks with disbelief and faces her.

"I'm staying, Jax. *We're* staying. Blaire has been through enough shit, and so has that little girl." Her usually happy expression vanishes and a very pissed female emerges. "So someone in this goddamn room is going to explain everything to us." Her eyes land on Hyde and me. "Aren't you?"

I give Hyde a questioning look, waiting for him to agree to blow protocol once again. I'm not just ruining my cover but his as well.

He smirks and rubs his palms together. "Why the hell not? Anything to ruin that fucking place I'm game for. Plus, if Massey is out, then we're basically non-existent to them. He's the one who kept tabs on our asses."

He's right. Massey was our one connection with The Reform. Our *only* connection.

That night Jax and Trudy are still around after we tell them who and what we are. Trudy is in disbelief her ex was involved in the Russian cartel. As she holds Jax, I can't help but think of Red in the other room. She didn't want to hear any of it again, so she decided to keep her distance. Who could blame her? The girl has been shot at and attacked in less than a week's time. On top of that, she's met her long lost sister.

Without thinking of anything other than making it better, I stand from the chair I'm straddling and make my way down the hall. The closet light is on and shines on two matching redheads lying cuddled together on the bed.

"You can stop staring," Red whispers. She's lying on her side with her back facing me. Savannah is wrapped horizontally across her body. "I've had enough creepiness to last me a while."

Walking over to the bed, with my heart pounding, I take advantage of this moment. "Can I sit, then?"

"Do what you want. You always do." Her words are bitter and cut me deep. I deserve them though. To her, I do what I want, but in reality, I do what I'm told.

She is the only thing I've wanted and took for myself. She has to know that before this goes any further, before her bitterness turns to hate. I need her to trust me again. I just *need* her. My arms slide under Savannah's small body before I carry her to Trudy, who happily takes her from me. When I turn, Red remains in her previous position, so I lock the door.

Kneeling beside the bed, I'm prepared to beg her to forgive me. "Please, look at me?" My head is bowed because I'm terrified of seeing hate in her eyes. She's had everyone who was ever supposed to love her, betray her and I'm no different. The bed squeaks with her careful movements and relief washes through me.

"I know you've lost all trust in me. I've fucked up. *I'm fucked*

280

up. There's no excuse for hurting you. You don't deserve this shit. But you weren't supposed to happen. You weren't supposed to walk in and conquer my every thought. But you did. You changed everything about why I was there. I wasn't there for revenge or a mission anymore. I wasn't there to be a government-issued vigilante. I was there to find you, protect you, and love you. And I *did* find you. I *do* love you, but I couldn't protect you. I'm so sorry Red... or Blaire... or whoever you want to be." I finally look up in her eyes and plead. "I'm sorry."

She slowly sits up, her eyes never leaving mine. As much as I want to touch her, I stay in my kneeling position. I want her to take control for once. Either tell me to get the fuck out or forgive me. I'll do whatever she wants.

"This past year has been so fucked up. First, living without my brother. Next, living to damage people because I was so bitter and full of hate. Pure hatred. Then Janet. I've never been a tough person, and I've always needed someone to take care of me, make decisions for me. They were my crutches in life. I was so naïve and stupid at times. I believed my brother walked on water, and what he did to himself every day was okay because of what I put him through." She wipes away a tear and my fingers dig into the mattress to keep them from reaching for her.

"I know you had no choice in lying to me. I understand that. But what I don't understand is why you wouldn't leave me alone. Every turn, you were there." She tilts her head and touches my cheek while looking down at me. "Now I do. I couldn't stay away from you either. I could have left town or stayed with Janet from the get go, but deep down, I wanted to be with you. You made me feel different. Wanted... beautiful. Normal." She pulls her hand away and leaves coldness to replace its warmth. "I just don't want you to be another crutch, Lyric."

I close my eyes as dread sinks in from her words. This is it.

She's pushing me away. When I feel her soft lips on my cheek, I know it's a kiss goodbye. "I'm sorry."

She kisses my cheek once more. "I want you to be my everything." She kisses lower toward my mouth. "My equal." *Kiss.* "My lover." *Kiss.* "My friend."

When her lips settle on mine, my hands grab hold of her tear-streaked cheeks to keep her close. I heard her words, but I still can't believe them or understand why she's not kicking my ass out. I won't question it though. I'll count my blessings and never lie to her again.

Red's hair cascades across my naked chest when I wake to a loud knock on the bedroom door. An urge to tell whomever it is to fuck off takes hold because I want to stay right here and make love to her like I did last night. It was slow and unrushed. It was sweet and pure vanilla. It was about her and only her. Pleasing her and showing her how much she means to me. Then Hyde yelling my name brings me back to reality. *Dammit.*

"What?" Yanking the door open, I don't give a shit I'm butt ass naked. He throws my phone to me. The serious look in his eyes puts me on guard. I step back into the bedroom and shut the door, and when I read Massey's number on the screen, I answer. "Yeah."

The thick accent on the other line is not who I expect it to be and is definitely not Massey. "Mr. Devereux, I'm rather tired of the games. It's time for a face-to-face meeting. Would you not agree?"

"Where's Massey?" I ignore his question and ask about my friend.

"With his wife and young daughters, who are both very

beautiful and *innocent,* I might add. The youngest especially could bring me in *mnogo deneg.* Now, Mr. Devereux, it's your call. Should I shoot your friend now and set a trade with one of my partners, or do you want to meet?"

"When?" I ground out while imagining my fist slamming into this sick fucker's face.

"Tonight. At that nice bar you always seem to be at. Jay Jay's I believe is the name. Open it back up. Let the crowd in. I'm in the mood to celebrate." He laughs and I'm about to push end just to shut him up, but he calls my name. "One more thing. Bring my daughter. I believe a family reunion is long overdue." He hangs up and I'm wondering how the *fuck* am I going to get Anya here.

CHAPTER TWENTY-SEVEN

"Courage is simply the willingness to be afraid and act anyway."
-Robert Anthony

Blaire

Something is wrong. He's angry and tense, but he's trying to hide it. I know from the tick in his jaw. The old me wouldn't ask because I know he's secretive, but the new me, the new us, is all about being honest. "What's wrong?"

"Nothing," he says automatically while pulling on his jeans.

"Lyric, no more lies. I know something is wrong so spill it." Sitting up, I hold the sheet to my naked flesh.

He looks as if he's about to speak, but before he can say anything, a very hyper Savannah runs in and jumps in bed with me. She hugs me tight and tells me all about the funny pancakes Jax made her for breakfast. I look up from her excited face and see relief in Lyric's face and know he's glad for the distraction. "I'll explain after we've all eaten so we can brainstorm. K?" He gives me a smirk as the look in his eyes beg me to drop the subject. So I do. For now.

Vannah is dressed and settled in front of the TV to watch cartoons before I sit in Lyric's lap with Hyde, Trudy, and Jax looking to him for answers. He tells us about the phone call this

285

morning from Polesky and the threat he's made on Massey and his family. Then he tells us of the party at Jay's and that Polesky wants Anya there.

"That's good, right? Y'all have him at an advantage. Your bar. Your territory," I say. "Surely he wouldn't kill a bunch of innocent kids. Right?"

"He'd enjoy putting a bullet in everyone's head, young or old. I'm telling you he's that demented and sick," Lyric says from behind me. "I still don't know how he got Massey, but it's not worth worrying about right now. We need a plan."

"Maybe Anya can talk to him. Maybe he only wants her to come back," Trudy says while listening intently beside Jax on the futon.

"Anya is missing."

Hyde sees my surprise when his words reach my ears. "What?"

He nods his head. "She's been gone for over a week now. So if he only wants her, then he's shit out of luck."

"And we're fucked." Lyric's deep voice vibrates against my back and his arms tighten around my waist.

I sit there, thinking of the situation and what needs to be done. "Y'all can't contact *friends* that will help? People you trust to have your backs? People like you two?"

"Massey was our only contact with The Reform. It's not like the military. We can't just call buddies up for help. We have no contact with any of them unless we're put on same case. Like Hyde and me."

"I can go. Lyric and I both have the same training." Hyde volunteers. "But I won't be able to watch the surveillance videos for anyone trying to fuck us over. And we need eyes on the building. We don't know how many of Polesky's men will be there, but I'm sure it's going to be a shit load. He never travels light."

"Mason is good with computers," Trudy says.

"Absolutely not. I'm not bringing my family into this shit, Tru. I'd rather neither of us be here as it is. So Mason, Jazz, and Fin are out." Jax yells.

Lyric nods his head. "I agree with Jax. No more civilians need to be involved."

"Actually, he wouldn't need to do anything but watch screens and report to us through a microphone and ear piece. No action. No identity involved." Hyde looks between Lyric and Jax. "It would make a big difference to have an extra gun at Jay's and extra eyes here."

"Ryan is a tough fighter. Bring him in," Jax says.

"Then that would be bringing someone in direct contact with the enemy. Ryan is unpredictable, and fighting in the ring is different from fighting for your life." Lyric sits quiet for a few minutes while we all try to figure out what needs to be done. Then he stands and places me on my feet before grabbing his phone and shooting a text to someone.

"Want to fill us in on who you just texted?" Hyde asks before I can.

Lyric doesn't say anything until after he gets a reply. His bleak face morphs into his sneaky sideways smirk and his eyes shine with amusement. "Seems we got some extra guests for tonight's party. I'm sure Polesky won't be anticipating the Knight family making an appearance."

Hyde's eyes widen before he smiles. The whole one-eighty of emotions confuses me even more

"Who?" I ask.

"Just some *business* partners who owe me a favor."

Understanding takes hold. Business as in *not the legal kind*. "Now that we have help, that still leaves us with one problem." They all look at me like I'm crazy. I roll my eyes. "Anya? Hello? What are we going to do about her?"

Lyric looks at me. He's scrutinizing every part of my face and body. Then he says something I'm not prepared to hear.

"You."

One box of brown hair color later, I'm closer to looking like Anya but still feeling like a ball of nerves.

Lyric, Hyde, and I head to his house to prepare. I have the dress from our New Orleans trip and some makeup there. As I apply the last bit of smoky eye shadow, I look at the dark brunette in the mirror and let Lyric's words run through my head while I prepare for the night.

I will protect you.

Stay at a distant table.

You know her mannerisms and know how she carries herself. No one will suspect a thing. People will have your back the entire time. I promise.

We decide my hair needs to stay down to guard my face from Polesky's watchful eye, so here I am. Dressed, ready, but not ready. My body needs Lyric so I exit the master bedroom and go look for him. When I see the mysterious bedroom door ajar, I slowly walk up to it before knocking. After Lyric opens the door, his eyes assess my new look and a whistle comes from behind him.

"Damn, Blaire. You look hot as a brunette."

"Um… thanks Hyde," I say while bouncing on the balls of my feet.

"I still miss the red. But I love you no matter what color your hair is," Lyric says before giving me a wink.

My smile is instant as his words sink in. That's the second time he's mentioned love to me, and even though our circumstances are fucked up right now, that one word has helped settle down my anxious fear. When my arms wrap around his waist, his warmth and scent surround me. When his arms don't wrap around me like I expect, I pull back only to see a huge-ass gun in each hand. "Where the hell did you get those?"

"My artillery room." He smiles and nods his head for me to look behind him. "Come on. I need to get you fitted."

He leads me into the third bedroom that only has two file cabinets against the white walls. Noise from the closet grabs my attention so I look over and take in all the different knives, ammo, and guns lining it from floor to ceiling. "Why do I have a feeling when you say fitted, you're not talking about clothes?"

"Lift your skirt." Lyric bends down and waits for me to do as he says. But I don't. "Lift your skirt, Red. I need to check this holster and gun's placement."

"Gun? Me?" I squeak out and step away from him in surprise.

"Yes, you. I'm not letting you do this without something for protection. And didn't you say you took lessons?" He grabs me by the waist and pulls me toward his body again. He raises my skirt enough to show my upper thigh then straps something against my skin.

"Y-y-yeah. But that was shooting a target. *In pants.*" He

ignores my rant and continues doing whatever it is he's doing. Then he pulls the strap so tight it pinches my skin. "Ouch you dick... that hurt." I swat the back of his head but it doesn't deter him.

"It needs to be tight so it doesn't fall off from the gun's weight." He finishes adjusting the garter holster and I can hear Hyde snickering in the closet. Who knew he had a personality? "Now, which are you more comfortable with? Revolver or automatic?"

"I've shot both. But I used to have a revolver." Before I know it, a 38 revolver hangs on my upper left thigh. It's strangely scary and exciting at the same time. Lyric and Hyde check ammo, grab guns, and tuck away a few big knives. As each second passes, I start to feel like a bad ass, like someone who can go up against a Russian drug lord and kick ass. But then once we finish loading up the car, that adrenaline-induced reaction vanishes. The nerves start kicking back in and I'm a jittery wreck.

What the hell am I doing?

That question runs through my brain as the place opens up for whatever is in store tonight. Even as I sit at a vacant table, it's there. As people pass and pay me no mind, I suddenly need a drink. Then I see Chris behind the bar and I forget about the drink.

"Um... Mouse? What's with the look?" he asks while cleaning glasses.

Leaning in close so nobody hears me, I look him in the eye. "Chris, tonight I'm not Blaire. Don't ask. Just keep the shotgun under the counter close."

Turning, I head back to my table without the drink, hoping he doesn't think this is some joke. I don't know what is going to happen, but I wouldn't be able to live with myself if I didn't at least try to save my friend.

Once I'm settled, I observe the unusual crowd surrounding me. Most are dressed in casual jeans and shirts, but a few stand out in sports coats, pleated slacks, and ties. My ritual of counting starts as I concentrate on the music playing in the background. But my brain can't focus on anything for too long because I'm so restless.

How do I know the good guys from the enemy? The only person I recognize besides Chris is Lyric until I see Cory's ex-boyfriend walk in with some new blonde arm candy. When he looks my way, I cast my eyes down at the table, praying he doesn't recognize me.

"You're acting scared. Remember, Anya isn't scared." Lyric's warm whisper in my ear fills me with calm. "I got you, baby." He kisses my cheek before disappearing into the crowd.

He's right. I'm not Red or Blaire tonight. I'm in disguise. I'm Anya fucking Polesky, and I own this bitch. My posture straightens as I sit erect in my chair. Turning slightly, I cross my legs, and just like that, I feel different, sexy, and strong. *Ready.*

A good-looking guy with black hair and intense blue eyes places a glass of red wine in front of me as he sits down across from me. He's one of the customers who seems overdressed, but who am I to talk. I'm wearing a black Vera Wang dress that deserves to be at a Red Carpet event instead of a grungy bar.

Smiling in true Anya/Mandy form, I tell the guy thank you while wrapping my hand around the stem of the glass with feminine grace.

"You're very welcome, Ms. Polesky," he says with a wink. "Name's Cole. Cole Knight."

Understanding takes hold. He's part of the plan, not the bad guy. Part of the Knight family that Lyric called early this morning. My body relaxes just a bit from at the thought. "Mr. Knight. What makes you think I like red wine?" My voice is seductive just like hers would be on a job. Cool and strong. I remember all the nights I watched as my tutor seduced men. How she watched them… studied them… used them. I need to be her.

"Because I hear Anya Polesky loves anything that looks like blood."

"That she does." Lifting the glass to my lips, I savor the pungent yet sweet taste that brings me back to my time with Mandy… Anya… whoever she is.

"Actually, Lyric sent me over. He wanted me to reassure you that you're in good hands." He folds both hands on the table. "See. And they're talented too… Just sayin'." He smiles with pure cockiness before he leans in. "But really… I'm ready to give lead poisoning to any asshole that looks at you wrong. Just say the word."

"I will. Thank you." We sit there in silence and study the ever-present crowd. He discreetly points out who's part of the Knight family and playfully tells me not to shoot them. When my wine is almost gone, I decide to be brave. "So, who are you and how do you know Lyric?" The guy I've fallen in love with still has too many mysteries and I want to discover them all.

He grabs a glass of amber liquid from a passing waitress. "I already told you the answer to your first question, and as for the second, let's just say we do *business* together." He drains his glass and smacks the waitress's ass when he's done.

Point taken. So instead of any more questions, my fingertips circle the rim of the glass. Lyric passes several times to check on me or kiss my cheek. Plus he gives Cole evil looks that only cause him to laugh as Lyric walks away.

When Cole straightens his jacket after sitting up, I know things are about to get real. "Looks like good ol' daddy's here."

My heart rate picks up as the reality of the situation hits me. I take a deep breath, ready to look at the man Lyric hates so much, but Cole shakes his head no. "Why?" I ask, not understanding his reasoning.

"Don't let him see you until Lyric is ready. He'll give me the signal, then I'll let you know. Let the fucker sweat. He might want to kill her, and if you're her, at the moment that means you're dead."

It makes sense, so I do as he says. I'll wait and try to stay calm. Keeping my cool, I watch Cole's face as if I'll be able to see what's happening. "What are they doing?" I ask with a fake smile plastered on my face.

"Sitting at a table," he says vaguely.

"Is anybody with him?"

"Yeah. One of his guards and another guy who's sportin' one helluva black eye."

"What about Lyric? Is he okay?" The noise of the crowd is overpowering. My head is starting to pound from the tension, and my worrying isn't helping either. My hands rest on the table and my nails dig into my palm.

"He's fine." His blue eyes land on mine. "Relax. My boys are close by, so don't worry. He's in good hands."

"Easier said than done. I've never been one to relax, and this shit isn't helping."

"Well, smile and get it together because it's show time."

Seductively I reach up and bring my hair over one of my shoulders to obscure my face before turning around slightly in my chair. That's when I see Lyric's nemesis sitting across the room in his expensive tailored suit. A black goatee decorates his slender face, and his dark hair is neatly slicked back. He gives me no indication that he doesn't believe our ploy before turning back around. Lyric seems to be relaxed, so my eyes move over to the big guy. He's standing by the table, mean mugging everyone who gets close, wearing a long, black trench coat. Beside him is the guy with a black eye. It's Massey, sitting beside Lyric in the booth with his back straight and hands on the table. When I look past the black eye, that's when I see scratch marks.

CHAPTER TWENTY-EIGHT

"Love alone is worth the fight. Freedom is just a bonus."
-Lyric

Lyric

As I set up extra cameras around the bar, I keep my eyes and ears open. Hyde's linked into Janet's older security system, and with the added cameras, Hyde will monitor every inch of the place from the hotel. He'll keep me posted of anything suspicious through the earpieces Cole and I are wearing. Both will be listening to every comment made throughout tonight's exchange. But Hyde is the only one I'll hear on my end. I turned Cole's microphone piece off. I didn't need the distraction of Red's voice, or Cole's ass flirting with her just to piss me off. I need to focus on what needs to be done and then I'll kick his ass if I need to.

The larger the crowd becomes, the tenser I grow. People have really packed in tonight even though we reopened unannounced. No concerts or live performances are on the schedule. Only live action and some fatalities, and with any luck, no innocent people be killed or be injured. The Knight crew has flown in a dozen men to help tonight and they will keep their eyes open and guns down until I say so. And even though Cole Knight and I both like to make our own rules, he's aware that tonight, I'm in charge.

Lou, Javier, and Joe are here, along with some of my men

from the cartel side. Joe brought in some of his *waitresses*. Most of them are part of some biker association that usually hangs at The Hole. They know how to handle themselves when it comes to bar fights and violence. Plus their men are here as well, watching and waiting.

Now I sit across from the monster I've despised for almost a decade. He's within arm's reach but, to make sure tonight goes smooth without people dying, I need to play it cool. And that means keeping my eyes off Red while she sits with Cole. Even though he's aware she's mine, I also know he takes what he wants and that isn't helping one fucking bit.

"So, Mr. Devereux, this little war between us has dearly cost us both. Me... my brother, you... your son and beautiful fiancé. Wouldn't you agree?" His thick Russian accent brings me back to that night in the alley. His features remind me of his brother and I'd love to do the same to him. But I restrain myself. "And in light of all the deaths, I don't see why we don't have a... a... What's the word? Truce? Yes... yes, truce, to finally put an end to all the killing."

I just stare at him from across the table, not answering. He snaps his fingers and the gorilla on his left reaches into his trench coat.

My hand immediately reaches for the guns that rest on my left side under my leather jacket. "I wouldn't fuckin' do that if I were you." My warning gains their attention.

Polesky only smiles as Gorilla continues. "It's a peace offering." He takes the bottle of liquor and places it on the table. "One of my favorites. Stolichnaya Elit is a rarity to taste. It's not like these imitators you Americans like. This is vintage Russian vodka. Worth dying for." He sneers and waves over a blonde waitress with dark roots. She's older, but smiles flirtatiously all the same. Polesky doesn't return it. "Two glasses. Chilled."

I feel Massey's eyes on me, but keep mine on Polesky. I don't need to look at him to know he's showcasing a black eye and some other non-fatal wounds. Other than that, he seems okay. I didn't see his family come in and that worries me. For all I know, they're already dead. "So tell me what you want, Polesky, for Massey and his family to be released? I know you. You don't show your face for nothing."

Just then, the waitress brings over two frosted glasses. Polesky brings out a cigarette and lights it, deliberately taking his time answering. "Right now, I want to drink," he says and once again snaps. His Gorilla comes to pour us both a great amount of his *peace offering.*

Since he wants to take his time, I decide to ruffle their feathers. "Must be nice, having your own personal bitch at the snap of your fingers," I say as his gorilla recaps the bottle. His eyes meet mine for a stare down but he quickly goes back to his post.

Polesky laughs from the insult just delivered to his guard. I feel eyes on us from all parties involved in tonight's meeting and I'm sure they're wondering why he's laughing so hard. The gorilla says something in Russian and Polesky answers him the same way.

"English," I demand to show my ignorance to their conversation. But I know what was said because Hyde is translating in my ear. Gorilla wants to put a bullet in my skull and Polesky promised him he'd get his chance. But I continue to play a dumb American for him and his monkey. "If you're in my bar, you speak English."

"My apologies, Mr. Devereux. I forget that my language is too intense for you Americans." He raises his overflowing glass. "Now, let us drink so we can get down to business, shall we. To peace." He toasts before tossing back the clear liquid.

"To peace." I repeat to placate him while listening to Hyde as

297

he keeps watch on the building. Seems at least thirty of Polesky's men are standing around, some outside the building while the others are inside.

He waits until I put down my drink before getting down to business. "Now... you have something I want back. I want my daughter to come home where she belongs. She's been gone too long and her dear mother misses her very much. It's that simple."

"Where's Massey's family?" I ask. I don't believe it's that simple. Nothing ever is.

"Where's Anya?" he counters.

Turning, I nod my head in Red's direction where she sits with Cole. Her back is to us, so after Cole tells her to, she turns. I watch as they make eye contact, and thankfully, her hair obscures her face like we discussed. I turn my eyes away from her and watch Polesky's reaction, hoping he buys it. Because I don't know what is going to happen if he doesn't. Finally, after a minute, he looks at me but gives nothing away. "Who is the man with her?"

"Collateral damage. You fuck me over, he has a gun ready to kill her." He doesn't speak, only nods and steeples his fingers. "Now, what about Massey's family?"

"They're outside with my men. Collateral damage." He winks and takes another drink before sitting back. Once again, he snaps his fingers, but Gorilla doesn't move. I guess his cue is from the hand Polesky rubs him off with. After a minute, another guy in a similar trench coat walks up with an iPad and hands it to Polesky. He turns it in my direction to show the video of Massey's family. They're inside a grungy van on their knees, hands tied, with pillowcases over their heads. Men on either side of them have rifles, ready to take them out with a signal. Polesky turns the device for Massey to see how his family is being treated, but training has taught him how to mask his emotions and that's exactly what he does. Nothing. Just the same face I saw earlier.

"How do I know that's not a recording?"

"Do you really want to ask that question, Mr. Devereux?" I give a nod of my head because, for all I know, that was yesterday and they're dead somewhere. He pulls out his phone and makes a call. "It seems I'm a liar. Bring me proof of the girls." He hangs up and turns the monitor once again in my direction. "You asked."

Massey's leg twitches under the table. He knows as well as I do that something bad is about to happen. And it does. When one of his men brings out a pair of wire cutters, I know what's about to come. Face placid, I watch as another one of the Polesky's men holds the youngest daughter's hands steady as the another proceeds to cut off her pinky finger. My stomach drops as Red's face enters my mind. I can't imagine what Massey is feeling at this moment as her tortured shrieks enter our ears. She bucks, trying to get free, but she's no match for the man who holds her still. Finally, she goes limp from the pain and passes out. Nobody seems to have heard anything because the music is blasting loudly and drowned out her screams.

If I could take out the fucker right now, I would. But the girls would be dead within seconds. So I take what I can and brace myself for what's to come. Ten minutes pass before someone brings the finger to me in a box. My mind scrambles to think of a way to get someone to that van before it's too late.

"See. I'm not a liar," Polesky says with a grin. "In fact, I'm a very generous man to only cut off her pinky. I could have done her thumb or entire hand instead, and made living a lot worse for her."

"So, how do you want to do this? You bring them in or drive the van up front for one of my boys, and I give you Anya?" I'm tired of the small talk and ready to kill this sonofabitch, get Massey's family back to him, and live my life with Red.

"Well, that depends on you, Mr. Devereux. You have two options. I will let your friend's family go with your men *if* you agree to marry my Anya and we unite our two businesses." He smiles and wags his bushy black eyebrows. "You get a beautiful wife, lots of fortune, and this war will be over. I'll forgive you for killing my brother, even. A man like you is what I need in charge of the business when I'm gone. Strong, clever, good at what you do. Marrying Anya will be good for you."

"And what's the second option?" I ask, showing no interest in the first, which results in insult. But hey, I really don't give a fuck.

His smile falls as he takes in my unresponsive features. "Second one is not as good. I walk out with Anya and I let go of only one of your friend's family. That's it." He slams his fist on the table as his angered face turns red. "Now which will it be? But be smart because I won't offer this again. You say no and the trigger is pulled."

As my hands rest in my lap, I allow my face to look contemplative. With careful movements, I reach under the table, wrapping my hand on the grip of the gun held under the table by a magnet. But before I can blow his ass to hell, a giggling, drunken blonde stumbles her way over to our table and falls straight into Polesky's lap. Then hell breaks loose.

In slow motion, Polesky's face morphs from anger to disbelief to pain. At first, I'm not sure if she landed on his junk or not, then Gorilla goes to grab her away, and that's when her arm comes up. I see the glint of a knife right before she slits his throat. Gunfire and chaos erupt around me, but my eyes stay focused on the blonde as she grabs Gorilla's gun out of his jacket and shoots the guy in a trench coat headed her way.

As people run past our table, I jump out and come in direct contact with a Russian thug. His gun stares me in the face, but I swiftly grab his wrist and twist it into until he drops it and I hear a pop. My head slams into his skull, and he drops to the floor. My eyes focus on Polesky just as he stands from the booth. Blood steadily spreads on his white shirt, and he stumbles just a bit. I start in his direction, but he grabs his phone and yells, "Kill them," to whoever's on the other end.

"Hyde. Where's the van parked?" I yell into the mike connected to my earpiece. A fist comes my way, but I duck my head. Grabbing the guy's head, I slam it into the wooden beam beside me and keep moving.

"It's not around the building," he says. "Hold up. I see Polesky's men running toward the public parking lot at the corner."

As much as I want to stay and finish Polesky right now, I need to get the van cleared for Massey. *Massey?* I look where he was a moment ago, but don't see him, so I continue through the crowd. Even though most people have exited the building, a lot of people remain inside. Everywhere I pass, people are either running away or fighting. I watch as Pete smashes his fist into someone's face before lifting a chair to slam into another one advancing on him.

"Where's Red?" I ask Hyde.

"Fuck if I know. Too many damn people and now she doesn't standout like before. And bro, cops aren't too far out. Reports are blasting the airwaves."

"Fuck the police. Just find her, and let me know as soon as you do." My eyes finally find Massey, but he's too far away. If he's headed to the van, I'm not sure he's going to make it in time. *Red. I gotta find Red.*

When I see Cole, she's nowhere around him. He's kicking some guy in the throat before grabbing his head to twist his neck forcefully. The guy falls into a crumpled heap on the floor.

I run in his direction. "Where's Red?" I yell over the screams and music still playing.

"She ran after you. I tried to stop her, but she was swallowed up when the shit hit the fan." Instead of beating the shit out of him like I want, it's not a priority. Finding her is. I hear Cole yell my name before I can leave. "I heard about the van. My boys are out there lookin'."

Nodding my head, I turn and see another one of Polesky's men come at me right before he lands on the floor with a bullet in his head. When I look where the shot came from, I see Cole put his gun away. "Now you owe me." He smiles and disappears.

I fight my way through the crowd, but it seems never ending. More men attack and more are taken down. Something heavy pounces on my back before an arm has me in a headlock. Once I regain my footing, I slam back into the bar repeatedly until he finally releases me. My elbow slams up to hit flesh, and I feel bones break. When I turn around to hit him once more, Chris has him over the bar and on the floor. Unmoving. "Go. I saw Blaire over there a second ago." He points to my left, and I know she's close to where I was sitting earlier.

My eyes continually look until I find her. My heart picks up, but I know she's not safe yet. She's huddled behind a speaker beside the stage. Her dark hair and dress camouflage her perfectly. When she sees me, she stands to head in my direction even though I shake my head no, trying to tell her to stay put. But she ignores it. Then my stomach hits the floor when Polesky grabs her by the hair when she passes by him. He yanks her back into his body, but his eyes widen when he realizes Red isn't his daughter. His face turns red with anger, and he slaps her so hard she falls to the floor. My wrath is all-encompassing, and I feel a new beast form as I head in her direction. *Nobody touches her.*

Any person who gets in my way eats my fist or lead as I rush to her side. Even though I want to put a bullet in Polesky's brain,

I'm still too far away for an accurate shot so I keep moving. Regardless he will die for touching her.

My gun's out and aimed as he pulls his and points it directly at Red. When a shot is fired, my heart sinks in fear that I'm too late. I'm not sure if it's his or mine. Then his body hits the floor as Red shakily stands up.

On the other side of where Polesky was standing, the blonde from earlier smiles, her gun pointing at his body. I'd know that sinister grin anywhere… Anya. I lower my gun right before she turns hers on Red less than a foot away. Kill shot. Lifting my arm, I aim, ready to take her down, but Red drops to the floor, swings her leg out, and knocks Anya to the floor just as I pull the trigger and miss. The impact causes her to drop her gun, so I kick it out of my way before I'm above her, ready to pull the trigger again. "Don't fucking move."

Her chest is heaving, but she doesn't look scared or concerned about my gun being above her. She's smiling. "Not so weak now, huh, Blaire?" she asks loudly. Then she addresses me. "I'm not the one you should be aiming that at."

Before I can look over my shoulder, Red screams. Massey has a gun to her head. Tears run down his face, and he looks unstable. I start to grab my other gun, but he shakes his head. "Don't!" he hollers. "She deserves to die. *You both do.* Because of you two, my family is dead. Because you led them to my home. Because you fell for this tramp. My girls are dead."

His words confirm my earlier suspicions. We are too late. But Red will not pay for something we couldn't control. "I tried to get to them on time, Massey. You know I did." With a quiet voice, I attempt to reason with him, to calm him enough to let Red go. Her eyes are wide with dread when I glance at her, so I concentrate on him once more. Sirens are now apparent, as they get closer.

"Why not take the deal? They would still be alive if you'd taken the fuckin' deal," he screams as spit and blood fall from his mouth.

He's grieving and not thinking clearly, not seeing reason. "You'd all be dead before you could walk out the door. You know that. Polesky doesn't do deals. *Think,* Massey."

He tightens his hold on Red and starts to ramble. "It was her they wanted to trade with. He knew you loved her. He knew she was your weakness. But she got away before I could get her to them and that fucked it all up." His voice breaks. "Now my babies are dead." His legs give out and his hold loosens when he falls to the floor in a heap of grieving agony.

Red runs in my direction as soon as she's free, and I put her behind my back. I watch my friend warily, not sure what he'll do. He's trained and can be deadly even though he hasn't been active for a few years. Gripping my gun tight, I'm ready to kill him even if I don't want to. He's been my mentor and advisor. He's been a brother to me for years.

After a few minutes of crying, he looks up at me with anguished eyes, takes a deep breath, and puts the gun to his head. "You're free now." *BANG!*

"Lyric? Lyric? Burn it. Burn the fucker down, and get out of there. Now!" Hyde's voice shouts in my ear, but my eyes stay focused on Massey's body lying on the floor. He's right. The place needs to burn to get rid of all evidence of what took place tonight. Evidence of me. Of us.

My arms wrap Red in an embrace, trying to take the death away she just witnessed. She's proven tonight how strong she is, not only to me, but also to herself. I'd kiss her, but I know we have no time. Lou, Javier, Chris, and Cole with his men, stand there watching. "Burn it." My voice shows my regret, but duty once again calls.

As they start lighting the place up, I remember Anya, so I look around, but I can't see her. It seems she's disappeared again. Fuck it. I don't have time to look for her sneaky ass. The place is quickly filling with smoke, so we make our way out the back exit.

CHAPTER TWENTY-NINE

"We cannot start over, but we can begin now,
And make a new ending."
-Zig Ziglar

Blaire

That night seems like forever ago even though it's only been four weeks. I still see the fire and flames lap over to engulf the place that held all my happy memories of my brother.

I watched it all turn to ash from a safe distance. I smelled the wood and flesh burn until I gagged and broke down in Lyric's arms. I felt so many different emotions that night. Fear, relief, disgust, and then sadness. Lyric eventually carried me to where Hyde picked us up and took us to the apartment. My brain was in such shock that I couldn't comprehend what was going on, and before I knew it, we were headed to the airport with our packed bags and loaded up on a private jet with the Knight family. I didn't argue or move. I didn't even notice Sissy with us. I just followed Lyric not saying a word while Hyde carried Savannah everywhere.

Once we landed, I finally gained my voice and asked where we were. The only answer I received was a safe place. Our first stop wasn't our final stop, our supposed safe place, because we were quickly routed to another plane for another long flight. But the closer we got to safety, the further we ran from what we were.

What and who we once knew.

I didn't know we would lose all contact with friends still in Mobile. I never expected to be cut off from the life I once understood. Plus, I didn't know how long we'd be gone.

However, it all made sense after a few days lying on a beach on Taveuni Island in Fiji. Lyric explained that if they wanted out, they had to be dead. The Reform would come looking once no word from Massey was received. They'd interrogate and watch everyone, looking for any sign of them. As far as everyone knows, we're dead. Except for Jax and Trudy. They knew we were at the hotel with Savannah until we left. And I have no clue what happened to them after that.

Lyric made sure Lou stayed in charge of the shipments in Mobile and assigned Javier to New Orleans. He doesn't want it anymore. I was terrified that, once people found out he was in with the government, they'd want him dead, as well. However, it was never about the drugs. Lyric said the government makes too much money off the shit. Too many dirty pockets in the White House. Polesky and his trading were the real reason for the mission. And now that he's dead, we were unsure what would happen. We knew he was trafficking more than just drugs and weapons. And the only clue we had to what it actually was, disappeared the night of the fire. Or so we thought.

The file that Anya promised to Lyric for his part in bringing down her father somehow magically appeared this last week. We sat at the table while they read it. I knew it would be bad, but I never imagined just how evil.

It's records of all Polesky's trafficking partners, from not only Russia, but also other countries. Mobs and gangs, as well as some administration officials, are involved. It also shows what he was trafficking. Criminals. Not robbers or thieves, but some of the world's deadliest and craziest. The worst part is, he not only traded drugs or money for these felons, he traded young boys and girls to some sick sons-of-bitches. Now these monsters are in our country as citizens and part of his team. No word on what exactly he plans to do with these men, but whatever it is, it can't be good.

Now we need to get this file into the right hands to bring them down. As far as the young girls or boys already traded, we might never get them back, I fear. And how we deliver the file, and whom to give it to is another question, but one we will face once we land back in the states.

Even with this new worry, I can't help but reflect on this last month, and how beneficial for us it's been. We've formed a family bond and built trust in one another. We've lived on a beautiful, white sand island away from people, and a few miles from the small market where we get the essentials we need to survive.

Lyric and I have become something unbreakable over the past weeks. After everything we've faced in life, we've molded into one another, breathed as one, and loved as one. We've learned to relax and have fun, how to smile, and most importantly, how to let go of our pasts and forgive. By no means am I cured, but I'm no longer blaming myself for what my father did to Benji or me. I no longer blame myself for my brother's addiction. And I no longer hold a grudge over life itself. I love my life and how it's turned out. I hate the road it took for me to get here, but I have Lyric and Savannah now and wouldn't change it. I'm truly happy for the first time in my life.

Now it's time to take that happiness back to Mobile and start a new life there. Rebuild old friendships while keeping a low profile the best we can. Lyric thinks that, since his mission is technically over because of Polesky's death, they won't pursue us anymore. I hope not. I just want to take what I have and keep it forever. No more deaths and heartache. No more worry. No more lies.

Throughout the entire plane ride, I think of last night.

The bonfire. The food. Lyric singing to me on the beach. The breeze blowing my blonde hair out of my face. The smell of salty air filling my nose. The way the orange flames reflect on his relaxed face as he strums his acoustic guitar. And the dominating, feral look he gives me before he stops singing.

He stands and walks over to me then picks me up and carries me to the outside shower that's covered with beautiful bamboo and greenery. He tells me he loves me with his mouth. Not only with words, but the kisses he places on every inch of my body, the thrust of him inside of me, and with his hands running across my skin. He loves me and will never let me down or lie to me again. He'll never leave me and make me feel small. He builds me up and makes me stronger. He's not my crutch. He's my best friend, and lover. My home.

When I wake from the impact of the plane landing, his sweet words run through my head. Feeling warm, I stretch out my stiff muscles and look at him sitting beside me. He's mine. Grabbing my things before taking Lyric's hand, I brace myself to face reality again. This time I'm not alone.

After we all load up in the limo Lou arranged for us, my nerves kick in and my hands start shaking. Lyric automatically reaches over and grabs them, calming me immediately. "What's wrong, Red?"

It's still funny he calls me that, even though I'm no longer a redhead. "Just thinking." I shrug. "What do you think people will think of us showing back up?"

"I'm sure they'll be a little pissed at first, but honestly, how many friends did any of us truly have?"

"You had Ryan. I was getting close to Cory. And Hyde," I stop and think about it, "Hyde didn't have anyone, I don't think." I look at him from across the limo. He's asleep with Vannah

310

snuggled close. He is now her *Uncle Hyde*. And he spoils her rotten.

"No. He doesn't get close to anyone. Well, except Vannah." He kisses my head. "So you see, baby, us reappearing won't matter to many people. And I'm sure the three or four that it actually does mean shit to, won't care. We'll tell them we had family business and had to get your sister back. You didn't have a way to contact them."

My eyes take him in, and I sigh. Even without his guitar, he's the same sexy guy he was on that stage the first night I saw him. His hair is still dark, and his lip still pierced. His eyes are still a stormy gray that reminds me of thunderclouds, and his stare is just as unbreakable. But he loves me in everything he does. I know that, not only from the words that he tells me every day, but also from the sacrifices he's made. For us.

"What about Ryan? Your band? I know you miss it."

"Ryan might be a little pissed, but he always knew I had a fucked up job. He just didn't know what." He kisses me and bites down gently on my lower lip. "I'll worry about the band after we get settled. Might open a new bar. I don't know. The insurance money should have gone to you. But let's worry about that later. Right now, I just want to get you home and have you make me some more disgusting bacon."

His tongue invades my mouth, caressing every inch of its warmth. But I can't help but smile from his words even as heat pools in between my legs. "You like my bacon. I've gotten better at cooking it."

"No." *Kiss.* "I eat it because you make it. Even Sissy turns her nose at it."

We pull into the three-bedroom house outside the city and I'm immediately in love. The one-story red brick home has a seating area on the small front porch with brick columns, as well as a cute sidewalk that leads to the driveway. Oak trees shadow the front yard to block the view from the road. A privacy fence hides the backyard that accommodates a guesthouse behind the pool. The open floor plan and furnishings make it feel more like an actual home. Our large bedroom has slate gray walls, and navy blue and red bedding. Vannah's room is every little girl's dream with a princess canopy bed and an overflowing wooden toy box. I don't know how Lou did this, but it's perfect. Every detail is taken care of from floor to ceiling.

Walking back into the kitchen, I see three new cell phones sitting on the russet-colored, granite counter, with new numbers for each of us. All that's missing now are our friends.

Lyric calls Ryan repeatedly with no luck. I decide to call Cory, and when she doesn't answer, I leave a message. When after an hour passes and no one returns our call, we decide to head to Mobile and show up in person. Opening the two-car garage, I see a white Chevy Tahoe, a blue Audi, and to my surprise, Benji's bike parked in the back. My fingers glide over its polished metal before Lyric wraps his arms around me. I don't know how it got here, but I'm so relieved that it's okay.

"You know I'm going to teach you how to ride that thing now, don't you?" he whispers in my ear. Chills surface and I shiver.

I turn and kiss his lips. "Yes, but first, I need to practice. We also need to break in that big new bed, too," I say seductively.

"We will. Hyde's checking the place for bugs, and then we

312

can do it everywhere you want." He grabs my butt to lift me before placing me on Foxy. "Now let's go find where the fuck everyone is." He passes me a helmet as his new phone rings. At that exact moment, Vannah runs out, begging to go with us. I tell her not this time, and she needs to play with Uncle Hyde until we get back. She shows pure attitude for a four-year-old, but after a minute of pouting, she finally stomps her foot and heads inside.

I'm soooooo dreading the teen years.

I finish adjusting the chinstrap of my helmet when Lyric walks back out. "You ready?" I ask, but his eyes immediately tell me something's wrong. His facial features and body language are stiff and angry. "Baby, what's going on?"

"That was Ryan's uncle. Turns out Ryan was found a few nights ago brutally beaten, and he's in a coma."

EXTRAS

Want to hear the Music mentioned in Learning to Forgive as well as Inspired this crazy love story? Then here's the link.

http://open.spotify.com/user/1293710976/playlist/OOYWRCNxTKjeMiL ex19hqc

Omnious Clothing so you can rock out some amazing fashion:
http://www.ominousclothing.com/

Ink Army Clothing: http://inkarmy.com

Photograph courtesy: https://m.facebook.com/randipphotography

R.D. Cole is a lively person with a determination to make it in life. Once her mind gets set on an idea she pursues it with passion. As long as she has God and her family she feels she can conquer every day. Besides reading and writing she loves to sing, dance, and go mudding on her Souped-up Can Am. Her hubby is 9 years younger but he seems more mature than her at times and they level one another out. She has a beautiful daughter named Bethani who is a miracle and a fighter. She's the only known living survivor of Matthew Woods Syndrome and when no one thought she'd live R.D. said "yes she will." R.D. takes nothing for granted when it comes to life. "Everything can be ripped from your fingers before they can grasp it. So if you want something in life, do it. Go for it."

That same mindset has helped R.D. write small pieces of her life mixed in to fictional settings and characters that will capture your heart.

"Read on. Dream on. Write on." -R.D. Cole

Support Indie Authors

You can stalk me at:

Website: www.authorrdcole.com

Email: authorrdcole@gmail.com

Facebook: www.facebook.com/r.d.coleauthor

Twitter: www.twitter.com/authorrdcole

Goodreads:
https://www.goodreads.com/author/show/7134270.R_D_Cole

On the Edge by Mari Brown

SNEAK PEEK OF THE HIGHLY ANTICIPATED NOVEL: ON
THE EDGE

Coming June 2014

Blurb:

Katarina Roberts has grown up with an abusive mother and a
brother who's part of the town's notorious Knight crime family.
Drew does everything he can to help her, but her only goal is to get
the hell out of Belmont and attend school at UCLA. The further
away the better until Cole showed up in her life.

Cole Knight is sexy and dangerous. Being groomed to take over
the family business, he has no interest in a relationship until he
meets Kat. Cole has decided he wants Kat, and will stop at nothing
to have her and keep her, making her part of the 'family'.

Kat now faces the hardest choice of her life; does she stay with
Cole or does she stick to plan she has developed over the last
couple of years and get as far away from Belmont as she can? Can
she give up her dreams for Cole?

On the Edge

Chapter One

As I take a sip of coke, my eyes dart around the crappy diner where I wait for Drew. Only my brother would pick a hole-in-the-wall, shit shack. After all, he's into all kinds of shady things. I'm thankful that when I called him, he dropped everything to come meet me. He could hear in my voice how upset I am. I didn't want to go into detail over the phone, so I asked him to meet me wherever he wanted.

I'm pissed off, and our dear mother is of no help in the situation. In fact, she's part of the damn problem. She always picks the biggest assholes to date, and the latest one has already moved in with us. I've tried to keep my distance from him, but Mom left for a weeklong business trip this morning, and of course, Jim, the asshole, decided to start slinking up on me now that she's gone. Yeah, not happening, buddy. I was out that door as fast as my ass could carry me.

I'm a senior and set on getting the hell out of this town, one way or another. I want a fresh start where I don't have to deal with my bitch of a mother who cares more about her boyfriend than her kids, and my brother who is always busy with stuff. I don't want to know what the stuff is, but I'm not stupid either. I know my brother is involved in the criminal world and the Knight family, even though Knight's Construction legitimately pays him. I hear what people on the streets say about gunrunning, gambling, and lord only knows what else he's done.

The bell above the door rings, and when I look up, Drew is entering the diner. His 6'3" frame makes him look as if he could take you down with one swing of his muscular arm. We share the same hair color, but he keeps his cut short and spikes it up all over.

Our brilliant, emerald green eyes leave little doubt that we are related.

Drew scans the restaurant and, when he sees me, he heads straight in my direction. Two guys I've never seen before flank him on either side. One guy is so humongous that he couldn't hide if he wanted. I mean Hulk huge. His hard, scary face gives the impression that he would show no mercy if you crossed him. In fact, some of the diners warily look at him as he walks by them. The other guy catches my attention for a whole different reason. I've seen some good-looking guys in my eighteen years, but damn, the eyes on this guy just draw me in like a fucking magnet. They are the most striking shade of Mediterranean Sea blue, and I can't get past them to look at the rest of him. I need to stop staring before I embarrass myself.

Drew slides in next to me while Pretty Eyes and Hulk sit across from us.

"So, what's going on, Kat?" Drew asks, with no preamble.

"Well, let's see. Mom left on a trip today, her new boyfriend is living with us, and when I got home from school today, he tried to put the moves on me."

My brother stiffens and, from the looks that cross the other guys' faces, they don't much like what I have to say, either, and they don't even know me.

"So, what happened?" Drew manages to ask me through clenched teeth.

"So, I may have punched him in the face, kneed him in the balls, grabbed my keys, and got the fuck in Mom's car." I fiddle with the napkin holder on the table while I talk.

The three guys exchange a shocked look, then Hulk smirks at me, Pretty Eyes' lips turn up in a faint smile, and my brother full-out laughs. Seems all three of these guys find my actions amusing.

When he finally pulls himself together, Drew turns towards

me. "So, what do you need from me?"

"I need somewhere to stay until Mom gets home. I am sure as hell *not* staying in that house with him, and I don't want to go to a hotel for a whole week."

"Done, but first, I want to pay the asshole a little visit." This visit will not be the 'let's sit down and have a beer together" kind. "You're gonna pack your shit and come stay at my place until the bitch gets home."

There's no love lost between my mother and brother. Since she's always been more concerned about her love life than her children, it's always been just the two of us. Shit, we aren't even sure we share the same dad.

"So, are you going to introduce me to the two guys sitting across from me, or should I just go with the names I've made up in my head?" I ask my brother.

"That's Pete, right there," he nods his head towards Hulk, "and this is Cole."

I turn towards Pretty Eyes and smile. Then it hits me.

"Cole Knight?" I question.

Surprise registers across Cole's face at my recognition. My brother shakes his head in the affirmative.

I find myself intrigued. My brother works for this guy's family. I soak in more details about Cole while staring at him. His dark hair sticks up in a sexy messy way that makes a girl swoon, and his small bit of facial hair is just enough to rub me the right way. Tattoos peek out from beneath his shirt, and I wonder just what is hiding under there. I want to lick those tattoos without even knowing what they are.

I shake my head, trying to clear my dirty thoughts. This guy is 23 and as badass as they come. I can't go there with someone like him if I want out of this fucking town. I have heard so many stories about Cole. He likes women, weed, and beating the shit out of people, and that's just the tip of the iceberg.

Drew decides that since they walked to the diner from wherever they had been, we will all travel in my mom's car back to my house. I end up in the back seat with Pretty Eyes, and struggle not to move in closer to him. Something about him draws me in and makes my pussy clench and become dripping wet just from being close to him. I need to get away from this guy before I do something stupid. Images of me straddling him run rampant through my mind, and I don't even care that my brother is in the driver's seat.

When we pull up at my house, the guys get out of the car and follow me up the walkway. I open the front door, and Jim shouts out at me. "Hey, Kitty Kat! You smarten up and change your mind?"

Tremors travel throughout my body. The man totally creeps me out. At Jim's words, Drew and his friends growl in anger. Unaware that I have company, Jim walks around the corner, but stops short when he sees the three guys behind me.

"Who the fuck are these guys?" Jim yells at me.

Drew steps in front of me as a set of arms wrap around my waist and pull me back. Hulk steps up next to Drew.

"I'm her fucking brother, shithead, and I take it you're the fucker who tried to put the moves on my little sister?"

Jim registers the threat in Drew's voice, and his face pales at my brother's words.

"Kat, go upstairs with Cole and pack your shit! Pete and I are gonna have a little chat with Jimmy boy here."

Drew doesn't turn to look at me, and Cole gently guides me towards the stairs. As if floating on a cloud, my brain doesn't register what is happening around me.

When we reach the top of the stairs, Cole whispers, "Where's your room, Kitten?"

His voice brings me out of my haze. With his body pressed right up against my back, his heat radiates through me and heads straight to my throbbing pussy. I want to turn around, fuse my mouth to his, wrap my legs around his waist, and devour him, but I'm frozen in place. As if sensing what I'm feeling, Cole turns me so that we're face to face. I look up into those gorgeous blue eyes, and my brain goes fuzzy. I can't breathe right. His eyes darken, and at that moment, I realize that we're in a shitload of trouble because he's just as attracted to me as I am to him. This is so not good.

I shake my head to clear the fogginess from my brain, turn around, and head towards my room. Cole closes the door behind us. I pull a suitcase out of the closet and start tossing my clothes in it while Cole sits down on my bed to watch me. The desire burning in his eyes distracts me from what I need to be doing.

"Fucking stop looking at me like that, asshole!" I yell in a low tone so that they don't hear me downstairs. "I can't hook up with you, no matter what my body is saying to me. My brother would fucking flip."

"Your brother won't say shit. He answers to me, not the other way around. When I want something, I go for it, and Kitten, I want you, so I will have you."

"Stop calling me Kitten. My name is Kat. K.A.T. Kat. Got it?"

"Well, you're Kitten to me, and that's what I'm going to call you."

I go back to packing my bag. Cole checks out my underwear as I toss it in my suitcase. I roll my eyes, but don't say anything else to him because this sexual tension in the room is getting to me. Since we're quiet, the elevated voices and sounds of the fight drift upstairs into my room. Something tells me that Drew and Hulk's fists are talking more than their mouths are. I can't say that I'm sorry Jim is getting his ass handed to him. I wish I could be the one to do it, but I wouldn't be able to beat a man twice my size.

When all the clothes I'll need are packed, I make my way to the bathroom for my toiletries and cosmetics. I certainly can't live without that shit for a week.

My thoughts travel to Cole, the arrogant bastard who's made himself at home in my room. I can't even explain what draws me to him. He is the opposite of everything I've ever wanted in a guy. I've always said that I would never be with a controlling man like the ones my mother always chooses. I like being in charge of myself, and don't want to give it up for anyone. With Cole, I have to, but somehow it seems different with him. This bastard is being groomed to run the Knight Family business, so he doesn't take shit from anyone. If I'm truthful, that is part of what attracts me to him. I think I *need* him. He can even me out, put up with my attitude, yet keep me in check at the same time.

The look he gives me is intense, almost as if he knows who I am. At the same time, I feel as if he's my other half. It sounds crazy because I'm only fucking eighteen. It's probably nothing more than lust and hormones, but it seems like so much more right now.

I finish in the bathroom and walk back into my room where the sight of Cole lying comfortably on my bed stops me. He smirks at me. I take in his lean, toned body and, once again, find myself wanting to jump him and scream for him to fuck my brains out.

I start to grab my bags, but Cole jumps up and takes the suitcase from me.

"I got it, Kitten." Jesus, even his smile can stop traffic. "Let's head out. Things are quiet downstairs for now."

When we make our way back downstairs, Jim is laid out on the sofa in the living room while Hulk and my brother sit there watching him. Jim looks as though it may be a few days before he recovers from the beating. Drew looks up when we walk in the room.

"Got everything you need, Kat?" Drew calmly asks me.

I nod, not finding any words and too overwhelmed with all the emotions swirling through me.

Drew turns back to Jim. "Now, don't forget, Jimmy, you will be gone when my mom comes back next week. And if I find out you've come near my mom or sister again? Know that I will kill you."

Well, ok, who knew my bro could scare the piss out of people. I think now is a good time to get going.

"Right, then off we go. Come on, Drew and Hulk," I squeak out. My erratic emotions are messing with my head, and I just want to get the hell out of here.

When we get out to the car, Cole places my bag in the trunk. I've never been to Drew's place because he doesn't want me to be around the shit he does. He's breaking his own rules to keep me safe from that asshole.

I'm so lost in my own thoughts that I fail to hear the three guys talking until Cole says, "She can share my bed."

"That's my fucking little sister, man. She's still in high school, for Christ's sake."

"I'm eighteen," I blurt. *Yeah, don't think that was helpful.* Cole gives me a knowing look. Then it hits me. "Wait, you live together?"

A big, shit-eating grin covers Cole's face. "Yes, Kitten, the three of us share a house."

Well, fuck me sideways. I'm in big trouble now. How will I avoid Cole for a whole damn week if he lives there, too? It's not possible. *Fuck! Maybe I should check into a hotel.* Yeah, that's a good idea. Who am I kidding? Drew wouldn't go for that shit, but damn, I can't be in the same house as Cole. He's already declared that he wants me and that I can share his bed with him. Um, hell no. I can't be involved in this shit.

I don't know what to do. This is new territory for me. I have *never* had a guy turn me inside out like this. I usually can take 'em or leave 'em. I'm no virgin, but I've never been with a guy who makes my body hum by just standing next to me. I'm so in over my head here. I have no doubt Cole is experienced. His lifestyle and good looks almost guarantee that he is going to rock my world. I haven't figured out yet if that's a good or bad thing.

Times like this, I wish I had a mother that I could go to or even a girlfriend who has my back. Nope, the only girl I talk with at school will not be the one I can talk with about this shit. Number one reason is that Cole is her older brother. Also, we don't actually talk outside of school. These feelings are going to send me to the loony bin.

When the car stops, we are parked in the driveway of a nice home, nothing fancy, but not a dump either. This is where my brother lives? A fucking middle-class neighborhood? Are you fucking kidding me right now? I step out the car, knowing that when I walk in this house, my life from this point forward will never be the same.

www.ingramcontent.com/pod-product-compliance
Lightning Source LLC
Chambersburg PA
CBHW062014170626
46813CB00001B/152